MOURNING BAY

A Port Stirling Mystery **BOOK 6**

KAY JENNINGS

Mourning Bay/Kay Jennings — 1st ed.

ISBN (Hardcover edition): 979-8-9855544-7-2
ISBN (Paperback edition): 979-8-9855544-6-5
ISBN (E-book edition): 979-8-9855544-5-8

Publisher's Note: Mourning Bay is a work of fiction. As of this publication date, the events and circumstances that occur within are a product of the author's imagination. While certain locales may draw on real life, they are used fictitiously to add authenticity to the story. The cast of characters are fictitious and are not based on real people, businesses, or organizations.

Cover design and Port Stirling Map: Claire Brown
Interior design: Steve Kuhn/Kuhn Design Group

Printed and bound in the USA
First printing 2023
Published by Paris Communications
Portland, Oregon, USA

www.kayjenningsauthor.com

OTHER BOOKS BY KAY JENNINGS:

Shallow Waters

Midnight Beach

Code: Tsunami

Dark Sand

Phantom Cove

For Marion, Doug, and Michele,
with whom we've shared a difficult year.

MOURNING BAY

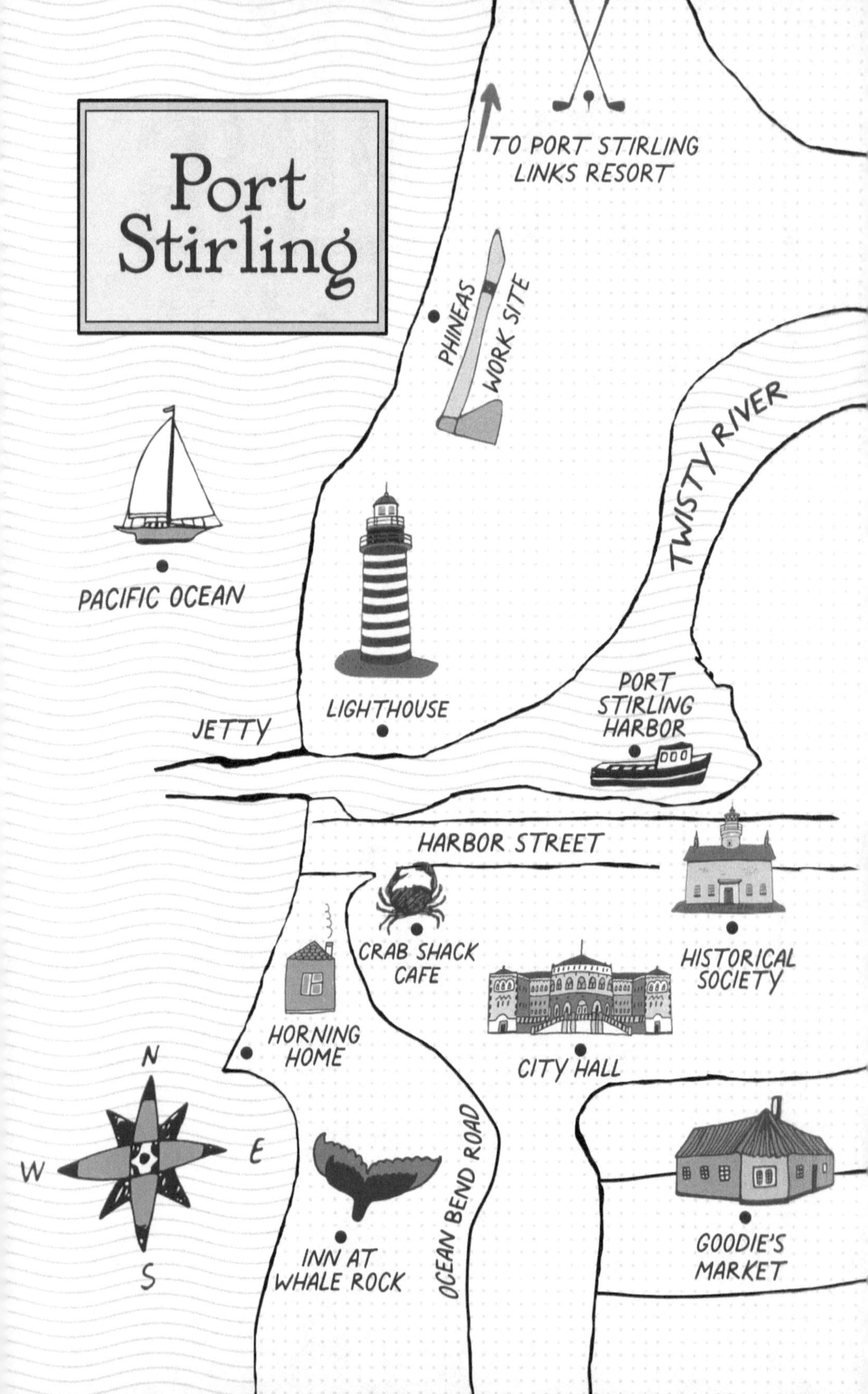

Port Stirling
TO PORT STIRLING LINKS RESORT
PHINEAS
WORK SITE
TWISTY RIVER
PACIFIC OCEAN
LIGHTHOUSE
JETTY
PORT STIRLING HARBOR
HARBOR STREET
CRAB SHACK CAFE
HISTORICAL SOCIETY
HORNING HOME
CITY HALL
OCEAN BEND ROAD
N
W E
S
INN AT WHALE ROCK
GOODIE'S MARKET

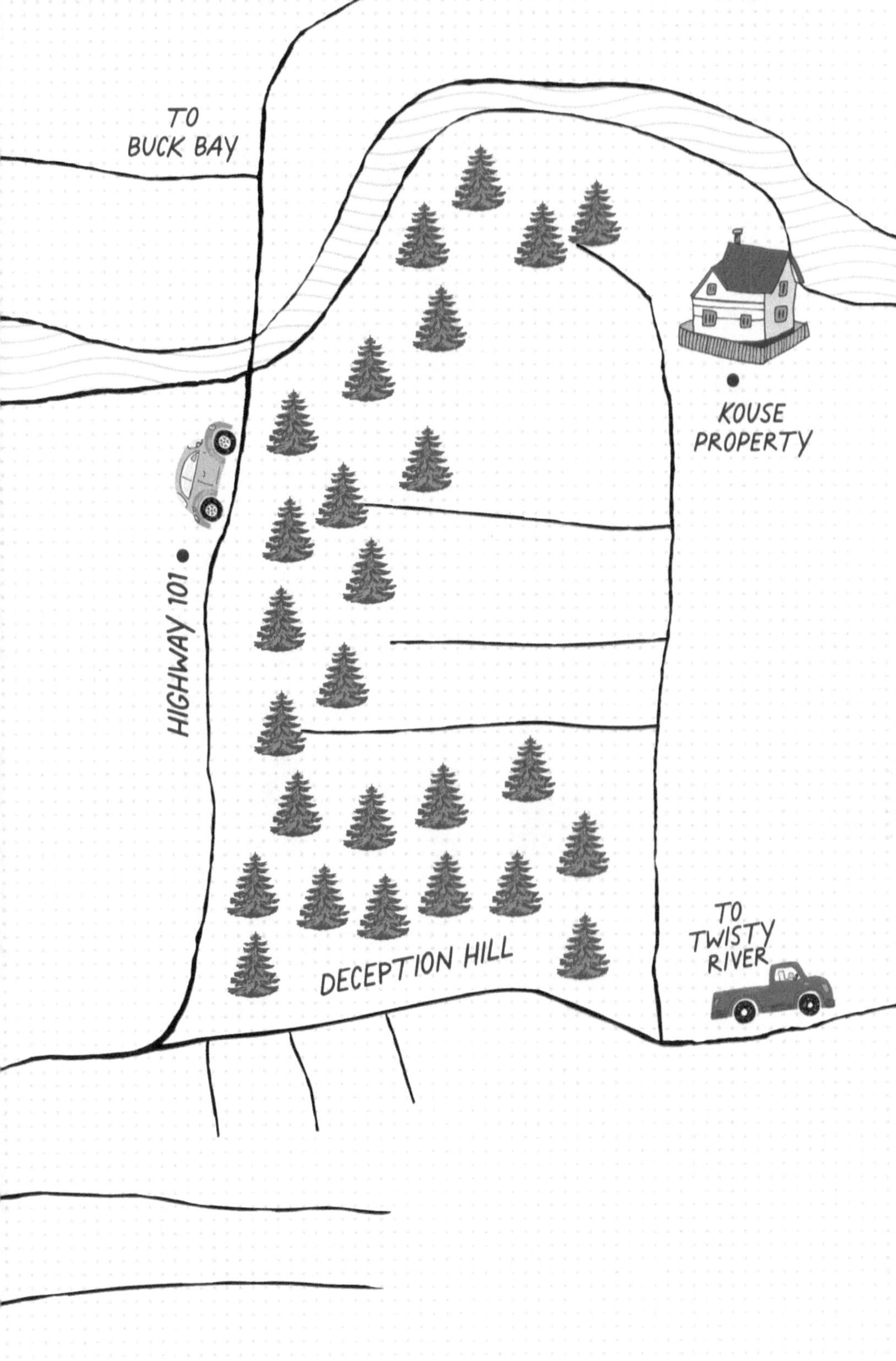

TO BUCK BAY
KOUSE PROPERTY
HIGHWAY 101
DECEPTION HILL
TO TWISTY RIVER

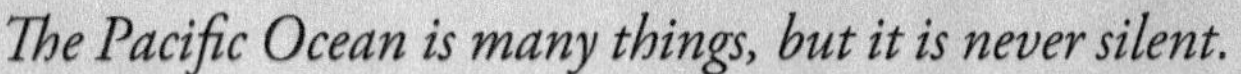

PROLOGUE

Mourning Bay got its sad name after a tragic shipwreck off the southern Oregon coast near Port Stirling around 1700. A Spanish galleon headed to South America was caught in a sudden January storm and smashed into the rocky coastline protecting a beautiful but notoriously dangerous bay. All aboard perished, leaving many wives and children to mourn their sailors.

A few scattered remnants of the hull remain on the south end of the bay, buried most of the time in the ancient sand. Occasionally, winter storms will re-arrange or uncover new relics, but the shipwreck itself has never been found. It is said that when the winds are blowing hard from the northwest, the sound of crying can be heard in the waves lapping the shore of Mourning Bay.

CHAPTER 1

Port Stirling police chief Matt Horning stopped suddenly in the aisle of the Chinook County courtroom and did a double-take at the man sitting in the aisle seat in the next-to-last row.

Walking beside him, Fern Byrne, Horning's wife of almost three months, tugged the hem of his jacket and whispered in his ear, "Let's go. You're still recovering, and we should get you home."

Gently, he shrugged her off and said, "It's OK. I need to talk to this gentleman."

Matt smiled as the man rose from his chair and extended his hand to shake. The man did not return the smile.

"You're Robert, aren't you?" asked Matt. "I barely recognized you."

"That's because the last time you saw me, I was wrapped in a filthy blanket, drunk, and sleeping in the doorway of the Whale Rock restaurant. Name's Robert Oakley."

Still shaking hands, Matt clapped him on the shoulder with his other hand. "Man, you look better. All cleaned up." Robert, in his early sixties, was wearing black slacks, a white dress shirt open at the neck, and a tidy maroon crew sweater over it. His shoes were polished and scuff-free. His non-descript brown hair was trim and combed into place.

"Cleaned up, yes," Robert said. "Better, no." He hesitated. "Would it be possible to talk to you for a few minutes? Or, can I make an appointment to see you in your office?"

Before Matt could answer, Fern reached out her hand to Robert and said, "I'm Fern, Matt's wife." She gave him a warm smile, but her tone was brisk. "If you've been sitting in this courtroom for a while, you heard what the chief has been through. We really need to get him home to rest—it's been a long day for him."

"Yes," Robert said. "I know you got shot, and I'm very sorry about your ordeal. I wouldn't be bothering you if it weren't real important." He started to move out into the aisle. "But it can wait till you've had some rest, Chief."

Matt took Robert's arm to halt his progress. "No, no, it's OK, I'm fine." He winked in Fern's direction. "She's a little overprotective."

"I am not," Fern said. "But he's stubborn"—she jerked her thumb toward Matt—"so we might as well go to the café across the hall and talk. Is it alright with you if I tag along, Mr. Oakley?"

"Sure. I read about you and those Brits. I could use some of your toughness about now," said Robert.

Matt detected a slight sway in the man and reached out to steady him. Fern dashed to Robert's other side, and together they walked him out of the courtroom and into a green plastic chair at a square table in the café. Once both men were settled, Fern brought three glasses of water to the table.

"What can I do for you, Robert?" asked Matt when Fern sat down.

"It's about my wife," Robert began haltingly. "My late wife, Hannah."

"Hannah Oakley was your wife?" Matt asked. He tried to not sound incredulous that Robert was married and that he'd been the husband of a woman so widely respected in the area.

"Yes." What little color there was in Robert's face went somewhere else, and he turned white as a piece of paper.

"I'm so sorry, Mr. Oakley," said Fern. She stretched across the small table and placed her hands on top of his. "It was suicide, I understand," she said quietly.

"It was not," he said, violently shaking his head from side to side. "It was not suicide. My wife is a missing person. Her body has not been found."

"But the coroner ruled it a suicide," Matt said, trying to not sound judgmental. "I read the file."

Robert took a deep breath and gathered himself. "I'm here," he began, looking directly at Matt, "because you helped me once, and I'm hoping you can help me again." Now he looked at Fern. "I don't know how much of my story you know, but let me start with the night I met your husband."

"Go on, Mr. Oakley," said Fern.

"Please call me Robert." Fern motioned at him to continue.

"Chief Horning picked me up from that doorway, bought me a hotel room for the night, and then sent one of his officers around the next day to check on me." He glanced at Matt. "I never had a doubt that if you hadn't been up to your eyeballs in the murder case of that poor little girl, you would have come back for me yourself. I knew you cared."

Matt nodded.

"Your officer took me to a shelter in Buck Bay. I stayed there for a few days while I dried out. Just about the time I was leaving—mainly because I wanted a drink—a man named Ted Frolick came to see me. I believe you both know Ted."

A close friend of Matt and Fern, Ted was married to Detective Patty Perkins of the Twisty River police department, a valuable colleague of theirs in local law enforcement.

"We not only know him," Matt said, "we love the guy. His wife Patty, too."

"Well, I love him, too," said Robert, with the slightest smile starting to form. "Ted saved me. Pure and simple. Two decades ago, he and I taught middle school together, and he'd heard I was in trouble."

"How did you get from being a teacher to…" Matt started to ask.

"To sleeping rough?" Robert interrupted. "Valid question. But the answer is simple. I showed up to teach one morning, drunk as a skunk, and they fired me. I was single, no relatives, had very little money saved and soon drank what I had left."

"That seems impossible looking at you now," said Fern.

"It's a very short, very slippery slope," Robert said. "I'm descended from Scottish immigrants by way of Canada and come from a long line of heavy drinkers. It can be difficult to fight your genes. It took me more than one long, hard year with the help of some good people to overcome it. Ted helped me get back on my feet and back into teaching."

"Wow," said Matt, almost speechless.

"The other person who saved me was Hannah Sorenson. Ted took me to Rainbow of Hope, the homeless and substance-abuse organization in Buck Bay."

"That Hannah Sorenson founded and ran," said Matt.

"Correct," said Robert. "Obviously, that's where we met. This is going to sound like a cliché, but Hannah saw something in me, something that no one else had bothered to look for. Something worth saving." He looked down at his hands on the table, still covered by Fern's.

Just when Matt feared it was about to get maudlin, Robert sat up straighter, removed his hands from Fern's grip, and briskly wiped away a tear on his chin. "And now, I need to get justice for Hannah," he said. "My wife did not commit suicide. She did not walk into Mourning Bay. She did not write the note the sheriff found. Or, if it is her handwriting as they say it is, it was taken out of context. And she most definitely did not leave me. I need you to help me figure out what happened to Hannah. Will you do that?"

Matt stared at him. "In my limited experience with suicide, Robert, remaining family and friends often say, 'It's not possible'. It's a standard reaction when it comes out of the blue. Is that what's going on with you?"

"I've mulled it over, thinking about our last few days before she disappeared, trying to be as objective as possible, and I am certain she did not drown herself in that bay," Robert said, his voice clear and calm. "Something has happened to her. I can't live with myself unless I make every move possible to find out what. You and your beautiful bride"—he smiled wanly at Fern—"are my best hope to help me."

"What do you think has happened to her, then?" asked Matt. "If she didn't kill herself, where is she?"

Robert stared at the wall behind Matt. "If it was possible for her to contact me, she would have by now. Therefore, she is unable to get in touch, which can mean only three things. She's somewhere injured and can't call me, or she's been kidnapped, or…she's been murdered."

CHAPTER 2

Matt and Fern looked at each other, and as they'd done so often ever since they'd met three years ago, read each other's mind.

Fern knew that Matt was thinking; "Robert is a hopeless case, and simply not facing up to the reality of his wife's suicide."

Matt knew that Fern was thinking; "We have to help him even if he's crazy."

So, of course, Matt said to Robert, "I'll look into Hannah's death, but I'm not making any promises. These things often turn out to be exactly as they look."

"Disappearance, not death," Robert corrected.

"Her disappearance," Matt said in a softer tone. "I'll go back over her file and talk to the sheriff."

"Do you promise?" Robert was a proud man, but he was begging now.

"I promise," said Matt firmly. "And, I'm sure I can speak for Fern, too, that we are very sorry for your loss. No matter how this turns out, this is a horrible thing to go through. How can I contact you?"

Robert scribbled his phone, email, and address on a piece of paper he pulled from a small notebook in his back pants pocket, and pushed it across the table to Matt.

"You live in Buck Bay now?" Matt asked.

"Yes. Hannah and I just finished building a new house across the bay from town. We had married and bought our former home just before the earthquake hit. The tsunami flattened it, and we rebuilt a little higher up the hill when the insurance money came in. This is one of the reasons I don't believe she killed herself. She was so excited about our new house and was busy nesting and making it perfect."

"Hmm," said Fern. "That does sound like odd timing. Suicide, if it's not mental illness, is most often about a lack of hope. What else was going on in her life?"

"It was all good," Robert said. "She'd just been awarded a big national grant for Rainbow for Hope. She was planning to announce it this week. It was a major coup for her and Chinook County. It's the kind of money that would be life-changing for people in our area, and she was beyond excited about it."

"Were you happily married?" Matt asked. He hurriedly added, "I'm sure you were, but I have to ask."

"Yes, we are happy," Robert said, his voice quavering. "Deliriously so." He looked down at the table. "Even though she's younger than me, we are like souls. I never expected to find this kind of love in my life."

"How much younger?" Matt asked.

"Eighteen years."

Matt shot a quick look at Fern and raised his eyebrows.

"That's quite an age difference," Matt said bluntly.

Robert lifted his eyes from the table and looked at Matt. "Yes, I suppose it is," he said. "When you're twenty and she's two, it sounds like a lot. But when you're sixty-four and she's forty-six, it tends to level out and not feel like a big deal."

"Did Hannah have any qualms about marrying an older man?" Matt persisted.

"If she did, she didn't share them with me. We talked a great deal before we decided to marry, and neither of us had any misgivings."

Matt suddenly stood up and moved to pull out Fern's chair for her. "We'll swing by my office on our way home and pick up Hannah's file. I'll study it and then talk to the sheriff as soon as I can."

"As soon as he has a rest," Fern added, rubbing her husband's arm.

"Right," Matt eyerolled, "as soon as I have a rest." He shook hands with

Robert. "It's very nice to see you again. Wish it was under better circumstances, but we'll see where we go."

"Thank you, Chief. You're a good man." He teared up and looked at Fern. "Take care of each other because you never know."

Close to tears herself, Fern whispered, "We will."

• • •

Matt and Fern left the café, and she started to turn right to the courthouse's front exit. Matt pulled on her arm and said, "Wait a sec. Let's go down to Earl's office and see if he's there."

"Do you not listen to anything I say?" she asked.

In spite of the stern look on his wife's face, Matt had to laugh. "You know I listen to every word that comes out of your beautiful mouth. But this won't take long, I promise. If the sheriff is in, we can get his quick take on Hannah's case."

Fern stood, feet planted, hands on her hips with the look that said, "Are you kidding me?"

Even with the stress of the trials and the ongoing challenges of Matt's recovery, Fern still looked gorgeous in his eyes. Today, she was dressed in a white blouse tucked into a black straight skirt and topped by a soft pink cashmere open cardigan that flowed easily when she moved. Pink was "their" color, dating back to a case they'd worked on together before they knew they were in love. Matt understood she'd picked it to wear today as a symbol of their future. The color flattered her, giving her complexion a peaches and cream glow. He would never get tired of looking at her.

"I love you, Matt Horning," she said now. "But you are a piece of friggin' work. C'mon, let's go see Earl." She grabbed his hand and took off toward the staircase that led down to the sheriff's office.

Earl Johnson had been the elected sheriff of Chinook County for over thirty years, and both Matt and Fern had a years-long relationship with him. Before she'd entered the law enforcement field, Fern had worked for the county as a victim's advocate, mostly in domestic abuse cases, and she and the sheriff had a close, warm, working relationship.

Matt met the sheriff shortly after he arrived to take the new job as police chief in Port Stirling. Earl recognized Matt Horning as the breath of fresh air the local law enforcement scene—with its well-entrenched hierarchy as small towns are wont to have—desperately needed. The two cops bonded immediately and were now, three years later, fast friends.

The normally rotund sheriff had lost some weight during Matt's recent ordeal. The attack on Matt and the subsequent emotional conclusion of the case had taken a toll on the nearing-retirement sheriff. Seated at his desk as the Hornings entered his office, Matt thought that Earl looked healthier than he had in recent months.

"You're looking good, Earl," Matt boomed now.

"And you look like shit," Earl retorted as he stood to greet two of his favorite people on the planet. "Shouldn't you be resting?"

"Jesus, I'm surrounded," Matt laughed.

Earl winked at Fern. "I only said that because I was pretty sure you'd just said the same thing."

"I did," Fern said. "I didn't realize that when you married the man of your dreams, you have to pay extra for ears."

Earl slapped his thigh and bent over laughing. "How in the hell did you get so lucky to grab this one?" he said to Matt.

"Luck had no part in it. It was pure skill," Matt said. "If you're finished laughing at my expense, do you have a minute?"

The sheriff gestured to the two chairs facing his desk. "Have a seat. What's on your mind? Other than the fact that the bad guys are off to start the party in prison. I don't often say this, but we did good, didn't we?"

The three cops and friends fist bumped.

Sliding into a chair, Matt said, "We want to know your thoughts on the Hannah Oakley suicide."

Earl leaned forward and put his elbows on his desk and made a steeple with his fingers. "Suicide note, her glasses, and her car found at Mourning Bay. No contact with anyone, including her husband. No sighting of her in the six days since. She walked into the bay, Matt."

"You're absolutely positive?" Fern asked. "No doubts whatsoever?"

"I didn't say that, did I?" said Earl.

"You have doubts?" probed Matt.

The sheriff shifted in his chair. "Maybe one or two."

"Such as?"

"I know—knew—Hannah Oakley," said Earl. "I know a lot of people, including several who if I heard they committed suicide, I wouldn't be surprised. Hannah surprised me. She just isn't the type. She's pragmatic, down-to-earth, and has a joy of life aura about her. She gives life and hope to people who have none—why would someone like that take her own precious life? It doesn't make any sense to me."

"Her husband feels the same way," said Fern.

"Robert. Yeah, I know. He's been pestering me to do more. But my department and Chief McCoy in Buck Bay have investigated, there aren't any leads and we're at a dead end. Not to mention our finite resources and budgetary limitations."

"Why didn't you bring me in to help?" Matt asked.

Earl shrugged his shoulders exaggeratedly, palms up, and looked at Fern as if to say, "Do you believe this guy?" What he said to Matt was, "Oh, maybe because you almost died and might need some more recovery time?"

"I need people to understand that I'm fine," Matt said, sounding frustrated. "I've concluded that I'm not Superman after all, but I'm good at listening to my body and taking care of myself. Better than most men, I would guess. I'm officially declaring that I'm back at work, and you two—along with Ed, Jay, Sylvia, Patty, and Bernice—need to back off and let me do my job. Got it?"

Fern looked down at her shoes, not answering. Earl said quietly, "We almost lost you. In fact, we thought we had. That was a tough moment for all of us. Especially her," he nodded in Fern's direction. "You can't blame us for wanting to make sure you come all the way back." He cleared his throat. "But if you tell us you're ready, that's good enough for me."

"I'm ready," Matt said. "And I've just promised Robert Oakley that I would look into his wife's disappearance. So, what do we know about the day Hannah disappeared?" asked Matt.

"It was last week, Wednesday, and she went to work at 9:00 a.m. like usual, worked in the clinic until 12:30 p.m. Then she told her receptionist that she was going to grab some lunch and then go to a meeting offsite. Said she'd be back about 2:30 p.m., but she never came back."

"Where was her meeting?" asked Matt.

"No one knows. She didn't say, and it wasn't noted on her office computer calendar, or in her assistant's calendar. We questioned everyone in her organization, her friends, her doctor, her dentist, her manicurist—everyone—and no one had a scheduled meeting with her that afternoon."

"So, who did she meet with?" Fern asked.

"The simple answer is 'no one'," said Matt. "She lied to the receptionist so she would have time to do what she wanted to do. Or, she did meet someone, and that someone killed her. Or, she did meet someone and the two of them disappeared together."

"Like a lover?" Fern asked.

The sheriff shook his head. "Nope, not buying that one. Hannah and Robert Oakley were very happily married. Everyone we talked to said the same thing. 'Lovebirds' is the word that keeps coming up. The consensus is—and I mean one-hundred-percent consensus—is that neither one of them would even look at another person and would definitely not be involved in any kind of affair. If Hannah did meet with someone Wednesday afternoon, it was most likely business."

"Then why wasn't it on her calendar?" puzzled Fern.

"Yeah," grunted Earl. "Like I said, none of this makes any sense."

"Did forensics go over her car and personal belongings?" asked Matt.

"Yep. Only traces of her and Robert were found. And their dog," added Earl.

Matt rubbed his chin. "Where was Robert Wednesday afternoon and evening?"

"Do you know his background?" asked Earl, staring at Matt.

"Oh yeah, better than most." Matt filled him in on how he'd first met Robert Oakley.

"So, we went after Robert pretty hard," admitted Earl. "Chief McCoy had a theory that Robert only pretended to love Hannah until she agreed to marry him so he could get her money."

"Was she well off?"

"Not rich, by any stretch of the imagination, but when you've been homeless, it's all relative, right?" said Earl. "All things considered, with Hannah's business, which has a very healthy bottom line, an inheritance from her late mother, and personal investments, she was worth about $450,000. Enough to certainly get the attention of a man without a roof over his head."

"Where was he last Wednesday?"

"Airtight alibi, and Robert behaved as any distressed husband would have," Earl said. "Between the hours of 8:00 a.m. and 5:00 p.m., he was in the high school, most of that time in class. He teaches math and algebra. Dozens of students and other teachers vouch for him, and he never left the campus. We have witnesses who say his car was parked in the exact same spot all day."

"What about after school?" Fern asked. "Where was he when he left?"

"He and another teacher, Jim Greenley, regularly run together after class. They did so between 5:00-6:00 p.m. A camera perched on the roof of the high school track grandstand shows them running a few laps and then heading off toward a road that leads down the hill from the school. Greenley told me he and Robert said good-bye at their cars in the school parking lot just a few minutes after 6 o'clock."

"Did Robert report Hannah missing, and, if so, what time?" Matt asked.

"Yes." The sheriff looked down at the file on his desk and shuffled to a page, pulling it out. "He called the Buck Bay PD at 7:38 p.m. and said his wife was missing." Earl looked up. "I calculated that if he drove straight home from the school, it would've taken him about twelve minutes to get home—they live on the other side of the marsh. Then our investigation showed that he called several people, both in Hannah's business and friends, to see if she was with them or had seen her. They all told us that he was edgy because he and Hannah had planned to go out to eat at 7:00 p.m, and it wasn't like her to not phone him if she was going to be late or if something was wrong."

Fern looked at Matt and bit her lip. "This is awful," she said. "That's just what you or I would've done under the same scenario."

"Yeah," Matt muttered. "How did McCoy and his department respond?"

"Well, at first, they told Robert that it was too soon to report a missing person—that she had to be missing overnight. But Robert reacted badly to that and demanded to talk to Chief McCoy personally. He convinced Dan that this was highly unusual behavior for Hannah, and they needed to start a search. Dan caved and sent out some teams to begin looking for her and/or her car, which Robert said was not at their home or her office. Long story short, two of Dan's officers found her car with her handbag and keys still in it in the Mourning Bay parking lot about 10:00 p.m. The suicide note and her glasses were discovered shortly after that. Which, for the record, is the second reason I didn't call you in. Mourning Bay is a county park, therefore, my responsibility as county sheriff. And, Hannah Oakley is a resident of Buck Bay, not Port Stirling, therefore, McCoy's responsibility. You don't have a horse in this race."

Matt leaned back in his chair. "You know that the Chinese say that if you save a life, you're responsible for it forever?"

"I've heard that one, yes," said Earl.

"Well, Robert Oakley seems to feel that I helped save him once upon a time. So, I guess I'm linked to him now. I have to at least snoop around a little, Earl, and give him something."

"Be my guest. I only wish I had something more to give him. All the signs point to Hannah Oakley walking into that bay."

"Was her cell phone in her purse?" asked Fern.

"No, and we and the forensics team went over that car with a fine-tooth comb. Her wallet with $122 was in it, and all of her ID and credit cards. The inside of her handbag looked mostly undisturbed to Bernice. But no phone has been found, and according to her staff, she used it all the time."

"Have your county guys or the Coast Guard dragged Mourning Bay?" Matt asked.

"Yes, we have two divers, and the CG sent two of theirs, along with their small sonar boat. Nothing. No sign of her."

"And you looked around the rocks guarding the bay?" asked Fern.

Earl looked at her. "Yes. We know how to look for a dead body in the water, Fern." Exasperated. "She's either at the bottom of the Pacific far out to sea, or she's somewhere else. She's not in Mourning Bay."

CHAPTER 3

Matt and Fern took the old highway that followed Twisty River home to Port Stirling. In late January, the days were beginning to get a little longer as they marched toward the end of winter. Longer, but not necessarily more pleasant, as hard, cold rain beat down on the windshield of Matt's Lexus SUV.

The windshield wipers kept up, but it was a close race. Fern, uncharacteristically quiet, gazed out her side window at the pretty river, gracefully winding its way to eventually meet the Pacific Ocean. The deciduous trees hugging the banks of the river were still bare of their fallen leaves, while the evergreens showed off their deep green colors, looking like jewels set against an ivory sweater. North of the river, the meadows off in the distance were dotted with cows and sheep, each keeping to themselves. Fern thought, as she always did while traveling the thirty-minute drive between Twisty River and Port Stirling, that the animals who lived in the lush Twisty River Valley were indeed lucky. At least, until they weren't.

"You're quiet," Matt observed.

"For a change, you mean?" she said.

"No, that's not what I meant. Just making an observation."

She didn't reply.

He tried again. "Have I done something to upset you?"

"Yes."

"Are you going to tell me what?"

"I don't like it when you make fun of me in public when I'm trying to care for you."

"I don't do that."

"You just did it with Earl. It embarrassed me."

"I'm sorry, then." He paused, eyes on the road. "I don't like it when you treat me like a baby."

"I don't do that."

"You just did. First with Robert Oakley and then with Earl."

"Being solicitous of my husband's health who almost died is not treating you like a baby—it's loving and caring about you. There's a difference."

"And I appreciated your love and your care when I needed it. You were there in my darkest hours, and it meant the world to me. But now, I need to feel like a man again instead of your patient. Can you understand that?"

She turned to look at him. "So, I'm just supposed to turn off all my feelings like turning off a lamp?" she said, her voice rising. "All my fears—just throw them out the window and pretend like you didn't get shot? Like it might not happen again the next time you're out of my sight?"

"Fern, we work in law enforcement. It's a risky field. You're in just as much danger as I am, some days even more so. Some worry is normal, but you can't grab ahold of me every time I leave the house. It's not going to work."

"I know. But I'm scared." She reached over and put her hand on his thigh.

"You don't think I was scared shitless the night you went after my shooter? I could barely breathe for hours waiting for your call. But we have to trust each other and know that we're both good at our jobs. I'm great at mine, actually… except for that part when I got shot."

Fern laughed. Even arguing, he could make her laugh. He was so darn cute with his black curly hair that was too long for a respectable police chief. They had let some things slide while he was recovering, including a haircut, but he needed one now. However, this was not the time to tell him that, she suspected.

"OK, I won't play nurse anymore. You're on your own, Tex, and if you end up back in the hospital, don't bother calling me."

"I'm never going back to the hospital. But if I did, you'd come and see me, right?"

She turned, silently, back to her window.

• • •

Matt ran into his office at city hall and picked up the file on Hannah Oakley, and then they stopped at the fish market on the wharf at Fern's request.

"I'll go in," Fern said, as Matt pulled up to the curb and parked. "What's your pleasure tonight? I'm cooking. My turn."

"How about some halibut?" he suggested.

"That's what I was thinking," she said. "It sounds good, doesn't it?"

"Yeah, fresh halibut is one of the only good things about Oregon in January," he said, pointing to the rain gushing down their windshield. "And get some fresh shrimp, too. I'll cook it with linguini tomorrow night when it's my turn. And make it snappy," he said with a smile. "I'm looking forward to having a drink with my beautiful wife."

"I put martini glasses in the freezer this morning before we left for the courthouse," she smiled back. "Had a feeling we might want to celebrate tonight. Be right back."

• • •

Darkness had descended by the time Matt and Fern reached their home on Ocean Bend Road. They moved from the garage into the warmth and light of the beautiful house that Matt built after the earthquake had destroyed his rental cabin on the bluff.

Although he would never forget that terrifying night—no one in Port Stirling ever would—he wasn't afraid to build his dream house on that same three-hundred-foot bluff overlooking the Pacific and the six-mile-long breathtaking beach below. His career in law enforcement, begun in Texas and now in Oregon, had taught Matt to play the odds. In crime, going with the statistics was often the solution to the case. He applied those same odds to another huge earthquake, and the stats said it was not likely to happen for another four hundred years. He would roll with that because his life would not be the same without this view.

Even in the dark, with the rain pounding the floor-to-ceiling windows in the living room, the ocean's waves were still visible, their whitecaps jumping up out to sea, and the foam remnants crashing ashore. Driven by the storm, some of the waves looked ten-to-fifteen feet tall. He moved to flip on the gas fireplace, strategically placed in a wide pillar between the two large windows. Its flame roared to life, immediately cozying up the high-ceilinged room.

"You make the drinks while I deal with the fish," Fern said, heading to the adjacent kitchen.

A few minutes later, Matt brought the icy martinis into the kitchen and placed Fern's on the far edge of the kitchen island where she was working on the halibut. He held his drink out to her and said, "I have a toast." She picked up her drink with her one clean, not fishy hand. "Here's to those three bastards beginning their well-deserved time behind bars," Matt said.

They clinked glasses and each took a sip, thinking their own thoughts about the recent horrifying case. Fern took another sip and then spoke first. "Mmm, that tastes good. Watching them, one by one, being led away in cuffs and shackles, I felt the weight of the world lifting off my shoulders." She clinked Matt's glass again. "May they rot."

"And may we appreciate our lives together, and never go through anything that hard again," he added.

"Yeah, we've had more than our share of bad luck," Fern said. "I thought the earthquake and tsunami would be the worst thing that could happen to us, but when I watched that LifeFlight copter take off with you in it, I thought my life was done, too."

Matt pulled out a barstool and started to sit, but Fern said, "No, let's have our drink in the living room while the fish is cooking, and take a quick look at Hannah Oakley's file." She smiled slyly at him. "You know you want to."

"I do. Let's see if we can help Robert Oakley avoid what we almost endured." He took Fern's drink from her hand and moved effortlessly to the white leather sofa facing the fireplace, setting a drink on the small art deco end tables at each end. Fern washed her hands in the sink, speared four jalapeno/garlic stuffed olives from the jar in the refrigerator, and joined him.

She kicked off her boots and curled up cross-legged on the sofa. Matt opened the file and picked up the piece of paper on top that had an official Chinook County stamp in the upper corner. He read out loud, "Under my jurisdiction as medical examiner for Chinook County, I hereby declare that in the matter of Hannah D. Sorenson Oakley, a resident of Buck Bay, Chinook County, Oregon, that to the best of my knowledge and belief, there is sufficient circumstantial evidence to indicate that she has died in waters contiguous to the county as a result of suicide on or about January 25, 2023. Evidence consists of a suicide note written by the victim's own hand, the victim's eyeglasses, and the victim's automobile, all found at or on the beach of Mourning Bay, a county park in the county of Chinook, Oregon, in the hours following her reported disappearance by her husband, Robert Oakley. It is probable that Mourning Bay is the place of death, and it is unlikely that her body will be recovered. Therefore, as Medical Examiner in the county in which the decedent was last known to be alive, I am issuing this certificate of presumed death, and, in the absence of her unrecovered body, it shall be the legally accepted fact of death."

Matt swallowed and looked up at Fern. "It's signed by Bernice B. Ryder, M.D."

"So, presumed death, not presumptive death?" noted Fern.

"Right."

"If I recall, that law was modified when they couldn't recover bodies of the presumed dead following the Mt. St. Helens eruption," she said.

"It gives the authorities an out if they find the body at a later date, and have to change the death certificate," Matt said.

"I'll bet Bernice hated this one," Fern said softly.

"You know she did," agreed Matt. "Bernice likes facts, not questions, and this case has some unanswered ones. I'll talk to her tomorrow morning."

"What else is in the file?"

"It looks like there are three separate reports," he said, shuffling through the file. "One is Earl's, and it's followed by Buck Bay Chief Dan McCoy, and then by the Coast Guard detailing their role in the search. Earl's and

McCoy's contain the interviews with the people in Hannah's life." He peered more closely at the file prepared by Earl; it contained a photocopy of the suicide note. It read simply, *It's over*, and was on a piece of white paper with jagged edges on two sides as if it had been torn. Matt would want to see the original note.

He abruptly closed the file. "Tell you what," he said, "you and I are entitled to one night of celebration before I go back to work in the morning. Let's eat and drink." He grinned at her.

Fern moved across the sofa and climbed into his lap.

CHAPTER 4

Fern was up first on Tuesday morning, quietly rising and tiptoeing into their closet to find her robe and slippers. She closed the door behind her before turning on the closet's overhead light, hoping Matt would sleep another hour or so. Maybe he didn't want a nurse, but she knew he still needed all the sleep he could get. The human body has only a few requirements to perform at its best, and Fern believed that proper rest and deep sleep were right up there with food, exercise, and love.

She pulled her butter yellow robe tightly around her and slipped on her favorite heather grey fuzzy slippers. It felt chillier than normal this morning. She headed downstairs, pausing on the staircase landing in front of the big window to peer out at the early morning surf. Dawn was just breaking.

Snow! There was snow on the beach! That almost never happened on the Oregon coast. She stopped to watch it come down, and it was obvious to her that it was tapering off. It was so quiet. She toyed with the idea of waking Matt, as she was certain he hadn't seen much snow in his lifetime. *Nope. Let him sleep. Coffee. That's what we need.*

She walked softly into the kitchen and put the coffee on, and then took her cup and cell phone and plopped down in her favorite chair in the far corner of the living room next to the big window. It faced out to sea, and she could look for miles in three directions.

I need to call my boss, she thought. Joe Phelps, head of covert operations for the U.S. Department of State in Washington, D.C., had hired Fern last year to keep her eye on the west coast. She had been instrumental in identifying a Chinese connection to major crime in two recent cases impacting Oregon and California, including the one that just wrapped up in both Portland and Port Stirling courtrooms.

Fern had had a text exchange with Joe Phelps at the end of yesterday's proceedings:

> Fern: Guilty on all counts.

> Joe: Nice work. Take one day off. Only one.

That, in a nutshell, was Joe. She checked her watch — 7:06 a.m. — a good time to catch him in his office. She touched his name in her Recents list.

"Good morning," Joe answered. "How are things on the left coast today?"

"Amazing," Fern replied. "We have snow on the beach. It rarely happens and it's so beautiful."

"We have it here, too, but it's not so beautiful. Mostly brown slush today. How's your husband feeling?"

"He's good. Wants me to stop being his nurse."

Joe laughed. "Yeah, I saw that coming. I imagine there's a big celebration going on around your place. You guys did a good job on this one, Fern. Took out some real bad actors. I can tell you that I'm breathing a little easier today, too."

"I'll take today off as you offered," she said. "Reality is setting in, and I need to do laundry. But after that, what's next? What do you want me to do tomorrow?"

"Well, all is currently quiet on the western front. There's some potential shit going down in the Seattle area that might have some Korean involvement, but it's being handled locally."

"You don't want me to take a look?"

"Not currently. It might require you at some point, but I want to give the locals a few days." He paused. "I'm somewhat concerned that there might be a backlash of some kind in your area. Chen was a big fish, and there might be some smaller fish in your pond that will try to fill the gap he's leaving. I want you to keep your eyes open and your ears to the ground in your south coastal area. Even a little north into southern Washington and south into California. Nothing overt, just pay attention to your world."

"I can do that," Fern said.

"I know I don't have to tell you to mind your p's and q's, but the last time I said 'pay attention' to one of my operatives, he got his head cut off."

"We've been over that, Joe, it wasn't your fault. Clay made a mistake. I won't do that. I'll look around this week, check in with my local sources, and see if things have calmed down now that the trials are over."

"That sounds perfect. Keep me posted. Anything else going on down there?"

"Matt's working on the suicide of a well-known local woman that might not be one."

"What's that about?"

Fern filled him in.

Joe said, "Suicide of a loved one is a tough gig. I hope Matt can help the poor guy."

They agreed to check in soon and ended the call. Fern scrutinized the local weather forecast on her phone and saw that the snow showers were expected to end by noon. *Might as well start some laundry.*

· · ·

Matt stood on the staircase landing and said, "Why is the sand white?"

Fern, coming out of the laundry room, laughed. "It's snow."

"It never snows here. What the hell?"

She met him at the bottom of the stairs and accepted his good morning kiss. "Isn't it pretty?" she said. They stood together watching the gentle flakes flutter down.

"It truly is," Matt said. "Is it gonna keep snowing?"

"Nope. Ends at noon."

He tugged on the belt of her robe. "Then let's hurry and get dressed and go outside to take some pictures."

"Back in a flash," she said and jogged up the stairs. "There's coffee."

By the time Matt and Fern got down to the beach, they'd been joined by dozens of neighbors and townspeople. Not to mention about a hundred dogs, all barking like crazy and running to the surf and then back up the beach, rubbing their noses in the foreign white stuff.

Matt felt comfortable on the open beach, especially surrounded by people he knew, but he still took a hard look around, up and down the beach, checking for anything or anyone who looked out of place. *Is that an outcome of getting shot, or just the cop in me doing my job?* he wondered. *Probably a little of both.*

Fern noticed his vigilance and said, "Everything OK?"

"Yep. Not a hair out of place." He squeezed her hand.

"And you feel good this morning?"

He stopped walking, turned to face her, and said, "Yes." Firm voice.

Fern smiled. "Just asking."

They resumed their walk, heading south into the sun, which was beginning to peek out from the leaden clouds. The snow was apparently over, but it lingered on the chilly sand. The snow coated the driftwood with a white layer, and it clung to the grasses, bending them over with the weight. Footprints led up to a lone bench near some stairs, empty now.

"Joe wants me to keep my eyes and ears open for a couple of weeks until he's confident there won't be any activity from our friends headed off to prison," she said. "He thinks it's possible someone might try to step into Chen's shoes around here."

Matt nodded. "He's right, it's worth being on the lookout. But my gut says Chen was such a control freak that there's no one else in his circle primed to cause us any grief. I'll be surprised if you uncover anything."

"That's my take, too," Fern said. "So, while I do my job, I might have more free time than I've had in weeks, and I have an idea what to do with it."

"You want to have a baby?" he looked at her expectantly.

Fern laughed. "No, not yet. We agreed to wait a year or so to enjoy our lives together first, right?"

"Well, we didn't write it in blood," he said.

"Are you changing your mind?"

"Not necessarily," Matt said. "I want what you want."

She hesitated. "I want to wait a little longer. I need time to establish myself in my new career, and there's something else I want to do, too."

"What?"

"If it looks like the crooks are taking a break for a while, I might have a few hours to establish our foundation. Remember, we talked about it after your hospital stay?"

"Yeah, I remember. It's a great idea."

"Good," she said. "Our money just keeps growing, and we can do some good in the world—or, at least, in our corner of it. I still like the idea of something in the health care realm, do you?"

"Yes. Especially after I looked at my hospital bills. Holy moly!" he exclaimed. "We have good insurance and personal resources, but what the hell would a family without means have done in my situation?"

Fern knew Matt's question was rhetorical, but she answered anyway. "They likely would've died. If we're smart about creating this foundation, maybe we can help prevent that. There's just one problem."

"Which is?"

"Neither one of us knows a darn thing about setting up a non-profit organization and running it," she said. "I want to take this slow time in my job to learn how to do it."

"It can't be that hard. You probably need to figure out the paperwork, maybe consult with someone who knows how to run a non-profit, and then dump some money in."

"I thought I would do that, but then what? How do we decide which projects to fund? How do we get the word out? How will we know what kind of startup expenses we'll have?"

"We'll need a process, for sure," he agreed. "We should take some time and decide on criteria, for starters. Even within the realm of healthcare there will be lots of choices. Do you fund capital equipment, for example, or people, or organizations who may have new solutions?"

"Yeah. And do we want to focus on one or more disciplines?" Fern asked. "Talking to Robert Oakley yesterday got me thinking. What about addictions? Mental health? Or, going back to your experience—more security for hospitals and clinics?"

"The need is enormous, Fern. Just in Oregon. And we should probably open up some access in Texas, too, since that's where our money came from."

"Yes," she said. "We don't have billions to cover the world, so we'll have to be specific, and I think Oregon and Texas are good starting points."

Matt heard a bark close by and turned to see Mr. Darcy, Lydia Campbell's border collie, approaching him at a fast clip. The dog skidded to a stop by Matt's leg and looked up, demanding an ear scratch.

"Hiya, boy," grinned Matt. He reached down, grabbed a fistful of snow, and rubbed it on the dog's nose. Mr. Darcy barked again, shook his head from side to side, and then nudged Matt's thigh. Matt squatted and gave the pooch what he wanted. They were old buddies, having met on Matt's first day in Port Stirling, when the inquisitive collie had discovered little Emily Bushnell's body in the beach cave.

Lydia came up to Matt and Fern, having given up pulling on Mr. Darcy's leash. She laughed and said, "You're his favorite police chief, you know. How are you doing?"

"I'm fine," Matt said standing and giving her a hug. "Sorry for all the racket around here on Thanksgiving." Lydia Campbell was a neighbor who lived about four houses up Ocean Bend Road from Matt. Her home had been spared in the earthquake, although she'd lost some cliff to the violent shaking and liquification that followed.

She waved her hand as if to dismiss his apology. "A few sirens. We're all just so relieved you came out the other side. And, you, poor thing," she said to Fern, taking her in a big hug. "How awful for you both. It's so nice to see you out here this morning. Isn't it, Mr. Darcy?"

The dog barked once and moved from Matt to Fern's thigh. She responded appropriately.

"Do you think we might be able to take a break from murder and mayhem for a while?" Lydia asked Matt, with a twinkle in her eyes.

"You mean, just enjoy this beautiful place we live?" he smiled at her, spreading his arms wide to take in the snow-covered beach, the powerful surf, and the sun starting to warm them just a bit.

"We're counting on it, Lydia," added Fern. "We could all use a break after the past year or so, don't you think?"

"I do," she replied crisply. "Mr. Darcy and I will do our best to not find any dead bodies." He barked in total agreement with his owner. "And you two, please keep any more bad guys at bay, OK?"

Matt was quiet, thinking about Mourning Bay and wondered if he would be able to do as Lydia asked.

Fern said, "We promise."

CHAPTER 5

Back in the house, Matt and Fern breakfasted, showered, and he headed off to city hall. Fern stayed at the house to make some lists and get organized to return to work tomorrow.

Although Matt loved being a cop, he'd never been so happy to go into work. Just driving the familiar route, parking in the space marked "Chief of Police", and strolling into the building gave him complete joy on this brisk early February morning.

The squad room was still quiet, with only Sylvia in attendance and at her desk, typing away on her computer. Seventy-something Sylvia Hofstetter, the police department's administrative assistant, was now a legend in Port Stirling, after her important role in the previous case. The plaque, awarded for her well-done job that earned her "City Employee of the Year", hung proudly on the wall immediately behind her desk. As she liked to say, "It's no trip to Paris, but it is a nice plaque."

"Our parking lot is still full of snow," Matt said. He stamped his boots on the floor and shook out his parka. "Can't we get the snowplow to plow us?"

Sylvia laughed, followed by a snort. "Port Stirling doesn't have a snowplow. It never snows here."

"Might want to look out the window," Matt told her.

"Freaky, huh? I've never seen snow on our beach. Must be climate change. What are we working on today?" she asked. Although Sylvia had enjoyed the breather between major cases while the trials were front and center, she was starting to get a teensy bit bored.

And, oh, how she had missed her boss during his recovery. Their small department was tight, working closely together and watching each other's backs, and the local law enforcement teams were collegial and cooperative, but it hadn't been the same without the chief running the show. Not to mention that being down two detectives—with Fern leaving to take her new job—the remaining officers were working heavy shifts.

Matt waved the files in his hand in Sylvia's direction. "Hannah Oakley."

"The suicide?"

"Yeah. Did you know her?"

"Not personally," said Sylvia, "but I know of her. She helped a friend of my daughter-in-law's after her daughter had OD'd on fentanyl. Saved the teen's life apparently. Based on her reputation and what I've heard about her, Hannah doesn't seem like the kind of person who would commit suicide."

"That seems to be the general consensus," frowned Matt. "But something has happened to her."

"And we're going to find out what, aren't we?" Sylvia asked. "What do you want me to do?"

"I don't know yet," Matt said. "First, I need to talk to Bernice. And then I need to read the files that Earl and Dan McCoy collected. It's been made clear to me that Hannah's case is not really my business. She lived in Buck Bay, and probably died in a county park, so, technically, it's got nothing to do with us."

"That's never stopped you before," she pointed out.

"I don't butt in," he said, somewhat offended. "Other than telling the State Department what to do." Sylvia shot out a big laugh. "But this case belongs to Earl with Chief McCoy on his flank. They don't need me riding in on a big horse kickin' up dirt."

"So why are you interested?"

Matt filled her in on Robert Oakley.

"Ahh," she said. "See, this is the problem with helping people. It never stops."

Matt looked at her sideways and raised an eyebrow.

She winked at him and turned back to her computer.

• • •

Matt took a few minutes to get comfortable in his office. He hadn't spent any real time there for weeks, and he wanted to reorganize a few things. He was, by nature, a tidy man and hated disorder.

Sylvia had left all the files relating to his shooting — major crime team meeting notes, surveillance on all the principles, virtually anything to do with his case — on top of his desk. Wanting to make a statement, mostly to himself, he took a round stamp from his desk's center drawer, and methodically stamped 'CLOSED' on each of the files. He filed them away in his cabinet without opening a single one.

Moving on. It's been about me for too long. Time to help someone else.

In the newly bare area of his desk, he placed the two files on Hannah Oakley, picked up his phone, and tapped Bernice's number.

Dr. Bernice Ryder answered after two rings. "I've missed your calls, chief. But please don't tell me you have another dead body on your first official day back at work."

"You need to stop blaming me for every crime that happens in Chinook County," he said playfully. There had been a rash of local murders that began literally the day Matt Horning had arrived in Port Stirling. Coincidence, but Bernice delighted in calling her friend, with whom she shared a gallows sense of humor, "Dr. Death".

"My call is about the suicide of Hannah Oakley," he continued. "Earl and Chief McCoy gave me their files; say they're done with this case. I've been asked by Robert Oakley to dig a little deeper. He's positive she didn't kill herself."

"I know that's what he thinks, Matt, and he was beside himself when I ruled it a probable suicide," Bernice said seriously. "But there was no evidence of anything else. Everyone loved her. There were no signs she'd been abducted. No forensic evidence in her car. No one ever called for ransom. There's been no sign of her phone, no credit card usage, no bank withdrawals. I think you'll see in Earl and Dan's files that no one they talked to had any motive whatsoever to want Hannah dead. And she did leave a note. Which had only her fingerprints on it. We swabbed it five times just to be sure."

"Well, *someone* left a note," Matt said slowly. "Do we know for sure it was her handwriting?"

"Yes, forensics matched it 100 percent to other handwritten notes from her office. It was even the same paper and pen McCoy took from her desk. She wrote it."

"But it could've been in reference to almost anything, couldn't it? There are lots of things that could be 'over'."

"True," Bernice allowed. "But someone tired of life, too tired to write a manifesto, might write those two words."

"I guess. But they could also have been written by a married woman who'd been having a love affair with another man. Imagine he'd gotten the note from her ending the relationship, he didn't like it, killed her, and left those two words in her handwriting for the world to find."

"Possible, but if you can find one person who believes that Hannah Oakley was cheating on her beloved husband, I'm a monkey's uncle."

Matt chuckled. "Darwin was right, you know. Your uncle was a monkey at one time."

"Har har," said Bernice. "She walked into that bay, Matt. But knock yourself out."

• • •

After Matt and Bernice hung up, he went back to Hannah's file. But soon after, a sharp rap at his office door was followed by city manager Bill Abbott, his boss, entering while simultaneously saying, "Can I come in?"

Matt stood to greet him, and the two shared a man hug.

"So happy to have you back, chief," said Abbott. "But I guess you know that goes without saying."

"Thanks for sticking with me, Bill," Matt said earnestly. "Not every manager would have done so."

Bill waved his hand as if to brush away the notion. "Never entered my mind. You're my police chief."

"Well, it meant a lot." Matt leaned back in his chair as Bill took an armchair facing his desk. "Is this a personal or business visit?"

"Both," Abbott said. "I needed to know you're here and healthy, but I also have a favor to ask. We need to replace Fern. Your small team worked very hard—and smart—while you recovered, but we need to fill our empty position as soon as you can get around to it. It's in this year's budget, so no issues there."

"I know, and it's on my list," Matt agreed, nodding. "We're lucky it's slow right now, but Jay, Walt, and Rudy are splitting the fourth shift since Fern's departure and it's catching up with them."

"Not to mention that they worked around the clock while you were out, all while under tremendous stress," Bill said. "Let's get an experienced law enforcement pro in here; someone you won't have to spend weeks training. We can go a little higher in salary if you need to. I'll deal with HR. But don't forget our diversity goals. You've got four white men and one senior woman currently, and we need a little more balance."

"Got it," Matt said. "The good news is that I don't necessarily have to get someone with loads of management potential. Jay proved he's got what it takes in my absence. All the reports on his performance in a crisis were stellar."

"Add mine to that, too," Bill said. "The kid was a superstar. Steady, diligent, resourceful, and a tougher leader than I expected when I appointed him interim chief. I'll write it up for his file, just haven't had time yet. I hated to bypass Walt, but he didn't seem to want to step up. Jay was the right choice."

"I'm square with Walt, don't worry. We had a good talk. He doesn't want a promotion. Likes his life the way it is, and he praised Jay's work." Matt scratched his chin and looked thoughtful. "What I'm most proud of is how they all worked together. Did their job but took it up a notch that the situation required."

"And more than that," added Bill, "the PSPD took charge. Sure, Lt. Sonders, Patty, and Earl came to the table in a big way, but it was our show. That makes me proud." Abbott stood up. "And now it's time to get them the missing officer and let them breathe a little."

"On it."

• • •

Matt spent an hour writing up the job description for the new officer, and then emailed it to Cindy in HR, along with a short list of police apps and recruiting sites he'd used in the past. He instructed her to keep diversity goals in mind and get with him when she had five or more candidates to review.

• • •

After a quick department meeting to set the shift rota for the week and catch up with everyone's life, Matt spent the rest of the morning carefully reading Hannah's files. Both the county sheriff's office and the Buck Bay PD had done their jobs…but that was all they did, no more, thought Matt.

Oh, sure, they talked to everyone in Hannah's immediate circle—family, work colleagues, and a couple of friends—but no one went beyond the bare minimum. It looked like suicide, and the cops seem to have taken it at face value. *Didn't the life of a woman of substance warrant a closer, deeper look? Didn't every woman's life?*

Like it or not, Matt agreed with Robert Oakley; his wife's disappearance deserved more rigorous inspection. *I'll probably piss off everybody, but it needs a more thorough effort.* He hit the intercom button on his phone. "Sylvia, come in and talk to me when you have a minute, OK?"

Thirty seconds later and in she came looking sleeker and dressed more professionally than usual. Personally, Matt loved Sylvia's 'look'; yards of flowing material, scarves that streamed behind her as she moved, lavenders, reds, brilliant blues, her colors. Today he noted her trim black pants, black turtleneck sweater, and a cropped camel and black checked jacket that fitted her small frame closely. Only her burgundy flat shoes with a proper small gold trim delivered any color.

He knew it was dangerous waters these days commenting on an employee's looks, but he couldn't help himself. "What happened to your stylist?" he asked, smiling.

"Oh, I fired her," Sylvia shot back. "As the city employee of the year, I feel that I need to set a standard this year. Believe me, there are some employees in this building who could stand to up their game."

He chuckled. "Worthy cause, but I'm not sure you need to go out and buy a whole new wardrobe. Although, you do look highly turned out today."

"These aren't new clothes. I had a professional wardrobe all the years I lived in New York, and I never throw clothes away. I bought some new shoes in the January sales because, you know, feet, but I've got lots of looks coming."

"Well, suit yourself."

"Did you read the files I left?" she asked.

"Yep, and I'm formulating a plan. We're gonna dig a little deeper into Hannah's disappearance."

"Good."

"I'll have Jay, Walt, and Rudy help us, but we're gonna be quiet about it. Earl and Dan McCoy might not appreciate it."

Sylvia shrugged. "You snooze, you lose," she said. "Earl won't mind because his department is strapped right now. He had to cut two positions at the end of the year due to budgetary issues, and then, of course, the locals will run wild."

"Yeah, that's what he told me." He paused. "Just between you and me, the Buck Bay police department was a little lackadaisical on this case. I'd never say that outside these walls, of course, but they shut down their investigation too early, in my view. Took everything at face value. That's not how it should work when a person disappears."

"What can I do, chief?" she leaned forward eagerly, pad and pen at the ready.

"Well, from what I can tell, they hardly looked into Hannah's past at all. Just talked to local family and colleagues. I'd like to know more about her. Where was she born and raised, schools, family, old friends, former boyfriends, or husbands, that sort of thing. Figured that's right up your alley."

"She was married previously," Sylvia said. "Before Robert Oakley."

"Weren't we all?" said Matt ruefully. Sylvia knew all about Matt's first wife, the famous Susie Longworth from Dallas, Texas, and she fervently hoped she'd never see that woman again in her lifetime.

"Her first husband was a local man, Justin Sorenson. He still lives somewhere around here, maybe down in Silver River," she said. "I don't know much about him, but I remember it surprised people both when they married, and then again when they divorced."

Matt leafed quickly through the files. "I don't see him mentioned here. Find him and I'll have a chat. I'd also like to know what she did professionally before Rainbow of Hope."

Sylvia was busy making notes, and he could tell she was a woman on a mission already. Matt smiled inwardly.

"While you get started, I'm going to talk to Robert Oakley again."

"Yes, chief," she said, briskly moving out of Matt's office and back to her desk.

How lucky am I to have an admin like Sylvia? May she work until she's ninety.

• • •

Matt picked up a Reuben sandwich from the Wave Schmave café down by the wharf. Owner Sheldon Weinstein and Sylvia thought they were being mum about their relationship, but Matt knew the two were seeing each other on a regular basis. They didn't want everyone in Port Stirling to know, but good luck with that. It only took an appearance together at Matt and Fern's big holiday bash to celebrate the outcome of the previous case, followed two nights later with a dinner in a corner booth at the Whale Rock restaurant for the tongues to start wagging. Jay told him about that dinner; he knew everyone in town, and was a classic 'old lady gossip', even though he hated it when Matt called him that.

It made Matt so happy. People who are in love want everyone else to feel the same, and he was very fond of Sylvia. He'd been covertly scrutinizing Sheldon since he'd figured out what was going on, just to make sure, you know, that he was good enough for her. The New Yorker had passed with flying colors; Matt decided he was a great guy.

Sheldon was working the counter today. "Checking up on me again, chief?" he teased Matt. "How's my girl doing today?"

"If, by your girl, you mean my assistant, Sylvia, she's awesome as always."

Matt grinned. "I believe she's happy to have me back at work and giving her something to do. She gets bored easily. You might want to keep that in mind."

"I am many things, but boring is not one of them," Sheldon said. "But thanks for the tip. Since I'm not handsome and brave like you, I have learned to develop other skills." He winked at Matt. "What can I get you today?"

Matt disagreed with Sheldon's assessment of himself. He was nice-looking in a dignified, New York way, albeit with eyes that rarely stopped twinkling. His salt-and-pepper hair was lush and brushed back neatly. Although he usually only saw Sheldon with an apron on, he remembered how well he'd worn his suit and tie at Matt's party—he cleaned up well. They were a good couple, and he hoped neither one of them would screw it up.

"What's good?" he said.

"If it were me, I'd get the Reuben today." Sheldon kissed his fingers. "It's magnificent."

"Can I eat it in my car without getting it all over me?" Matt asked. "I'm driving to Buck Bay."

"I'll load you up with some big napkins. No prob."

* * *

True to Sheldon's word, Matt safely devoured the Reuben on his drive. He'd lost weight during his ordeal, and he was starving all the time now. *That man is an asset to Port Stirling*, he concluded.

The sun was still trying to establish itself, hanging in a hazy sky mixed in with some low clouds and fog as Matt headed north on Highway 101. The snow was all melted, and it was 47 degrees by noon. *Guess that was our big snow event.*

Robert Oakley was thrilled to hear from him this morning, and they agreed that Matt would come to his house. He lived across the bay from downtown Buck Bay. Matt had only been to that side of town once, to go to Bernice's home for dinner with Fern and the Ryders. He could tell from looking at Google that Robert's home was along the road and not at the top of the hill in Bernice's high-rent district with her million-dollar views.

But as he pulled into the driveway, he was pleasantly surprised by the Oakley house. *Way better than sleeping outside in a doorway*, Matt thought. The new house was set back from the road in a small grove of fir trees, and was a nice two-story, neatly painted in sage green with crisp white trim. A large brick chimney spanned the two stories at one end, and smoke curled up from it today. Even in February, the lawn and landscaping were clipped and tidy.

Robert opened the front door and came out onto the large, covered porch. He waved as Matt exited his car and wiped his face one last time to make sure he got all the Reuben off.

"Nice place," Matt said climbing the four stairs to the porch and extending his hand.

"Thanks," Robert said. "We built this house after the earthquake and mostly enjoyed the process. It turned out like we wanted it to, and we're almost finished with the final touches. Please, c'mon in."

They took seats in the bright cream-colored living room in facing club chairs, angled in front of the warm fire. "I can't tell you how much it means to me that you're here," Robert started.

"I've read the files on Hannah's disappearance," said Matt. He tried to make his voice sound flat and professional because he didn't want to get Robert's hopes up. "I'm not convinced that we investigated as fully as we could have. I have some additional questions for you."

Robert threw up his hands and said, "Hallelujah!"

"No promises, you have to understand that," Matt said firmly. "This could still have a bad ending. It probably will."

"I get it. Most of the answers to the question are unpleasant," Robert said. "Believe me, I've answered them all in my head. Where will you start?"

"My assistant is looking into Hannah's background a little further. We want to know everything we can about her. Even though there's no mention of him in the files, she tells me that Hannah was married before she married you. Name of Justin Sorenson."

"I was wondering when someone would get around to him," Robert said. His face looked angry.

CHAPTER 6

"Yes, Justin Sorenson was Hannah's first husband," said Robert. "I have a photo of the two of them in the desk." He rose from his chair, went to a utilitarian oak desk in a corner of the large living room, and opened a lower drawer.

Taking the photo from Robert's hand, Matt realized he didn't have a good photo of the missing woman. "Do you have a sharp photo, like a headshot, of just Hannah that I can borrow for a few days?"

"Of course," Robert said, returning to the desk and picking up a framed photo from the desktop.

Matt stared at the couple's photo. The first thing that jumped out at him was that Justin appeared to be several years younger than Hannah. He was also extremely good-looking, as in the Brad Pitt category. Hannah, although pleasant looking, was not exceptional in any way. Mousy brown hair, narrow face, and thin lips, but her deep brown eyes exuded a warmth.

Matt took the single photo of Hannah from Robert, and this one told more of a story about the woman. Smiling broadly, her eyes crinkled, an effect that made her look even warmer and more welcoming. Matt thought she looked nice; someone you'd want to get to know. There was also intelligence there. Matt took an immediate liking to her.

"What can you tell me about their marriage?" Matt asked. "How'd they meet, how long were they together, and why the divorce? I'm sorry if this is painful for you."

"It's OK. They were married about four years. It took Hannah that long to figure out that Sorenson was—still is—a con man." Robert spoke clearly and calmly. "Hannah's parents were killed in a car crash on Hwy 101, foggy night, drunk driver. She was obviously devastated. In the aftermath, Hannah and her brother, George, were left some money in their estate, which they split evenly."

"How much was Hannah's share?" asked Matt.

"About $200,000. Not a lot by today's standards, but still not chicken feed." He hesitated.

"Go on," urged Matt.

"I hate this part." Robert rubbed his hands on his thighs. "Shortly after Hannah came into the money, she met Sorenson at a bar in Buck Bay. She was there with some girlfriends, and he singled her out. You've seen their photo. Does Hannah look like the type of woman a man like him would go after?"

Sidestepping the question, Matt said, "Let me guess. Justin Sorenson was charming, he brought the heat, swept Hannah off her feet, and they were married within weeks. Is that about right?"

"In a nutshell. She had money, owned her own home, and had a good job. Sorenson had none of those things. Hannah was blinded by 'love', and never had a chance."

"What happened?"

"She's a smart woman, chief. She eventually figured him out and booted him. But he did not go gently. He sought and was awarded Transitional Spousal Support because he was unemployed and even if he managed to get a job, he would be a lower wage-earner than his spouse. He told the court that he was going to seek additional education to become more employable and they bought it. That was eight years ago, and she's still paying him."

"He sounds like a real sweet guy," Matt offered.

Robert snorted. "Yeah. Funny thing is, Hannah and I had just been to see a lawyer about pulling the plug on good ol' Justin."

"Oh? When was that?"

"About three weeks ago."

"And what was the outcome?" Matt asked.

"The lawyer said, "Go for it, the guy is a parasite, which will be clear to the courts now.""

"Were you planning to follow through?"

"Yes. It took Hannah a while to get over whatever remaining guilt she had wrapped up in him, but she decided it was time. Past time, in my view. Even at my rock bottom, I never sponged off a woman." He shook his head.

"Had she told Sorenson the bad news?"

"She and the lawyer were working on it, and the lawyer advised her to write him a letter first telling him of her intentions. I think she just did that."

"Did she mail it?"

"I believe so, but we hadn't heard boo out of him, so I'm not sure where it stood." Robert paused. "Are you thinking what I'm thinking? 'It's over'?"

"That's exactly what I'm thinking," said Matt.

• • •

Matt made some notes and got some contact information for some key people in Hannah's life who he wanted to talk to—Justin Sorenson, for sure, Hannah's brother, her best friends. Earl and Dan had covered her current business colleagues thoroughly, but Matt still wanted to talk to them himself.

As he and Robert walked through Hannah's life, Matt decided he would bring in his officers—Jay, Rudy, and Walt—on a proper investigation. Matt was getting the feeling that there was more to Hannah's disappearance than it looked on the surface. He had that sharp thing in his gut he'd learned to listen to over the years. *Why in the hell hadn't Earl and Dan talked to Justin Sorenson?*

He looked up now, directly at Robert and asked, "I assume that you are the beneficiary of Hannah's estate—is that correct?"

"I assume so, but I don't know for sure. We made wills shortly after we were married, naming each other. There aren't any children involved, and we agreed our siblings can take care of themselves. I think she left a painting to George that their grandmother painted and maybe some cash, but that's all. Whether or not she changed her will at any point after that, I have no idea."

"I'll have to check. Please give me your attorney's name and contact info."

Robert did so, paused, and then said, "You can't possibly believe that I would harm a hair on Hannah's head? Not for a few dollars?"

"No, I don't think that," Matt said. "But I always follow the money. Standard procedure."

"Do what you have to do, then," Robert said brusquely. "What else can I tell you?"

"Is there anyone, other than Justin Sorenson, who may have had any reason to harm Hannah? Any feuds in her background, professional disagreements, or conflicts? Long-standing grievances?"

"I've racked my brain trying to think of someone who could be involved in her disappearance," said Robert. He looked pained. "There just isn't anyone. Her friends, relatives, employees—they all love Hannah. And the non-profit world she works in is very friendly and collegial…they help each other all the time. She has a wonderful reputation in the community. It's just baffling to me." He looked at Matt as quiet tears fell from his eyes onto his sweater. "But I know—I know!—she did not kill herself."

Matt rose from his chair. "Well, I guess we'll see where this goes. I'll give it my best, Robert. Take care of yourself in the meantime."

"Will you keep me posted?" he said, wiping his face with his sleeve.

"Of course. I'm going to bring in some of my officers to help me interview and it will take us a couple of days. Hang tight. I'll be in touch, probably with some more questions as we begin to talk to folks. Do you have friends or family who can help you?"

Robert attempted a smile. "I'm not going to start drinking again if that's what you're worried about."

"You're under a lot of stress. The devil finds souls at times like this," Matt said quietly.

"He's not going to find me," Robert said firmly. "And, yes, I've got buddies and neighbors beating down my door on a regular basis. I'm not alone anymore, chief. I'll be fine no matter what you discover about Hannah. I just need to know the truth."

"Then I'd better get a move on and find it."

● ● ●

Back in the squad room, Matt gathered his crew and told them the plan for further investigating Hannah's disappearance. He began with how he'd met Robert Oakley and brought them up to speed on his life since then.

There was some wariness among his officers. Matt invited them to share their thoughts. Jay went first.

"I know you have a connection with Oakley, but this might not sit well with Earl and Dan. They already investigated and agreed it was suicide."

"I'm concerned about that, too," admitted Matt. "It's kinda not done in our world, especially with a team like ours that works so closely on area crime. And, Bernice. She doesn't declare the cause of death lightly. She had to believe in it, too."

Rudy spoke. "But Bernice can only go on what the forensics and the cops tell her when there's no body. If they didn't do a good job on the investigation, she had no choice."

"Good point, Rudy," said Matt. "But I don't want to get on the bad side of anyone. These people are our friends as well as our colleagues. And, there's also the not insignificant fact that I trust their judgment, especially Earl's."

"You sound like you're trying to talk yourself out of this case," said Jay. He looked around the room. "If you believe that Robert might be right, and there's any chance at all that Hannah didn't die by suicide, we should work on it. We trust your instincts. And, we can handle Earl and Dan."

There were nods around the room.

"What if it turns out that they didn't do a good job on their investigation?" asked Matt. "And we find out new info. How can we make sure they don't look bad?"

"Hannah and Robert Oakley should be our concern," spoke up Sylvia. "Not whether some cops get their little feelings hurt. You can finesse it, chief. Include them when you need to. If you need to."

"I will absolutely include them if we uncover anything useful." Matt frowned. "It's just that I know how I would feel if one of them started going over my case. But Sylvia's right; the focus needs to be on the victim and spouse, not whether I get invited to McCoy's BBQ this summer."

They all laughed.

"And, besides, it's not like these slackers are working on anything meaningful anyway," Sylvia said. She waved her arms around the squad room.

"OK, then," Matt said, "let's go." He pinned the photo of Hannah that Robert had given him and wrote her name under it on the squad room's white board. Then he wrote down several questions they needed answers to as they began investigating:

1. *Who is the beneficiary of Hannah's will?*

2. *Did Justin Sorenson know that Hannah was cutting off his spousal support? Did he receive a letter from her stating so?*

3. *Was there anything going on at work out of the usual? Was anyone in Rainbow to Hope pissed off about anything?*

4. *Was there anything in her recent past that indicated trouble with friends or family?*

5. *Had Hannah been to see a therapist, or shown signs of depression?*

6. *Was there any hint of an affair, or problems in her marriage to Robert?*

At that last question, Jay asked, "Why would Robert ask you to investigate further if it might throw any suspicion on him?"

"Who knows? But stranger things have happened," Matt replied. "I don't suspect him of being involved in her disappearance, and I strongly believe his motivation is pure, but that doesn't mean I won't still ask the question."

• • •

Tuesday was wearing on; the squad room clock read 3:45 p.m. when they'd covered the case basics. They decided as a group they wanted to start working on it this afternoon, and they had time left in the day to start through their list of questions.

Matt took Jay with him to track down Justin Sorenson. Robert thought he had moved from Silver River back to Buck Bay recently and worked part-time at a pool hall in the downtown area. The cops decided to try there first.

Walt was going to Oakley's lawyer to see what he could discover about Hannah's will.

Rudy, who had remained on good terms with a woman he previously dated in the Rainbow to Hope office, thought he would talk to her first and see if there was any dirt her colleagues hadn't shared with the Buck Bay PD.

Sylvia did what Sylvia did best; attack the internet in her quest to learn what she could about how Hannah really lived her life. It was amazing what social media could reveal these days. Her main objective was to unearth good friends who the cursory investigation might have overlooked. Matt had taught her that the more they could learn about the victim, the more obvious the 'why' of the crime might become. Sylvia absolutely loved her job.

In the car with Jay driving back to Buck Bay for the second time today, Matt said, "Fern tells me you're going to buy a house."

"I am. I'm a grownup now."

Matt chuckled. "I don't think it's official until you're thirty."

Jay held up his hand. "Stop. Do not say that number. It's evil."

"Thirty. Thirty. Thirty. When does it happen?"

"April."

"Well, you'd better have a house bought by then," Matt said. "You know, since your life as you know it will essentially be over."

"Thanks, man, funny. Fern found two online she thinks I should go look at."

"She's good at this, so you should. Do you have a realtor?"

"Not yet, but I'm gonna call Sandy Vox, you know, she helped us on the Anselmo case."

"Right. She also found my rental cabin, which, alas, is now at the bottom of the Pacific Ocean."

"You've had a couple of real bad nights in Port Stirling, my friend," observed Jay.

"Yep. But in my world, that means it's only good times ahead. Right?"

"You'd think," said Jay.

"How's it going with Amy Rose? Have you seen her this month?" Matt saw them dancing at his holiday party and thought Jay could do worse.

"Yes."

"Details, man," Matt persisted. "Are you getting any?"

Out of the corner of his eye, Matt saw Jay's mouth twitch upward.

"As a matter of fact, I am. And it's good."

"You'd better bring her over for dinner at the house then so Fern and I can pass judgment."

"I'd be happy to bring her over. But it won't matter what you guys think."

"Uh-oh," Matt grinned.

• • •

Justin Sorenson was tending bar at the Growler Pool Hall in downtown Buck Bay. Matt recognized him immediately from Robert's photo. Still a real good-looking guy but starting to grizzle around the edges just a bit.

The two cops approached him, showing their badges.

"Are you Justin Sorenson?" asked Matt, taking the lead.

"Guess so," he replied, shrugging a shoulder.

"I'm Matt Horning, police chief in Port Stirling, and this is Detective Jay Finley. We'd like to ask you a few questions about Hannah Oakley."

Justin looked around the nearly empty room and said, "Good a time as any. What can I help you with?"

"Had you seen your former wife recently?"

"No, not for a couple of years. I was sorry to hear about her suicide."

"Were you surprised by that news?" Matt asked.

"Yeah, I guess I was. Didn't seem the type. Too damn cheerful."

"Had you talked to her recently?"

"Like on the phone, you mean?" Justin asked.

"Yeah."

"No. Haven't seen her. Haven't talked to her."

"What about email or text?" Jay asked.

Justin looked over at Jay and said, "No. No contact with Hannah at all."

"Did you receive a letter from her in the past week or so?" asked Matt.

"What is this, guys?" Justin said irritably.

"Please answer the question, Mr. Sorenson," said Matt.

"No, I have not received any letters from her."

"Have you had any communication from Hannah's attorney?"

"Like recently, you mean?"

"Yes, in the past two weeks," clarified Matt.

"No."

"So, you didn't receive a letter from either Hannah or her attorney informing you that they were petitioning to end your spousal support?" Matt asked.

To Matt and Jay's surprise, Sorenson laughed.

"Wondering when they would deal with that," he said.

"Eight years, I understand," said Matt. "Seems like more than enough time to get back on your feet after the divorce."

Justin glared at him. "She had plenty of money. It didn't hurt her to share a little of it with me. She was the one who wanted the divorce."

"And why was that?" Jay asked. "Why did she want a divorce relatively soon?"

Another shrug. "Marriage is tough," Sorenson said. "We just kinda drifted apart."

"I heard she kicked you out for sponging off her," Matt said.

"Believe what you want. She's dead now, so I guess it doesn't really matter," Sorenson said.

CHAPTER 7

As they drove back to Port Stirling, the late winter sun was beginning to set. Coming up on the bluff just before town, Matt pulled off at the viewpoint. The retiring sun was turning the ocean many shades of gold, pink, and crimson.

"This is why we live here, huh?" Jay said.

Matt nodded. "Takes my breath away. Did you believe Sorenson? That he didn't get a letter from Hannah or the lawyer?"

"I kinda did," Jay said hesitantly. "At the time, he seemed sincere."

"But?"

"But the more I think about it, the more I think even I would have lied under those circumstances. I wouldn't want the cops to know that I'd just been cut off from her money, and then she turns up dead."

"We don't know that she's dead," Matt corrected. "Just that she's missing. We have to operate under that scenario for now."

"I know. But you know what I mean. If he tells us that yes, he got a letter from her saying no more dough, it would be suspicious timing," Jay said. "I would keep it to myself, and hope Matt Horning didn't find out otherwise."

"So would I," Matt agreed. "We'll see what Walt learns with Hannah's attorney before we pursue this any further. If she says she or her client sent Sorenson a letter, then we go to Plan B."

"What is Plan B?"

"Don't know yet."

. . .

Rudy Tomaselli felt uncomfortable going into Rainbow of Hope, which was one of the reasons why he was no longer dating Sarah Forrester, a counselor there. Rudy had a heart of gold, but he felt hardened around the non-profit's clients. Oh, he had sympathy for those with mental issues or just down on their luck, but it was the druggies he had a problem with.

Rudy had always taken care of his body, even when he was a kid. Both of his parents were athletes, and they'd instilled that discipline in him. His grandparents on both sides were from the 'old country', still living in the Naples area of Italy. They believed in pasta, not exercise. His dad's favorite refrain when he thought Rudy was dogging it in the gym or on the field was, 'Do you want to look like Nana when you're old?'

He decided when he was ten years old that he did not want to look like Nana, and he'd made time for his body pretty much every day since then. Sure, he liked a beer or a glass of wine as much as the next guy, but he was always careful to keep it under control. The clients that Sarah dealt with had let the booze and drugs control them, not the other way around. Oregon had made it easy for the druggies with its loose 'recreational drugs' policies, and Rudy had a problem with that. But he still didn't have much sympathy for them.

Sarah came out to greet him and pointed to a small conference room at one side of the larger space. "Shall we go in there?"

He followed her in and closed the door behind him.

"You look good, Sarah. It's nice to see you," Rudy smiled.

"You, too." She scooted her chair closer to the small round table. "I presume this is about Hannah?" she ended the sentence with a question in her voice.

"Yes. Thanks for taking time to talk to me." Rudy took out his notebook, while Sarah looked around the windowless, non-descript room. Ivory walls, brown indoor/outdoor carpet meant to show no dirt. One framed photo of a lone pink flower in a vase for decoration.

"No problem," she said. "We're all in shock."

"How did you hear about it?" Rudy asked.

"Probably the same way you did," Sarah said. "The sheriff's office called us the morning after she disappeared. I'm still having trouble processing it." She looked sad.

"What's the scuttlebutt in the office? Do people have any theories?"

Sarah leaned back in her chair and twirled a length of blond hair that reached past her shoulder. *I always go for blondes,* Rudy thought, *maybe that's my problem.*

She hesitated a split second too long, and Rudy said, "You can tell me the truth. We don't have an agenda. Just want to find out what happened to her."

"Most of the staff and several of the clients who worked with Hannah don't believe she killed herself," she said.

"You included?"

"Me included."

"Why?" Rudy asked. "What are you basing that on? The evidence points to her walking into Mourning Bay."

"I have several reasons," Sarah said. "It's just not the sort of thing Hannah would ever do. And even if she did decide to commit suicide, she'd never do it that way. She was afraid of the ocean. Her brother almost got swept out to sea when they were kids. He was rescued, but it left a scar on Hannah. She would have taken pills. But the main point is that she truly was not the type."

"Family and friends often say that, you know," Rudy said.

"I know. But family often miss the warning signs; we're experienced at detecting those things in this building, and not one person here will tell you they saw even one sign that Hannah was suicidal."

"OK," said Rudy. "You said you had several reasons—what are the others?"

"She and Robert are deeply in love. She wouldn't do this to him. It was like they found each other after half a lifetime of searching."

"Did she tell you that personally?"

"Yes. We were friends and we shared our personal feelings," Sarah said.

"I even told her about you when we were dating." A hint of a smile flashed across her face.

Rudy, much to his horror, felt himself blushing. "Women talk, I guess," was all he could get out.

"And, she recently got some good news about the business." Sarah continued talking quickly to spare Rudy any further embarrassment. "She was informed last Monday that Rainbow to Hope had been awarded a big grant from a major west coast foundation. It was a very competitive process, and we really didn't expect to win, but Hannah gave it her all. The grant secures our funding for the next five years." She looked down at the table. "At least, we hope it does now that Hannah is missing. Hopefully, they won't reconsider."

"Who was your competition?" Rudy asked. "Who lost?"

"Over two hundred non-profits applied, and they narrowed it down to ten in December. Then they did site visits the first week in January, and ours went very well, but we still didn't think we had a chance. Our competition included well-run operations in Newport, Eugene, Vancouver, and Seattle. Hannah thought one of those four would win."

"Why do you think you won?" Rudy asked.

"Our results over the past couple of years have been terrific. We high-lighted our track record, and it proves we're getting the job done." There was pride in Sarah's demeanor. "Plus, Chinook County's need for our services is unfortunately very high. We were able to show that as well."

"A new addict born every day, huh?" said Rudy.

Sarah bristled. "You know better than that, Rudy. It's not just the local substance abuse problem which, yes, is significant and getting worse not better. You know that word 'Hope' in our name? Well, lots of folks around here don't have much hope for a brighter future. We try to show them the way to hope. And, we're seeing more and more serious mental health issues. Put it all together, and the foundation apparently decided that their money would be well spent in Buck Bay."

"Did you hear from your competitors after the grant was announced?"

"Yes, I believe that they all phoned Hannah to congratulate us. It's a friendly, professional group, and it's too bad we couldn't all win. But we'll take it."

"Who's in charge of the money here?" Rudy asked.

"We have a CFO, and she and Hannah are both overseen by a three-person board of directors."

"Are all checks signed by both the CFO and CEO?" Rudy asked.

"Yes. Exactly. And if the amount is over $2,500, it requires a board signature as well."

"So pretty hard to pocket any company funds."

Again, Sarah bristled, and leaned forward across the table. "That would never happen here," she said firmly. "Nobody works in the non-profit field expecting to get rich. We do it because we're each on a mission. You never understood that, did you Rudy?"

"I understand it just fine. Cops are the same. You think we get into law enforcement to get rich? That the risk of getting shot every day is all about a couple of bucks? It's not, let me tell you. We may have different methods of helping people, but we're in it for the same reasons you are."

Sarah raised her hands, palms up, gesturing at him. "OK, I get it. Calm down. But the next time you're arresting an addict, ask yourself if I could do more to help him. Can you do that?"

Rudy frowned. "I'll keep that in mind, but no promises."

She raised her arms in victory. "Progress!"

Rudy had to smile. "OK. If Hannah didn't kill herself, what do you think has happened to her? Where is she?"

"That's the mystery, huh?" Sarah said. "I think somebody's got her. Something bad has happened to her. All I know is that last Wednesday she told me she was going to get some lunch and then to a meeting offsite, and she'd be back at 2:30 p.m. She left about 12:30 p.m."

"Did you ask her who she was meeting with?"

"I didn't. She's the CEO, it's none of my business unless she tells me. Wish I had now."

"The Buck Bay PD report said she got takeout at the Thai restaurant around the corner. Does that sound normal?"

"Yes, she loves their food. Probably eats lunch there three times a week. They even make her a special dish."

"Can you take a stab at who she might have been meeting?" Rudy asked. "Any guesses?"

"I don't think it was to do with Rainbow or she would have told me."

"Pretty sure I know the answer to this next question, but I have to ask it," Rudy said. "Is there any chance she had a boyfriend? A lover not named Robert?"

"No. There is no chance."

"Would she have told you if she was?"

"Not necessarily," Sarah answered. "But I would've known."

Rudy raised an eyebrow. "How?"

"Hannah was an open book. She would've given herself away. We're not best friends, but I could still read her pretty well. She did not go to meet a lover."

"Who is her best friend? Do you know?"

"She has several good friends, mostly from school days here. If I had to pick one, I'd say Blake Bowen."

Now, Rudy's eyebrows both shot up. "The rock 'n roll singer?"

Sarah laughed. "Yeah, odd, huh? Blake and Hannah went to kindergarten through twelfth grade together, and the way I heard it, were mostly inseparable growing up. Obviously, there was the period when Blake hit it big and moved to L.A., about the same time as Hannah left to go to college in Colorado. But I think they even kept in touch then, just less frequently. When Blake's star burned out, she moved back to Buck Bay and lives here now. They get together regularly."

"I had no idea Blake Bowen moved back here," Rudy said.

"And that's just the way she wants it. She and her husband live a quiet life, although he works. He runs the Eugene non-profit I told you about, but he works mostly remotely these days. Hannah told me that Blake still pulls in the royalties and makes sporadic appearances. They live in a fancy gated house on several acres, still technically Buck Bay, but on that spit overlooking the Pacific southwest of here."

"I think I know the house you mean," Rudy said. "Always wondered who has to live behind a gate."

"I don't know that they *have* to, but there's probably still the occasional fan that's a nuisance."

"Do you have a phone number or email for her?"

"I think I have both, but I'll have to look it up. I know for sure I have Alex Bowen's—that's her husband. They're both really nice people, and I'm sure they'd be happy to talk to you if it would help find Hannah."

"Great. Please shoot them to me when you get a chance. And if you know of other friends we could talk to, add them, OK? Robert Oakley has given us a list of family, so we're covered there." Rudy jotted down a note in his notebook. "Is there anyone you can think of who would want to harm Hannah?"

"Robert asked me the same thing. He and I put our heads together after she disappeared, and we can't come up with a single person. There's no reason. Nothing makes any sense. And the more I think about it, the more puzzled I become. I'm sorry."

"Thanks, Sarah. It was nice to see you again."

Sarah smiled.

Rudy talked to a few more of the Rainbow to Hope staff, and the story was the same. Hannah Oakley wasn't a saint, but she was darn close to one, according to her colleagues. It was inconceivable to them that someone would want to hurt Hannah. But even more unthinkable that she would kill herself or just disappear.

But as he drove back to Port Stirling, Rudy thought of the possibilities. *Either someone did hurt her, or she killed herself, or she just took off. Or, maybe she was a saint and walked across the water in Mourning Bay.*

CHAPTER 8

Back at the office at 5:15 p.m., the group gathered in the squad room to report on their findings. The PSPD worked in a room much like every other police department, with the exception of a wall of windows on the west side that had distant views of the Pacific Ocean.

Walt had tracked down Hannah Oakley's attorney. She told him that Hannah had made no changes in her will since she and Robert made new ones shortly after their marriage.

"So, does that mean that Robert essentially gets everything?" asked Matt.

"Lawyer wouldn't let me read it yet. She's kinda stuck in purgatory, although Bernice's Presumption of Death clarifies the legal status somewhat, she said. But I asked her if Robert Oakley was still the prime beneficiary and she nodded."

"Follow the money," said Matt quietly.

"Can't do that in this case," said Rudy, shaking his head. "I talked to my pal Sarah Forrester at Rainbow to Hope, and then to another six colleagues of Hannah's. They all said the same thing. She and Robert were apparently the love story of the century. No boyfriend or girlfriend on either side, and they were blissfully happy."

"That's the same story I got from Robert, too," admitted Matt. "He is truly devastated, and I'm pretty sure he's not faking. What's your gut telling you, Rudy, after spending the afternoon there?"

"I don't know, man. There doesn't seem to be anybody that we could classify as a suspect in Hannah's circle. My gut says one of the addicts got ticked off at her and did her in. But I didn't get to the 'clients' today."

"We're putting Justin Sorenson, Hannah's ex, on our list," said Jay. "He told us he didn't know she was cutting off his allowance, but we're not sure we believed him." He looked over at Matt, who nodded in agreement. "Did the attorney know if Hannah had sent him a letter?"

"She didn't know for sure," said Walt. "But she thought Hannah was planning to send it last week."

"Before she disappeared?" asked Matt.

"She doesn't know, chief," said Walt. "All she knows for sure is that Hannah didn't send her a copy of any letter she may have written, and she didn't tell her whether she had or not. It was her view that only Robert might know. And, of course, Justin himself."

"Robert doesn't know," said Matt. "He knew she was mulling it over but didn't know if she'd gone beyond that stage." He looked at the wall for a moment. "Here's a thought: maybe the attorney could call Justin and inquire if he'd received the letter from her client, Hannah? Make it sound like she knew about it and was just confirming it with him."

"He'll lie to her, too, don't you think?" said Jay.

"Yeah, probably," agreed Matt. "But it wouldn't hurt to have another take on whether or not he's lying. Lots of lawyers have good radar on people."

"I like it," said Walt. "She's a sharp cookie, and she wants to help any way she can. Very upset. And, for the record—which is sounding like a *broken* record—she doesn't think Hannah offed herself either."

"Sylvia, have you found anything interesting yet?" Matt asked.

"I've been looking at her social media accounts—Facebook, Instagram, and Twitter. She was most active on Facebook and posted something almost every day. Also has tons of friends there, several hundred. Most of her friends are around Chinook County, but she has a good number in Colorado, too."

"Sarah Forrester told me that Hannah went to college in Colorado," said Rudy. "So that makes sense."

"Ahh," said Sylvia. "I haven't gotten to her education records yet, so that's good to know. Hannah also has a lot, as in 'a lot' of FB friends in the non-profit world. Many of them are CEO types like her, but she also has a lot of connections in the philanthropic foundations and grant worlds. The one thing I can tell you in my early going here is that she is extremely well-connected in her professional sphere."

"Anything else jump out?" asked Matt.

"Hannah seems to spend regular time with local friends. There are hundreds of photos showing dinner at their houses, picnics on the beach, shopping trips and concerts in Portland — that kind of thing."

"Any pictures of Blake Bowen?" asked Rudy. "Sarah told me that Hannah and Blake had been besties since kindergarten."

"Is she the washed-up rock 'n roll star?" asked Sylvia.

Rudy smirked. "That's kinda harsh, Syl. She retired and moved back to Buck Bay, that's all."

"Whatever," said Sylvia. "And, yes, there are many photos of her and Hannah together. They are always smiling and having fun."

"Who exactly are we talking about?" asked Matt.

The others laughed.

"Only the most famous person to ever come out of Chinook County," said Jay. He filled in his newcomer boss on Blake Bowen's story. "We had a golfer who made it to the PGA, but he didn't last long, and a couple of successful writers, but Blake is our claim to fame."

"Where does she live now?" asked Matt.

Rudy consulted his notes. "In Buck Bay. You know that bluff that runs southwest of downtown? She and her husband live out there on a big ocean-view property. I think I know the house because it's the only one with a gate on the driveway."

"We should talk to her," Matt said. "Did you get contact info?"

"Sarah's going to email it to me, she had to look it up."

"OK, people, that's a start," Matt said. He stood up. "Thanks, and I'll see you all bright and early tomorrow morning. I'll get everything we know on the white board before I leave, and we'll see how it all feels tomorrow."

· · · ·

Fern was a little bit at loose ends, home alone for the first time since Matt came home from the hospital. She finished the laundry, washed the vegetables for dinner and made a salad. She walked out to the road and their mailbox, then answered a text from Beverly, Matt's mother, telling her he felt 'great!' and was back at work full-time.

At 4:00 p.m. she wandered out to the deck and scanned the horizon and the beach. Once the snow melted, it warmed up in a hurry, and had turned out to be a lovely day, especially for this time of year. Although the more she thought about it, the more she realized that much of the Oregon coast would frequently get a burst of pleasant weather in February.

The sky was pale blue, just one shade lighter than Tiffany blue. The ocean, vigorously hitting the shore with bright whitecaps, showed bands of blue hues as it marched to the horizon. For the first time since early last fall, Fern thought the air felt soft today, caressing her skin rather than beating it up. She lifted her face to the sun that was now low in the sky, preparing to dip where the sea and sky met. *I seem a little down today, maybe some extra vitamin D will help.*

She stood like that for several minutes, thinking about what was causing her mood. *Matt doesn't need me as much now as he did during his recovery. True. But that's a good thing. Is it a letdown after all the excitement and success in wrapping up his case? That would be understandable*, she told herself. *Please don't tell me you're missing the rigid structure of your job when you worked in the Port Stirling PD. You wanted a job with more flexibility and the freedom to put your own stamp on it.*

Yes, but.

But what?

Maybe I'm not sure exactly how to begin. We're not in crisis mode at the moment. Also true. So, for the first time, you have to figure out how to proceed. You need a plan, Sam.

She went back inside and strolled to her home office. Her workspace was on the opposite end of the house from Matt's and was smaller and not appointed as luxuriously as his. But she couldn't love it more. This space was empty when she moved in, and she had set about furnishing it early on. Matt said it was empty because he didn't think she was ever going to come around and marry him, but he'd left it bare…just in case.

Fern had found a white L-shaped contemporary desk online that fit perfectly into the southwest-facing corner of the room. That corner, near the backyard steps to their deck, had one of the best views, and the windows ensured that her room was filled with light all day. She'd set up her computer monitor in the corner, pushing it as far back as she could so it didn't interrupt the view more than was necessary. She'd also bought a contemporary yellow/grey/black area rug that gave a splash of color over the neutral carpet. Two small bookshelves, a couple of silver task lamps, and a good ergonomic desk chair, and she was done. A beam of sunlight was hitting her rug and made the lemon-yellow colors dance.

Fern created a new Word file and sat for a moment thinking what to write.

'GOAL', she wrote at the top of the page: *Keep the west coast safe from bad actors*. Under that, she wrote 'STRATEGIES', and started a bullet list:

- Establish and work with contacts in the major and local law enforcement agencies in her territory.

- Contact former bad guys in prison on a regular basis: Who might be a good snitch?

- Contact people who interact with the public daily. Vicky springs to mind—more like her in other cities and towns, especially on the coast from San Francisco to Seattle.

Fern finished her plan just as she heard Matt's car in the garage. Her Joe Phelps' induced day off was over. She needed to get out there tomorrow.

• • •

"Your mother texted me and wanted to know why you hadn't answered her texts," Fern said. She smiled sweetly at Matt as he stood at her office door.

"I was busy," he gruffed. "You know, doing my actual job. She can't expect me to be in touch with her every day." He shrugged out of his jacket and ran his hand through his hair.

"You almost died," Fern said. "It's going to take her a while to get over it. Humor her when you can and don't worry about it when you can't. I'll cover for you for another few days until she realizes we're back in our routine, and all is well."

He grabbed her in a tight hug and planted a long kiss. "Thanks. I owe you. Again." He grinned. "What are you working on?" He looked over her shoulder at her open laptop.

"Trying to figure out how the heck to do my job. Could you take a look at this and tell me if I'm on the right track? What's missing?"

He stepped around her and sat down in her desk chair, while he scanned her document. "Looks thorough to me," he said after a few minutes. "The only thing I might add—and I can't believe I'm saying this—is to maybe talk to Arlette Sherwin and see if Clay had any tricks of the trade that she knows and might share with you."

Clay Sherwin was the State Department's spy before Fern was hired.

"That's a good idea, Matt. I don't want to overlook anything."

"As long as you overlook getting your head cut off like poor Clay," he said.

"Well, except for that last part, he was successful," Fern said. "He did uncover the early days of the Anselmo operation, and he was onto the bad guys. We know that now. How do you suppose he learned what was going on? I'm so afraid I'll miss some obvious signs because I don't really know what I'm looking for."

"Clay didn't either," he said. "Maybe he got a tip. Or maybe he was jogging on the beach and saw one of their amphibious duck boats. Or maybe he overheard Octavio and Juan talking in a restaurant. We don't know. Joe Phelps said he never asked for a wiretap, so it was all local snooping around. My bet is somebody heard Octavio yapping and thought it sounded suspicious, and Clay heard about it. Something made him track down Octavio and start following him."

"He and Juan were out and about around town, weren't they?" Fern remembered.

"And don't underestimate old men in coffee shops," Matt smiled. "They see things going through towns that don't belong."

"How was your day?" Fern asked.

"Hell if I know. I can't figure out what to believe in this Hannah Oakley case. My head says she drowned herself in Mourning Bay. Case closed."

"And your heart? Or gut?"

"This woman did not have a single reason to kill herself, and the whole thing is highly suspicious. But without a corpse, I don't have a murder." He filled her in on what transpired today. "Jay and I are going to Buck Bay first thing in the morning to talk to her best friend, a woman named Blake Bowen. I'm hoping she can shed some light on Hannah's mental state."

"Blake Bowen and Hannah Oakley are best friends?" Fern's eyebrows shot up and her mouth gaped open.

"Apparently," said Matt. "You know her too, I suppose?"

"Everyone in this part of Oregon knows Blake Bowen."

"Why are you surprised they're friends?" asked Matt.

"Well, they couldn't be any more different," Fern said. "At least, not on the surface, except that they are both well-known in the area. Blake is flashy and loves attention. Hannah is unflashy, and while she gets the attention because of her work and success, she doesn't appear to welcome it."

"Opposites attract?"

"More like the tortoise and hare, I think," said Fern. "Blake took off like the hare immediately after high school, while Hannah was slower and steadier. Have they stayed in touch all these years?"

"According to Rudy's contact at Rainbow to Hope, yes. Especially since Blake moved back to Buck Bay."

"You and Jay remember that she's too old for you," Fern joked. "She's very beautiful. And, I always thought, slightly dangerous."

CHAPTER 9

Cindy from HR buzzed Matt first thing Wednesday morning, and said, "Are you busy? I've got some resumés for you to look at. I only have three, but two of them look really good."

"Already?" He was genuinely surprised and could tell she was excited. "I thought it was difficult to recruit good people these days?"

"It is," she acknowledged. "But more people want to live on the coast than maybe some other places. Also, after one day of research, it looks to me that police officers move around some."

"I did."

"Right. Plus, we're kind of famous now because of your recent high-profile cases. I think I'll get several more hits, but I want to show you these early ones. Can I come over to your office now?"

"Sure." Matt took a drink of his coffee. "Let's see what you've got."

Cindy, a perky, young, relatively new hire herself, barreled into Matt's office. "Oh, good, you've got coffee," she gushed. "I brought mine, hoping you wouldn't mind."

Matt thought she didn't need any more caffeine, but he held his cup up and said, "Cheers." He drank from his while she settled her files on his desk.

"So," she started, "we received three hits overnight from our post on Policeapp.com, one of the sites you gave me. The first one," she handed him a resumé, "is from a detective with the Eureka, California, PD. That's south on 101, not too far over the Oregon/California border. He's got lots of the experience you're looking for."

"Did he say why he's leaving?" Matt asked.

"Yes. In his cover letter, he said they are restructuring, and he doesn't like his new role."

"Hmmm." Matt stroked his chin as he scanned the resumé. "Could be a whiner. Will you do a phone call with him first to make sure he doesn't have two heads?"

Cindy giggled. "Yes, chief, I'll vet any you think fit the broad parameters of our opening."

"Can we ask them about ethnicity? Mr. Abbott would prefer we not hire another white male."

"No, not directly. But if they are candidates of color, they will sometimes offer that in the phone interview. And if they merit an interview with you, that can be a ZOOM call…a face-to-face over your computer," she clarified.

"I know what a ZOOM call is. I'm not ready for the nursing home yet," he gruffed. "OK, this one is in the good pile. Next?"

As he watched Cindy sort and pick up her next candidate's file, Matt thought she might vibrate out of her skin with excitement.

"This one is a female from Boston! Her resumé is terrific—maybe even overqualified for our position. And her cover letter was perfect." She proudly placed the papers in front of Matt.

"Tamryn Gesicki. Boston PD." Matt read from the top of her resumé. "Do you think she understands where Port Stirling is? And how small we are? Boston is a major city police force."

"I was very clear in our posting that we are a small-town police department in southern Oregon," Cindy said. She was slightly offended. "And may I remind you that you yourself moved from a big city to our town. People have reasons."

"Touché." He spent a few minutes reading and could see why Cindy was excited. Gesicki was highly decorated, well-qualified, and checked all the boxes. "Talk to her first, and then I'll talk to her if you approve."

"Yay!" She put the third file in front of him. "I would rule out this one, but I'm obligated to show you everything."

Matt looked. "Male. Boise, Idaho. Why don't you like him?"

Cindy nodded at the papers and said, "Keep reading."

"Ahh," Matt said, reading the cover letter. "Let go for bullying the female employees in the department. Nice. But he says he didn't do it." He looked up at her with a smile.

"Of course he didn't," she smiled back. "Isn't that what they always say?"

"Yep. He gets a 'thanks, but no thanks' letter. OK," he arranged her paperwork in a neat pile and handed it back to her. "Let's see what you think after a phone call with these first two, and then what the rest of the week brings in. Nice work. Keep me posted."

"Thanks, chief. They won't replace Fern, but I will find you someone good. Let's get the right person!"

Was I ever that cheerful? Matt wondered.

• • •

Stella and Mac Walsh, along with their good-natured basset hound, Archie, were camping in Hedgehog Mountain state park, about thirty miles south of Port Stirling in the forests of the southern Coast Range.

The park, drippy, foggy, with a chilly mist, was mostly deserted this time of year, which was precisely how the Walshes liked it. They lived mostly off the grid and spent much of their time foraging for food and saleable items the land and sea gave up.

This Wednesday, on a soft and damp forest floor, they would dig up giant ferns they could sell to florists and nurseries up and down the west coast. It was a lucrative business and accounted for much of their yearly income. Today they were after sword ferns, the king of Northwest ferns.

A well-known nursery in Sausalito, California, would pay Stella and Mac enough for the magnificent ferns to cover what few household expenses they had for a few weeks. They had harvested a treasure trove of mushrooms—Chanterelles, American matsutakes (they'd been one of the 250 lottery winners of the annual permit!), hedgehogs, lobster mushrooms, and the Porcini-like king boletes!—late last fall, and the income they derived from selling to fancy restaurants in Portland and San Francisco would last them until the spring morels mushroom harvest season.

And, if they had time before sunset, they would also catch some rainbow trout in the big lake near the top of Hedgehog Mountain. The mom-and-pop fish shop in Silver River, near where the Walshes lived, always wanted fresh-water trout, and would buy as many of them as they could catch.

They cooked some eggs on their camp stove, fed Archie his breakfast, and set off on the trail. The rule was you could only harvest plants in the 'road prism', generally defined as about 100 yards off the road. Stella and Mac tried to follow this rule, and it usually worked; Oregon's forests were extremely productive.

And it worked today. They'd hiked only about 50 yards around the first bend in the trail before they'd come upon an abundant display of about one hundred of the giant sword ferns, each one five feet across.

"Did you bring our permits?" Mac asked Stella.

"Yeah," Stella pointed to her jacket pocket. "We've got two, each worth $20. Small ferns $1 and these big boys are worth $2 each. Let's get twenty of these since there's so dang many right here, don't you think? These are spectacular."

Mac chuckled. "Aren't we smart? This is like taking candy from a baby. These are so easy to harvest," he said as he approached one perfect fern. He dug a small circle around the shallow root base, and the majestic plant popped right out.

Stella and Mac set to work with their shovels, while Archie sniffed along beside them. They dug twenty beauties and piled them into the back of their large pickup.

· · ·

Matt pressed the buzzer on the gate. He and Jay had difficulty finding the Bowen residence, but they were now sure they'd arrived at the right place. They had taken the left turn onto Angels Road off 101 just north of Port Stirling Links, but then the trouble started after that. GPS took them north of the golf course as expected, but then it seemed confused when the road split. They'd wound around a couple of one-lane roads, one of them unpaved, and ended up at a dead-end before circling back to the road they were on now.

When they'd called to schedule a meeting, Alex Bowen said they were the only lane with a gate, so this had to be it. Finally, a voice in the black box said, "Yes?"

"This is Chief Matt Horning and Detective Jay Finley from the Port Stirling Police Department. We spoke earlier this morning."

The gate began to swing open, and Matt drove up a hill until he came to a house. It was a giant A-frame with a wall of windows overlooking the Pacific Ocean, several hundred feet below. A wrap-around deck extended the living space, and a man stood on it now, waiting for them to approach the front door, which was up a flight of stairs.

"You found us," he said, walking toward them, and sticking out his hand. "Alex Bowen."

"It wasn't easy," replied Matt. "I'm Chief Horning and this is Detective Finley." The men shook hands.

Alex smiled slightly. "I know. The GPS doesn't always find the way. Please come in." He indicated a pair of wide French doors, and they went inside. "I wish we had a better day for the view," he said. It was grey and misty with reduced visibility.

"I live on the beach in Port Stirling, and I see the view every day," said Matt. "Thanks for meeting with us, Mr. Bowen. Is your wife here?"

"She is, but I wanted to greet you first. Blake is very upset about Hannah's death," he warned them. "They've been friends for forty years, and she's not dealing with it very well."

"We can imagine," said Matt. "This is a tough one, and we're sorry for your loss. We'll be as gentle as we can, but we need to ask her some questions. Can you get her, please?"

"Of course," said Alex. "Make yourselves comfortable and I'll be right back." He walked to the back of the house and turned down a hallway to his left.

Matt and Jay settled in two chairs facing a large black leather sofa, leaving it for the Bowens. Their experience in dealing with bereaved family and friends taught them that they often liked to sit close to each other during times like this, and they respected that.

"Nice house," said Jay. "Think they'd sell it to me?"

Matt looked over at him and laughed, trying to be quiet. "Doubt it."

Alex led Blake into the room, and the woman was clearly in distress. Her face was red and swollen from crying, and her black sweats were wrinkled. She was barefoot and clutched a handful of tissues in her right hand.

The two cops rose to greet her. "We're so sorry about your friend, Mrs. Bowen," said Matt.

"Blake. My name is Blake," she choked out.

"Why are you here, Chief Horning?" asked Alex Bowen. "None of the other cops called us, so we figured Hannah's suicide must be cut and dried." He was a good-looking man, about fifty, tall and lean, lots of brown hair nicely styled, but starting to grey at the temples and around his ears. He would have to decide soon whether to let it go or keep its natural color.

"Well, in my book, death is never cut and dried," said Matt. "I've been asked by Robert Oakley to take a look and tie up any loose ends on his behalf. He is, as you probably know, distraught." He turned his attention to Blake Bowen. "What can you tell us about Hannah? You've been good friends for a long time, we understand."

Blake's face, which Matt could tell was normally quite beautiful when it wasn't red and puffy from crying, reddened and crinkled as more waterworks began. "We weren't just good friends, we were best friends," she wheezed. She attempted to pull herself together, patting her eyes with tissue and then running both hands through her white-blonde spiky chin-length hair. She let out some air and continued.

"Han and I met in kindergarten, and we've watched out for each other ever since. We had all sorts of wild adventures together, which most of the kids who grew up in Chinook County had, too." A flitting smile came and was gone in an instant. "This was a fun place to be a kid."

"I've been told that by my wife and friend," Matt said, pointing his thumb in Jay's direction. "They both were raised here."

"You're not from around here, are you?" Blake said. "Do I hear Texas in there somewhere?" She tried another small smile.

Jay, sitting quietly beside Matt, thought, *She's flirting with him! Her best friend committed suicide a week ago, and she's flirting with Matt in front of her husband? What the hell?*

Matt shifted in his chair. *He knows it, too,* thought Jay.

"Yes, ma'am. Dallas area." He paused. "Did you have any inkling that Hannah was depressed or considering suicide? Were there any signs? Was she acting different around you?"

Blake shook her head violently. "No, nothing at all. I would've known if she was in trouble. I would have known." She gazed out the window to the ocean and took some deep breaths.

"But you've been away much of this month," Alex interjected. "You hadn't seen her for, what was it, about three weeks before her suicide?"

Blake glared at her husband. "I still would've known if Hannah was in distress. I would've felt it."

Matt and Jay exchanged a quick glance, and Jay jumped in.

"How did you learn of her death?" Jay asked.

"Robert called me the night she disappeared to ask if she was here with me," Blake said. "Then we found out later they'd found her car."

"How did you find that out?" Jay again.

Blake looked at her husband. "I don't remember that part, do you?"

Alex shook his head. "I don't remember either, but someone in her office must have called Blake to give her the news. Maybe Sarah Forrester, she's kind of in charge now, I believe."

"Where were you when Robert called?" Matt asked. "Were you home?"

"Well, that's the thing," said Blake. "I was at a spa in Baja. As Alex said, I hadn't talked to Han and didn't know anything that could help Robert. I felt so helpless because I immediately knew that something was wrong."

"How did you know that?" asked Matt.

"Because Han never acted impulsively these days. She always did the normal thing. If she didn't show up at home when Robert was expecting her, then something had to be wrong. But I couldn't do anything to help him. I feel so guilty."

She put both hands up to her face and started crying again. Alex patted her on her thigh. "It's not your fault, sweetie," he said.

"He's right, Blake," said Matt. "You couldn't have saved her even if you'd been here. If she was determined to kill herself, she'd have found a way. And if Hannah met with foul play, well, you wouldn't have been able to stop that either."

"Were you with Blake in Baja?" Jay asked Alex. He was getting an uneasy feeling in the pit of his stomach for some reason.

"No, she goes there alone regularly," said Alex. "I'm not invited." He smiled and squeezed her leg. "I was home. My work takes me to Eugene twice a week most months, but I was working from home last week."

"Why the departure from your usual routine?" asked Jay.

"I'd been working hard on a big grant and decided to chill for a couple of days at home. My work is cyclical. Big moments of high stress, followed by lulls."

"You work in the non-profit sector, correct?" asked Jay. "Like Hannah."

"Yes, that's right," Alex responded. "We did similar work, both of us running organizations to try to help those in our communities who need a leg up. We worked together frequently, and I will miss those collaborations."

Jay noticed the past tense.

"You sound sure she's dead," Matt said, catching it, too.

"If the sheriff and the medical examiner rule it, I guess we're forced to believe it," Alex said. He shrugged his shoulders.

"What about you, Blake?" Matt asked. "Do you believe Hannah is dead?"

Her hands trembled and she had a glazed look in her eyes. Jay thought for a minute she wasn't able to talk.

"I have to," she said finally. "Han would've contacted me by now if she was alive."

"Do you believe she walked into Mourning Bay? Killed herself?" Jay asked. He wanted to hear her say it.

Blake took another deep breath to compose herself. "I'm trying to get a grip," she whispered, sounding apologetic. "I agree with my husband. If our sheriff says that's what happened, who am I to argue with him."

"You're her best friend," said Jay. "Who better to argue on Hannah's behalf?"

Blake fidgeted on the sofa and crossed her legs. "Part of me feels she would never have killed herself. But the other part of me feels like the other possibilities make even less sense."

"Can you think of anyone who might have wanted to harm her?" Matt asked.

Again, Blake looked unable to speak, and was now shaking visibly.

"That's just it. I can't," she whispered. "It's impossible. Everyone loved her. I loved her so much." She was sobbing now, and the cops knew the interview was over.

Matt stood up first and said, "Thank you for meeting us. Please take care of each other. We're very sorry for your loss. If you think of anything else, will you call me?" He handed his card to Blake.

Blake nodded, and Alex said, "Of course, chief. We'll do anything we can to help you."

"Appreciate that," Matt said. "We'll be in touch if we have additional questions or if we learn anything."

"We'd like to be in the loop," Alex said. "Blake needs closure just like Robert."

Matt said, "Will do. We'll let ourselves out. Thanks again for your time."

"It's no problem," Alex said. "The gate will open automatically for you as you approach it. Just leave room for it to open inwardly."

Matt and Jay walked down the sandy path to their car. Jay looked back up at the house as he opened his car door. Alex was looking out the window at them. No sign of Blake.

Putting on his seat belt, Matt said, "What do you think?"

"I think we've just seen a good actress perform," Jay said.

CHAPTER 10

The mist off the ocean had now turned into a full-blown fog as Matt and Jay made their way inland from the Bowens' residence. Matt drove carefully on the unfamiliar one-lane road with the fog swirling in and out as he made their way off the bluff and back into downtown Buck Bay. Once he was clear of the Bowens' road, he spoke into his cell phone: "Call Robert Oakley."

His phone did as it was told.

"Robert, hi, it's Matt Horning. I've got one of my detectives with me and we're in Buck Bay. Can we stop by and see you?" He paused. "Great. We should be there in about fifteen minutes."

He pressed 'end call' and turned to Jay. "I want you to meet Robert and give me your take on him as I tell him what Walt learned from the lawyer about Hannah's will."

"You mean, that he gets everything?" Jay asked.

"Yeah. I want both of us to observe his reaction."

"OK, but you don't suspect him, do you?"

"Nope. But I'm not ruling out anyone or anything yet. Gathering the facts. So, tell me why you didn't believe Blake Bowen. What was it she said?"

"It's more what she *didn't* say," Jay replied. "The Bowens are the only people we've talked to that didn't swear that Hannah didn't kill herself. They both left the door open to that possibility."

"Maybe that's because Blake knows her better than anyone, even Robert. Maybe she saw something in her friend that leads her to believe suicide was a possibility."

"Then why didn't she tell you that?"

"Because she didn't want to break Hannah's confidence?"

"Even if it would help us close this case?" Jay asked. He shook his head. "I don't think that's it. I think they want us to believe that she walked into that bay."

"And why would the Bowens want us to think that?" Matt asked his smart detective friend.

"They want our investigation to end there."

"And why would they want that?"

"Because they don't want what really happened to Hannah to become known," Jay responded.

"And why would they care about that?"

Jay looked at Matt. "You agree with me, don't you?"

"Yep. Just wanted to know if we are on the same page," Matt said. "My takeaways are that Blake is distraught over her friend's death, that she was out of town and therefore couldn't have had anything to do with it, and that the official verdict of suicide is indeed possible, and that she and Alex have accepted it. So, we cops should just forget the whole thing, and everyone move on with their lives."

"Are we going to do that?" Jay asked, knowing the answer.

"Nope."

• • •

A woman was standing on Robert's front porch, and the two were chatting. He waved when he saw Matt pull into his driveway.

"Howdy," Matt said, as he and Jay approached the house. "This is Detective Jay Finley and he's helping me with Hannah's case. Robert Oakley," he said to Jay.

Robert and Jay shook hands, and Robert said, "This is my neighbor, Tina Bigelow. She just brought me a casserole." He smiled at her.

"We're all very upset," Tina said. She greeted the cops. "It's this not knowing for sure what happened to Hannah. So hard on Robert." She gave his arm a squeeze.

"Did you know her well?" Matt inquired.

"Just as neighbors for a couple of years," Tina said. She was attractive in a middle-aged sort of way. Coiffed blond hair worn in a short pageboy, red-frame glasses, and a slim, slight build. Looked like she played golf several days a week. "Hannah and Robert were very nice to me when my husband died last year. I want to repay the favor. Wish I could do more."

"Sorry about your husband," said Jay. "Was his name Bruce Bigelow? If so, I knew him."

Tina smiled. "Yes, that's my husband. How do you know him?"

"He and my dad played high school football together and were friends."

"Ahh, Bo Finley is your father? Bruce loved him."

"Yes, that's my dad," said Jay. "Small world, huh?"

"Oregon is a small state, for sure," said Tina. "Well, I should be going. Let you gentlemen get on with your business. Please tell Bo that Tina said 'hi'." She gave Robert a quick hug, said, "Call me if you need anything, honey," and headed across the lawn to her home.

"Do you have any news?" asked Robert. He headed into the house and held the door open for the cops.

"Nothing big, no," said Matt. "We just want to update you on a couple of things, and I have a few questions. First, my sergeant talked to Hannah's lawyer about her will. We wanted to know if she'd changed it recently."

"Since she and I wrote new ones after our marriage?" Robert asked.

"Yes," Matt said. "And the lawyer said that Hannah had not made any changes since you both filed the new wills. She wouldn't confirm the details, but she did say that Hannah had not made any changes to the beneficiary since you signed them."

"So, essentially, I get everything?" Robert asked. "House, her investments along with our joint property?"

"That's my understanding," said Matt. He and Jay studied Robert closely. There might have been a slight twitch in his left eye, but otherwise, no outward emotions.

"Michelle Wayne wanted to wait until you contacted her," Matt said. "Didn't want to move on from Hannah's death until you were ready."

"That's considerate of her. Nice woman."

"Weren't you at least curious if you were still her beneficiary?"

"I don't care about the money." Robert looked bereft.

"It feels like a substantial amount for a man who was unhoused until a couple of years ago," noted Matt. "Some people might think that's motivation for you."

"To kill my wife, you mean? You don't really mean that, Matt."

"I didn't say I believe it," Matt said quietly. "But money and greed are often at the bottom of these kinds of cases. You stand to benefit the most from Hannah's death, and we are trained in law enforcement to follow the money. I'm sorry, but did you kill your wife for her money?"

Robert looked from Matt to Jay. "Is that what you think, too, young fellow?"

"I don't think anything, Mr. Oakley," said Jay. "We're doing our jobs, that's all."

Robert leaned forward, placed both hands on his knees and looked at the floor for a minute. Then he raised his face to confront Matt directly and said, "I did not. Why on God's green earth would I call you in to investigate her disappearance if I'd killed her? What fool would do that?"

"As a diversion, perhaps," offered Matt. "It's not unheard of."

"I asked you to help me because I'm desperate to know the truth. You heard what Tina said—it's the not knowing that's the hardest."

"How did Bruce Bigelow die?" asked Jay. "Dad probably told me, but I can't remember."

"The big C," answered Robert. "He had colon cancer and ignored it until it was too late. Awful." He shook his head as if to unload the bad memory.

"Is Tina a close friend?" asked Matt, trying to make it sound like an innocent question.

Robert's eyes opened wide, indicating he hadn't fallen for Matt's innocence. "What the fuck? You think Tina and I killed our spouses so we could be together with lots of dough? What the hell is going on here, Matt?" He stood up, his face splotchy, clearly in a rage. "You need to go now."

"Sit down, Robert," said Matt. "We don't think anything of the kind. Just don't want to leave anything unasked. Please sit down," he implored again. "We've got a few more questions and then we'll leave."

Robert tapped one foot angrily on the floor, but he eventually sat down. "What?"

"Did you call Blake Bowen when you first realized that Hannah was missing?" asked Matt.

"Yes. She was one of my first phone calls. I figured Hannah had gone out to Blake's beach house and they got to talking and lost track of the time. But she said Hannah wasn't with her."

"Did you talk to Alex, too?" Jay asked.

Robert thought for a minute. "No, Blake said she was in Mexico. I don't think Alex was with her. She goes to some spa down there. Hannah went with her once, but it wasn't her cup of tea. Said it was boring."

"Did you ever talk to Alex that night or the next day?" Jay again.

"Yeah, he called me Thursday morning to tell me that Blake was coming right home. Said he'd just heard the news that the sheriff found Hannah's car, and how sorry they both were."

"Did you get along with them?" Matt asked.

"Blake and Alex? Sure. She was Hannah's best friend." Robert's face closed off.

"Well, I couldn't stand my first wife's best friend," Matt said. He smiled at Robert.

"I wouldn't have picked Blake as a best friend," admitted Robert. "But she's OK. Lots of fun on occasion. And Alex is fine."

"We're going to check the Bowens' alibis for the time Hannah disappeared," Matt told him. "Please keep that under your hat for now." He and Jay stood.

"So, you're not going to arrest me?" Robert asked, looking into Matt's eyes.

"Nope. You're already in jail, my friend. I'm trying to make it better for you, not worse. I'll call you tomorrow." He patted Robert on the shoulder. "Hang in there."

"What now, boss?" Jay asked, back in the car. They were headed home to Port Stirling. Matt was concentrating on the windshield. The fog was now so soppy and thick, he had to turn on the wipers, and still couldn't see more than twenty yards in front of the car.

"Talk to your dad about Bruce Bigelow. What he knows about his death. And, what are his thoughts on Tina Bigelow?"

"Does this mean you actually think Robert and Tina might have a thing?"

"She's an attractive woman, don't you think?"

"S'pose. But Robert's a good guy. He's your friend."

"The only thing I know with certainty about Robert is that he used to sleep in doorways," Matt said. "Do I like him? Yes, I like him. But I don't know that he's a good guy. While you talk to your dad about the Bigelows, I'm going to talk to Ted Frolick about Robert. Let's see if any dirt comes out in the wash, OK?"

• • •

Hannah Oakley's lawyer, Michelle Wayne, looked up Justin Sorenson in her Contacts folder, and punched in his cell phone number. She expected her call to go to voicemail and had the message she wanted to convey to him in mind, but, to her surprise, he answered his phone.

"Mr. Sorenson, this is Michelle Wayne, Hannah's attorney. Do you have a minute to talk?"

"Yeah, but I can't think why I'd want to talk to you," he said.

She ignored the rude remark. "I won't take much of your precious time. I'm calling to ask if you received the letter Hannah sent to you informing you of her intention to file a petition to end your spousal support."

"I'll tell you the same thing I told the cops—I didn't get a letter from Hannah. When did she send it, or is this a figment of your imagination?"

"She mailed it to you about four days prior to her disappearance," Michelle bluffed. "Are you being truthful?"

"You people need to get a life," Justin snarled. "I didn't get a letter from her, alright? I haven't seen or heard from Hannah in months. I would tell you if I had because I have nothing to hide. Leave me alone."

"I'm afraid I can't do that," she said. "But I can guarantee you will only hear from me one more time. That will be when I send you formal notice that with Hannah's death, your support ends. No more gravy train, Justin."

"Fuck off."

• • •

Archie, the basset hound, veered off the path in front of Stella and Mac as the three of them hiked through the dark, heavy Chinook County forest. They were deep into Hedgehog Mountain now, breathing in the damp air and respecting the cavernous silence surrounding them. The dirt path was barely two feet wide, and it was edged by lush woodland foliage that brushed their hiking boots. The overhead canopy was dense and soggy, and an occasional drip of drizzle fell on the trio.

"Archie," said Stella. She called the hound back to them, while wiping the mist off her face with a red-checkered handkerchief from her jacket pocket. But uncharacteristically, Archie kept going. He was moving faster now off to the right of the path and was growling. It was a low, mild growl, as Archie was getting on in years and rarely got excited about anything.

"Archie!" Stella repeated, with a bit more force behind her command. The hound kept going and was now twenty yards to the right of the path. He suddenly pulled up short and came to a complete stop. Turning toward his parents, Archie began to bark loudly, standing his ground. They could hardly see him in the undergrowth, almost up to his eyes.

"What is it, fella?" said Mac. He headed off the path, trudging toward his dog. Stella plodded along behind him.

Archie kept barking.

"Mac, wait for me," Stella said urgently. "There's something wrong. Archie never acts like this. It's freaking me out."

Mac slowed and waited for Stella, taking her hand as she approached him.

"It's OK, he's probably just found some animal poop or something," Mac said to reassure her. He did a 360-degree circuit of the forest around them. There was nothing. They were profoundly alone.

Mac leaned down and scratched Archie's ears, but the hound wasn't having it. He turned away from Mac and began pawing at the ground they were standing on, a small clearing in the underbrush. He never stopped his baying-like bark.

Stella bent over and inspected the clearing. "Someone's been digging here," she said.

"Yeah, it looks that way to me, too," Mac said. "Wonder why? There's nothing but undergrowth."

The couple stood and watched their frenetic hound digging away, hell-bent-for-leather, and drooling more than usual.

Stella saw it first and let out a scream that reverberated through the forest. A woman's face.

Mac pulled Archie away, and the hound gave him a look that proudly said, 'Look what I found.'

"Oh my god!" Stella said, her hand flying to her mouth. "It's a body."

"A dead body," Mac said. Shaking, he carefully brushed the dirt off the woman's face, and with his bare hands began to pull more earth away from the corpse. "It's a woman," he said after a minute or two. He stood up and took Stella by the shoulders. "We need help. Let's find a couple of branches we can use as stakes to mark the trail."

"Leave her here alone, you mean?" Stella looked up at him.

"We can't help her, honey. She's dead. We have to tell the authorities. We'll mark the spot so we can lead them here, but we have to go quickly. I don't know if it's safe for us to be here."

Stella started crying. Mostly out of fear.

Archie moaned quietly behind them, and when Stella and Mac looked at him, he lowered his head to the ground and licked the dead woman's face.

Mac swooped his dog up in his arms, and they took off running for their truck.

CHAPTER 11

Matt's phone buzzed. Sylvia.

"Howdy. What's up?"

"Milton just called me," Sylvia said. "He took a 911 call from a couple who are down at Hedgehog Mountain. Says their dog found the body of a woman buried in the forest. Says it looks recent."

"Oh, no." Matt gripped the steering wheel tightly, his knuckles turning white. "Do you have their coordinates? I've only been there once and I can't remember much about that area," Matt said. "Jay is with me."

"Put me on speaker," Sylvia instructed. "Jay knows it well."

"Hi, Sylvia," Jay said.

"Go to the campground entrance," Sylvia said. "It's off 101 before you get to Silver River."

"I know it," said Jay.

"OK, once you're at that entrance, stay on the road and veer to the right. There's another road in a short while that takes off and goes up over the mountain. Still paved. Follow that for 1.2 miles and then look for a dirt road on your right just before you go around a sharp left corner. He said their red truck is parked just off the pavement on the dirt road, a few yards in. They will meet you there."

"Got it," Jay said, scribbling in his notebook.

"Did they tell Milton if they marked the location of the body?" asked Matt.

"Yes, they had the presence of mind to put stakes in the trail they were on."

"What are their names?"

Sylvia consulted her notepad. "Stella and Mac Walsh."

"Got it." Matt repeated the names aloud.

"Where are you now?" she asked.

"Just driving into Port Stirling," Matt said. "We'll keep going on 101."

"They're scared, Matt," Sylvia said. "Want you to hurry."

Matt floored it, and Jay turned the siren on, and then called Bernice and requested her forensics team. He gave her directions and then hung up his phone. The two friends didn't talk during the drive. They didn't have to.

• • •

The cops found the entrance to the state park and followed Sylvia's instructions. The road wasn't much as it started up the mountain, and Matt had to slow down. He noted the mileage as he drove. The instructions had been good, and they found the dirt road with Stella and Mac's truck down it a few yards deeper in the forest.

As they approached, they saw the couple madly waving.

"Thank god you're here!" exclaimed Mac. Archie barked.

"I'm Matt Horning, police chief in Port Stirling, and this is Detective Jay Finley. Thank you for calling us."

"I'm Mac Walsh and this is my wife, Stella." He pointed at the dog. "This is Archie. He's got a good nose on him. Somedays, I wish it wasn't quite so good."

"We're thankful for your nose, Archie," Matt said. He bent down to pet the hound, and Archie allowed it. "Can you take us to your dog's discovery?" he asked Mac.

"We marked the trail to show the way to where we found her," Stella said, her voice shaky. "Everything in the forest looks alike."

"I know this is a horrible experience for you, ma'am, but we're grateful. You guys did the right thing, and this could really help us. I'm afraid it might be connected to a case we're currently working on. Please take us there."

The four people and one dog took off down the dirt path, led by Archie.

One of the stakes had fallen over, but the second one was standing tall, and Matt saw it immediately. As they hiked, he surreptitiously took out the photo of Hannah Oakley from his inside jacket pocket. Jay scanned the forest, swiveling his head in constant motion.

Archie ran ahead as fast as his short legs would take him and made the right turn into the undergrowth.

"Guess we didn't need the stakes after all," said Mac, his voice a whisper. "That dog never forgets anything."

"Why don't you and Stella stay here," Matt said, moving in front of the Walshes. His tone was soothing. "Let Jay and I do our thing. In fact, the three of you should go back to your truck and watch for our forensics team. The county's medical examiner is on her way with three of her staff. Her name is Dr. Bernice Ryder. Tell her we're here, and show them the way, OK?"

Stella looked around nervously. "Can we sit in our truck?"

Immediately Matt understood her fear. "Of course, and lock the doors. I don't believe you're in any danger though. I think whoever buried this body here is long gone; I'll know for sure if I can identify the victim. Please don't leave until we're finished here. It won't take Jay and I long once Dr. Ryder's team arrives."

"Sure thing," said Mac.

Matt and Jay followed Archie to where the hound was pawing at the earth. Jay turned back toward the couple before they took off and asked, "Why are you here today?"

They glanced at each other. "We come here regularly," Mac said. "We harvest the hedgehog mushrooms and Sword ferns to sell to our customers. Today we were after the ferns. Why?"

Jay looked around. "Just wondering. It's a pretty deserted place."

"That's why we come here," said Stella. "It makes for pristine foraging."

"Did you happen to be here last week?" asked Matt, hands on his hips. He hoped to get lucky that the couple might have seen something. "On Wednesday afternoon or anytime Thursday?"

"No," answered Stella. "We only come here twice a month usually, and it's been at least two weeks since we were here last."

Matt leaned over Archie, getting closer to the ground the dog was protecting. "Too bad," he said under his breath, pulling on latex gloves.

Mac pulled Archie out of Matt's way and held his dog close to him. He put his other hand lovingly on Stella's elbow and guided her back down the path toward their truck.

Jay moved to the other side of the rough grave, as Matt knelt near the woman's head and carefully brushed away more dirt from her face. He held the photo of Hannah Oakley next to the buried woman and let out a long sigh.

"It's her, Jay. Hannah. Shit."

"You're sure?"

"Yep. You take the photo and get closer."

Jay did as he was told. There was no question it was the same woman.

Matt stood up and conscientiously backed away from the body. Jay did the same. The two stood quietly for a moment, absorbing the hush of the forest. The only sound was the stirring of small critters, squirrels probably, in the undergrowth. They breathed in the cool, misty air, redolent with fresh fir trees and the rich earth below their feet. There was a slight whiff of decay.

Matt spoke first. "This is why you don't get personally involved in cases. Robert's life will be ruined forever, and I have to tell him."

"We now know she didn't walk into Mourning Bay to kill herself," said Jay, "that should give him some degree of peace. Don't you think?"

"I suppose it might. But his wife was murdered. Did you see the strangulation marks on her neck?"

"I did."

"How is that better than suicide?" Matt asked rhetorically. "Dead is dead, and I think that's all Robert will care about. Just when he finally got his life back on track. Dammit!" Matt slapped his thigh hard.

"I'm sorry. It totally sucks. If I were Robert, I'd want to know who killed her. It would make it easier for me to stomach if we caught whoever did this to her. Don't you think?" Jay asked.

"Yeah, you're right. We'll get him," said Matt, his jaw tightening. "Or her."

. . .

Fern spent her morning calling around to some of her friends and local contacts at the county level. They knew she had a new job with the State Department and were proud of her advancing career. Her cover of Public Liaison for the west coast gave Fern quite a lot of leeway with the locals because most didn't understand what that truly meant.

So, when she called the county sheriff's admin assistant, Clare, — a long-time friend — and asked, "Anything exciting going on this week?", she wasn't suspicious of Fern's motives.

Clare informed her that no, nothing was going on at all, and, in fact, it was boring around her office. Earl was in court, there was no crime action, and she was reading at her desk, as she'd accomplished her duties this morning.

"That's a good thing, Clare," Fern offered. "We could all use a little break from the chaos, don't you think?"

"I guess," Clare agreed. "It's not like I'm an action junkie or anything, but sometimes it's nice to be busy."

As Fern made her phone call rounds, Clare's story was repeated. All quiet on the western front. Nothing going on. Residents and tourists alike all behaving themselves. No suspicious activity around the area towns. The local law enforcement departments were using this time to plan and gear up for March's spring break, always a busy, troublesome time on the Oregon coast as hoards descended from far and wide on the beach communities.

Once she'd completed her phone calls, Fern grabbed her jacket and headed out. She would have lunch at Whale Rock and pick Vicky's brain, and then drive up to Buck Bay and walk around to some of the hotspots… see if anything was shaking in the county's largest city.

Even the restaurant at Whale Rock was slow today, and Fern had been careful to arrive at the peak of lunch hour to check out the activity. Vicky greeted her friend with, "Thank goodness, a customer. Tired of making your hubby lunch already?" she said with a broad smile.

Vicky didn't know Fern's real job beyond what had been announced publicly, and it wouldn't matter even if she figured it out; Vicky was discreet and knew how to keep her mouth shut when it mattered. She was very protective of her buddies on the police force.

Fern laughed. "I've had enough of him for a while," she joked. "I need to see my friends. Besides, he's back at work full-time, and he doesn't know I exist."

"I don't believe that for a minute." She led Fern to her favorite table by the window and said, "Do you need a menu?" Vicky, unusual for her, was wearing pants on this chilly morning, topped by a powder-blue turtleneck sweater.

"I do not," replied Fern. "Bring me a large bowl of clam chowder and a tuna melt. And a cup of coffee." She looked around the mostly empty restaurant and added, "If you can, get yourself a coffee and join me for a few minutes. Let's catch up."

"Brilliant idea. I'll get a check to that couple," she nodded at a table on the other wall where an elderly couple sat, "and then we can talk."

While she waited for her food, Fern jotted down some notes from her morning phone calls. *Slim pickings*, she thought. *Will Joe think I'm not doing my job? I can't invent trouble, for crying out loud.*

She checked her phone messages, but there were no calls. She was anxious to hear what Matt and Jay thought about Blake Bowen. Blake's husband, Alex Bowen, was one of the people on Fern's list of non-profit CEOs she would contact when she was ready to get organized about their new foundation. He was recommended to her by Bernice as someone who worked in the health-care field and could likely offer philanthropic guidance. Fern forgot to tell Matt that, and she hoped he would meet Alex today, too, and give her some feedback on him. It was a small world in Chinook County.

Vicky came with Fern's order and two coffees. She pulled out the chair opposite Fern and said, "I'm on a break. Let's dish."

"I got nothing," laughed Fern. "Matt's doing great," Fern told her before she could ask. All of his friends had been so upset when he got shot and was fighting for his life. She expected to answer questions about his recovery for weeks. "My husband is feeling like Superman again, and we are settling into a dull, married couple routine."

"And it feels like pure heaven to you, doesn't it?" Vicky wisely noted.

Fern nodded and turned serious. "It does. It was so scary, Vicky. Everyone kept telling me he was going to die."

Vicky reached across the table and patted her arm. "But he didn't. And he put away the assholes that wanted him dead, and now we can all get on with our lives."

"Amen to that. Kinda slow, isn't it?" inquired Fern, looking around the dining room.

"Been this way for a couple of days now," Vicky said. "We always have a lull between New Year's and spring break. Not great for the business, but I don't mind taking things a little easier for a while."

"What's the latest around here? Anything exciting happen while we were in the trials?" Fern asked.

"People are talking about the suicide of Hannah Oakley. Nobody can believe it."

"I don't believe it either. I didn't know her personally but killing herself sure doesn't jive with her public reputation. Don't tell anyone, but Matt's taking a second look into it."

"Glad to hear that," Vicky said. "But if the sheriff is convinced…"

"Yeah, that bothers us, too. Earl is a smart cop, tough to fool."

"Maybe Earl's getting tired. It's been a rough couple of years, and he's been at this a long time."

"Oh, I don't think so," Fern countered. "He will die with his boots on trying to do the right thing for the county. But that's why Matt wants his investigation to be quiet; he doesn't want to embarrass Earl."

"A woman's dead, Fern. Or, at the very least, missing. I would expect our local law enforcement to be completely positive before closing the door." Vicky frowned.

"Earl said both he and Chief McCoy are sure. It's Hannah's husband, Robert Oakley, who got Matt involved. They have a past."

"Don't I know it!" Vicky exclaimed. "They met in the doorway here. That was also the night I met Matt for the first time. I decided there and then that your husband was one of the good guys. Nobody had ever bothered to help Mr. Oakley before, including me, I'm ashamed to admit."

"Well, now he's determined to help him again if he can. Matt said it's probably suicide, but he's going to look into it and make sure there aren't any loose ends so Robert can move on."

"Does he know about Justin Sorenson? Hannah's first husband?" Vicky asked.

"Yes, he and Jay talked to him yesterday. What's your impression of him? I assume you know him." She took a big spoonful of the hot and heavenly clam chowder, a big swirl of butter on top.

"Justin Sorenson is a piece of doo-doo on the bottom of your shoe."

Fern had to laugh. "OK, then, tell me what you really think of him. This is sooo good." She pointed at her clam chowder.

"Chef made a fresh batch this morning. Outdid himself, didn't he? Sorenson is a parasite who's been mooching off women for all of his adult life. Everyone knew Hannah was just a meal ticket to him. Everyone but her, I guess. Sad, really."

"She figured him out, though," Fern said. "And divorced him, I understand."

"Finally," Vicky said, shaking her head. "And when I heard she got rid of the con man only to turn around and marry a homeless alcoholic, I thought that's a smart woman making a second dumb mistake. But it turned out she read Robert Oakley better than all of us. That's what makes this a real shame. Sometimes life sucks."

"Matt will get to the bottom of it, whatever the bottom is. What else is going on?"

"Nothing much," said Vicky. She took a sip of her coffee. "We were busy during the holidays, and then we were jammed all day every day for about three weeks with golfers and plain old tourists. After those folks left town, we had a rush from some big tour groups coming to see the new Native Cultural Center."

"Has everyone been behaving themselves?" Fern asked, trying to sound innocent.

"The golfers were rowdy, but then they always are. I don't care because they're great tippers." She smiled. "They make up for the young families, who can be stingy with their dough. But no real trouble from any holidaymakers."

"What about the tour groups?" Fern asked. "Where are they coming from?"

"Mostly from around the west and Canada, but we had one big group from Tokyo, and another one from Germany. The German group was about forty people, and they stayed for several days. We got the Japan group, about fifty, but they were only here for a dinner and then breakfast the morning they left." Vicky said. "Other than that, things are quiet and mostly good," Vicky said.

"You haven't heard any noise about the three trials or the prison sentences, have you? Nobody complaining about the cops?"

"No. Everyone was shocked when they learned what happened to Matt, and you-know-who's role in it. I think the general consensus is 'Thank God' we took those vermin off the streets."

"Obviously, I'd want to know if there is any grumbling," Fern said.

"Will your new job bring you in touch with our foreign visitors?" Vicky asked. Fern thought she detected a slight smirk on Vicky's face. *Play it straight.*

"Yes, it will be up to me to make sure that they all leave the U.S. with a good impression," she said briskly. She patted her face with a napkin. "Any new tourists in town this week? Any internationals?"

"There's a small group of golfers from Scotland. Staying at the Links, but they were here for dinner last night. Eight men, having a rollicking good time. Their bar bill was bigger than the food bill. I couldn't understand one word they said, but it didn't seem to matter. We all had fun." Vicky laughed.

"Anyone else around lately speaking other languages? Spanish? Chinese?" Fern asked.

"We had a family from Oklahoma last night, too. They might as well have been speaking Chinese," Vicky said, laughing again. "I could barely understand them. But, no, not nearly the foreign languages we had in the previous months." She leaned forward, arms crossed on the table. "You did get all the bad guys in this last go-around, didn't you?"

"Yes, we think so. Doesn't hurt to stay alert, right? Are the geologists all gone?" Fern asked. She shivered at the thought of Phineas Stuart and his family.

"There was a guy from South America. Chile, I think. A scientist of some sort—went right over my head. I talked to him in January, but I think he's gone now. I'd like to read some of their reports," Vicky said, surprising Fern. "Wonder how I'd get ahold of any?"

"My understanding is that we'll have to wait until they publish them in the scientific journals. I heard it could be as soon as April. I'll find out and let you know. It should be fascinating to read about our earthquake and tsunami."

"I think so. We had a once in six generations event they tell me," Vicky said. "I'd like to learn about it. Those scientists were practically giddy when they'd come in here to eat. I figure it's some good stuff."

"If you see or hear anything suspicious, please let me know, OK? I want to make sure that our international guests are treated well. We want them to go home and tell all their friends about us, right?"

"You betcha," Vicky nodded. "I saw your home office the night of the party in December. Is that where you're working out of?"

"Sometimes, but I have an official office down at city hall. I'll be going there more now that Matt is on the mend."

"My tax dollars at work," Vicky smiled. "I don't mind if it means you're on the job keeping the status quo." She stood up, smoothed her hair, and said, "Back to work. Keep in touch."

• • •

Fern paid her bill and walked to her VW bug in the parking lot—there were only two other cars in the lot on this chilly February day. The drive to Buck Bay was uneventful if you didn't count the occasional powerful gust of wind coming off the ocean that threatened to pick her car up. The rain held off for now, but she knew it was coming; enormous, jagged clumps of clouds moving at rapid speed were racing ashore.

Once in Buck Bay, she stopped in at the police department to say 'hi' to some of the officers she'd worked with there. Chief Dan McCoy wasn't her favorite, any more than he was Matt's favorite, but they were cordial.

McCoy said the same thing as everyone else she'd talked to today, "Nothing going down. Humdrum, just the way I like it," he told Fern. "If it wasn't going to rain this afternoon, I'd go fishing. How's your patient doing?"

"Matt is recovering brilliantly. Thanks for asking. He's back at work."

Chief McCoy lifted a doubtful eyebrow. "Really? Isn't it a bit soon? I could understand him being in the courtroom for the trials, but back in action?"

"He thinks he's Superman," Fern joked. She wasn't about to tell McCoy about Robert Oakley's plea for Matt's help.

She got back in her car, sitting quietly for a few minutes, thinking about her next move. *That's it, there's nothing happening and I'm wasting my time.* She decided to stop by Hannah Oakley's office and ask them about their work and upcoming projects. Her goal was to learn something about how the non-profit world works. If her real job was going to be a snooze like today, she might as well get started on creating their foundation.

On the drive to the other side of town, Fern called Joe Phelps in D.C.

"I feel guilty," Fern told Joe when he answered his phone.

"Why?"

"Because you're paying me for doing nothing. It's deader than a door-nail around here."

"I'm not paying you for nine-out-of-ten days you're at work," he replied. "I'm paying you for that tenth day when you get a lead, and all hell breaks loose."

"Well, it doesn't appear to be breaking loose today." She filled him in on how she'd set the stage with some of her best local contacts.

"That's good. If anything does happen, you're squarely in the loop. Check in with your other contacts in Portland, Seattle, and northern California tomorrow. Your approach is perfect. Non-threatening, but available to help them."

"What am I looking for, Joe?"

"Oh, you know, brilliant Chinese guys running evil businesses through your part of the country. The usual."

Fern could tell Joe was smiling into his phone. *Not funny.*

• • •

Fern pulled up to the curb in front of Rainbow to Hope. She had worked with several of the employees here when she worked for the county as victims' advocate, and knew the organization was solid and a true godsend in the community.

Like Rudy, Fern knew Sarah Forrester, too. *Well, maybe I don't know Sarah quite like Rudy knows her*, she smiled to herself. She approached the reception desk and asked the pleasant older woman if Sarah was available. She was, and came out to greet Fern.

"Haven't seen you in a while, Fern," Sarah greeted her with a quick hug.

"I've been busy. You may have heard."

"Getting married, solving murders—yes, I heard," Sarah grinned. "What brings you here? Come into my office." She turned and went down the hallway. "Is this to do with Hannah's disappearance?"

"Actually, no. My husband is working on the case, though, at Robert Oakley's request. I think Rudy talked to you. Terrible thing. I'm sorry for you and your organization; it must be a difficult time."

"The worst. We're all like zombies. Just stunned. Have a seat." She pointed to a chair in front of her desk, and Fern sat down.

"I'd like to keep our conversation private, if that's OK with you," Fern requested.

Sarah made the zip gesture across her lips. "No problem."

"Matt is a wealthy man. His family owns a huge ranch in Texas and there's lots of oil on the property," Fern told her.

"Lucky you," Sarah smiled.

Fern fidgeted in her chair. "Yes, but it came as a shock to me. I didn't know it prior to our marriage; he told me on our wedding night."

"Ha. That's princess stuff."

Fern laughed. "I guess so. Anyway, we want to do something for others with a portion of the dough. After his shooting, we decided to start a foundation, with the primary focus on health care in our region and in Texas. His hospital experience was life-changing for both of us and opened our eyes to several things that need fixing. Not that we can fix it all," she hurriedly added.

"Sounds good. How can I help you?"

"We don't know the first thing about setting this up, and how to run it once we get going. I'm here for advice."

"What kind of money are we talking about?" asked Sarah.

"We thought we'd start with five million, with the intention to grow it to ten over a few years. The money comes into his bank account every month."

"I can help you get started, but you should also talk to Alex Bowen. He runs a non-profit in Eugene—but he lives here—and his budget is in the ten million range. We're smaller than that, so it would be helpful for you to understand operating principles in two different-sized organizations, I should think."

"That sounds good," Fern nodded.

"The first thing to do is to identify your philanthropic objective, and it sounds like you're part way there on that," said Sarah. "But as the two of you have no doubt seen during Matt's experience, healthcare is a broad topic. I suggest you focus on one or two pieces of the whole and create a mission statement. Do you have any ideas on how you want to narrow the focus?"

"We've been noodling it, and have it confined to three areas," said Fern. "Two of the three involve hospitals in Oregon and Texas. We want to increase hospitals' ability to provide better security. Matt's shooter walked right into OHSU and opened fire." She shuddered as the images flooded into her mind. Sarah reached across her desk and placed her hand on Fern's arm.

"How awful," Sarah said quietly. "But you're safe now."

"It was as bad as it gets," whispered Fern. "We don't want that happening again, and the hospital folks tell us that it's a struggle to fund proper security. So, that's going to be number one on our mission. Number two is providing more capital equipment—life-saving equipment—to the smaller hospitals throughout Oregon and Texas."

"Like the Buck Bay Hospital?"

"Exactly," nodded Fern. "Do you know Dr. Bernice Ryder?"

"Yes, I know Bernice well," Sarah answered. "She's excellent and we're lucky to have her in our community."

"Yes, and as good as Bernice is, she didn't have everything she needed to save Matt's life. She told me she didn't have the surgical skill to perform the vital operation he needed, but she also didn't have the state-of-the-art equipment required. As we've talked it through further, we've discovered that most of our smaller hospitals don't have everything on their wish list.

Matt and I won't be able to get them to Level 1 Trauma hospital status, but we can beef up capital equipment budgets that might make a difference in a case like Matt's in another small town."

"This is a dream come true for me," said Sarah. "We have so many wonderful people doing good work around here, but funding is always - *always*—an issue. What's your third priority?"

"The third one is also tied to Matt's case. When we looked at his hospital bills—ICU, LifeFlight, round-the-clock care—he made a comment about what do poor people do."

"They die, usually," responded Sarah.

"That's exactly what I said! We have great medical insurance and private resources, but many people aren't as fortunate. So, how can we provide funds for more people to access the care they need? That's priority three."

"This one is trickier and more complex than your first two priorities, but that doesn't mean you can't make a dent in the huge need. The first thing you'll want to do after you write a clear-cut mission statement—and you've outlined it succinctly for me today—is to set grantmaking guidelines. That's where Alex Bowen could help you, he's a genius at that. Hannah is, too, but..."

"Were you involved in writing grants for Rainbow to Hope?" asked Fern.

"Yes, certainly, but Hannah was the genius at it. Both she and Alex are so good at reading between the grant guidelines to get at the heart of what's required. That's why it's important you nail down your guidelines to give organizations like us a hard look at whether we can qualify or not. The less ambiguity the better."

"Do you have an example of a well-written grant with guidelines you could share with me?"

"Absolutely." Sarah turned to a file cabinet on her right and pulled out a file. "Here's a recent one. I'll have a copy made for you—it's public material. Also, do you and Matt have a lawyer or financial advisor? I ask because you'll need someone to help with compliance and record-keeping, taxes, that sort of thing."

"We don't currently, but we've got a couple of people in mind we want to talk to," Fern said. "We've relied on Port Stirling's city attorney, plus

Matt's family has a long-time lawyer in Dallas, but we know we need our own. We've just been waiting on Matt's full recovery."

Sarah ticked off her fingers: "Get your objective and mission statement down on paper, solidify your grant guidelines, hire a lawyer or financial advisor. Then you're off and running. This is so exciting," she added with a smile.

CHAPTER 12

While they waited for Bernice and her forensics crew, Matt and Jay roped off a good-sized space around the body. Then they began a meticulous search of the area, carefully moving aside rotting leaves and other woodland debris. Jay was precise in every movement he made, while Matt's pace was a bit quicker, which mirrored their personalities. Both were rigorous in their searches, but Jay's innate fear of missing something crucial often led him to things no one else saw, including Matt.

But today, nothing turned up. No weapon, no discernible footprints, no blood. Only some broken twigs, squished ground cover, and the obvious attempt to cover up the body provided evidence.

"The SOCO team isn't going to have much to work with," Matt lamented.

"You never know with Bernice and those guys," Jay said. "They found the second bullet in your wall when Ed and I missed it."

"True. But you and Ed weren't exactly in full cop mode that afternoon." He slapped Jay on the back a couple of times to, once again, display his gratitude for his friends' action on Thanksgiving.

They turned to look up the path at the sound of someone approaching.

"Talk about the middle of nowhere," Bernice ranted. "Why can't you find a body on a downtown street?"

"Sorry, Bernice, we'll try to do better next time," Matt said sarcastically. "I know this is an inconvenient location for you."

"Well, I guess it's better than your house," she smiled and gave him a warm hug. "Set up over there," she instructed her team of three men, pointing further down the path and on the opposite side of where the body was buried.

"What've you got?" she asked.

"It's Hannah Oakley, I'm afraid," Matt said. "I've got a photo from her husband, and Jay and I are sure it's the same woman. You knew her, right?"

Bernice gasped and briefly put her hands over her face. "Yes, I knew Hannah, and I was afraid of something like this. Dammit!"

She ducked under the crime scene tape and followed the cops, pulling on latex gloves as she walked to the burial site.

Bernice stood looking down for a few moments, breathing shallowly. Then she said in a halting voice, "I am formally identifying this as the body of Hannah Sorenson Oakley. Somebody write that down, please."

She took out a fine, small brush, and began brushing the dirt off Hannah's face and clothing. Then she worked to free her neck and shoulders from the ground, waving off offers of help from the cops. With a magnifying glass, she looked at the marks on Hannah's neck. She motioned for her team.

"Please dig her up as gently as you can and place her on the stretcher. Get her out of the fucking dirt." They did as they were told, and the process took about twenty minutes. Once Hannah was on the stretcher, Bernice resumed her inspection of the corpse.

"As you can see," she said, "decomposition and putrefaction of the body has begun."

"So, she's been here for a while?" Matt asked.

"Yes, at least five days and probably longer," Bernice said. "I'll be able to tell you more after the autopsy when I can check the extensiveness of her cellular destruction, but from what I can observe now, it indicates she likely died around the time of her disappearance. Probably about the time I declared her death by suicide." She bit her lip and shook her head sadly.

Matt put his arm around Bernice's shoulder and whispered in her ear, "You went with what you had available to you at the time. This is not your fault."

Bernice took in a deep breath and slowly let it out. "I asked Earl and Dan to keep searching for her, but they said it was obvious." She looked up at Matt's serious face. "What on earth are we going to tell Robert?"

"The truth," Matt answered simply. "Jay and I think it looks like she was strangled. Can you tell yet?"

Bernice moved closer to the stretcher and bent over Hannah's face, and then lifted her head. "Yeah, it looks like manual strangulation. There's bruising all around her neck." She gently placed Hannah's head back on the stretcher and picked up her right hand. "Her fingernails look normal. No blood. No broken nails."

Matt and Jay peered at the hand Bernice was holding. Both cops nodded.

"No defensive wounds indicates that she knew and trusted her killer," said Matt.

"Looks like it," Bernice agreed. She pointed to another mark at the top of Hannah's chest, just visible in the V-neck of her blouse. "See this? My guess is she was wearing a pointy necklace of some sort, and it dug into her skin during the fight."

"Bingo," Jay said behind Matt and Bernice. He crouched down and reached into the empty grave. He stood up, holding Hannah's cell phone out in front of him for them to see.

* * *

While forensics did their thing, Matt and Jay went back to the car and talked to Stella and Mac Walsh.

"Sorry to keep you so long," Matt said. "We have just a few more questions for you and then you're free to leave. Have you ever seen the woman in the grave before?"

"We don't know her," answered Mac. "But we've been talking since we found her, and we think it's that woman who disappeared last week."

"Except they said she committed suicide," added Stella. "So, we guess it's not her. But she looks like the woman in the newspaper."

"It is her—Hannah Oakley," said Matt. "The police had evidence that she had killed herself, but obviously now, that's not the case. The coroner believes she's been murdered, so we need you to keep quiet for now about your discovery. Can you do that?"

"We live off the grid, chief," explained Stella. "We talk to very few people. Keeping quiet is what we do."

"Right," Mac said. "No problem. We understand that you want to keep the details secret."

"That's it," Matt said. "We don't know exactly what we're dealing with yet, so the less information that gets out into the community, the better. Where do you live?"

"In the woods between here and Silver River," Stella said. "Can we go home now? It's creepy here." She rubbed her arms.

Matt ignored her question. "Have you ever seen anyone suspicious around here? Not just lately, but anytime?"

They looked at each other and simultaneously shook their heads. "No," said Mac. "Not really. Occasionally, there are some rowdy campers down below. But no one I would call suspicious."

"Stella?" Jay asked.

"No," she said. "There were two guys yelling at each other two weeks ago down by the road, but they didn't come up here. And they were gone by the time we'd finished our work and headed home. Nothing out of the ordinary. Sorry."

"Do any of your friends know Hannah Oakley?" Matt asked. "Do you know?"

"Don't think so," said Stella. "Everyone knew *of* her because of her do-good rep, but none of our friends knew her personally, I don't believe."

"Can you think of any reason why anyone would want her dead?" Jay asked.

"Listen, guys," said Mac, sounding frustrated. "We just found her body, OK? We don't know her, and we don't know anything about her. We're going home now, OK?"

"Yes," said Matt. "We're sorry to keep you, and, again, thank you so much for calling us. You've been a big help. You especially, Archie," he said, petting the dog, who looked up at him with mournful eyes.

• • •

Forensics wrapped up and left the scene, with Bernice's promise to call him the minute she had any results. Matt told her that he and Jay would tell Robert in person this afternoon, and Bernice gave him a peck on the cheek and said, "Thank you. I'll hold off on the autopsy in case he wants to see her one last time."

"Is that a good idea?" asked Jay.

"Probably not," Bernice said. "But he might insist. Sometimes family members do. But try to talk him out of it. It's healthier for him if he remembers her as she was."

Before they took off, Matt and Jay went back to the gravesite and covered it up with leaves, branches, and other forest debris as best they could. Jay took some pretty pictures of the woodland around the site in case Robert asked to see it. Then they left for Buck Bay and the unpleasant task ahead.

As they turned on Highway 101 for the drive north, the rain that had been threatening all day finally burst through the clouds. It was a soft rain, although the heavier, steely clouds off to the southwest looked more determined.

Jay, wearing gloves even though forensics had already dusted it for prints, plugged the dead cell phone into the squad car's charger. They had three different types of chargers in the car at all times, and the first one Jay tried worked. Hannah's phone sprung to life.

The screen had a background photo of a red amaryllis in bloom and, unfortunately, a keyboard to type in a passcode over it. Jay made a few attempts at it, trying 'hope' and 'rainbow', along with a stab at a few years in which she might have been born. No luck.

"Hope her husband knows her passcode," Jay said.

"I would think he might, or at least know where she might have written it down. I know Fern's."

"Yeah, but you guys are cops."

"I think it's more a matter of being close to each other, and Robert and Hannah, by all accounts, were," Matt said. "Help me remember to ask him for it. I sometimes forget crucial details when giving this kind of awful news."

Once on the way, Matt called Chinook County Sheriff Earl Johnson. "This won't be fun either," he said to Jay as his phone rang. Earl, just leaving the courtroom where he'd testified, picked up.

"What's up, Tex?" he asked. "Don't tell me you're actually back at work?" He chuckled.

"Hi, Earl. Yeah, I am. Feeling good." He hesitated. "I need to tell you something. Are you alone?"

"Now what? Yes, I'm alone."

"We just found the body of Hannah Oakley. Buried in the forest on top of Hedgehog Mountain. She'd been strangled. You're my first call."

"Oh, good god. You're sure it's her?" Earl sounded strangled himself.

"Yes, it's her. Bernice came with her team, and she identified her. They were friends. They've taken Hannah's body back to the morgue, and I'm on my way to tell Robert. Jay is with me."

"I'll meet you at his house," said Earl. "And don't tell me I don't need to do this. I do. I let him down, Matt, and this is the least I can do now."

"I thought you might say that. It's not necessary, but if you want to, I understand. You'll probably arrive first, so wait for us, OK? Don't go in until we get there."

"Agreed. Did Bernice think she'd been there long? Buried?"

"Yeah," Matt said. "Probably around the time she disappeared. I don't think you and Dan could have prevented her murder if that's what you're getting at. She met somebody on Wednesday afternoon and whoever it was killed her and then disposed of her like you'd bury your dead dog."

"Damn," Earl said. "This one never felt right from the start, but I let the meager evidence we had cloud my gut feeling. I promise you I won't ever do that again."

"You don't have to promise me anything, Earl. But you and Dan need to realize that this might make you look bad in the public's eye. You should be prepared for some backlash."

"Do you think I don't know that?" Earl bellowed, loud enough for Jay to hear. "We didn't do our job, and I don't need a young gun cop to tell me that." He ended the call.

"That went well," Jay said.

"I'm going to bring in Ed, which will probably piss off Earl even more than he already is. What do you think?" Matt asked.

"I would," Jay said. "You know I'm no good at PR, but I think we need more of a show toward solving this case than usual. There's no getting around that Earl and Dan dropped the ball, and the public might be uneasy that there's a killer out there."

"Hell, I'm uneasy. We need to make some quick progress." He pressed Ed's number.

"Howdy," Matt said. "What are you doing tomorrow morning?"

"That depends on what you've got to say," Ed answered. "If you want to go fishing, I would tell you that it looks like rain tonight. If it's business, I'm in."

"Business, I'm afraid. The worst kind." He filled in Ed on the details.

"Oops," Ed said. "This will be a stain on the local constabulary."

"Yup. We need a major crime team meeting first thing tomorrow and figure out how to handle this. Can you call Patty and pick her up in the morning? Be in Port Stirling by 8:00 a.m? I'll ask Sylvia to call the others."

"Will do. You'd better call Earl first."

"Already did. Not sure he's talking to me, but he's going to meet Jay and me at Robert Oakley's house in a little while."

"Rough," Ed said. "But I know you'll find a way to make it as easy on Oakley as possible. So sorry, Matt. I'll see you tomorrow morning."

. . .

In the end, there was no way for Matt, Jay, and Earl to make it easy for Robert Oakley. He broke down completely and was inconsolable. To their huge relief, he didn't want to see her body in the morgue. All he wanted was to know what they would do to catch her killer.

Earl had insisted upon delivering the news, and Matt and Jay agreed it was best. The sheriff had apologized to Robert in heartfelt and honest terms, and Robert seemed to appreciate Earl's sincerity. He asked one question of him: "Would you have been able to save her if you'd believed me that night?"

Earl gave Matt an imploring look.

"No, I don't think so," Matt responded quickly with strength. "We'll be following the evidence, but right now, it looks as if a person or persons unknown took her on that Wednesday afternoon. We think she was killed almost immediately, probably at Mourning Bay, and soon after taken to where we found her. It was almost certainly too late by the time the sheriff and Chief McCoy found her car."

Unable to speak, Robert nodded as the floodgates opened again. Earl held his arm and helped him to the sofa.

After a respectable length of time had passed, and Robert had calmed down some, Matt said softly, "Can you answer a question for us?"

"What?" Robert croaked, rubbing his hands on his thighs as he bent over in pain.

"Do you know the passcode to Hannah's cell phone? Jay found it in her grave and we've charged it up, but it requires a passcode. We'd really like to take a look at her calls and texts from the days before she disappeared."

Robert stared at Matt for a few seconds as if one of them was on an alien planet. Then he said, "0505. The day we got married. May 5, 2021."

"Thank you. It may help us find out what happened to Hannah," Matt said. He placed his hand firmly on Robert's arm. "We're going to help you get through this. I know you think you can't, but you have friends and we're going to make sure you're not alone in the battle ahead of you. Is it alright if we go see if Tina is home and can come stay with you for a while?"

Robert nodded, staring at the floor.

Jay slipped out quietly and walked across the lawn to Tina Bigelow's house next door. While he walked, he tried 0505 on Hannah's phone and it unlocked successfully. He slipped the phone back in his pocket; they would search it later.

Thankfully, Tina was home.

"Jay, isn't it?" she asked, opening her front door. She took one look at his ashen face and said, "Oh, no, what's wrong?"

"We found Hannah's body today. She's been murdered, and we just told Robert. He's not doing so great. Could you come over and stay with him? Maybe help me figure out who to call that could help him?"

"Let me grab a sweater," she said and hurriedly retreated into her living room. "I'll take care of him, and we'll figure it out together. I'll call Jim Greenley, too, he's Robert's best friend."

They quickly made their way back across the lawn and into the house of death.

. . .

After she left Rainbow to Hope, Fern drove around Buck Bay for a while, just observing the pace of the county's largest town. She did a full circle, east to the other side of the bay, and west to the beach, as well as driving around the downtown core. While there were people around, going about their business, it was mostly quiet as opposed to bustling. The slow time of year for tourism meant even the traffic through town was subdued.

Once she was convinced she had nothing new to report to Joe Phelps today, she headed to her new cubbyhole office in the Port Stirling city hall to write a brief report on her activities. It was essentially a broom closet that the city manager had found for her, but it would work perfectly well for her State Department role needs. She was determined to keep her official work separate from the work she would do on her and Matt's behalf with the new foundation; that business she would conduct from her home office.

Fern had called the number for Alex Bowen that Sarah had given her before she left Buck Bay on the off chance that she could connect with him today, but her call went to his voicemail, and she left a message explaining who she was and why she wanted to talk with him. Bowen sounded pleasant on his recording. In the meantime, she had enough to get started on with Sarah's grant info and her other suggestions on how to proceed.

And, while it wasn't spying on bad guys or killing murderers with a fire poker, she was excited about this new direction in her life. *I can do both jobs. My work with Joe Phelps comes first, but it's clear I'm going to have enough down time to get our foundation running. Doing work I love to help the country, and possibly making life better for our local folks—how lucky am I?!? All the while, side-by-side with the man I love. My life is pretty perfect right now. Uh-oh*, she thought, recalling what had happened the last time she'd had the same thought.

At city hall, hoping to catch a glimpse of her handsome hubby, Fern poked her head in the police department squad room on her way down the hall to her broom closet. Sylvia, who was alone in the room, waved her in and said, "Come in for a minute. I have news."

"What's going on?" Fern said. "Is Matt here?"

"No, he and Jay are at Robert Oakley's home in Buck Bay. They've found Hannah's body. She was murdered and buried in the forest on Hedgehog Mountain."

Fern gasped, and her hand flew to her mouth. "That's awful news. I wondered why I hadn't heard from Matt for several hours. How was she discovered?"

Sylvia shared the details with Fern, admonishing her that it was, of course, top secret for now.

"So, Robert was right all along," Fern mused. "Do we have any clues yet? Any evidence? I assume Bernice was called in?"

"Yes. The body's been taken to the morgue. I don't know many details yet," Sylvia said. "Matt was anxious about getting to Robert. I do know that Jay found her cell phone. It was apparently buried under her body. Dreadful scene, I'm sure." She stared directly at Fern. "So now, it looks like we have another killer running around Chinook County."

Fern shuddered. "The big question is whether Hannah was targeted specifically, or if it was a random grab and kill."

The two women locked eyes.

CHAPTER 13

Matt welcomed the Chinook County major crime team to the Port Stirling police department conference room in the bowels of city hall. It was Thursday morning, 8:00 a.m.

He and Jay were the first to arrive, and Matt gestured to the chair at the head of the big mahogany table. "You want to sit there?" He had a sly smile on his face.

"No, I most certainly do not," Jay said firmly. He had filled in as acting chief when Matt was recovering because the city manager had asked him to, but he was far more comfortable in his detective role. "Maybe some-day when you're senile and decrepit, but not now."

"You'll be waiting a long time for that," Matt said.

"That's fine by me."

Next to arrive was Sylvia, escorting Oregon State Police lieutenant Ed Sonders and Twisty River detective Patty Perkins, who gave Matt a hug. "So nice to see you, chief, even if it is in this depressing room." The team only met here when there was big trouble in the county that required all hands on deck.

Ed and Patty were followed by Buck Bay police chief Dan McCoy and the interim Chinook County district attorney, Jeri Schrader, who arrived with Sheriff Earl Johnson. They drove together from Twisty River, the county seat where they both had their offices.

Jeri, the assistant district attorney, was in an acting role until the next election in May. She would be on the Oregon primary ballot for the top job. There were two men running against her, but they were both known yahoos in the local area, and Jeri's campaign for district attorney was looking good.

"It's nice to see you back in that chair, Matt," Jeri greeted the chief. "We owe you a lot at the county, and everyone sends their regards."

Matt knew to what and to whom Jeri was referring, but he demurred. "Actually, if you folks owe anyone at all, it's Sylvia. She did the legwork on my case."

"I took Sylvia to lunch a couple of times during the trials. She's a spark-plug," she whispered in Matt's ear. "Hope I can find someone just like her for my admin assistant if I get elected."

"You'll get the job. But hands off Sylvia," he joked, meaning every word.

Bernice was the only team member missing. She was busy with the autopsy and would join them tomorrow morning with her results. While the team exchanged greetings with their colleagues, Matt moved to the room's large white board, and taped up the photo of Hannah he'd been carrying in his pocket. He wrote her full name under the photo.

"Let's get started," he said, and everyone took their seats around the table. The room had been remodeled after the earthquake had taken out one of its walls, but it was still a soulless, standard-issue government conference room. Only the new cream wall paint, and a few fabulous black-and-white photos of the town's lighthouse and local beach scenes livened it up.

Dan had been advised of the situation yesterday after Matt had told Earl, and Matt wanted to smooth it over for the both of them this morning as best he could.

"All the initial evidence pointed to suicide," he said. "It was only pure, dumb luck that led us to the position we're in now." He explained how Stella, Mac, and Archie had stumbled across the grave. "If they didn't have a basset hound, we'd in all likelihood never have known what happened to Hannah."

He looked around the table, and all heads were nodding. It was a fluke, and the cops knew it.

"What made you reopen the case in the first place, Matt?" asked Jeri.

He shuffled uncomfortably. "Robert Oakley asked me to look further into his wife's disappearance. I had known him before this happened. He was convinced she never would have killed herself, and I agreed to take another look. But I wasn't getting anywhere either," he hurriedly added. "There was simply no trail that suggested anything other than the official verdict."

In his heart, Matt knew that wasn't the complete truth. He was already suspicious of Justin Sorenson, Hannah's first husband, and he'd gotten a weird hit off both Blake and Alex Bowen. Rudy's point about the addicts that Hannah had worked with opened some doors in his mind, too. And there was still the nagging "follow the money" refrain in his head about Robert Oakley. It had all begged for more investigation, and now their hand was forced.

"Matt's being kind," growled Earl. "I dropped the ball."

"Right behind you, Earl," frowned Dan McCoy. "I took the lazy way out, and you humored me. I've considered resigning, but I'd rather see this thing through. Maybe I can still bring some justice to Hannah and Robert." He was desolate, a stricken look on his face.

"It's a mess, for sure," said Patty in a brisk tone. "But hanging your heads and whining won't move us forward. We need to nail the bastard that did this, and we need to do it fast before anyone gets fired." She shot a glance at Matt.

"Patty's right," he agreed with her. "We've had success before working as a team, and we can do it again. And I'm more worried about the killer doing it again than I am about people getting fired."

"Do you have any indication that Hannah was specifically targeted?" asked Ed.

"No," said Matt. "It's too early. My department just started investigating earlier this week. But there are some things that got our attention surrounding Hannah and gave us the feeling that it might not be a random crime." He ticked off his suspicions and made a column on the white board for each one: Justin Sorenson, Blake Bowen, Alex Bowen, Rainbow to Hope addicts, and, finally, Robert Oakley.

"She met with someone that Wednesday afternoon, we believe," Matt continued. "Jay found her cell phone in the grave, and we went through it last night after we got Robert settled at home with some friends. She had six calls and two outgoing on the day she disappeared. Jay, can you take us through the calls and the timing?"

Matt sat down and Jay rose to take his place at the board.

"Hannah's calls on the day she disappeared, Wednesday, started at 9:33 a.m, when she placed a call to Alex Bowen's cell phone. We have confirmed that Alex uses this phone for business. The call lasted approximately six minutes."

"Alex Bowen runs a non-profit in Eugene that has essentially the same mission as Rainbow to Hope," Matt added. "They deal with substance abuse and mental health issues in Lane County."

"And he's married to Hannah's best friend, Blake Bowen," said Earl. "We talked to him, but Blake was out of the country. I should've followed up with her. There just didn't seem any point."

When Jay was sure Earl was finished, he continued. "Next on Hannah's list of Recents is an incoming call from the Debbie and Martin Longfellow Foundation at 9:54 a.m. This call lasted about ten minutes and is from area code 415."

"Who are they?" Patty asked. "Do you know yet?"

Jay shook his head. "No, we will track it down after this meeting. We think they might be the outfit that just gave a big grant to Rainbow to Hope. Hannah's staff told us it was from a west coast foundation."

Patty Googled it on her phone and nodded. "Foundation headquartered in San Francisco," she told the team.

Jay wrote another entry on the white board to the right of Robert Oakley's name: Longfellow Foundation, and then returned to read from his notes.

"The next incoming call is Blake Bowen," Jay told them. "At 10:45 a.m. Call lasted eight minutes. Next incoming was at 11:30 a.m. and there's no caller ID, might be a spam call. Call lasted twelve seconds and there's no corresponding voicemail."

"At 11:58 a.m., Hannah took a call from Robert Oakley, duration about four minutes." Jay looked at Matt.

"Robert has confirmed that he called Hannah 'around noon' on a break between his classes to see if she wanted to go out to dinner," Matt said. "He told us that they often went out on Wednesday night...called it their hump day celebration. They agreed to go to an Italian restaurant near their home at 7:00 p.m, and Robert told her he'd make a reservation." Matt paused. "That's how he knew something was wrong when 7:00 p.m. passed and Hannah hadn't arrived home."

"Did you check to see if they had a reservation?" Ed asked.

"Yup. And they did," Matt answered. "Owner knows them."

"At 12:20 p.m," Jay picked up where he'd left off, "Hannah received a call from the Blue Door Motel that lasted under a minute."

"Is that the dive motel downtown by the library?" asked Dan McCoy. His eyebrows rose. "Why would that dump be calling her?"

"It is," said Matt, "and that's what we want to know, too. We didn't talk to them last night, but they're on our list today. Our theory is that they might have been having a problem with a Rainbow client."

"Makes sense," agreed McCoy. "They get a lot of drop-in business. Addicts sleeping it off, that kind of thing. Let's just say it's not a family destination motel."

"Could you go talk to them after we're through here?" Matt asked McCoy. "Jay and I will need to go back to Buck Bay, but I'd like to get some things done here first."

"Yes." McCoy made a note in his journal. "Consider it done."

"I'll track down the Frisco foundation," Earl volunteered, needing a bone thrown his way, too.

"Sounds good, sheriff," Matt said. "Jay?"

"At 12:45 p.m," Jay said, "and this is juicy for several reasons, Hannah took a call from Justin Sorenson, her first husband." He hesitated to let the drama of that announcement sink in. "It's juicy because he told Matt and me that he hadn't talked to his ex-wife in months. The call lasted about five minutes."

"So, he lied," Patty mused. "Earl, did you talk to him?"

Earl tapped the pen he was holding on the table. "No, I didn't."

"Nobody mentioned she had an ex-husband," Dan McCoy said. "We didn't know."

Everyone suddenly found the conference table very interesting; they all looked down at it.

"Not only did he lie to us," Matt said, to break the silence, "we believe there is a good chance that Hannah had recently written to Justin telling him that she was petitioning the court to end his spousal support that she'd been paying him for over eight years. He told us that he had not received anything from her saying that, but Hannah's attorney thought she might have sent it the week before she disappeared. I will be talking to Mr. Sorenson again."

Jay consulted his notes one more time and said, "The last call on Hannah's phone was an outgoing call at 1:16 p.m. to White Orchid, the Thai restaurant around the corner from Rainbow to Hope. Her office told us she often got lunch there. We think she picked up some takeout, and then headed off to the meeting she told her staff she was going to. There are no further phone calls on her phone, and the charge had died by the time we recovered it."

Matt said, "As you can see, finding Hannah's phone was a stroke of luck—saves us from getting her records from the phone company. It gives us several leads to follow. I want to bring in the Bowens for further questioning, and I think we'll split them up into two rooms and interview them separately this time. Jay and I met with them together at their home in Buck Bay. Patty, I'd like you to come with me to talk to Blake Bowen—I need a different perspective on her."

"Just tell me where and when and I'm there," Patty said.

"Dan, could we borrow a couple of your interrogation rooms for the Bowens? Easier for them than trekking down to Port Stirling."

"Sure," Dan said stiffly. "When do you expect to bring them in?"

"Sooner rather than later," Matt said. "But I'll try to work with their schedule so as not to scare them off with urgency. Jay, can you and Ed take Alex Bowen?"

Both cops nodded.

"We need to know why Hannah called him the morning she disappeared," Matt said. "And, there's something about Alex that rubbed me the wrong way. Not sure why. He was pleasant enough, but he felt a little fake to me."

"What about Justin Sorenson?" Earl asked. "I'd like a shot at him."

"We'll get him into Buck Bay PD, too," Matt said. "Hannah's lawyer wants to go with me to talk to him, but if you want to come along, too, that's fine. Your bullshit meter could be really helpful with this guy."

"It will be my pleasure," said Earl somewhat formally.

"Sylvia is digging into Hannah's background," Matt said, gesturing to her. "She was the one who told us about Hannah's first marriage."

"I'm looking at her entire life," Sylvia said. "So far, nothing out of the ordinary jumps out at me except that first marriage to Justin Sorenson; they were an odd pairing no matter how you look at it. We need to know *exactly* how they got together." She looked at Earl, and he nodded, getting the point.

"Anyone have any early theories on who might have killed her, or why she might have been targeted?" Matt asked. "I know you've just absorbed the facts of Hannah's death, but y'all have been around these parts a lot longer than me. Any random notions swirling around your brains?"

"I keep coming back to her work," Patty jumped in. "There doesn't seem to be anyone who didn't like and respect her personally. But what about on the job? Could there have been some professional jealousy about Rainbow to Hope winning that big grant?"

"For every winner, there's a bunch of losers," agreed Matt. "Maybe one real sore loser. We need to check on the other finalist organizations." He made a note.

"It bothers me that everyone *did* seem to love her," Jay said. "It's not real. Everyone has enemies. How can there not be one or two people in Hannah's circle that don't think she walks on water? It's unrealistic."

"Everyone likes you," smiled Matt.

"No, they don't," Jay said, shaking his head. "I've got some former buddies from school that hate me now. And all I did was make something with my life while they got left behind. So, even lovable me isn't loved by everyone. My point."

"He's not wrong," Sylvia said, looking at Jay. "No one is a saint. There must be some past disagreements in Hannah's life, jealousies, or just opposite personalities. I'm looking for that, too."

"I wonder about her customers," said Earl. "The people she dealt with, some of them low-lifes, always bothered me in this case. Substance abusers would kill for things you and I can't imagine. Hannah may have been an easy target because she was so darn nice and trusting."

"Did you interrogate any of the current clients?" Ed asked, keeping his tone neutral.

"A couple," said Earl. "They saw nothing, knew nothing…you know the drill."

"Don't want to get involved, right?" said Ed.

"You know it," said Earl. "If I had it to do over again, and I guess I do, I'd bring in four or five of them for official interrogation."

"Let's do it, Earl," said Dan McCoy. "I'll help you. My guys made a short list of some of the clients our department sent to her recently. Mostly, it's guys who sleep in the city park even though we keep telling them they can't."

"Round them up," Matt said firmly to Dan. "Friends time is over. Somebody killed Hannah, and it's no more Mr. Nice Guy until we find out who."

"There is one elephant in the room," said Jeri, speaking for the first time. "None of you have mentioned Robert Oakley. In our line of work, it's almost always the husband. Maybe his plea for help to Matt was a ruse to throw us off."

The room went silent for about ten seconds until Matt spoke. "There's your next district attorney, folks," he said with a tight smile. "As much as it pains me, I'm the first person to consider that possibility, Jeri."

"He did," Jay said. "I told him he was too cynical for his own good."

Laughter around the table.

"It doesn't make sense to me," Jay continued, "that Robert would bring in Matt when she'd already been officially ruled a suicide. Why rock the boat at that point if you'd killed her and gotten away with it?"

"Maybe because you were worried someone might find the body—hello—and if you got out in front of that, it would put you at the bottom of the list," Earl answered. "Look at Matt's board. Robert's almost near the end of suspects. So, it kinda worked."

"But everything points to their marriage being extremely happy," Jay argued. "Why would he throw that all away after his past few years of hell?"

"The money," Dan McCoy said. "It's been known to happen. A guy with nothing meets a woman with something, and decides he wants it all."

"He was crushed when we told him Hannah was dead," Jay said. "Absolutely crushed. He wasn't faking it."

"No, he wasn't faking," Matt agreed. "But it could be guilt, a recognition of what he'd done and what he's lost forever. The finality of it. Grief has many facets."

* * *

On the way out of the room, Matt pulled Patty aside and asked, "Is Ted home today? I want to talk to him about Robert Oakley."

"Yes, and that's a good idea. He knows Robert inside and out." She hesitated. "In spite of what Jeri said, you don't really suspect him in Hannah's murder, do you?"

Matt shook his head. "He's a person of interest only because he inherits everything from her. We can't rule him out just yet."

"Following the money?" Patty asked.

"Always. He was sleeping rough and drinking mightily when I first met him. Money in his pocket might be a welcome thing to him."

Patty looked pensive. "Ted said the exact same thing to me."

CHAPTER 14

Cindy in HR had now conducted initial interviews for the open police detective position with five potential candidates. Two of those five were the cream that rose to the top, and one of them was the cherry, but she wouldn't tell Chief Horning which candidates she preferred. It would be more thorough if he had a phone call with all five, and then they could narrow it down together.

She placed the five resumés on his desk with a note that read: *'All five are qualified professionals, and none has two heads. ☺ I told them that you would be in touch soon.'*

Matt found them with Cindy's note when he returned to his office after the crime team meeting. *She actually drew a smiley face,* he thought.

Unlike many cops who worked their way up to management, Matt didn't mind the personnel part of his job. And the truth was that just covering their rounds, even during a slow time, had resulted in too many double shifts for his department. Now that they had a real case to work on, they would be stretched even further without Fern.

He skimmed the resumés and noted that three were on the west coast, one from Boston, and one in Plano, Texas, his old stomping ground. He saw the name at the top and recognized a former colleague, someone he also remembered as a dumb, racist cop. Matt threw the resumé in his trash can. *Then there were four.*

Checking his watch, 11:10 a.m., he decided to call the woman in Boston first and then work his way to the west coast applicants. He carefully read through her application and jotted down some notes before he picked up his phone.

He reached Tamryn Gesicki's voicemail and left a carefully worded message. "This is Matt Horning, and Cindy Baird suggested I give you a call. Please call me at your convenience on this number. Thank you."

Impressive resumé and an intelligent voice on her message, he thought. *Next.*

Matt was about three paragraphs in on the second resumé when his phone buzzed. Boston area code.

"Matt Horning."

"Chief Horning, you mean," corrected a pleasant female voice with a deep, mellifluous tone. "This is Tamryn Gesicki returning your call. Thank you for calling."

"I didn't want to leave my title on your phone, not knowing who had access to it."

"That's considerate, and I appreciate it. But this is my personal cell, and no one knows my code but me. Please feel welcome to call it at any time during this process." She paused. "So, you have an opening for an experienced detective, I understand."

Take charge. I like that. "Yes. We are looking for a new officer. It's to replace a detective in our little department. We're a small town, but one opening can leave us short-handed, and that's where we find ourselves today."

"What happened to the former officer? Why do you have this opening?"

"She was offered a job with the U.S. State Department and accepted it."

"Wow. That's something. Did she leave on good terms with you?"

In spite of trying to maintain his professional demeanor, Matt laughed. "You might say that. I married her."

"The police chief married one of his detectives?" Now she laughed.

"It's complicated," Matt said, trying to regain control of the interview. "But now that you know my secret, let's talk about you. Your resumé is very impressive, and you appear to have a solid career underway. Regular promotions and several commendations over the past six years."

"Thank you. I've worked hard," Tamryn said. "And I like to think I've worked smart, too. I'm not sure how it is in Port Stirling, Oregon, but in Boston it's more important to use your brain than your gun. Let's just say that often gives me an advantage over some of my colleagues."

"Smart is even more important out here," Matt told her. "We're a small community, and if we lose the public trust, we're all toast. Looking at your record, there's one thing that's bothering me. Boston PD is a major police force; why would you want to leave a successful career there and go 3,000 miles across the country to a small town?"

There was a brief silence on the other end of the line, and then she spoke. "Because my husband beat the shit out of me, and no one in this 'major police force' seemed to care. Since we're being honest with each other."

"Oh. I didn't expect that," Matt said. He gulped and hesitated. "Are you alright now?"

"Fit as a fiddle now, but he put me in the hospital for a few days. And, as painful as that was, it was almost more painful when my sergeant refused to arrest my husband, or even talk to him, for that matter. Said it was a domestic issue that I should be able to resolve on my own."

Now Matt was truly speechless. "That's unbelievable."

"Right? That's what I thought, too. But none of my colleagues had my back, and everyone acted like nothing had happened. And it gets worse. I come from a large Polish family, four brothers. And their advice after the 'incident' was to suck it up and try to be a better wife. My father and my four brothers. Mom kept her mouth shut. So, you see, chief, I'm done here."

"Where are you living now? Are you safe?"

"Yeah. I rented a furnished apartment when I left the hospital. No one knows where I'm living. I've filed for divorce, and I'm only showing up for work until I can land a new job. I'm a skilled detective, chief. You could do a lot worse out there in the boonies."

He chuckled. "Yup, I've got worse resumés on my desk right now. But I want to be crystal clear; you need to consider what a different life it is out here. The culture, the weather, the food—it's completely different from the east coast."

"It's completely different from Texas, too, but you've thrived."

"Ahh, you did your homework," he conceded. "I needed a fresh start."

"And you don't think I do?!?"

"I think you do, yes, but I want to make sure you've really thought this through. The lifestyle change."

"I want a change. I need a change. And I like what I know about Oregon. It's progressive, with lots of beautiful open space. People leave you alone and mind their own business."

"All true."

"I'm choking here, chief. My family, my work, they're all choking me, and I can't breathe. I will work hard to fit in because I know I'll be different. But I'll win over your department and your town because I'm good at my job, and I want it to work. What do you say?"

"I say that we both need to sleep on this tonight and talk again tomorrow. Is that good enough for now?"

"You're the boss." Tamryn Gesicki ended the call.

• • •

After lunch, Matt spent the rest of the afternoon talking to the other three candidates—none of whom left the impression on him that Tamryn Gesicki had. Then he did due diligence on all of the candidates' qualifications and references before heading for home at 6:00 p.m.

He thought about Robert Oakley calling his wife the day she disappeared to ask her if she wanted to go out to dinner that evening. When he'd heard that was what their phone call was about, it dawned on him that he hadn't taken his wife out to dinner since they'd been on their honeymoon in Maui. *What a crappy husband I am.*

He called her on the way.

"I'd like to take my beautiful wife out to dinner tonight," he told her when she answered. "How about it?"

"Excellent, excellent idea," Fern said. "I'm sitting here staring at the freezer trying to decide what I can make in a hurry."

"Close that freezer, babe. I was thinking we might go somewhere nice, like The Links dining room. How does that sound? I'll call them if you approve."

"I approve! I'm walking upstairs to change out of my sweats. Call them!"

* * *

Upstairs, Fern stood in the middle of her closet. *A date with my husband. I'd like to look good.* She chose a black-and-white print silk dress with a wide boatneck and full, swishy skirt, and grabbed a wide, red patent-leather belt. She rarely wore heels because she'd developed a bunion on her right foot—a fact she was keeping secret for now because she was too young for this kind of crud thing to happen to her. She'd been buying shoes for comfort rather than style lately, but she dug out a pair of red kitten heels that were several years old, but still looked good. They would hurt a little, but they were perfect for this dress, so she'd tough it out.

Fern wondered what had inspired Matt to want to go out tonight. Since his shooting, they had, by necessity, stayed home almost every night. While he was recovering, it was their only choice, and now it had become routine, a nice routine. But she didn't want them to fall into routines; she wanted their marriage to be, if not exciting, not predictable either. She would have to be mindful of doing her part to ensure things didn't get too mundane on the home front.

He'd been tired last night, and hadn't arrived home until almost 9:00 p.m. They had talked briefly about Robert Oakley, but she could tell he was too exhausted to go into much detail, and she didn't want to press. She'd made him a peanut butter and jelly sandwich, which he accepted gratefully and wolfed down with a glass of milk. He'd taken a quick shower to wash off 'the stink of death' as he called it, and was in bed and sound asleep by 10:00 p.m.

She had woken at 6:45 this morning, and Matt was already gone. It would be nice to sit across from each other tonight and catch up. She added a little makeup, brushed her hair, and started down the staircase just as he came in from the garage.

Spotting her across the living room, he let out a wolf whistle. "You're a sight for sore eyes," he said, and rushed to give her a hug. "That dress deserves a kiss."

"Bet you say that to all the girls," she teased. But she met him way more than halfway on the kiss.

Reluctantly, he pulled back from her and said, "I'll be right back. Going to put on a better shirt."

They had a favorite table in The Links dining room; in the corner by the window and across from the fireplace, which had a welcoming roaring fire tonight. Fern appreciated the subdued lighting, the plush carpet, and the crisp white tablecloths and small lamps at each table. Being a Thursday night, the room wasn't packed like it would be over the weekend, but they still had company with several tables full of animated diners.

It was dark out, but a three-quarter moon was moving from east to west over the Pacific and was visible through a thin layer of fast-moving clouds. It cast a silvery light on the whitecaps outside their window.

Matt pulled out Fern's chair — a plush, comfy armchair — just ahead of a waiter bearing an ice bucket and a bottle of champagne.

"We didn't order that," Matt told the waiter, who they knew well.

"I know," the waiter smiled. "It's on us, chief. We haven't seen you since you got shot, and we're all so happy you're better. And don't give me any nonsense about you being a public servant and can't accept gifts…blah, blah, blah. This is for Mr. and Mrs. Horning, our friends."

Matt raised his hands palms up and shrugged. "Then you'd better pour my wife a glass. And thanks, it's kind of you."

"Here's to you, darlin', and being freed from cooking tonight," Matt said, lifting his glass to her.

"And to you, handsome," Fern toasted. "You didn't look so hot last night, but you seem to have some sparkle tonight."

"Yeah, that's me, sparkly." He laughed and took a sip. "I feel grateful to be alive, and grateful that you're alive and we're together. Let's not take it for granted, OK?"

"You know I don't," Fern said. "After everything we've been through, every single day is worth celebrating. I can't have champagne every day or I'd double in size, but it hits the spot tonight. And I have a small thing worth celebrating."

"What's that?"

"I made progress today on setting up our foundation. I talked to Alex Bowen. Sarah Forrester gave me his name and number as someone who could show me the ropes. His foundation is in the ballpark of what we're planning, and he was helpful."

"He's a suspect in Hannah Oakley's murder, Fern," Matt said, his face clouding up. "You should have asked me first before you called him."

"I didn't mention you or the case," she said defensively. "I used my own name, and we only discussed the non-profit world and how things work. I took lots of notes and will use a lot of what he shared with me."

"How did he seem?"

"Well, he was very nice and pleasant," Fern said. "We got on well, and he said I could call him anytime for advice. He's been in this business for twenty years and knows the ropes."

"Did he mention Hannah?"

"No. It was nothing to do with her, Matt. He's the best person locally to help me. It was all about business. I don't know why you're being so hinky about this."

"What if Alex Bowen turns out to be our killer? I don't want you holding hands with him across a conference table."

"Oh, for crying out loud, you are way off base on this one. His wife was Hannah's best friend, and our phone call was harmless." She took a big gulp of her champagne. "But I won't talk to him again until you've ruled him out of your case."

"I'd appreciate that." He refilled her glass. "Now, let's look at the menu, and then I'll fill you in on where we are on the case, and you can tell me more about your progress. It feels like a lot has happened since I've seen you. I liked it better when we worked together."

Fern ignored his remark as their waiter reappeared. She ordered oysters on the half shell for them to share as an appetizer, and a steamed Pacific cod dish that they cooked to perfection here. Matt ordered a Caesar salad that they would also share, and his favorite pan-fried halibut. He cooked it at home better than any restaurant, but The Links did it justice, too. Matt still loved a good ol' Texas BBQ on occasion, but he was beginning to wean himself off meat and more in the direction of the fresh fish and seafood Oregon offered. He let Fern believe it was her healthful influence, but the truth was when he learned how good the fresh bounty was here, he was hooked.

They devoured the dozen oysters — six Pacific and six Kumamoto grown just north of Buck Bay — and washed them down with the champagne.

"That's a perfect pairing," said Fern. "Yum." She wiped her lips. "Did you check in with Robert Oakley today?" she asked him. "How is he doing?"

"I called him, but his friend Jim Greenley answered his phone. He said Robert was resting, and not doing very well. Won't eat, etc. I actually wanted to talk to Greenley because he's Robert's alibi for the time period Hannah disappeared. He's a teacher, too, and they run together several times a week after school."

"Did he confirm he was with him that day?"

"Yep. In class all day, Robert's car stayed in the same parking spot, and they went for a run until about 6:00 p.m."

"Any wiggle room?" Fern asked.

Matt stared at her. "How come you're not like everyone else telling me that Robert can't possibly be a suspect in Hannah's murder?"

"Because I've learned from you that the spouse is always the most likely." She smiled sweetly at him.

"You've met him. Do you think he's a suspect?"

"No, I don't. But I also know that you won't rule him out until you're one hundred percent sure he's innocent. Was there time after he left Greenley and before he called the police for him to kill her?"

Matt shook his head. "Not really. Maybe technically possible, but it's awful tight. And he took the news hard. Real hard. Jay says there is no way he could've faked his reaction. And I think I agree with him."

"But he's the only person who benefits financially from Hannah's death." It came out like a question.

"Yes. As far as we know, Robert gets everything."

"And that bothers you."

"Yeah, it bothers me."

"Not everything's about money," she said.

"That statement from a woman who's sitting here eating oysters and drinking champagne." He smiled to let her know it wasn't a criticism.

"True," she said. "But if I couldn't afford this meal, I wouldn't kill someone just to beef up my bank account. And I don't think Robert did either. What does the crime team think? Any ideas from your meeting this morning?"

"We kicked around a couple of theories, but it's too early and we don't have enough evidence yet. Bernice will join us tomorrow morning and give us the autopsy results. We'll go from there. The team misses you, by the way."

"That's nice," Fern said with a smile. "I miss them, too. We need to entertain so I can see them."

"Agreed. But I do have an interesting development on another matter."

"Oh?"

"We're doing a search to replace you. Not replace you, I mean, but fill your old position."

Fern grinned and playfully slapped his hand. "That's a better way to put it."

"Cindy in HR came up with five potential candidates, and I had a phone call with four of them this afternoon. The fifth one is a cop I worked with in Plano, and he's a dirtbag, so he's out. Finalists are three men and one woman."

"Bill Abbott wants you to hire with diversity in mind," Fern said. "He told me. But he also wants you to hire the best cop you can get."

"Well, because I'm so brilliant, I may have covered both those requirements in one person. Her name is Tamryn Gesicki, and she is a decorated detective in the Boston PD."

"Boston? Wow."

"Wow is right. She's pretty amazing, and she wants our job bad."

"Why?"

"Well, that's the big question. Which I asked during the course of our interview. And here comes the baggage. Which is highly confidential, of course."

Fern nodded her understanding.

"Her husband beat her badly enough to put her in the hospital, and the Boston PD and her family didn't support her when she needed it most."

"What?" Her eyes widened.

"It's a bad story, Fern. And, she's doing the only thing she can do — start over someplace new. She's divorcing her husband…"

"Duh," Fern interrupted.

"…leaving Boston and quitting her job as soon as she finds another opportunity. And the beauty of it is she's incredibly qualified. She's done everything we need and more."

"Would she be a good fit with your team? Culturally, you think? Big city PD compared to our small village?"

"She's a strong proponent of community policing, and she's in this profession for the right reasons. She might be a bit quirky, and she's got the heavy Boston accent, but she's smart and wants to build a new life. I think I've totally lucked out."

"Will you have anyone else interview her?"

"Sure. Abbott told me to hire who I want, but I'm going to have him talk to her, too. She's a bit of a risk, but I think she's worth it. I'm thinking I'll ask Sylvia to have a chat with her, too. Nobody can fool Sylvia."

Fern frowned.

"What?" Matt asked.

"Darn. I was hoping you wouldn't find anyone as good as me right out of the gate so people might miss me more."

Matt laughed and slapped the table. "You have no filter, Mrs. Horning. And everyone misses you. You know that. And Gesicki may or may not be as good as you, or this might blow up in my face."

"I want it to work for you. And I already love her."

CHAPTER 15

On Friday morning, the major crime team got busy with their assignments on the Hannah Oakley murder investigation. The day dawned calm and clear, yesterday's relentless rain and wind moving inland from the coast. This week's changeable weather was classic late winter in Oregon: cold, miserable one day, and a hint of spring the next.

Today, the air was soft with a hint of fragrance mixed with the fresh tang of the ocean. Both sea and sky were bluer than blue, and the sandy beaches took on a golden hue. Even the seagulls were mellow, silently riding along on top of the ocean's now-gentle waves.

Matt started his day in a chair on his deck facing the ocean — he would never again sit with his back to it — and made a phone call to Ted Frolick. Before he picked up his phone, he drank from his coffee cup and thought back to the day he'd first met the older man. Ted had been a suspect in Matt's first case in Port Stirling, the murder of little Emily in the shallow waters of the beach sea stacks, but after spending thirty minutes walking on the beach with Ted in front of his house, Matt knew he wasn't a killer. He liked Ted almost immediately and admired his intelligence and dignified demeanor.

Matt looked south down the beach, searching for the stretch by Ted's old house as he recalled that momentous day. When Ted and Patty had married, it'd been a far more joyous day than the day Matt first arrived in town.

He checked his watch. 7:30 a.m. *Too early to call most people.* He looked out to sea and enjoyed his coffee. *Roger!*

The seal was looking up at Matt on his deck and appeared to grin. He bobbed under and resurfaced, still watching Matt.

"Ted will be up," Roger said.

"You're probably right," Matt said. "How've you been?"

"Wet. And you?"

"I'm good. Back at work and happy."

"I'm sorry I let you down the day you got shot," Roger said. "I should've been paying better attention."

"Not your fault. I'm glad they didn't shoot you, too."

"I've been here for ten years. Probably good for another fifteen," Roger said.

"Hope so."

The harbor seal bobbed under a wave. Matt dialed Ted's number.

"Top of the morning to you, chief," Ted said.

"It's not too early, is it?"

Ted laughed. "I've been up since 5:15. Almost ready for my first nap."

"Is your bride awake, too?" Matt asked. He didn't want to disturb them.

"Sitting right here at the kitchen table with me. She's looking at an expensive Mexican spa on her laptop. Should I be worried?"

"Nope," Matt answered, chuckling to himself. "It's all in the line of duty. She's gonna check an alibi for one of the suspects in our case. But it wouldn't kill you to take Patty to a nice Mexican resort, you know."

"She may have just mumbled something of that nature," Ted said. "Do you want to talk to her?"

"Actually, it's you I want to talk to. About our case, though. Have you got a minute?"

"Lots of them. I'm retired. What's on your mind?"

"Robert Oakley," Matt said. "He told me you saved him once upon a time. Got him cleaned up and back into teaching."

"He was ready," Ted said. "Robert was never cut out to be a bum. Too smart. Too valuable as a human being. It's so unfair about Hannah's death, just when they had everything going for them."

"Patty tell you she was murdered?"

"Yes. Terrible thing."

"You know Robert well. Any thoughts on who could have killed his wife?"

"What you really want to know is if I think Robert could have done it."

Matt hesitated. "Yes, that is what I want to know. Could he?"

"He could. But do I think he did kill her? No, I don't."

"Are you sure?" Matt had to ask.

"No, I'm not sure," Ted answered simply. "And if I were you, I'd go to all lengths before I'd rule him out."

"Why do you say that?"

"The same reason you're asking me this question. The money. You met Robert at his low point, and you've seen how he's rejoined society. Hannah made that possible for him."

"But he got a job and was taking care of himself."

"True. But Hannah gave him a hand up. She provided a lifestyle for the two of them that he couldn't have done by himself that quickly. I think he loved her deeply, but I also think he relished living the good life."

"Nothing wrong with that, Ted."

"Not a thing, certainly. But now, I understand, he's got all the moola to himself."

"It's not that much money. Not enough to kill for."

"Says the man with his own millions," Ted said. "I'm not saying he killed her. But your question was could he. And my answer is yes, he could kill if motivated. Robert's a nice guy, but he's been down in the gutter and that changes men. I think he's capable of most things a man could imagine, simply because of his time living rough. You know that saying: 'Don't judge a man till you've walked a mile in his shoes?' It's appropriate when you're talking about Robert Oakley."

• • •

After Ted hung up the phone with Matt, Patty dressed and kissed him good-bye. Ted had asked her if he'd done the right thing by telling Matt his feelings about Robert.

"He asked you what you thought. You answered him honestly. That's all you could do," she told her husband. "At this point, nobody knows who killed Hannah, but everyone will have an opinion. It's our job to turn those opinions into evidence, or to discard them. I'm outta here. See you early evening, about 5:30 p.m."

She headed to her office in the basement of the Chinook County courthouse where the Twisty River police department was headquartered.

'Department' was a loose word for their force. It consisted of Detective Patty Perkins, her boss, who was in reality a glorified spokesperson, and two beat officers. Yes, Twisty River was the county seat, but it was, and had been for decades, a small, somewhat dying town that held onto the county seat with clawing fingernails. It was mainly the judges and local attorneys who resisted every effort by Buck Bay to relocate the county seat to their town; they loved the diner around the corner from the courthouse in Twisty River.

Patty had a small office that had only one redeeming feature—a door. She closed it now and settled at her desk, removing her uniform jacket. Opening her laptop, she went to the website she'd bookmarked at home, Rancho Miguel Splendida, and dialed the phone number she'd found in the Contacts section.

She had boned up on her Spanish earlier this morning, and she could communicate, barely, if necessary. But much to her relief, the phone was answered by a nice sounding woman who said, "Good morning, Rancho Miguel Splendida. How may I help you?"

"Buenas Dias to you, ma'am. I'm Detective Patricia Perkins with the police in Oregon, and we're investigating a homicide. I would like to talk to someone who can answer a few questions about a guest who stayed with you earlier this month. Can you direct me to that person?"

"Si. You will need to talk to our director of reservations who works in our general manager's office. If you'll kindly hold, I will try to find her now."

"Gracias."

While she held, Patty fished out a yellow legal pad from her top desk drawer. She'd tried to get used to taking notes on her laptop, but she still preferred the pad. *Guess that makes me a dinosaur. Tough cookies.*

The line came alive, and a voice said, "Hello?"

"Yes, hello," Patty said, and introduced herself again to the new woman. "What's your name, please?"

"I am Luna Perez, and I manage all of our reservations. How may I assist you?"

"I want to know if an American woman named Blake Bowen from Oregon was a guest with you during the week of January 22 this year. Can you get that information for me?"

"I can tell you that, yes, Mrs. Bowen stayed with us that week. She is a favorite guest of ours and we see her regularly. I myself had breakfast with her that week."

"When did she arrive and when did she leave?"

"Let me check my records; I have them here. One moment, please."

Patty waited, pen poised over her yellow pad.

"Ah, si, here it is. Mrs. Bowen arrived on Saturday, January 21, and she was due to depart on Friday, January 27."

"Did she leave on Friday as scheduled?"

"I assume so."

"Can you be sure? Do you have a checkout time for her?"

"We don't have checkouts at our resort," Luna sniffed. "We believe it's insulting to our guests."

"How do you know when someone has left?" Patty sniffed back. *How bizarre*, she thought.

"We provide a shuttle to our airport for our guests on their day of departure. It's part of our excellent service. Mrs. Bowen would have taken the shuttle on Friday."

"Does someone on your staff check the rooms after the shuttle leaves to make sure the guest has left?"

"Of course."

"And Mrs. Bowen was not in her room on Friday after the shuttle departed?" Patty asked, trying to be as clear as possible.

"That's correct. She was gone, along with all her luggage on Friday."

"Can you verify that she was on the Friday shuttle for me? It's very important."

"Of course, but I don't have that information here at this time. I will need to talk to the Friday driver and host."

"Please do so at your earliest convenience," Patty instructed, and then asked, "When is the last time you personally saw Mrs. Bowen?"

Luna hesitated for a moment. "I believe it was Wednesday morning. She had been out on our early morning walk, and was in the gift shop at the same time I stopped in."

"How did she seem? Did she act normal?"

"I would say so, yes. We exchanged greetings, but it was brief as she appeared to be in a hurry to get cleaned up after her hike."

"And what day did you have breakfast with her?"

"It was Sunday, the morning after she arrived. I always greet her personally to make sure we provide everything she needs."

"How did she seem that morning?"

"Normal. Happy to be here. We laughed and talked freely. Is she alright?" Luna asked worriedly.

"Yes, she's fine. Don't worry. But a friend of hers was murdered, and we must talk to everyone who knew the victim and understand where they were when we think the crime occurred. Please call me when you've talked to the Friday staff. Here's my number." Patty gave her the phone number and thanked her for her time.

• • •

Sheriff Earl Johnson started his workday at 9:00 a.m. with a call to the Debbie and Martin Longfellow Foundation in San Francisco. He was put through to the executive director, Ginny Vincent.

The sheriff explained why he was calling and asked her specifically about the phone call from their number to Hannah Oakley's phone on Wednesday, January 25.

"That was me," Ginny answered. "I called Hannah to discuss next steps now that the grant had been awarded to Rainbow to Hope." Her voice cracked and she said quietly, "I'm having trouble believing I'll never talk to her again. Is there any news on her disappearance?"

"I'm afraid it's bad news," Earl said. "We've found Hannah's body, and it appears that she was murdered."

"Murdered?!? How is that possible?"

"That's what we're trying to find out."

"But she was declared a suicide, I thought. I'm confused."

Earl cleared his throat. "That was my fault. We didn't find her body, and all the evidence we had pointed to suicide. We should have investigated more fully, and I take full responsibility for that. I'm sorry to deliver such awful news."

Ginny gathered herself. "It is awful news, sheriff, on two fronts. I got to know Hannah well during our grant vetting process, and I liked her enormously. But beyond my personal feelings, she was the primary reason Rainbow won our grant. She was a leader with tremendous vision and had the track record to prove she knew how to get results."

"Will the grant still go to Rainbow now that they'll have to find a new manager?"

"That's a good question. Hannah wasn't just a manager and counselor; she founded Rainbow to Hope. She was the heart and soul. We may have to review the grant."

"There are other good people who worked with Hannah," Earl said. He felt like he had to defend the local organization.

"Yes, that's true, but there were also some other organizations that we liked as well, and that finished very close to Hannah's operation."

"What can you tell me about the other finalists?"

"We had narrowed it to three finalists before we selected Hannah. Our mission calls for us to focus on the west coast, and the other two finalists are in Seattle and Eugene, Oregon."

"Is the Eugene organization run by Alex Bowen?" Earl asked.

"Yes. Do you know him?"

"He lives in Buck Bay with his wife, who was Hannah's best friend from childhood days. We know that he and Hannah often worked together on projects because their business model is the same. Our investigation has talked to Alex and his wife."

"Alex's organization is well run, and, if I'm honest, we chose Rainbow to Hope because of the need in your community. Eugene has major problems, too, but Chinook County is close to the edge with substance abuse."

"Don't I know it," sighed Earl. "We estimate that over 70 percent of our crime is related to drugs. I really hope you don't pull your grant from Buck Bay. We need help."

"I wish I could promise we won't, sheriff, but we will have to do some further due diligence with Hannah's death. Please keep this confidential until we have time to evaluate the situation."

• • •

After his call with Ted, Matt phoned Robert Oakley. The call went straight to voicemail, and Robert's voice in happier days instructed him to leave a message. Matt did, telling him he would be in Buck Bay later today, and planned to stop by to see him. Also told him to let him know if he needed anything.

Then he called the Bowen residence, and Alex picked up.

"Hi, Alex. It's Matt Horning here. We've had a development in the Hannah Oakley case, and we need to talk to you and Blake again."

"What kind of development?" Alex asked.

"I'd prefer to not discuss it over the phone," Matt said. "I'm afraid your wife will be upset, and I'd like to deliver our news in person. We'd like you to bring her to the Buck Bay police department this afternoon if you're available. Can that work for you?"

There was a brief hesitation, and then Alex said, "Sure, chief. We want to help you in any way we can. Will it be you we meet with?"

"Yes. And I've asked Detective Patricia Perkins, she's with the Twisty River PD, to join us. She's one of the best detectives in Chinook County." Matt threw that out there to rattle his cage a little.

"I really don't see what this has to do with us, or how we can help you," Alex said. "We've told you everything we know, which is essentially nothing useful."

"That's probably true, but we just have a couple of things we want to clear up. Can you make it by 2:00 p.m?"

"I think so. Blake is reading in her room, and I'm doing some paper-work and am almost finished. Where is the police department?"

"It's in city hall in downtown. Do you know where that is?"

"Yeah. We'll be there." He hung up.

You'd better be there, Matt thought. He called Jay to let him know and asked him to round up Ed for the 2:00 p.m. meet. They would take Alex Bowen while he and Patty took on Blake in a separate room.

Patty was next. "We're on with the Bowens at Buck Bay PD at 2:00 p.m."

"Terrific. I've got some questions for the missus," Patty said. "She was definitely at the Baja spa the week in question, but it seems that none of the staff is quite sure when she left."

. . .

Matt dressed in his uniform and headed to city hall. Sylvia and city man-ager Bill Abbott were huddled at her desk in the squad room.

"Just the man we're looking for," boomed Abbott. "Your employee of the year and I have news, don't we Sylvia?"

"We do," smiled Sylvia.

"Let's hear it," Matt said.

"We've talked to Tamryn Gesicki in Boston as you requested," said Abbott. "We like her."

"Now, Bill, I didn't say I 'liked' her," objected Sylvia. "I said we'd be lucky to get her."

Abbott waved his hand dismissively. "She would be a major-good hire, that's what I meant by 'like' her. She's very professional on the phone, and she might come off as a little…"

"Brusque?" Sylvia finished for him.

"I was going to say 'blunt'," Abbott said. "But she's super experienced with excellent references. I talked to two of them, and they said she was the bravest cop they'd worked with. She's got commendations, Matt!"

"I know, her record is admirable," agreed Matt. "Tell me your thoughts, Sylvia."

"I agree with Bill on her background and proficiency. And she appears to be highly intelligent. She's a little..blunt. But she doesn't have to be Fern, she just has to get the job done, and, on paper, she looks extremely competent." She smiled at Abbott. "We think you should hire her."

"And get her here fast if you can," added Abbott. "We have a killer on the loose."

CHAPTER 16

"You're hired," Matt said into his phone.

Tamryn Gesicki let out a whoop that nearly traveled 3,000 miles.

. . .

OSP Lieutenant Ed Sonders and Port Stirling Detective Jay Finley greeted Alex and Blake Bowen as they entered the lobby of Buck Bay city hall. Matt and Patty were already there, and Matt explained how this was going to work.

Confronted with the four police officers in their uniforms, Alex and Blake, dressed casually in jeans and sweaters, looked uncomfortable the minute they walked through the double glass doors. There was nowhere to hide in the large, empty space. The building was modern, with open parking under the one-story city offices, and walls of windows that brought the outside in. Huge baskets of purple and yellow pansies were evenly spaced along the entire front of the building.

Alex spoke first. "We don't understand why we're here, chief," he said to Matt. Blake remained mute at his side.

"Like I told you on the phone, we just want to dot our i's and cross our t's," Matt said in a friendly tone, keeping his voice neutral. "Just routine. You'll be out of here before your parking meter expires," he smiled at Alex.

"Lt. Sonders and Detective Finley will go with you to a room down that hall," he pointed to his left. "Detective Perkins and I will go with you, Blake."

Blake looked at her husband in what Matt would call total panic. She said, "You're going to split us up? Can you do that? We'd really prefer to talk to you together."

"Look here, Horning," Alex said. His friendly 'I'm a good guy' demeanor was now shot to hell. "We're trying to cooperate with you, but I need to stay with my wife. She's having a hard time." He squeezed Blake's arm as if to punctuate his statement.

"I understand," said Matt. "And I'm sorry, but this is standard procedure. We won't keep you long."

Ed stepped up to Alex and said, "Please come with me, sir."

Alex looked up at the 6'4" officer and said, "Do I have a choice?"

Ed smiled. "Of course you do. You're not being detained. We just want to ask you a few questions. It will go faster this way." He started to move down the hallway, and Jay moved beside Alex to herd him along. Alex looked over his shoulder at Blake, smiled and blew her a kiss. Off they went.

Jay opened the door of the interrogation room and indicated a chair for Alex; the chair that faced the camera recording their meeting. He and Ed took the chairs to Alex's left and right.

"I want to emphasize for the record that you are here voluntarily, and are not a suspect in custody," Jay said. "We would like to record our conversation, but only if you agree. Is it OK with you if we record our talk?"

Alex hesitated. "I suppose so. I've got nothing to hide, and I'm just here to answer a couple of questions, right?"

"That's correct," Jay said. "And you're free to leave at any time, or not answer anything you don't want to."

"OK."

Ed gave a 'thumbs up' sign to the recording device booth.

"We're talking to Alex Bowen regarding the homicide of Hannah Sorenson Oakley," Jay began. "Mr. Bowen, Lt. Ed Sonders of the Oregon State Police, and me, Detective Jay Finley of the Port Stirling PD, agree to record our conversation. Mr. Bowen is here voluntarily at the request of Port Stirling police chief Matt Horning."

"Homicide?" Alex interrupted Jay. "What do you mean?" A shadow of fear crossed his face.

"We found Hannah's body yesterday, and this is now a homicide investigation," Jay replied. "She was murdered."

"How? Where? How could this happen?" Alex blurted, losing his cool.

"We can't say anything about the circumstances until the county medical examiner performs an autopsy," Jay said promptly and nodded at Ed.

"Hannah Oakley's phone records show that she called you on the morning of Wednesday, January 25 — the day she disappeared," Ed said. "She called you at 9:33 a.m. and the call lasted approximately six minutes. Why did she call you? What did you talk about?"

Alex, who'd been sitting with his hands clasped on the table in front of him, leaned back and placed his arms on his chair, fingers splayed out. He took a deep breath and composed himself. "Did she?" he said. "We talk regularly but I don't recall the specifics on that day."

"She did," Ed said. "And her records show that she hadn't talked to you — at least, not on her cell phone — for almost three weeks before that Wednesday. Anything you can remember about the call may be helpful to our understanding of her mood, or what she was doing that day."

"Oh, wait, I do remember talking to her then. She called to give me her condolences for my organization not getting the grant that the Longfellow Foundation gave to Rainbow to Hope. I already knew she'd won, of course, but it was nice of Hannah to call me. We were friendly competitors in this one, but we often work together. Our organizations run the same kind of programs."

"How did you feel about losing out to her?" Jay asked. "It must have been tough to do all that work and not win. We understand it was a lucrative contract."

"Well, it wasn't fun to lose, for sure," Alex smiled. "But I was happy the money was going to Buck Bay — our community needs the help. And, besides, it wasn't that big of a grant to my organization. Big for Rainbow to Hope, but I run a larger program." He paused and then, "Are your colleagues telling Blake the bad news now? I really should be with her."

"Matt and Patty will break it to her gently," Jay said. "She'll be well taken care of." He continued his line of questioning. "How did Hannah seem that morning when you talked?"

Alex thought for a moment. "Normal, I would say."

"Happy? Sad? Angry? Upset about anything?" asked Jay.

"She wasn't angry or upset, I don't think. Just sort of her normal self. It was a courtesy call, that's all. I would have done the same if the shoe was on the other foot."

"Were you surprised when you heard she committed suicide?" asked Ed. "Not a 'normal' thing to do—walk into Mourning Bay and kill yourself?"

"Both Blake and I were totally shocked when we got the news," Alex said. "My wife was Hannah's best friend, you know." He shifted in his chair. "Hannah gave no indication when we talked that morning that she was depressed or upset. We couldn't believe it."

"But when Chief Horning and I talked to you, you indicated that both you and your wife had accepted the official ruling of suicide," Jay said. "What changed your mind?"

"Well, when the police and the coroner release a statement saying so, you have to believe it, don't you? They obviously knew much more about the circumstances than we did. We didn't really have a choice after that."

"Hannah's husband, Robert Oakley, never believed she killed herself, no matter what the official verdict was," Jay said flatly.

"He was in denial of her death," said Alex. "That's probably pretty normal, I would guess."

"Did Hannah mention what she had planned for that day?" Jay asked. "Not that I recall."

"Did you tell your wife that you had talked to Hannah? Did you call Blake after you and Hannah had your conversation?" Ed asked.

"I can't remember," Alex said. "I don't think we talked that morning, but I'm not sure. Blake was in Mexico, you know, so we usually only spoke once a day or so. She goes there to chill out."

Jay consulted his notebook. "Blake called Hannah at 10:45 a.m. on that same morning." He looked up at Alex. "Do you know what they talked about?"

Alex tapped his right index finger on the arm of his chair. "No. But they talk almost every day, so it's not unusual."

"Did Blake tell you she'd called Hannah on the day she disappeared?" Jay again.

"No, I don't think so. Maybe later on she might have mentioned it to me."

"Isn't it a little odd that Blake would call Hannah from Mexico?" Jay asked.

"Not really. Like I told you, they talked frequently."

"But it seems like quite the coincidence that Hannah called you, and then about one hour later, Blake called Hannah," noted Ed. "While she's supposed to be chilling out. All on the day Hannah disappeared, and, we think now, on the day she was murdered."

Alex shrugged. "I can only tell you that both Blake and I were friends with Hannah. Friends talk to each other."

"When did Blake get back to Buck Bay?" Ed asked.

"Friday morning. Late morning, I think."

"Not Thursday?" asked Ed.

"She tried to, but she couldn't get a flight," Alex answered.

"What airline did she fly home on?" Ed asked.

"Well, she usually flies on Alaska, and that's how she got there," Alex said.

"That doesn't exactly answer my question," Ed said. "How did she get home?" He couldn't hide that Alex's waffle perturbed him.

"All the commercial airlines were booked, so she called her agent, and he got a private plane to come and pick her up."

Jay and Ed exchanged a quick glance.

"But didn't she have a return flight scheduled for Friday afternoon anyway?" asked Jay. "Why not wait for that one and keep to her original schedule?"

"As you can imagine, Blake was beside herself over the news of Hannah's disappearance. She got antsy and wanted to get home quickly to help in any way she could." Alex delivered that line with cool composure. *That sounded rehearsed*, thought Ed.

"Who is her agent and who flew the private plane here?" Ed asked. He gripped his pen over his notebook to show Alex he was serious about following up on this new development.

"Her agent is Simon Towers. I honestly don't know who owned the plane or who flew her home. Probably some other client, or someone in the agency," Alex said.

"We'll need contact information for the agent, please," said Ed.

"Sure," Alex nodded. "No problem. I don't have it with me, but Blake can provide it for you once we get home."

"What do you think the Longfellow Foundation will do about their grant now that Hannah is dead?" Jay asked, changing tactics.

"I have no idea."

"Have you talked to them in the last two days?"

"No. I did think about calling them this morning," Alex admitted. "To see if they knew about Hannah."

"But you didn't make the call?" Jay asked.

"It didn't feel right when I thought about it. Kind of bad taste, you know?" He hesitated. "Have they heard?"

"I believe Sheriff Johnson was planning to call and tell them today," Jay said. "That's all we know."

"I'll wait to see if they call me," Alex said. "I would think they might reconsider their award with Hannah gone, but it's not for me to suggest. And, honestly, I'd hate to win it that way. The money doesn't seem that important anymore."

"Yeah," said Jay, "murder can put everything else into perspective, huh?"

• • •

Down the hall, Matt and Patty were trying to calm down a highly agitated Blake Bowen.

The trouble started when Matt asked her if they could record their conversation. Unlike her husband down the hall, Blake reacted badly to that suggestion.

"No, you certainly may not," she said. Her voice quavered but was somewhat louder than usual. "People pay to record me."

"Well, that's your choice," Matt said calmly. He tried out a little smile. "I understand that you get paid to perform, but we're not asking for a performance here. Just have a few questions to ask you. Very informal."

"Ask away," she said belligerently. "Take notes if you have to. No recording."

"OK, no problem," Matt said. "I'm afraid we first have to tell you some bad news. Terrible news." He paused to let that sink in.

Blake knew immediately. She bent over and brought her hands to her face, shoulders heaving and sobbing loudly.

"We found Hannah's body, and she's been murdered. This is now a homicide investigation. I'm so sorry, Blake."

Matt and Patty let her cry until she dried up. Matt stood and went to her, patting her on the back silently while she struggled for self-control.

After a few minutes, Matt looked at Patty. "We just have a few questions for you. I'll be brief," Patty said. She opened her notebook. "Rancho Miguel Splendida told me that they weren't sure when you left the property. They checked, and you weren't on the scheduled shuttle to the airport on Friday afternoon. When did you leave Mexico?"

"Friday morning," Blake said. She sat still as a stone, now locked in on Patty. Her face was splotched with grief, and her lower lip trembled.

"Why didn't you wait for the shuttle and your scheduled flight home?"

"Because I was eager to get home and see if I could help find Hannah. My agent sent a plane to pick me up."

"The staff at the hotel doesn't recall seeing you after Wednesday morning," Patty said. It wasn't exactly what Luna Perez had told her, but she wanted to see how Blake would react.

Blake placed an escaped strand of hair behind her right ear. "I stayed mostly in my suite. It's very comfortable and private, and I needed some down time."

"How did you get your meals on Thursday?" Matt asked. "Room service?"

"No," she said hastily. "I have a fridge in my room, and I snacked from it all day."

"That sounds heavenly," Patty smiled. "Yogurt, cheese, leftovers, wine?"

That got a thin smile out of Blake. "Something like that, yeah."

"On your private patio?" Patty again.

"Yes."

"What time Friday morning were you picked up?" Matt asked.

"It was early. Probably around 7:00 a.m."

"Where did the plane come from?"

"L.A. Los Angeles. My agent lives there."

"What kind of plane was it?"

"Small corporate jet," Blake answered. "Nothing fancy. I've flown in it before. It can land easily at Buck Bay airport."

"We'll need your agent's name and contact information," Patty said, trying to sound casual. "Just routine."

"Is that really necessary? I hate to bother him with this. He's a very busy guy."

"I'm afraid it is," Patty said. She didn't like Blake's tone.

"We'll be candid with you, Blake," Matt said, leaning forward. "We blew it originally with the suicide verdict on Hannah's disappearance. The pressure is on local law enforcement now to investigate her murder fully. As in 'no stone unturned' fully. We don't know if Hannah was specifically targeted, or if we've got some lunatic out there who might strike again. It's important that we eliminate people in Hannah's orbit first, and then we can spread the net further. We want to eliminate you and Alex today. Can you help us do that?"

Patty watched with appreciation as Matt gave Blake his winning Texas smile. It worked.

Blake nodded. "I'll email his info to you when I get home. It's on my laptop."

"Thank you," Patty said. "That's great. Just a couple more questions and then we'll let you get going." She checked her notes. "Hannah's phone log tells us that you called her at 10:45 a.m. on Wednesday, the day she disappeared. Why did you phone her?"

"We were best friends. We talked all the time."

"So, nothing specific?" Patty asked.

"I was just checking in with her," Blake said, her face expressionless.

"Telling her about Mexico? That kind of thing?"

She shrugged as if to reject Patty's questions. "I guess. Just talk."

"It seems like an odd time for a chat," Matt said. "A workday morning."

"I don't keep office hours."

"I meant, an odd time for Hannah," Matt said, waiting for a reaction that didn't come. He continued. "Did you know that Hannah had called your husband earlier?" Matt asked. "About an hour before your call?"

"No."

Matt and Patty exchanged a quick glance that any mind reader would know said, 'Wonder if that answer would pass a lie detector test?'.

"So, Alex didn't mention to you that he had also talked to Hannah on the day she disappeared?" asked Matt.

"I told you 'no'."

"Kind of a coincidence, don't you think?" Patty noted. "Both you and your husband talk to Hannah, and then several hours later she's never seen again?"

"I talked to Hannah almost daily," Blake said. "Like I told you. And Alex and she talked regularly. They're in the same business, and it was normal. Nothing unusual at all for them to have a phone call."

"Your husband often worked with Hannah, is that correct?" Patty asked.

Blake hesitated. "I wouldn't say 'often,' it was more like once in a while."

"Would you say they had a friendly business relationship?"

"Sure. Hannah was my best friend, and she and Alex got along well. No problems, smooth relationship."

"So, he didn't get angry when Rainbow to Hope beat him out for the big grant?" asked Patty. "Angry enough to strangle Hannah to death?" *Let's shake up this lovey-dovey party*, Patty thought. She and Matt watched Blake intensely.

Blake paled and shifted in her chair. "Of course not! You can't ask me that question."

"It seems as if I did," Patty said coolly. "And I'll ask it again: did Alex kill Hannah?"

"No." Her fingers closed tightly around the arms of her chair, and she glared at Patty.

"Did you really return home on Wednesday night and kill Hannah yourself?" Matt piled on.

Blake turned her attention to Matt and her eyes narrowed. "I loved Han. She was my dearest friend. Why would I kill her?"

"Maybe because Hannah was becoming more loved and more famous locally than you? Maybe you were jealous of her popularity?" Patty suggested.

Blake barked an ugly laugh. "Mousy Hannah? More famous than me? What are you, nuts?"

CHAPTER 17

Even though Matt worked weekends during a homicide investigation, he still looked forward to Friday night and wrapping up the official work week with his bride. The house lights were on, and he couldn't wait to see Fern. *What the heck did I do before I met her? You weren't all that happy, remember? Lots of friends and family, but you were lonely. No more.*

He parked the squad car in the driveway and bounded up to the front door. She opened it before he could get his key out.

"Come in, young police chief," she said, a big smile on her face.

"Are you happy to see me?"

"Always." She threw her arms around his neck and held him close. "But I'm dying to hear what happened today."

"Lots of action. On several fronts," he told her, kissing her cheek. "Let me change my clothes while you whip up the martinis, OK? We're celebrating tonight."

"A break in the case?"

"Maybe. But I'm also celebrating the hiring of Tamryn Gesicki. Or as I like to call her, Fern 2.0."

Fern didn't like the sound of that. Wordlessly, she retreated to the bar to mix their martinis.

Matt reappeared shortly in jeans and his favorite Texas sweatshirt. "I'll grab the olives," he said, moving to the kitchen.

"So, you hired her today?" Fern asked, setting their icy drinks down on the kitchen island. "Did Bill Abbott talk to her already?"

"Yep. Sylvia, too. Abbott was practically frothing at the mouth over Tamryn," he laughed. "She's a great get, Fern."

"When is she starting?"

"She'll arrive tomorrow late afternoon."

"What?!? So fast?"

"She quit her job immediately after I offered her our position, and they told her to take her PTO. She booked the red eye from Boston to Seattle" — he checked his watch — "and is in the air now. Says her mom will notify her landlord and pick up any personal items she left behind. It's truly a fresh start for her."

"I'm looking forward to meeting her," Fern said. "Please tell her if there's anything I can do to smooth the way for her, I'm all in."

Matt chuckled. "I already did. I knew you'd offer." He squeezed her thigh.

"How did it go with the Bowens today?"

"Well, after talking to Jay on the ride home — he and Ed took Alex, and Patty and I took Blake — we haven't ruled them out. Patty talked to the resort Blake was at, and no one there remembers seeing her after Wednesday. And she didn't ride the airport shuttle when she was supposed to on Friday."

"Where does she say she was between Wednesday and Friday?" Fern asked.

Matt told her Blake's story and added, "It's got some holes in it. We have to investigate more."

"What about Alex?"

"Jay said they thought Alex was purposefully vague. They asked him what he and Hannah talked about on the phone the morning she disappeared, and at first, he didn't recall they'd talked. It was only when they pressed him that he remembered the conversation. Ed thought that Alex hoped we didn't know about that phone call. Jay told me that a couple of things Alex said sounded rehearsed. Patty and I had the same hit off Blake."

"Are they hiding something?"

Matt nodded. "It sure feels that way to me. I'm eager to lay it all out for Tamryn and get her unbiased read." He leaned over and kissed her. "What's for dinner? Something smells good."

"Does that mean you're not taking me out again tonight?" she said playfully. "I rather liked last night."

"I can go get takeout, but I'd like to stay home tonight," he said seriously.

Fern laughed. "I'm kidding. I knew you'd be hungry, and I knew you wouldn't want to go back out. Do I know my husband or what? I've got half a chicken roasting in the oven with some potatoes, and I made a honkin' big salad." She jumped up. "Give me ten minutes."

His eyes followed her like a dog at feeding time.

* * *

Instead of meeting in person on Saturday morning to compare notes from their investigations yesterday, the county crime team settled on a conference call. As a group, they decided to take the rest of Saturday to follow-up on their individual assignments and catch up on the omnipresent cop paperwork. They would meet again Sunday morning to hash out their thoughts.

* * *

Tamryn Gesicki couldn't stop staring out the window of the small plane taking her from Portland's airport to Buck Bay. Even though she grew up within spitting distance of the Atlantic Ocean, she'd never seen a coastline as beautiful as Oregon's.

Where are all the people, she thought? Her window seat on the left side of the plane — no row of seats, just one on each side of the aisle — allowed her to follow the coast as the pilot took them south with a flight pattern just out to sea from the landfall. The towns, some of them no bigger than a wide turnout in the coastal highway, were sparsely placed, with richly green forests and high rocky cliffs in between them. The waves crashing onshore created dramatic plumes of spray that were visible from their low-flying elevation. Vast stretches of sandy beaches were completely empty of people.

The magnitude of what she was doing had just begun to creep into her head. She had doubts. *You will not second guess this decision*, she admonished herself. *You had no choice but to leave everything and everyone you've ever known. It's the safe and smart decision. Right. But did you have to come to the end of the world? Should you have waited for a job closer to your home? No! You have no home. Not anymore.*

Tamryn turned away from the window for a moment and closed her eyes. Only her mother had been upset at the news of her departure. Her father and brothers shrugged at the information but wished her well in her new life. She thought it was possible she might never see them again. Her sergeant and colleagues said all the right things when she resigned and walked out yesterday evening, but Tamryn knew they couldn't wait to show her the door. They'd never known how to deal with her.

She'd told her family where she was moving but asked them not to spread the word too far. No one at work had asked, and she didn't offer the information. Her mother had driven her to the airport, and they had a tearful parting. But both women avoided saying the real things on their minds. To make her leaving easier, Tamryn had promised to email and phone regularly, and, yes, mom should come out to Oregon, and Tamryn would, of course, come home for Christmas.

But that would never happen.

• • •

Late Saturday afternoon at city hall, Matt and Jay had just finished writing up the reports from their respective interrogations of the Bowens, when Matt's phone rang.

"Tamryn! Are you on the ground?" Matt asked.

"I am, chief. What now?"

"Detective Finley and I are finishing up some paperwork, and we'll come pick you up. We're about thirty minutes from the airport. Can you chill until we get there?"

"Sure thing. I'll grab a snack in the café. Take your time, no rush." They signed off.

Tamryn wheeled her suitcase into the tiny café and sat at a table by the window. She was hungry, tired, and desperately wanted a shower and a change of clothes. Her black knit travel pants, white waffle tee, and fleece jacket were rumpled after the long journey. *Three planes to get from Boston to here!* she exclaimed to herself. *Boston to Seattle, Seattle to Portland, and Portland to Buck Bay—good grief.* She'd taken a red eye last night to Seattle, and then flown from there this morning. *Maybe my new boss will know a better itinerary if I ever decide to go home again. Or maybe dealing with a small regional airport instead of Boston International is part of the culture change he's talking about.*

The waitress took her order for a coffee and a bowl of clam chowder. *Risky, because it won't be as good as what I'm used to. But the view!* An imposing steel cantilevered bridge with concrete arches spanned the huge bay adjacent to the airport runway. The main towers rose hundreds of feet above the water in a Gothic arch style, their green paint contrasting nicely with the brilliant blue sky. As she looked on, a massive ocean-going barge loaded with containers easily passed under the bridge's arches. Mesmerized by the slow-moving behemoth, she was surprised when her waitress brought her order.

"Where are you from, ma'am?" the waitress asked.

"Boston born and bred. But I'm moving here. To Port Stirling." Tamryn used her hands to try to corral her unruly, frizzy black hair, to no avail after fourteen hours of travel.

"Don't worry," the waitress smirked. "You will love our clam chowder, too. I guarantee it." Off she went.

I'll be the judge of that, Tamryn thought. She swirled the butter on top of her bowl and took a spoonful. It tasted freshly made. *Not bad.* She took another spoonful. *This is seriously good. I hope this is a sign that I'll like it here.*

She finished her chowder and went outside to soak up some fresh air after Matt had texted they were on the way. He had asked her how he would know her when they arrived. She texted back, "5'3" curly chin-length black hair, black pants and grey fleece jacket that look like I slept in them because I did. Not to mention, I'm the only person here."

Matt and Jay parked the squad car in front of the lone woman.

"Just like Boston's airport, right?" Matt grinned, greeting his new employee with a hearty handshake.

"Funny," she grinned back in spite of her tiredness.

"Hi, I'm Jay Finley," the detective said, and gave her a handshake, too. "Welcome to Oregon."

"Tamryn Gesicki," she replied, returning his handshake.

Jay looked from Tamryn to Matt and back. "I'm the only one without curly black hair. I feel left out."

Tamryn let out a loud belly laugh. "Yeah, but the chief's is neater than mine."

"Only because I didn't fly across the country," Matt said graciously. He looked down at her suitcase and noted her backpack. "Is that all the luggage you have?"

"Yes. My mother is holding onto the rest of my things until I get a place here. I think she's hoping I won't like Oregon."

"You will like it here," Jay said. "Maybe not the weather, but otherwise it's great."

She flung her arms upward to the azure blue sky, the sun on her face. "What the hell is wrong with the weather? It was snowing and 29 degrees when I left Boston."

"Yeah, Jay," said Matt sarcastically, "what's wrong with this weather? It's always like this, right? Sunshine, no wind, no clouds."

"Whatever you say, boss," Jay said. He rolled his eyes in Tamryn's direction. "And if you believe that, I'd like to sell you this bridge."

Tamryn looked in the direction of Jay's pointed finger, and said, "I was just admiring that bridge. It's spectacular. Mostly the setting with the wide bay and the forest beyond. Gorgeous."

"You ain't seen nothing yet," Matt said, holding the door open for her. "Hop in. Jay, take the back seat, OK?"

Jay nodded. "And so it begins. I'm now the second-rate detective."

"I seriously doubt that, Detective Finley," Tamryn said, taking an immediate liking to her new younger colleague.

"Just want her to see what her new home looks like," Matt said to Jay. He thought Jay was kidding, but there might be some truth to his remark.

• • •

On the drive to Port Stirling, they brought Tamryn up to speed on the Hannah Oakley murder case. Matt knew she'd worked as many homicide cases as he had, maybe more, and there was no reason she couldn't jump in immediately. He'd never hired anyone previously without meeting them first, but her work record spoke volumes.

"We have a county major crime team," he explained to her, "and we're all involved with this case. We meet every day while we're working on it. Do you think you'll be ready to join us tomorrow morning?"

"I can start tonight," she said. "Just need a quick shower and change of clothes."

"No need," Matt said, shaking his head. "We're taking you to the Inn at Whale Rock so you can settle in and get some rest tonight. We'll start tomorrow. The city manager's admin, MaryLou, has three or four possible places to rent for you to look at, and has volunteered to tour you around tomorrow afternoon, but you can stay at Whale Rock as long as it takes."

"Don't get too comfortable, he lives right down the road," Jay said from the back seat.

She laughed. "So, you'll pick me up in the morning before your meeting?"

"Yep. 7:30 a.m."

She started to say 'OK' but then interrupted herself. "Oh my god! The Pacific Ocean!" It sounded like 'gawd'.

They had climbed a hill where the first glimpse of the ocean presented itself out her passenger-side window. Matt pulled over and parked at the lookout, about four hundred feet above the water.

She jumped out of the car.

"Don't get too close to the edge," Matt warned. "You never know when a piece of it might fall into the water."

She slapped her thighs and stared out to sea. "This is incredible," she managed to say. Turning her head, she took in the full scope of the scene, north to south. Far below, the waves crashed against the rocky cliffs. Last night's storm had passed, but there was still a heavy swell, and Tamryn imagined what it would be like during a storm.

"I'd like to live right here, please," she informed the guys.

"Can't," Matt said. "State of Oregon owns this particular spot. But you never know what you might find in Port Stirling."

"Tell her your earthquake story," Jay snickered.

"Not right now. We want her to stay, don't we?"

. . .

After he'd dropped Jay off at city hall where they'd left his car, and taken Tamryn to Whale Rock with instructions to eat dinner in the restaurant and seek out Vicky, Matt gratefully turned into his own driveway.

Long day, he thought. Tired, he slumped in the seat for a moment. He was elated to add Tamryn to his department but frustrated with the case. Stealing a move from his wife, he flapped his arms like a bird flying into the sunset, and said, *Let it go*.

The sky was putting on a show out his living room window as the sun sank into the Pacific. "That's a hard-working man," said Fern as she moved from the kitchen to join him in front of the window. She handed him his beer and took a sip from her wine glass. "I know I'm not supposed to ask, but are you feeling alright?" She kissed him lightly.

"I'm OK. A lot going on today." He slid into his usual seat on the end of the sofa. "Paperwork always makes me realize that we haven't solved this damn case yet. Too many loose ends. Let's not talk about it tonight." He took a swig from his beer bottle.

Fern understood his frustration. She also understood that sometimes it was important to walk away from the case. Let it settle, at least overnight. She changed the subject.

"So. Tamryn," she said. "Did she get here as planned?"

"Yep. Just dropped her off at the Whale Rock Inn." That brought a smile to his face.

"I take it you like her," Fern said.

"I do. But even if I didn't, I'm glad I hired her. We got lucky, Fern. She's very experienced, tough, and shrewd. A bit of a smart ass, but in a funny sort of way. You will love her."

"What does she look like?"

"I don't know. Short. About my age, I guess."

"Is she attractive?"

He thought about how to answer this question as a husband. "I would say not. Her hair is kinda all over the place, and her face is too square for me, sort of flat. She's a little chunky."

"Good."

Matt laughed. "Tamryn's already intimidated by your cop record—wait until she lays eyes on you. Try to look bad tomorrow, OK?"

"Nope. I'll be pulling out all the stops," Fern smiled. "Can't she have a few days to get oriented?"

"She doesn't want it. Wanted to start tonight. I said no because she looked tired. She wants to pick your brain, and then after our team meeting in the morning, she'll go look at the rentals MaryLou has picked out for her. But I'm telling you she's eager. She wants this to work."

"Can't blame her," said Fern, "after what she's been through in Boston."

Matt scrunched up his face. "She keeps her personal stuff inside, but she looks wounded. The way she told it to me, it sounds like the Boston PD couldn't wait for her to leave. Her husband is on the force, too. Lower level than her, beat cop, real awkward for all. And her family really let her down."

"Aren't we lucky?" Fern said, wrapping her husband in a big hug.

· · ·

Tamryn Gesicki threw her backpack on the desk in her spacious room at the Inn at Whale Rock. *Nice*, she thought, looking around. Her new boss told her he reserved a King suite for her with a kitchenette and room to move around a bit since they weren't sure how long she'd be staying until she could rent a place. But she wasn't expecting anything this sweet. It also had a gorgeous stone fireplace, a big screen TV, and a whirlpool bath, which she began filling immediately, tossing in some bath gel. She knew you weren't supposed to put bubble bath things in a whirlpool, but she really, really needed it tonight. *Just this once and I won't ever do it again.*

While the tub filled, she slid open the door that led to a small balcony and a promised partial view of the ocean. *There it is! I can see the Pacific. Maybe I'll just live in this room forever.*

She unpacked her suitcase and hooked up her laptop on the desk. She dashed off a quick email to her mother to let her know she'd safely arrived and added, "This place is paradise."

After a long soak turning the jets on and off to suit her, she began to feel a little more human. *A quick nap and then dinner.*

Tamryn walked through a short, covered arcade and across the parking lot to the Whale Rock restaurant entrance, breathing in the fresh salt air. Darkness had descended on Port Stirling, and a mist had blown in from the sea. The fog seemed to swirl purposefully around her, creating some confusion as to her pathway. It was dead quiet and a little ghostly. A chill ran up her spine, but it was banished the minute she opened the door and entered the restaurant's warm, inviting dining room.

She was greeted by a somewhat older woman than her with a bleached blonde pageboy, long earrings dangling below the chin-length hair. She was dressed in a red above-the-knee dress and white patent-leather knee boots. Tamryn thought of a Nancy Sinatra record album that was one of her parents' favorites and felt a stab of homesickness.

"Hi," Tamryn said in return. "I'm supposed to ask for Vicky."

"You don't have to ask, hon, you found her. I'm Vicky. Do you want a table, or are you here for the bar?"

Tamryn smiled. "Both. Can I have a drink at my table?"

"You can have several drinks if you want. Follow me."

Anyone who asked for her got one of Vicky's favorite tables, and Tamryn was seated in a nice booth in the corner by the window.

"Are you visiting from somewhere?" Vicky asked, handing her a menu.

"It's my first time here, but I'm staying," Tamryn said. "I have a new job and I start work tomorrow. I'm from Boston."

"Good Lord, that's a hike," said Vicky.

"That's the idea," Tamryn said. Her face remained neutral.

"So, what fabulous new job brought you all the way out here?"

"I'm a police detective and I'll be working for Chief Horning. He told me to ask for you."

Vicky's eyes widened and she quietly slapped the table as the lightbulb went off. "You're Fern's replacement!" She stuck out her hand. "I'm very happy to meet you. What's your name?"

"Tamryn Gesicki. And do you have a last name, Vicky?"

And just like that and like so many others before her, Tamryn's first friend in Port Stirling was Vicky.

"That was fast," Vicky said. "It's only been a few weeks since Fern started her new job. I thought it would take longer for him to find a new detective."

"It was fast," Tamryn agreed. "But the chief needed help, and I was available, so here I am."

"Well, welcome to our little town. Let me get you a drink while you take a gander at our menu. What do you want?"

"I'll have a vodka martini, please. Whatever vodka you have is fine."

"A girl after my own heart. Be right back."

Vicky swished away, and Tamryn looked at the menu, immediately passing up the pasta section. Instinctively, she knew she wouldn't get the wonderful Italian pastas she was used to in Boston, and there would be literally zero chance of finding good Polish food out here. Her mother's saying: 'Bloom where you're planted' came to mind, and she started reading the seafood section.

"How 'bout a Dungeness crab salad?" she asked Vicky when the waitress carefully placed a very full vodka martini in front of her. "Is the crab fresh?"

Vicky put her hands on both hips and said, "Do I look like the kind of woman who would bring a newcomer frozen or fake crab? No, I do not. Get it, it's delish. I'd better help you with the dressing choice, too. Get the blue cheese. We make the dressing here and the cheese is from a cheese maker in southern Oregon. Served at the White House, I'll have you know."

"I love good blue cheese," Tamryn said.

"Then you will be in hog heaven. I'll bring some crusty bread and local butter with it."

Vicky had been right, of course. The crab and everything had been delicious. Just as she was starting to think about finishing with a piece of marionberry pie, Vicky reappeared and plopped down across the booth from her.

"Now, I don't gossip, and I don't tell tales," Vicky said, "but there are a few things you need to know before tomorrow."

"I'm all ears," Tamryn said.

"Matt Horning is one of the finest men you'll ever meet. And I can say that because I've met some real stinkers."

"Welcome to my world," Tamryn softly growled.

Vicky stared her in the eyes. "That's what I thought. Which is why I'm telling you that you can trust Matt. Fern, too. And don't be surprised if it takes folks a while to accept you as her replacement. She's done a lot for this place, especially after the earthquake ripped us all apart."

"I'm pretty good at my job, too," Tamryn said. She wasn't defensive, just matter of fact.

"And you will bring your own skills to the police, and you'll win over everybody. It just might not happen in one day, that's all I'm saying."

Tamryn smiled. "I can see why Matt told me to ask for you. Are you good friends?"

"We've been best buddies since his first day on the job," Vicky said, pushing herself up out of the booth. "I hope I'll say the same about you someday. But first, I'm bringing you a piece of marionberry pie." She held up her hand. "But before you ask, no, the berries aren't fresh, they're frozen — it's out of season. But you won't be able to tell." She smiled and disappeared.

I'm actually happy right now, thought Tamryn. *Must be the vodka. But with a full night's sleep, I'll be ready to face my new world tomorrow. Can't wait.*

. . .

In her cozy home at the bulbous end of a cul-de-sac on the north end of Port Stirling, Sylvia, in her flannel PJ's and favorite purple robe, was up late. *Almost midnight and I should go to bed.* But she wanted to find a tidbit or two in Hannah Oakley's social media feeds that might help Matt and the cops before tomorrow morning's meeting.

It was Sylvia's dogged research on the hired gun that tried to kill Matt that broke their last case wide open, and she rather liked all the attention that brought her. *I may be seventy-five, but I've still got it,* she smiled to herself. Matt had shared with her early on after his arrival in Port Stirling that it was most often persistent digging and/or forensic evidence that got results in homicide cases. Very seldom did they get a game-changing confession like you see on TV.

Sylvia and Patty had a telephone call after the detective and Matt had interrogated Blake Bowen. Patty had told her that she felt Blake was "lying through her teeth", and she wanted Sylvia to specifically look at any interactions between her and Hannah. That's what Sylvia had been doing since late this afternoon.

She had returned to Hannah's Facebook feed, going back a couple of years, but nothing had jumped out at her. Turning her attention now to Blake Bowen's social platforms, she was riveted. *What a beautiful woman.* She also listened to a couple of videos with Blake performing in her prime, and thought she was just as talented as she was gorgeous. *No wonder she was a star. Hard to believe she grew up around here.*

Scrolling through more recent posts by the singer, Sylvia found dozens of photos with both Blake and Hannah. It appeared they traveled together frequently, as well as all the local shots—beach, restaurants, etc. Blake almost always wrote a caption for her posted photos, and after Sylvia had been at it for a while, one in particular caught her eye.

A picture of just the two women that Hannah had posted on her feed had been shared to Blake's. Beneath it, Blake had written, "Bitch always looks thinner than me in the pics *she* posts." She had also hit the 'Angry' emoticon, and there was no sign of a smiley face to indicate Blake was kidding.

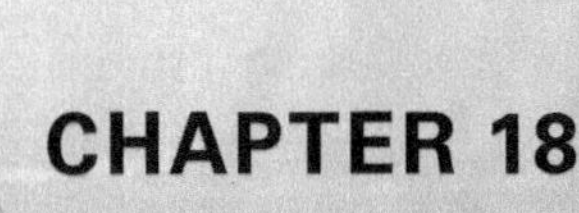

CHAPTER 18

Sunday morning at precisely 8:00 a.m, Matt kicked off the crime team meeting in the basement of city hall. "We have two special guests this morning, but only one of them is staying for our meeting."

A collective "Fern!" went up around the table as she entered the conference room, arm in arm with Tamryn Gesicki.

"I'm the one who's not staying," Fern said quickly. "I'm just here to introduce you to my replacement who, unfortunately, is going to make all of you forget about me in a heartbeat. Ladies and gentlemen, please give a big Port Stirling welcome to Detective Tamryn Gesicki."

The applause was polite, joined by a few scattered "welcomes". Only Bernice, closest to the door, stood to shake hands with the newbie.

"Thanks, Fern," Matt said to his wife. "I appreciate your willingness to show Tamryn how things are done around here. I'll see you tonight."

That got some laughs around the table.

"Guess I'm dismissed," Fern said, not smiling. She turned and left the room.

"That was a police chief move, not a husband move," Bernice said, as Fern quietly closed the door behind her. Her remark came out caustically, just as Bernice had intended.

The other four women around the table—Patty, Sylvia, Jeri, and Tamryn—all nodded in agreement.

"What!?!" Matt said, shrugging his shoulders and throwing his palms up in question. "I thanked her for her help." Nevertheless, a blush creeped up his neck.

"And then told her to get out," Tamryn spoke for the first time, looking at her boss. "Not cool." But her eyes crinkled just a bit, letting Matt know that she was on his side. She was wearing a severe black jacket and pants, with a pale blue blouse, but her demeanor was the opposite of severe, not exactly friendly, but warm and down-to-earth.

In her Boston accent that amused the others, and looking around the table, pausing on each member of the team, she continued, "I understand that I'm replacing a legend, and I will undoubtedly fall short on occasion. But I'll tell you what I just shared with Fern: There will not be one day in my employment here that I won't bring it. You will get my best, and I will have your backs. Count on it."

She leaned back in her chair and nodded at Matt.

"You're hired," Patty said with a broad smile. "We're all happy you're here, and we appreciate you wanting to jump right in and help us with this terrible case. Matt has told us you bring a lot of homicide experience…"

"Which, working for him, is a good thing," Bernice interrupted her good friend.

"And," Patty continued, "which it's beginning to look like we could use today. This case is puzzling for a lot of reasons, and your fresh take would be welcomed."

"Thanks." Tamryn returned Patty's smile. "Let's get going. What've you got, boss?"

Matt quickly jumped up and moved to the whiteboard, relieved that they were getting down to business. And not stoning him.

"Because there appears to be no reason why anyone on planet earth would've wanted Hannah Oakley dead, I thought we could start with a refresher on why someone would kill another person. Then we'll share our reports and interrogations from yesterday. That sound OK?"

Before anyone could say anything, Tamryn said, "There are only three reasons. Revenge, getting even for something they did to you. Greed— you want something they have, usually money or love. Or, they're afraid of you, somehow threatened. Maybe you know something about them they don't want anyone to know." She paused. "Maybe four — it was an accident. But I think we count out number four in this case. Strangulation is intentional." She'd ticked off her reasons on her fingers, and now placed her hands in her lap.

"One thing I'd like to add," said Jay, raising his hand. He didn't want Detective Gesicki to be the only one to contribute to the conversation. "Most female victims are killed by someone they know. I don't know the exact percentage, but it's about fifty percent."

"It's higher than that," Tamryn said. "That fifty percent number only applies to their partners or family members. When you add in acquaintances or colleagues, it's closer to eighty percent."

"OK," said Jay, frowning. "It's a strong likelihood then that Hannah was murdered by someone she knew. That was my point." He didn't love being corrected by the newbie.

"Anybody else?" Matt asked. He looked around the table.

"That about covers it," said Sheriff Earl Johnson. He looked at the list Matt was writing. "I think we can probably rule out revenge as the reason for Hannah's murder. We didn't uncover one single thing that she's done to make another person in her circle want to get even with her. It's not even like she got drunk and killed some stranger driving. Her family loves her, her staff loves her, her friends love her, even the addicts she works with respect her and don't harbor any grudges. No one has mentioned her ever doing something bad to them. Even her ex-husband still likes her."

"Maybe he does and maybe he doesn't," said Matt, still standing. "We need to confront him again and ask why he called her on the day she disappeared. Justin Sorenson is on our list today," he said to the group. "Hannah's lawyer is going with us to see him when we're done here. She thinks Hannah had told him about the spousal support ending, and she wants to be there."

"Was the ex-husband interrogated when she first disappeared?" asked Tamryn. "Seems like he might be a prime suspect."

"We didn't know he existed until a few days ago," said the sheriff.

"How could you not know in this small place?" Tamryn persisted.

"Nobody we talked to mentioned that she had a previous husband," Earl said.

"Not even Robert Oakley?"

"He didn't tell us about Sorenson, and we didn't think to ask about previous relationships."

Tamryn stared at Earl, and it was obvious she didn't know quite what to say next. Finally, "One of the first tenets in a murder investigation is to find out everything you can about the victim's life."

"We didn't believe it was murder," Earl said quietly. "All the evidence pointed to suicide." He paused. "I don't need to be told how to investigate a murder."

Tamryn flushed. "I didn't mean to imply that. Sorry."

Earl looked down at the file in front of him, lips in a tight line.

Patty jumped into the void. "I'm not sure all her friends loved her," said Patty. "I thought Blake Bowen reacted funny when I suggested she might be jealous of Hannah's standing in the community. Didn't you think that was odd, Matt?"

"Yep. I surely did," Matt said. "We'll tell you more about that interview later." He wrote Blake Bowen's name under Justin Sorenson's in the Revenge column.

"And, if we consider greed, we only have one suspect — Robert Oakley," Patty continued. "He's the only person in Hannah's orbit to benefit financially from her death. He gets everything, isn't that correct?"

"Yes," said Matt. "That's what Hannah's lawyer indicated to us. She wouldn't tell us everything in her will."

"Have you confronted him on that?" Tamryn asked.

"I have," said Matt. "He's very convincing about not caring about the money. And, it isn't a huge sum."

"I'm not sure Robert is the only suspect who stands to gain financially," Jay said.

"Who else does?" asked Matt.

Jay looked at Ed. "We think Alex Bowen is itching to have the Longfellow Foundation reopen the grant that Hannah won just before her death.

His organization was one of the finalists. If they do decide to take it away from Rainbow to Hope, Bowen might be the recipient of that decision."

Ed added, "He said all the right things, and he's smooth as silk, but there was just enough edge to his voice when we asked about it to get our attention. Alex Bowen struck Jay and me as a man who doesn't like to lose."

"Has the foundation indicated they might revisit their grant decision?" asked Tamryn.

"I talked to Ginny Vincent, the Executive Director of the foundation, yesterday," said Earl. "She indicated that with Hannah's death, they would review their decision. I made the case why Rainbow to Hope getting their grant was crucial for our community, but she stressed how Hannah was the heart and soul of the organization. My gut feeling is they may yank it and give it to the next finalist. Which is either Alex Bowen's Eugene org or some outfit in Seattle."

"And I believe that Alex Bowen probably knew that this was a possibility," said Jay. "Put his name under 'greed' with Robert's for now."

"There might be one more name to add to that reason," Bernice said, speaking almost in a whisper, unusual for the dynamic medical examiner.

"What do you mean, Bernice?" Matt asked.

She turned to Ed on her right and began passing out copies of the autopsy report.

"This is my final report on Hannah Oakley," she said. "I finished the autopsy yesterday, and before I share the results with Robert, I want to share them with you." She flipped open the report's cover.

"Hannah had been dead about one week when her body was discovered in a shallow grave in the Hedgehog Mountain forest. Death was caused by manual strangulation. You can see the bruise marks on her neck in photo #1. There is no indication that she tried to fight off her assailant, so no biological evidence under her fingernails, for example."

"So, that tells us that Hannah knew her killer," interrupted Matt.

"Looks like her mysterious meeting was with someone she trusted," nodded Tamryn.

Bernice smiled at Matt. "May I finish my autopsy report now?" she asked.

"Please continue," Matt said. "You want us to add a name to the 'greed' column. Who is it?"

"I can't give you a name, just a suggestion for further investigation. Without getting too technical, pregnancy and childbirth leave an imprint on the mother's bones. The pubic symphysis—the joint between your left and right pubic bones that separates to prepare for childbirth—and the adjacent sacroiliac in Hannah had a series of pits or craters that indicate childbirth. During delivery, the softened ligaments are stretched. Over a few weeks, things begin to repair, but this erosion is responsible for leaving the imprint of childbirth."

"Are you telling us that Hannah Oakley has a child?" Matt asked.

"I believe that Hannah gave birth at some point in her life, yes," said Bernice. "However, taking off my ME hat and putting on my friend hat, I can tell you that she has never mentioned a child. And I've known Hannah for twenty years."

"Well, this is a shocker," said Patty. "Do you think Robert would know?"

"I don't think so," said Matt, shaking his head. "He told us that Hannah's brother is her only relative. Now, I guess Hannah could have had a baby and was not involved in its life, so Robert didn't think it was relevant. But didn't we ask specifically if there were any other relatives, Jay?"

"I think we did. If there's a child somewhere, I don't believe Robert knows about it."

Sylvia stood up. "I will contact Oregon's vital records office and see what we have to do to get a certified copy of a birth record. I've got a friend I can call on Sunday. Should be easy. I think they go back all the way to the early 1900's." She almost ran out of the conference room. A woman on a mission.

"If Hannah had a baby in Oregon, Sylvia will find it," Matt said. "But if we don't find a birth record here, then what?"

"Didn't Sylvia tell us that Hannah went to college in Colorado?" asked Jay. "Maybe that's our next search."

"What's bothering me," Bernice said, "is that if Hannah had a child, it's completely out of character for her to have abandoned it or given it up for adoption. That's just not who she was as a woman. But she sure as hell couldn't hide a child in Chinook County; someone would know. It's baffling to me, and I didn't sleep all night trying to figure this out."

"But if there is a child out there, and if it factors into Hannah's will in any way, there's a strong motive," said Tamryn. "We need to see Hannah's will whether her attorney likes it or not."

• • •

Fern was irritated. Not so much at Matt for his dismissal of her at his meeting; she knew he was trying to make it easy for Tamryn to join the group. She missed being in on the action. Not being able to do anything to help find that poor woman's killer. It was making her grumpy.

Fern understood that her new job would have peaks and valleys, and she welcomed that — truly, she did. What was annoying to her today was that she didn't have a plan for how she would handle the valleys without going bonkers. Usually, she would talk over her problems with Mary, her mother, but in this case, Fern knew Mary would use the opening to discuss grandchildren, and she didn't want to have that talk yet. And Matt was totally consumed with the Hannah Oakley case, and she didn't really want to add her discontent to his plate right now.

Their new foundation needed to be her focus until Joe Phelps had a new assignment for her. She'd continued to check in with her sources on the west coast, and there was nothing shaking. She wanted to talk further with Alex Bowen and quiz him specifically about how he allocated his non-profit budget. His overall budget was bigger than Rainbow to Hope's and was more in line with what Fern believed her and Matt's foundation would be.

She'd done as Sarah Forrester suggested and created a mission statement with their objectives and had studied the sample grant application Sarah had shared with her. From that, Fern had a start on their grant guidelines, and Matt had agreed with Fern that appointing Michelle Wayne as the foundation's consulting attorney was a good idea, considering her experience with Rainbow to Hope. Michelle told Fern that a rough draft of the overall budget would be important for her to see sooner rather than later.

And that's where Fern had stalled out. She was good with numbers and budgets, but the scope of a seven-figure foundation was intimidating to her.

Knowing that Alex was still under suspicion in Hannah's murder, but also knowing that he was a respected CEO in the region, Fern decided to call him again anyway. *Matt might not like it, but we aren't joined at the hip, and I need to progress on my project in the hours I have available.* She picked up her phone.

Alex said, "Hi again, Fern. How can I help you today?"

"I'm sorry to bother you on Sunday, but I'm working on the budget for our foundation, and I'm stuck. Sarah Forrester told me that your budget is over $10 million, and we're going to be in that ballpark. I'm wondering if you might share with me your budget categories and a rough percentage dedicated to each. Is it OK for me to ask that?"

Alex laughed. "Of course it's OK. Non-profits are an open book — no secrets. I don't make copies of ours, but you're welcome to stop by the house and I'll go over it with you. Are you in Buck Bay now?"

"No," said Fern. "I'm home in Port Stirling." She thought for a second. "But I could run over there if you're free for an hour or so. I'm about twenty minutes from your place, I think."

"I'm just getting organized for my week ahead, so now would be a good time. That is, unless your hard-working husband calls me back to the police station again." He laughed again as if being interrogated was a social engagement.

Fern bristled. "He's just doing his job."

"I understand that, but Blake and I have told the police everything we know."

"Perhaps we have a bit of a conflict of interest here, Alex. Maybe I better not bother you anymore," Fern said firmly.

"Don't be silly. You're not a cop and there's absolutely no reason why I can't help you establish your foundation. I don't get involved in my wife's business, and I'm sure you don't get involved in law enforcement these days."

Oh, if you only knew, Fern thought. "OK then, I'll be there shortly."

CHAPTER 19

After Bernice's bombshell, the crime team continued reporting on their interrogations and activities.

"I'm still waiting for the contact info for Blake Bowen's agent," said Patty. "He supposedly arranged for the plane that brought her home early from Mexico," she explained to the group.

"She said she would email it to you when they arrived home after visiting the police station on Friday," said Matt. "She didn't do that?"

"Nope," Patty said. "And it's starting to annoy me. I could do some research and find his name, but I want Blake to provide me with her contact info. If I don't have an email from her by the time we're done here, I'll call her. We need to know when she left and where she was after Wednesday morning. That's the last time anyone at the resort can unequivocally confirm they saw her. Right now, in my mind, Blake Bowen does not have an airtight alibi."

"Thanks, Patty," Matt said. "Stay on this. It smells like old fish. Dan, did you guys get to the Blue Moon Motel yesterday?"

McCoy nodded in Earl's direction. "Yep, the sheriff and I paid them a call, and took your Rudy with us for muscle because their clientele can be unsavory. By the way, did you know Rudy caught a burglar for us when you were in the hospital?"

"Oh, yes," Matt laughed, "I've heard that story more than once. Rudy's turning into a good cop. I'm glad we have him."

"He is sharper than you think just by the looks of him. He's awful pretty, but he gets the job done," joked McCoy.

"My wife Milly has a major crush on him," Ed deadpanned. He flashed a mischievous look at Jay. "You'd be advised to keep your new girlfriend away from young Rudy."

Bernice was the first to pile on Jay. "You have a new girlfriend? How did we not know this little factoid?"

"Maybe because it's none of your business?" Jay said. "And because it's not an appropriate topic of discussion during a major crime team meeting."

"Nice try, Jay," said Patty. "We'll eventually find out who this lucky woman is, you know. We're detectives."

Jay sat smiling with his hands clasped across his stomach. It was a defensive, 'I'm not-talking' posture.

Matt knew that the last thing Jay wanted was for his girlfriend's boss, police chief Dan McCoy, to know they were dating, so he changed the subject and got his friend off the hook. "You were saying, Dan? The Blue Moon Motel?"

"Right," said McCoy. "Earl and I spoke to the general manager. He was the one who made the call to Hannah at 12:20 p.m. on the day she was murdered. He called her, as we suspected, because he had an out-of-control addict in his parking lot harassing customers."

"Why call her?" Jay asked. "Why not call your department?"

"That's what we asked him," McCoy said. "He and Hannah had a kind of agreement. Because he often deals with homeless people, and because many of them have mental health or substance abuse issues, Hannah asked him to let her organization try to help them first before automatically throwing them in jail."

"Did she follow up personally that day?" Matt asked.

"No. She sent two of her male counselors to talk the guy down."

"And did they? Talk the guy down?"

"Apparently, yes. He went with them to Rainbow to Hope, and he's staying in one of their 'recovery rooms'. We talked to him yesterday afternoon once we confirmed that Blue Moon guy was telling us the truth about his call to Hannah."

"And?" asked Matt.

"And, we rounded up some of the other recent 'problem' men who grace our city's sidewalks. Earl, Rudy, and I took five of them to the pizza parlor for lunch and had a good chat. All of them knew Hannah and several members of her staff. Earl, do you want to tell them your thoughts?"

The sheriff said, "Yeah, it was an interesting afternoon. Bottom line, we don't believe any of these guys killed Hannah. Two of them are too strung out to do anything that energetic, and the other three are 'clients' of Rainbow to Hope. They're mostly guys who are down on their luck, but also men who don't mind living rough. They occasionally take up their offers for help, but they revert to the streets."

"What did they say about Hannah specifically?" Matt asked.

"Four of them have dealt with her on a regular basis," Earl said. "The fifth guy kept calling her Harriet, he was one of the strung-out ones, and we're not sure he really remembers her. The other four were mostly positive about their interactions with her. Said she was 'a do-gooder,' but in a nice way. None of them felt threatened by her, and they all believed she was genuinely trying to help them back to civilized society."

"I would add," said McCoy, "that none of them knew anything personal about her—not where she lived, whether she was married or not, that kind of thing. Their only relation to her was through Rainbow to Hope."

Earl said, "And, honestly, as a group they seemed sad to hear of her death. We grilled them about whether they'd heard any scuttlebutt about her murder, but they all swore there was no talk or knowledge about it at all on the streets." The sheriff paused. "I've been in this business for a long time," he said, and it was clear he was still reeling from this case. "I may have blown it on Hannah's suicide call, which I will regret to my dying day. But I'd bet my reputation that none of Hannah's clients killed her. This murder is something way more personal."

● ● ●

Wanting to give Earl some time to regain his composure, Matt turned to Sylvia, who had rejoined the meeting after telling them that her state contact would start a birth record search first thing Monday morning. "Have you found anything interesting in Hannah's background yet?"

"Not much. It's all pretty vanilla," Sylvia reported. "There is one thing that caught my attention, but I'm not sure it's even worth mentioning." She looked at Matt and shrugged her shoulders.

"Your gut feeling helped us crack the last case," Matt reminded her. "Tell us."

"Well, there are lots of photos on both Hannah's social media platforms, and also on her best friend, Blake Bowen's as well. They are mostly what you'd expect," Sylvia said. "Arms around each other, clinking wine glasses together in a restaurant or someone's home…that sort of thing. What I like to call the 'If it's not on Facebook, it didn't happen' photos."

Laughter around the table at the truth of Sylvia's statement.

"But there was one photo on Blake's feed with a caption under it that had a nasty tone about it. Like she thought Hannah was trying to make herself look better than Blake on purpose. She even referred to her as 'that bitch'—pardon my language. Seems like a rude thing to call your best friend online, even if you are kidding."

"What was the context?" asked Patty.

"Blake looked voluptuous in the photo… you know, plump," Sylvia said, her mouth turning up in a slight smile. "And Hannah looked quite slim. It was somewhat the angle of the pose, but they are two distinctly different body types. Blake indicated that Hannah picked this photo on purpose to make her look fat."

"And Blake referred to her as 'mousy Hannah' when we interrogated her," Patty remembered. "It sounds like Blake wanted to always be the pretty one."

"Maybe there is something to your theory, Patty," Matt said. "Maybe Hannah was getting too popular in town, and perhaps Blake didn't like it. Especially with her own star beginning to dim with the passing years."

Patty nodded. "I think it's real. Women are competitive, even with friends. However, my theory hits a wall when I try to imagine Blake strangling Hannah. They're both fit and probably strong women, but Hannah was taller than Blake. I can't visualize Blake getting any leverage on her."

"Even small women, in a rage, can kill," Tamryn said. "It only takes about ten pounds of pressure on the neck to strangle someone to the point of unconsciousness. You just have to be determined and keep the pressure on for a few minutes. I've seen it."

"I've seen it, too," said Matt. "Up close and personal. A woman high on drugs and enraged almost got the better of me one night in Dallas. My partner had to pull her off right before she stabbed me."

That brought a silence to the table.

Matt grinned. "A story for another time. My more boring story for today is that I visited the Thai restaurant that Hannah's last known phone call went to. The husband-and-wife owners were probably also the last people to see her alive, except for her killer, of course. They told me that she did pick up takeout lunch on that Wednesday, and they remember because when they heard the next day that she killed herself, they were shocked and very upset. She was their favorite customer. They were both visibly upset, and clearly still shaken by her death."

"Do they have an alibi for Wednesday afternoon and night?" asked Tamryn. "Maybe they poisoned her Tom Kha soup and made it easy to strangle her."

"There was no poison in Hannah's body," Bernice reported with a smile and nod to Tamryn. "But good question. It's the first thing I look for now after what happened with the Brits."

"What happened with the Brits?" Tamryn asked. "I know I have a lot of catching up to do."

"I'll fill you in later," said Matt. "Recent case. And, trust me, you don't want to ask Fern about this one." He smiled. "Better it comes from me."

Tamryn looked puzzled, but said, "Sure, boss."

"And, yes, the owners were at the restaurant until about 10:00 p.m," Matt clarified. "I spoke with two other workers and all four of them were there together from 11:00 a.m. until closing. They're in the clear."

Matt jotted down a couple of things on the whiteboard, and then took his seat. "So, going forward, here's what I'm thinking. Jay and I, with Hannah's lawyer, will pay another visit to Justin Sorenson and see what he has to say about Hannah's call to him on that Wednesday morning."

Tamryn raised her hand. "I'd like to do some research on Bernice's theory about Hannah having a child. It seems odd to me that no one appears to know. No one would know in Boston, but here…"

"Agreed," said Matt. "Look into her parents' birth records and see if there's anything there. I'll talk to Robert and find out if he knows anything about this development. He would've mentioned it when he told me about Hannah's brother, so I'm not hopeful, but maybe there's a reason why it's a secret."

"I've directed my department to do a full-scale search of Hedgehog Mountain now that forensics has finished their work there," said the sheriff. "They're up there now. I know you don't think she was killed there, Bernice, but we figure it can't hurt to look more closely. And it beats the hell out of sitting around with a dead end."

"I do think Hannah was killed somewhere else and moved to her grave site," Bernice said. "But I'm with you, Earl, it can't hurt to look around. You all should take another look at Mourning Bay, too. My team is confident she wasn't killed in her car — we've been over it about a million times and there's nothing in it that shouldn't be in it. But we only combed the area between the parking lot where her car was found and the water. Somebody should search the entire park."

"We'll do that," said Dan McCoy. "My guys really want to solve this one, and they will search every inch of Mourning Bay. Plus the road to and from."

"Sounds good," said Matt. "Patty, you keep going on Blake Bowen's alibi. And don't be afraid to ruffle her hair a bit, she's acting funny."

"Me? Afraid to be obnoxious? What planet have you been on?" Patty said.

Matt laughed. "Yeah, silly me. Poor Blake."

Ed said, "And I'm going to keep looking at Alex Bowen, for the simple reason that I don't like him. We only have his word that he was at home on Wednesday. I want to put it on him to come up with someone who can verify his alibi. Plus, it occurred to me on the drive here this morning that we might want to think about a search warrant — or maybe, warrants — to look closely at the Bowen property. And perhaps for the Rainbow to Hope headquarters. I don't know, what do you think?" he said to Matt.

But Jeri jumped in. "You don't have enough probable cause for the Bowens. She was in Mexico, by all accounts. He said he was home, and no one has come forward to dispute that. Yes, they each talked to Hannah on the day she disappeared, but they both have good reasons for doing so. The only thing I've heard that sounds suspicious is what Sylvia reported about Blake's Facebook post. I don't like that either, Sylvia, but it's not enough on its own to get Judge Hedges to move. I'm sorry."

"You sound more like Dalrymple every day, and you haven't even been elected yet," joked Jay.

Sitting next to him, Jeri slugged him in the arm. Playful, but Jay felt it.

"Judge would probably allow Hannah's office to be more thoroughly searched, although it would feel more like a fishing expedition, and she's notoriously opposed to search warrants under those conditions. I'll request whatever this group deems is necessary, but I'm just trying to be honest about your chances. You need more."

"She's right, Ed," said Matt. "We don't have enough. But if we find out that Blake lied about when she returned to Oregon, or we can't verify Alex's whereabouts, or with the luck of the Irish, we find something either at Hedgehog Mountain or Mourning Bay tied to them, we might make a run at a warrant. Until then, we keep slogging."

"Hannah Oakley was killed somewhere," Bernice said. "You need to find out where."

. . .

Fern drove up to the gate protecting the Bowens' home from sightseers and pressed the intercom button. The afternoon had turned gloomy, with billowy black clouds threatening out to sea. Paired with the slate grey ocean and its mean-looking whitecaps, it was a bleak day, not to mention a little spooky.

As she waited for the gate to open while a thickening mist swirled around in front of the house, she had a flash of the Addams Family house. The Bowens' large 3-story house with its mishmash of stylistic elements was out of place on the coast of Oregon. *How do you make an A-frame look Victorian,* thought Fern? *But to each his own.*

"Is that you, Fern?" squawked Alex from the intercom.

"Yes."

"Come on up."

The heavy gate creaked and swung open slowly, as if it was asking Fern if she really wanted to come in. She headed up the paved driveway and saw Alex above, waving from the big deck that looked out to the ocean.

"Hi," said Fern, climbing out of her car. She shivered in the cold, damp air, and reached for her jacket in the passenger seat.

"Hi, yourself," said Alex. "Hurry and come in. It's much warmer in the house."

A seagull screeched overhead as Fern approached the front door. *Is this smart?*, she thought. *Don't be silly, Alex Bowen is a respected CEO, hardly the killer type.*

He held open the door and welcomed Fern inside to the huge open plan room. *Nothing like the Addams Family house inside.*

"This is kind of you to indulge me on Sunday," Fern said.

"It's no bother," Alex said. "Slow day, and I'm always happy to help someone new to the non-profit world. Who knows? Maybe someday you'll give my organization a grant." He smiled.

"You never know, I guess. I couldn't tell you today where our foundation is headed, but I'm hoping to set our parameters soon."

"Please, have a seat." He gestured to a round oak dining table in the room, closer to the kitchen, which she could see at the far end. There was a large file on the table, stuffed with papers and about two inches thick. Alex took a seat in front of it.

"Is Blake here?" Fern asked. "I haven't seen her in ages."

"No, I'm afraid not. She's in town getting her hair cut, to be followed by a mani and pedi. Must keep up the good fight, she told me this morning."

Fern laughed. "It is constant."

"I suspect staying beautiful is much easier for you than it is for Blake these days. She keeps whining about how getting older isn't fair."

Fern felt a warm flush climbing up her neck. *He was charming, no doubt about it.* "Thank you, but I have my moments, too."

He patted the top of his file. "Before we dig into the budget details, may I ask you where the funding for your foundation is coming from? This might be rude, but a police chief's salary can't be that high."

She chuckled. "No, it's not. And neither is mine working for the government. We don't say much about Matt's money, so I hope you'll keep this to yourself. His family has owned a ranch in Texas, the Dallas area, for generations, and his parents struck oil about thirty years ago. They have generously shared that revenue with Matt and his two siblings."

"A good reason to marry him, huh?"

Fern's smile disappeared. "Actually, I didn't know about the money until after we were married. It was a surprise." *How many times in my life am I going to have to tell this stupid story?* "We'd talked about what to do with some of his money right after our wedding, and then after his shooting, the idea of a foundation dedicated to local health care issues just seemed like a natural."

"The need is real," Alex said. "You're to be commended for recognizing it and doing something about it. Lots of women in your position would spend all the money on houses, clothes, and travel." He opened the file.

"I guess I'm not most women. I like all those things, but you can only spend so much, right? I do buy better wine now, and I like cashmere sweaters." She took out her journal and fished in her bag for a pen, not sure why she shared that with him.

"Life is too short to drink bad wine, for sure," he laughed. "Can I get you a glass now?"

She shook her head. "No, thank you. I can't stay long."

They both jumped as a loud thunderclap shook the house.

"Nice day, huh?" Alex said.

"Yeah," agreed Fern. "Shouldn't we be getting a pleasant little hint of spring by now?"

"That was ten minutes this morning. Climate change, I guess. All bets are off." He took out a sheet near the top of his file. "OK then, the first thing you need is the major categories of expenses. We break ours down into four categories, with sub-categories under them: Operational Costs, Functional Expenses, Administrative, and Development. Operational is pretty much like it sounds, mainly staff salaries, rent, utilities, plus other things like office supplies. The Functional category includes stuff like IT services, recruitment, advertising and so on. Administrative is a category we don't talk much about outside of management and our board, and includes legal fees, accounting services, human resources stuff, and board expenses."

"Why don't you talk about that?" Fern asked.

"Because most people don't understand what it takes to run a multi-million-dollar business, and they think paying attorneys and accountants is wasting money. I assure you it's not."

"I've already hired a lawyer. I get it," Fern said.

"And the fourth category, Development, includes fundraisers like auctions and banquets. In our case, it takes money to raise money. An example of this is my organization is sponsoring a road race next weekend. Eugene is a runner's town, and this will be our second year of putting on this event. Last year, we cleared $125,000 thanks to lots of volunteers, and this year will be even bigger. That's a whole new outreach program for us. But, since oil wells are your fundraiser, you won't need much in this category."

"No, but I like the idea of community volunteers getting involved," Fern said. "Maybe that's part of the real value of local fundraising."

"It doesn't hurt, but events aren't my favorite thing. I'm in it for the cash," he grinned.

His phone rang, and he pulled it out of his pocket and looked at the number. "Oops, I've got to take this call. I'll just be a minute." He rose and moved down the hallway.

Fern busied herself looking over the numbers attached to the various categories. As she expected, the Operations numbers were the highest, mainly staff salaries, which seemed high to her. *Must be lots of employees.* Everything else was close to what she'd anticipated. The Administrative category was blank with a note that read "See attached documentation."

She picked up the top sheet, but the second page included a breakout of rent, utilities, office supplies and equipment. She craned her neck to see down the hallway and didn't see Alex, so she snooped a little further into the file. Finally, she found a page entitled 'Administrative Expenses-2022'. Quickly doing the math in her head, Fern saw that those expenses were nearly one-fifth of the entire organization budget! *How can that be?*

This wasn't something she had counted on. *How much could it cost to hire an attorney and a part-time accountant?* Fern figured there must be more layers to Alex's organization than she knew about. Quickly, she grabbed her phone and took a photo of the budget detail pages. She didn't think Alex would mind, but this was the detail she needed, and she didn't want to risk him saying 'no'.

She slipped her phone back into her handbag's outside pocket just as Alex came back into the room.

"Sorry about that," he said. "Board chairwoman. You have to take those calls." He winked at her.

"How did you assemble your Board of Directors?" Fern asked. "For our starting funding level, it looks like we'll have to appoint four members. Does that sound right to you?"

"Yes. And again, your needs here will differ somewhat from mine. I needed pillars of the community—people who could open their wallets and the wallets of their friends. Because you're all or mostly self-funded, you'd be better off appointing people who would be more technical advisors. Like doctors, health care CEO's, people like that."

"That makes sense."

"One caution," Alex said, leaning back in his chair, "make sure you get people you can control, or who you trust to let you do your job. The last thing you want are board members who get down into the nitty-gritty and get in your way. This can be a problem with, say, doctors, who think they know everything and can run a business better than you. Thankfully, most of them are too busy saving lives to interfere too much, but be on the lookout for that type of personality."

Fern smiled. "Thanks. Good tip. What else should I know? Are there any amateur mistakes I'm likely to make?"

"Make sure your accounting is beyond perfect. The IRS is getting serious about the non-profit field, and you want everything above board."

"We would do that anyway, what with Matt's profession," Fern said. "Whatever we do has to be spotless."

"That's true. I keep forgetting who you're married to. I like your husband, but I can't figure out how he landed a beauty like you." He smiled his very white teeth smile and placed his hand on hers.

Fern pulled her hand away and rose from the chair. "Maybe people say that about you, too. Blake is a gorgeous woman."

"Touché," he laughed.

CHAPTER 20

Matt saw the others out of the conference room, and said to Jay, "I need some time in my office to make some phone calls. Can you hang for an hour or so while I figure out where Justin Sorenson and Robert Oakley are?"

"I'm gonna get some breakfast," Jay said. "I overslept and haven't had any food yet."

"By all means," laughed Matt. "The last thing I need is to be stuck with a cranky, hungry detective."

Matt sat down in his office chair and spun it around to take in the view. While he always enjoyed a sunny day and a view far up the coastline, he was increasingly fond of these stormy days. A lightning bolt jagged across the sky, looking like it came close to the lighthouse, and was followed almost immediately by a raucous clap of thunder. He was used to violent thunderstorms in Texas, of course, but it was unusual for the Oregon coast, and it jolted him. He sat mesmerized for a while and watched the sky and sea reacting. The waves were smashing into the jetty and exploding thirty feet in the air, completely covering the breakwater with their spray.

Tamryn and her behavior in the crime team meeting was on his mind, and he knew he had to talk with her. Matt had been the 'new guy' before, and he totally got how Tamryn was trying to prove her worth the first time in a group setting.

However, she didn't understand how tightly this group of officers worked together. And it wasn't just on major crimes; there was regular cooperation on law enforcement issues affecting the county. They covered for each other when necessary, and there was constant communication between the departments. Matt could tell that Tamryn had ruffled some feathers in this first meeting, especially Jay and Earl's.

Earl was still sensitive about dropping the ball earlier on this case, but Tamryn didn't know that. *That's on me. I should have prepared her better. But there was a prickliness about her that he would have to deal with. If she's going to correct another detective like she did with Jay, she needs to do it in private, and in a softer manner. Although, am I being sexist? If a man had done that to another man, would I think it's a problem? The best thing to do is just tell her what I thought about the meeting and let her deal with it as she will. I need her to succeed.*

Matt's phone rang. Earl.

"Where in the hell did you find her?" Earl bellowed when Matt picked up.

"If you're referring to Tamryn, you know she's from Boston," Matt said patiently. "I'm sorry if she was a little pointed in her comments. I'm sitting here watching the storm out my window and thinking about how to handle the Tamryn storm."

"I know I'm raw about this case, but she's gonna have to tone it down if she wants to fit in. You feel that way, too, right?"

"Maybe," Matt said tentatively.

"What does that mean?" the sheriff asked his good buddy.

"Well, maybe we could all use a kick in the pants. Maybe we're too set in our ways, and a fresh, tougher approach will make us more effective."

"I'd like to remind you that our recent collaborations have been highly successful in reining in the bad guys," Earl said. "Including solving a murder that was over one-hundred years old. I'm not sure anybody needs a kick in the pants, and I resented her implications. Keep her away from me if you're determined to continue her employment."

"She's part of the team, Earl. I need her."

"You have to earn membership on this team. You can't just hand it to her, chief."

• • •

Fern intended to drive straight home and start cobbling out a budget for their foundation that she could present to Matt and Michelle Wayne later in the week. However, the sign pointing to Mourning Bay County Park caught her eye, and she took the turnoff.

Arriving at the bay's parking lot, she pulled into a space facing the water and kept her windshield wipers operating on high in the now driving rainstorm. She looked around at her surroundings and tried to visualize Hannah meeting someone in this parking lot. *Who did you meet, Hannah? Who killed you?*

Fern couldn't get Robert Oakley out of her head. Part of her felt enormous empathy for his loss. *I know how I would've felt if Matt had been killed.* But another part of her, the logical head part, kept thinking about the law of averages when it came to murdered women. Unlike some of the other cops, she didn't think it was just about the money when it came to Robert. Yes, he went from a homeless alcoholic to a comfortable, sane life, and it looks like he gets it all, but for all intents and purposes, he already had it all as Hannah's husband. *Is there something else in their relationship that no one knows about?*

Fern pretended she was Hannah sitting in her car waiting for Robert to meet her, perhaps to share their lunch. He arrives and pulls up next to her in his car. She gets out, leaving her purse on the seat and the car keys still in the ignition, and jumps into his car. Robert strangles her, takes off her glasses, and removes her cell phone from her pocket where she always carried it. With the note 'It's over' in his pocket that he tore off something she wrote to him, Robert runs down to the beach near the tide line. Wearing gloves, he places her glasses and the note on the piece of driftwood where the cops found them. Then he drives her corpse to Hedgehog Mountain and buries her along with her cell phone. He drives back to Buck Bay, parks his car in the same parking spot he had earlier, and teaches his next class. As planned, he goes for a run after school with his mate, and then goes home and calls the police to report his wife didn't show up for their 7:00 p.m. dinner date.

It's possible. But why, Robert, why?

Maybe because she was recently married in a beautiful, loving ceremony herself, Fern thought about Hannah and Robert's wedding, wondering what it had been like for the bride. Had she been nervous about the decision, or was she overjoyed to find Robert at this point in her life as Fern had been to find Matt? Had Hannah worn a traditional white dress, or opted for something more personal to the couple as Fern had done with her blush pink selection?

She looked out her car window at the bay in front of her. Although Mourning Bay was mostly protected from the fury of the Pacific, the wind was blowing up a gale, and the generally placid waves were now thrashing onto the shore. Fern stared through the wild rain and felt close to Hannah. She had worn a white dress and had been overjoyed at her wedding. Fern was certain of it.

I need to talk to Matt.

. . .

Matt checked in with Robert Oakley and told him that he and Jay were headed to Buck Bay and would stop at his house. Then, he started to dial Justin Sorenson's cell, but thought better of it. *I think a surprise visit will be preferable. I want to stay one step ahead of that guy.*

Instead, he called Michelle Wayne, who was expecting him to call with the Sorenson plan and left a voicemail requesting that she meet them at the Growler Pool Hall at 11:00 a.m. to surprise Justin.

He told Tamryn, who was working with Hideki Ikeda, Port Stirling's IT manager, to get her electronics all set up, that he would be back by 3:00 p.m. and would like to meet with her then. *Nice of Hideki and MaryLou to come in on Sunday and help us out*, he thought. *I need to remember to tell Bill Abbott how everyone pulls together in a crunch.*

He and Jay took off in the squad car. Matt was deliberately quiet to see if Jay had anything on his mind. Didn't take long.

"So, this new hire," Jay said. "Do we like her?"

Matt knew this would likely be a serious conversation, but he had to laugh at Jay's start. "I like her, but I suspect you might not be a huge fan of hers yet."

"Correct. She's a fucking know-it-all. How could you hire her? She's not like any of us."

"And you base your impression on one ninety-minute meeting? Where she's probably trying to show y'all that she knows something about police work?"

"I get that. But she made Earl feel like a piece of shit. When he already feels bad."

"I know, and I've heard from him on this topic, too. That was my fault. I didn't tell her the background on the erroneous suicide call. But you don't know Tamryn's full background story yet either. Also my fault. I'm planning to have a retreat for our department at Whale Rock's new retreat center so we can all get to know each other better and ease her in. Just haven't had time yet to plan it with y'all."

"That's probably a good idea, as long as she doesn't take over that like she tried to do with our meeting this morning," Jay grumped.

"You said she's not like us, and that's true. It's also a big reason why I hired her. We could use a new set of eyes and experiences for how we approach things. If you give her a chance, she can only help us get better."

"So, we're not good enough?"

"C'mon, Jay, I didn't say that. The world around us is changing, and our little corner of it is attracting more attention. Our south coast is on the map these days with more tourists, which is a good thing, but also more crime and international attention."

"Which is not so good."

"Exactly. Which is why Joe Phelps hired Fern to keep an eye out, and why I don't think it will hurt us to have a new employee with experience in big city crime. I'll talk to Tamryn this afternoon about her tone, but I'm not going to ask her to back off—I want her to jump right in the middle and stir things up if necessary. And you need to support her. Your attitude about her will be important in city hall and around the county. Don't make this hard, Jay."

The young detective sat silent for a minute. "I want to like her. I know we need another detective to replace Fern. That's probably part of the problem; she's not Fern. But I'll try."

"We were never going to find another Fern," Matt said softly. "And we didn't need to because Fern will still be involved with us. Hell, between the two of them, they probably won't need me at all."

"Or me," said Jay morosely.

* * *

Robert Oakley looked a little better today, not quite as pallid, when he opened his front door to Matt and Jay. But he greeted them the same way: "Any news yet, chief?"

"Nothing definitive," Matt replied vaguely. "Can we come in?"

Robert stepped aside, holding open the door, and Matt and Jay walked into the living room.

"Are you alone?" Matt asked as Robert took a seat in his chair across from them. He was wearing a crisp white shirt open at the neck and clean jeans. Matt could tell that he was trying to overcome his grief.

"Yes, for a while," Robert said with a thin smile. "Jim and JoAnn Greenley are coming over soon with yet more food. Everyone's been so nice."

"People want to help you," Matt said simply. "Including us. We had a county crime team meeting this morning, and we're following up with a few items that came out in some of our interviews yesterday. Also, one question that arose during Dr. Ryder's autopsy of your wife." He hesitated, trying to figure out a sensitive way to say this.

"What?" Robert snapped to attention.

"Dr. Ryder believes there was a chance that Hannah gave birth at some point in her life."

Robert's eyebrows shot up.

"Would you know anything about that?" Matt asked directly.

Robert stared at him, his mouth open. The silence lasted about ten seconds. "No. No, I don't," he spit out, dazed.

"Well, obviously you're stunned by this possibility," Matt said gently. "She never mentioned a child at all?"

Robert shook his head. "No. Her brother is her only relative. That's what she told me."

"Maybe there was a child and it died?" Matt proposed.

"I think she would have told me if that were the case, don't you?" Robert's voice was shaky and uneven. "Bernice is sure about this?"

"She can't be one hundred percent positive," Matt answered, "but she said the evidence is strong. We had to ask because it might be important. And, we need to take a look at Hannah's will. We've asked for a subpoena so Michelle Wayne can show it to us."

"We should have a reading of the will now," Robert said forcefully. "I'm ready, and there's no reason to delay any longer on my account."

"I'm sure there's nothing to this, Robert, but we need to pull on every loose thread. We'll want to talk to Hannah's brother about this, too. If it's true, maybe it happened when she was real young, and he might have some info."

"He's never mentioned it to me," Robert said.

"Maybe there's a reason for that," Jay said.

• • •

Leaving a stunned Robert, Matt and Jay headed downtown to find Justin Sorenson at his place of employment, the Growler Pool Hall. Michelle Wayne was parked at the curb in front.

Before they entered, Matt greeted her and said, "We have some new information that came out of Hannah's autopsy, and I need to ask you about it before we go in."

Her face showed surprise, but she said, "Sure. What is it?"

"Dr. Ryder said there is evidence that Hannah gave birth at some point in her life," Matt told her. "Do you know anything about a child?" He and Jay both watched her face closely.

Which was stupid because Michelle Wayne was an excellent attorney, trained to keep her emotions in check. Which she mostly did now. "No," she said, "I don't. If that is true, Hannah never told me."

"So, there's no mention of a child in her will?"

"No, there is not."

"Any bequests to anyone you don't personally know or recognize?"

Michelle thought for a moment. "No, off the top of my head, I don't believe so. It's a simple, straightforward will. So is Robert's that was done at the same time. There won't be any surprises in either will."

"How long have you known Hannah?" Matt asked.

"I moved to Buck Bay in 2015 and met her shortly after that. So, probably a little over eight years."

"Did she disappear for any lengthy periods during the time you've known her?"

"That's a question for her best friends," Michelle said. "Hannah and I were friends, yes, but not the kind of friends who see each other every week. If you're asking me if she could have gone away for a few weeks or even months to have a baby, I couldn't answer that confidently."

"OK, thanks," said Matt. "Let's go see if Mr. Sorenson can answer that question."

Justin, behind the bar, saw them coming and said loudly enough for the four patrons elbowed up to hear, "Two cops and a lawyer walk into a bar…"

"And said what?" one guy drinking a pint asked, expecting a joke.

"And said, we need to talk to your bartender in private," Matt barked.

"I'll hold down the fort," the only woman in the room said, moving from a bar stool to the dispensing side. She glanced over her shoulder at Matt, taking in Jay and Michelle, too.

"Thank you, ma'am," Matt said politely. "Mr. Sorenson, step over here please." He indicated a booth in the far corner.

Sorenson did as he was instructed, but he glowered at the cops. "You can't keep coming in here and bugging me," he said.

"Actually, we can," said Jay and smiled at him.

"I'll talk to you guys, but I'm not talking to her," Sorenson said, pointing a vigorous index finger in the general direction of Michelle's face.

Matt said, "We'll try not to 'bug' you too much, Justin, but your name keeps coming up in our investigation of Hannah's murder. And Ms. Wayne stays. We have just two questions for you today. Answer them both truthfully, and we'll get out of your hair."

"What now?" Sorenson asked. "Let's get this over with. I do have a job, you know."

"Finally," said Michelle, and couldn't keep the snark out of her tone.

Matt stepped between them, subtly but making a point. "Let's all sit down, what do you say?" He herded Sorenson into the booth and took a seat on the aisle. Michelle and Jay slid into the other side.

"Detective Finley has some new information that he retrieved from Hannah's cell phone log," Matt started and nodded at Jay, noting that Justin's face paled a little at that tidbit.

Jay, not needing to reference his notes on this one, said, "On the day that Hannah disappeared, you called her at 12:45 p.m. and the call lasted for approximately five minutes. Why did you phone her?"

"It was personal," Justin said, clamping his mouth shut and leaning back against the wooden wall of the booth.

"A woman has been murdered," said Matt. "There is no 'personal' anymore. Tell us why you called her. Now."

Sorenson looked down and picked at a hangnail. "It was a family matter."

"Your family or hers?" Matt asked.

"I can't say," Sorenson said stubbornly.

"Was it about her ending your spousal support?" Michelle asked.

"I'm not answering any questions from her," he said to Matt.

"Was it about her ending your spousal support?" asked Matt.

"No," Sorenson said. "I've told you morons I didn't know she was planning to take action."

"Then why did you call her?" Matt asked again. "Surely you can understand how your unwillingness to answer this simple question makes you look bad in our eyes."

"I told you; it was about a family matter. Something I knew she would want to know."

"You have to do better than that, son," Matt said. "Or, you'll have to go for a ride with us down to the station for formal questioning."

"I can't tell you," Justin pleaded. "I promised Hannah I wouldn't tell anyone, and that seems more important than ever now. Do what you have to do, but I'm not saying anything more."

The two cops and lawyer exchanged looks, and then Matt said, "Time for question number two. Did you and Hannah have a child together?"

Justin's eyes opened wide, and he immediately said, "No!"

"You're sure about that?" Matt followed up.

"Yes, I'm sure," he said, collecting himself. "I would remember that, don't you think?"

"This is not the time for you to be a smart ass, Justin," said Matt. "Trust me on that."

"Well, it was a dumb question," Justin said.

"OK, then let me ask another one. Maybe this one will be smarter. Do you know if Hannah ever gave birth to a child?"

"I couldn't say."

"It's a yes or no question, Justin. And my patience is running on the thin side."

Sorenson considered for a minute and finally said, "Then, no. I don't know anything."

Michelle Wayne, who had shown immense restraint to this point, said, "You're lying. My take is that you know something, and this is the 'family matter' you're unwilling to disclose." She pounded her fist on the table between them. "Did Hannah have a child? And you knew something about it and that's why you called her on the day she was murdered. To tell her what you knew."

"Nope," was all Sorenson said in rebuttal.

A noisy group of five people entered the bar and took a table in the middle of the room about ten feet from their booth.

"I need to get back to work," Sorenson said. "Let me out of this booth or take me in — those are your choices."

Wordlessly, Matt slid out of the booth, Sorenson sliding right behind him. Jay rose, handed his card to Justin, and said, "If you want to add anything, you know, to correct the record or whatever, call me."

Sorenson took the card and shoved it into his too-tight jeans pocket.

• • •

"Lying turd," muttered Michelle Wayne as they stood on the sidewalk.

"I am starting to believe that Sorenson didn't know about Hannah's plans to cut him off," Matt said. "I don't think she'd pulled the trigger on that nugget yet."

"Yeah," said Jay. "I think the same, but I am starting to think there's a kid somewhere, and maybe Justin Sorenson is the only one who knows about it."

"Agree," said Matt. "There was something intensely personal about his phone call that day, and it seems like it was more about her than him."

"I'm not buying it," said Michelle, shaking her head. "Justin has never cared about anyone but himself, and he could care less about protecting Hannah, especially now. I think she wrote him the letter and he called her to whine, or to try to convince her to change her mind. There's no child. It's highly unlikely. And Justin Sorenson is probably your killer." She shrugged into her white wool peacoat and headed for her car. "Keep me posted," she waved over her shoulder.

"Or," Matt said slowly to Jay as they piled into the squad car, "When they were married, Hannah told Justin about having a child when she was younger—and *only* told Justin—and he just learned something about the kid and called to let her know. It upset Hannah, and she took off to do something about it."

"And it got her killed," said Jay.

CHAPTER 21

Tamryn Gesicki was hunkered down in her corner of the squad room, which was at the opposite end of the corner shared by Detective Jay Finley and the sergeant, whose name Tamryn couldn't recall offhand. They had the breathtaking view out to the Pacific, which was only right from her perspective. She hadn't done a thing to earn that view yet. But she would.

MaryLou was coming to pick her up shortly to scope out the rental properties she'd uncovered for Tamryn. *It was very nice of them to cut my legwork on finding a place to live. I'm grateful. How refreshing to work with nice colleagues. Hope I didn't piss off any of them in this morning's meeting. But some of the early investigation of this case—sheesh. Disaster.*

Before MaryLou arrived, Tamryn wanted to take a dive into birth records to look for a Hannah Oakley child. Sylvia was working on Oregon's records, and the two decided that Tamryn would take a look at Colorado, where Hannah had gone to college.

If Hannah had born a child, it would open up a whole new can of worms, and Tamryn thought it could be a key to her murder. Maybe Robert just found out, and worried he might have to share too much with an offspring of Hannah. Maybe Hannah wanted to keep the deep, dark secret it appeared to be in this small town, but someone knew and was blackmailing her. Maybe Hannah had abandoned the child, and the kid took it wrong, hunted her down, and killed her.

And how could Hannah's brother, George, not be aware if there was a child? *Kinda hard to hide from family for nine months.* Tamryn would talk to him asap if Matt agreed during their one-on-one this afternoon. Except for one phone call that the sheriff had made to George shortly after Hannah's disappearance, it didn't appear that the brother had been fully interrogated yet.

Sylvia had given Tamryn the dates of Hannah's enrollment at the University of Colorado, four years' worth. She would research if she had come home to Buck Bay during school breaks, including the summers, or if she had stayed in Boulder. According to her math, it was about twenty-five years ago, so the path would be stone cold. *But there are ways,* she thought.

She was on Hannah's second year of college in the Colorado birth records when MaryLou popped into the squad room. Sylvia pointed at Tamryn, and MaryLou approached her, holding out her hand.

"Welcome to Port Stirling," she bubbled. "I'm MaryLou, and I'll be your guide today." The cheerful woman, somewhere just north of fifty, giggled at her own joke, realizing she sounded like a waiter.

Tamryn stood, returned the handshake, and said, "You look like a young Sally Field."

MaryLou grinned and said, "I get that a lot. She looks pretty good now in her seventies. Hope I can keep it going! Are you ready to go?"

"Yes, I'll just grab my coat. It's nice of you to do this on my behalf, especially on Sunday. I really appreciate it."

"It's my job. A fun part of my job."

"How long do you think we'll be gone?" Tamryn asked.

"Not long. I've got four places for you to look at, but one of them is way better than the other three, and I suspect you'll make a quick decision."

"That sounds promising," Tamryn smiled.

"Your timing is good. We're several months away from the summer rental season, so there's some good places on the market. And the owners love to rent to city employees, so you'll get a good deal."

Tamryn wondered what a 'good deal' meant around here. She knew it would be less than Boston, of course, but she hadn't had time to look at property once Matt offered her the job.

"Let's go," she said. "I'm excited."

And she was. Her new home awaited.

. . .

In MaryLou's Volvo, she said to her passenger, "Will you be working on the Hannah Oakley case? We're all upset."

"Already started working on it. It's a bad one for a small community," Tamryn said, and looked over at the woman. "Are you scared?"

MaryLou bit her lip. "A little bit. Yes. Mainly because no one seems to know anything yet. But we all trust Matt to get to the bottom of it soon."

"He will. We'll all be working around the clock until we get some answers."

"Calling it a suicide and then discovering the poor woman was murdered has been shocking."

"Did you know Hannah?" Tamryn asked.

"Not personally, no. But everyone in Chinook County knew of her. That's why this is so difficult; nobody can understand why she was killed. It sorta makes you think we might have a crazy person running around."

"Well, I just got here, but I think that's unlikely. Most murders are personal. There's a reason Hannah was targeted—we just need to figure out what it was."

"Are you good at this sort of thing?" MaryLou asked. "Is that why Matt hired you?"

Tamryn smiled. "I am good at it. Some people think it's the only thing I'm good at."

"I'm sure that's not true," MaryLou admonished. "Maybe moving to Port Stirling will help you find what other things you're good at." She pulled up in the driveway of a small tan house and turned off the engine. "OK, so here's how we're gonna do this. I'm going to take you quickly through the three houses that I don't think you'll want, and then we'll finish with the fourth and probably the winner."

Tamryn looked at the small house in front of her that was sandwiched in between two other small houses, with only about five feet separating them. She could tell that the neighbors could look from their windows into hers.

"Why don't we just go to the house you like best," she said to MaryLou. "I trust your judgment."

MaryLou grinned and started up the engine.

Ten minutes later, they had crossed Highway 101 from the east to the west and driven south for a few minutes. Tamryn could tell they were on the same road as her hotel, but quite a bit further south. MaryLou turned right on a small gravel road that wound through some big trees briefly, and then emerged into an open area.

A one-level grey house with recently painted white trim sat in the clearing. MaryLou parked and they went up the four shallow wide steps to the roomy front porch with its bright yellow door centered between two glass panels. Tamryn did a three-sixty and couldn't see another house.

MaryLou took out a set of keys, selected one, and they went in. The owner knew they were visiting today, and had turned on all the lights, and the gas fireplace in the cozy living room. The house was spotless, and Tamryn looked around approvingly.

There was a roomy kitchen with a bright skylight on their left that looked out to the car park area. It had a dine-in, small octagonal oak table, in addition to the two barstools at the counter separating it from a tiny room that was used as an office/study/library—take your pick.

"It's furnished," informed MaryLou, "but of course you'll want to add your own things."

Tamryn did a quick survey of the kitchen, opening some cupboards and checking out the refrigerator. "All the kitchen needs is my Keurig and a year's supply of coffee."

"Let's go see the rest," MaryLou said, and she trotted down the hall to the living room. There was one step down into the open room, with the fireplace at the far end, and a large wall-mounted TV to its left. A beige sectional, coffee table, and two armchairs were arranged to face the fireplace, and it looked comfortable.

But Tamryn ignored the furniture, instead moving to the west wall of sliding glass doors.

She wheeled around to look at MaryLou. "Are you kidding me?" she exclaimed. "A view of the ocean? Are you frigging kidding me?" She didn't wait for an answer, vigorously pushing open the glass door and stepping onto the huge redwood deck. The deck ran the length of the back of the house, and was bordered on three sides by small, scraggly bushes. A small dirt path opened up to a lawn of sorts that extended about fifteen feet out from the house. Beyond that, she could make out another path, mostly sand and reeds, that worked its magic way down to the water.

Tamryn turned back to MaryLou, her hands forming a pyramid cupping her nose and mouth as if to hold back a scream of joy, her brown eyes twinkling.

With a trace of a smile, MaryLou said, "I thought you might like this one."

"I'll take it," she said, giving MaryLou's arm a squeeze.

"Don't you want to see the rest of the house?"

Tamryn laughed. "I guess we should, huh?"

The hallway continued on to the other side of the front door, where they found two bedrooms and two bathrooms. One bedroom, a smallish one but tidy and well-furnished with a functional bath off it, overlooked the car park. The other, the primary bedroom, was at the end of the hallway on the west side, and looked onto the redwood deck and, yes, the majestic Pacific Ocean. It was a lovely, calm room, painted a soft blue with navy carpet and white bedding. Even though the sea today was grey and stormy, Tamryn thought there would be days where the color of this room would be reflected in the tranquil water. The attached bathroom had everything Tamryn needed.

Now Tamryn faced MaryLou with fear on her face.

"What?"

"Can I afford this?" Tamryn asked her.

"Yes, or I wouldn't have shown it to you. Prices are lower here than you're accustomed to."

"But even so…an ocean view, privacy, and a perfect little house? It has to be expensive, doesn't it? What are we talking?"

"If you sign a one-year lease, the rent is $1,250 a month. You have to pay your own utilities, although garbage pickup is included in the rent."

"That can't be right." Tamryn looked stunned. "I couldn't get a closet in Boston for that. Are you sure?"

MaryLou looked down at her shoes. "Yes," she mumbled. "I'm sure."

"Look at me," Tamryn directed. "Why is it so cheap? What's wrong with this house?"

"Well, there is a story. Are you sure you want to hear it?" She looked Tamryn in the eye.

"I knew there had to be something. How bad is it?"

MaryLou cleared her throat. "There was an agent working for the federal government, and he was the last person to rent this house."

"Oh?"

"Yes. He was killed in the line of duty."

"He died in this house?"

"No, no" said MaryLou hurriedly. "He was killed somewhere else. But he was murdered in a particularly gruesome fashion, and word got around town. Everyone knew he'd been living here, and no one wants to rent it now because it's a creepy story. The owners are somewhat desperate for a tenant."

Tamryn laughed and laughed, bent over holding her thighs.

"That doesn't bother you?"

"Do you have any idea how many murders there were in a ten-block radius of my apartment in Boston over the eight years I lived there? Plenty, I can tell you. So, no, it doesn't bother me. In fact, I feel quite safe here." *Safer than in my Boston apartment with my lunatic soon-to-be ex-husband,* she wanted to add but didn't. *My own place!*

She looked out to the ocean again. "It feels like home. Let's hurry and close the deal before they raise the price!"

*   *   *

Jay deposited Matt at the PSPD shortly before 3:00 p.m. He was going to drop in on his retired father, Bo Finley, and talk to him about Tina and Bruce Bigelow, Robert Oakley's neighbors. Jay knew that his dad had known them since high school, and he wanted to hear his take on his old friends.

He wasn't sure what was bothering him, but there was some little stab in his stomach every time he thought about Tina and Robert. One of the strongest lessons he'd learned when Matt came to town as his new boss was to listen to his gut. It had paid off in the first case they'd solved together, and he would never again ignore an inkling of discomfort like the one he had now. It was more like a sense of foreboding.

Jay had been born inland about twenty-five miles from Port Stirling, but his parents had moved the family when Jay was in middle school. They'd bought a house with five acres on the southwest side of Deception Hill. The tsunami that had nearly claimed Matt's life hadn't reached the Finley property, but the earthquake had leveled their old house. Now that Jay and his sister were launched into adulthood, Bo and Alice had rebuilt a smaller, one-level home.

Jay loved the new house. It was better situated on the property to take advantage of their wonderful garden and landscape — Bo and Alice could grow anything! He parked in the parking apron off to the right of the sparkling house. Even though the fog had come in from the ocean and was doing the job of a fine rain, both his parents were outside. Jay waved.

"Well, this is a nice surprise," said his mother, coming in for the big hug.

"We figured you were up to your eyeballs on Hannah Oakley's murder," added his dad, following Alice. "Read about it in the newspaper. Terrible."

"Yeah, it's a bad one," Jay said. "It's why I'm here. Can you kids talk for a minute?"

"Sure, c'mon in," said Bo.

They went in through the garage, slipping off their gardening boots and jackets. Even though his shoes were mostly clean, Jay slipped them off, too. Their new carpet was butter yellow, for crying out loud — his mom loved yellow — and Jay wasn't about to be the one who got it dirty.

"Why do you want to talk to us about this case?" asked his dad, taking a seat on the sofa. Alice sat next to her husband, her hand resting familiarly on his thigh.

"This is a small world deal," Jay said. "Tina Bigelow is Robert Oakley's next-door neighbor, and she's good friends with him. Was with Hannah, too. I want to know if you can tell me anything about Bruce's death."

"Just what most people know," said Bo. "Nasty cancer. He slowly got sicker and sicker, and tried to ignore it. By the time he finally went to the doctor, he was already a goner."

Alice wagged her finger at Jay. "Go to the doctor."

"I do, mom. You raised a smart son. I wonder why Tina didn't step in sooner and insist they find out what was wrong with him?"

"I said the same thing," Alice said. "It was finally your dad that got him to go."

"Tina tried, but Bruce was a stubborn old cuss," his dad said. "I explained that he wasn't forty anymore and we couldn't get away with the stuff we could when we were younger."

"How did Tina react at the end?"

"She took good care of him after the diagnosis, but…" Bo's voice drifted off.

"But what?"

His mom spoke. "Your dad doesn't want to say it, but we both think Tina was relieved when the end came. Her life had been a living hell trying to manage his illness." She looked at Jay. "I see that look on your face, and it doesn't mean that Tina is a bad person. It just means she's human, like all the rest of us. Bruce became a real burden, and she did the best any wife could do."

"Would you say she was happy when he finally died?" Jay asked.

"Relieved. Not happy," Bo said. "There's a big difference."

"Have you ever seen Tina and Robert together anywhere?"

Alice and Bo looked sharply at each other.

"What do you mean?" Alice asked.

"Like out to dinner, or shopping at the garden nursery? Anything like that?"

"Like a date? Is that what you're getting at?" asked Bo. "I don't know Robert, so couldn't tell you."

"Do you know him, mom?"

"No, we've never met him. I did see his photo in the newspaper." Her mouth was set in a grim line.

"And?" Jay asked.

"I might have seen him with Tina once."

. . . .

Detective Patty Perkins had finally wrangled Blake Bowen's agent's contact information out of her. Blake had been reluctant and kept whining about what a busy man he was. Patty wanted so desperately to say, "So?", but instead restrained herself. "I promise I won't take much of his time." Blake was still unhappy about it but turned over this tremendously busy man's phone number.

Patty's call went to voicemail, and she left a message explaining who she was and why she was calling, and that it was urgent he returned her call. Then she waited. And waited. And waited. When he still hadn't called after four hours, she dialed him again.

"Mr. Towers, this is Detective Perkins again. Perhaps I wasn't clear on my previous message. This is a police matter, and it's urgent we hear from you. If you don't return my call by 4:00 p.m. today, I will have a colleague of mine in the LAPD drop by your office on Van Ness Avenue and wait until you're available to talk." She hung up.

Six minutes later, Patty's phone buzzed.

"This is Simon Towers. What do you want?"

"Thank you for returning my call," said Patty brusquely. "I have just a few questions for you and won't take long."

"You have five minutes."

"This is a homicide investigation, Mr. Towers. I have as long as I need." She deliberately rustled some papers close to her phone in the hopes that it would annoy him further.

"How can I help you?" His tone was still belligerent, and Patty knew he would be a hostile witness.

"You represent Blake Bowen, is that correct?"

"Yes, for twenty-five years."

"Did you send a corporate jet to Mexico to fly Mrs. Bowen home to Oregon earlier this month?"

"Yes. I often assist her with transportation and well, anything she needs. She's a valuable client."

"Even now?" Patty asked. "She's not much in demand these days, is she?"

"Blake Bowen is a star, detective. And I treat her like one."

"OK. This next question is important, so please think carefully before answering." She paused for drama's sake. "What day and time did your plane pick her up from the Rancho Miguel Splendida airport?"

"I don't have to think; I have no idea. All I do is call the captain and order up the plane."

"Alright, fair enough," Patty said through clenched teeth. "What day did you call the captain to order the plane?"

"I can't recall."

"Again, Mr. Towers, this is important. It would be so much easier for both of us if I don't have to subpoena your phone records."

"I think it was a Thursday."

"Did you call the captain from the phone you're on now?"

"Probably."

"Then please take a minute and scroll through your outbound calls for mid-week three weeks ago. I'll wait."

Silence.

"It looks like I called him on Friday that week," he said finally.

"Are you sure of that?" she asked.

"Yes."

"What time did you place the call?"

"Uh, a little after 7:30 a.m."

"I need your captain's name and phone number, please."

"He will only confirm what I've told you when you call him," he said. It came out smug.

"Oh, I'm not going to phone him," Patty said. "Going straight to a sub-poena on him."

• • •

Tamryn knocked on the door of Matt's office and entered. "Are you ready for me?" she asked, sticking her head around the door.

"Yep. Come in." He indicated a chair opposite his desk. He loved that visitors to his office had a marvelous view out the window behind him. "Nice view I have, right?" he said to her as she took a seat.

"I have a better one," she said.

"No, you don't. You're in the cubicle with no view."

"I'm talking about my new house," she said and couldn't help the grin from forming.

"You found a place?"

"MaryLou found it. All I did was write a check. It's so perfect, Matt. I'm over the moon."

"She found me the perfect rental house, too. Guess she's good at reading people. Good with people in general." He paused.

"Unlike me?" she helped him out.

"I wouldn't say that," Matt said. "You just don't know all the players yet. That's on me. This meeting is not to rag on you, but for me to fill you in on some recent history." He leaned forward on his desk, clasping his hands in front of him.

"The county sheriff has gone through hell and back in the past three weeks. Earl is a great guy and has become a wonderful friend to me since I arrived here. He's also a hard-working, savvy law enforcement officer who serves the people of this county extremely well. But he dropped the ball on the initial call of Hannah's disappearance.

"Just between us, he went along with Buck Bay chief Dan McCoy, who's been known to take a shortcut or two. Deep down, Earl knew they hadn't done all they could, but the evidence really did point to suicide, so he rolled with Dan's call. Now, he's beating himself up real hard."

"And I added to his personal angst," said Tamryn in a whisper. "That's a bad place to be in. I've been there, and it's not pretty. And, I won't ever go there again."

"Neither will Earl. We all have to help him get his mojo back, you included."

"Does he hate me?"

Matt chuckled. "Let's just say he's not inviting you out for a beer quite yet. But the thing I love about Earl is he'll give you a chance, even if he doesn't think so today. He'll come around, but you will have to earn it. Give him more respect. The more you're around him, the easier that will be for you to do because he's got a wealth of experience around here and he's smart as a whip."

Hannah nodded. "I can do that. What about Jay? Did I push his buttons, too?"

"'Fraid so. Jay's background is more complicated. He's very close to Fern. They worked as partners and balanced each other perfectly. In the aftermath of the earthquake and tsunami, the two of them were the face of our department with the locals…even more than me, because they grew up here. It was always going to be hard for whoever replaced Fern to be accepted by Jay."

"Fern hinted at that when we first talked," said Tamryn.

"Yeah, she knows," Matt said. "The two got even closer after I got shot. Fern leaned on him, and he leaned on her when Bill Abbott put him in charge. And that leads to the other complication with Jay; he's gone from running the department back to detective—which he welcomed, he didn't love being interim chief, even though he completely aced it. But now, he's looking at your experience and skill level, and I suspect he feels he's dropped even further down the ladder."

"Well, that's just not true. He and I have the same rank and the same job description. He has no reason to be defensive about that—we're equals. I welcome working with him, especially as he knows so much about the area."

"Tell him that," Matt suggested. "It is the truth. He was invaluable to me when I arrived not knowing anyone or how things worked. But I have an idea how to speed things up for you. We're going to do a one-day retreat here in town as soon as we solve this damnable case. It will be mainly our department, but I'll also invite Earl, Patty, and Ed in for part of it to get to know you better. We work with all the law enforcement in the area, but those three are the people I rely on the most."

"Are you saying the other police departments in the county aren't as good? Should I avoid them?"

"Nope, not saying that. At least not on record." He smiled. "But those three have been tested along with me in some rough situations, and I trust them with my life. We need them and it's important they accept you fully. Jay will come around. He knows we need you to succeed, and he's a team player above all else."

"OK. What do you want me to do in the meantime?"

"Be nice to everybody but be dogged on Hannah's case. Don't pull any punches. I hired you to bring relentless, experienced detective work, and I'm not going to put any holds on you. What have you been doing today?"

"I thought you'd never ask." She pulled her chair in closer to his desk and laid a file on it she'd been holding in her lap. Her face danced, mouth, eyes, and cheeks all aglow with some sort of anticipation.

"What have you got?" Matt asked.

"In 1998, a twenty-one-year-old woman named Hannah Haynes gave birth to a baby girl in Boulder, Colorado." Tamryn looked up from her notes and locked eyes with Matt. "Hannah's brother's name is George Haynes."

"Then it's likely our Hannah."

CHAPTER 22

Only Patty Perkins would have the tenacious spirit to get the captain of the corporate jet who flew Blake Bowen back to Buck Bay from Mexico on the phone for an actual conversation. And it took her five hours and several not-so-veiled threats to make it happen.

Geez Louise, these guys are reluctant to talk about Blake Bowen, she thought. Captain Woods, however, when faced with the reality of lying to an officer of the law or telling the truth, finally came down on the right side. He knew that Detective Perkins could check the filed FAA flight plan, as well as the flight records at Burbank Airport where he hangared his plane.

No matter how much Blake's agent begged him to say the flight in question was on Friday, Woods was unwilling to risk his reputation and license by lying to the cops.

"I left Burbank at 4:00 p.m. on Wednesday, January 25, and picked up Blake just before 7:00 p.m. I refueled at her airport, picked up some food, and we landed at Buck Bay Airport at 10:40 p.m," Captain Woods told Patty.

"What was her mood?" she asked.

"I only saw her briefly before we took off. There was a cabin attendant who took care of her during the flight," Woods said. "She seemed OK to me when we boarded in Mexico. Maybe not as lively as she usually is," he added.

"Did her agent or Blake give you a reason for the change in her plans?"

"No. I just go where and when I'm told. I don't ask a lot of questions. None of my business. My job is to fly the plane between Point A and Point B."

"Did you see who met her in Buck Bay, or did she take an Uber?" Patty asked.

"There was a black SUV waiting for her, and I think it was Blake's husband, Alex. I've met him previously, but it was dark and raining pretty hard, so I can't be sure. I was still in the cockpit doing my check-downs."

"Why do you think everyone wanted you to say you made the trip on Friday morning instead of Wednesday afternoon?"

"Beats me," said Captain Woods. "Hollywood peeps. Most of them are nutters. That's all I can say."

. . .

"Matt, it's Patty."

"Howdy. What's up?"

"I have a bombshell for you," she said. "I'm not exactly sure what it means, but it sure as hell means something. Blake and Alex Bowen lied about when she came home from Mexico."

"No kidding?"

"No kidding." She recounted her conversation with the captain.

Matt soaked it all in. "Why do you think they lied to us?" he asked.

"I think it's one of two possible reasons," Patty said. "One, they somehow knew that afternoon that Hannah was missing, and Blake was upset and wanted to come home. Or, two, Alex Bowen killed Hannah and needed his wife's help to bury the body."

"Yikes. Nobody knew until about 7:00 p.m. that Hannah was missing. So, why did that plane take off at 4:00 p.m. to fetch Blake?" Matt asked. "Maybe Robert told Alex a little before he called the police, but certainly not before 4:00 p.m. I guess it could be unrelated. Maybe she was just homesick."

"If that was the case, then why did they lie to us? Why not just say it?"

"Yeah. Guess we need to ask the Bowens that question."

"Like, right now?" Patty suggested.

"Like, right now."

• • •

Detective Tamryn Gesicki rang the doorbell of George Haynes' home in Buck Bay. Like his sister, Hannah's brother and his wife also lived across the bay from downtown, but in a poorer neighborhood about two miles from the Oakley's new house.

Back at the station, Tamryn had filled in Jay on her Colorado discovery, and asked him to join her after George agreed to talk to her.

"How in hell could she have kept a child a secret all these years?" asked Jay, driving the squad car. "It's mind-blowing. Nice work, by the way."

"Thanks. I think she must have given the child up for adoption, don't you? Hannah was too deep in the Buck Bay community for her to come home from college with a baby and keep it silent all these years. But let's see what her brother says."

"He had to have known," Jay said. "Why wouldn't he have mentioned it? Your sister gets murdered, and you don't tell the police about her past? It's crazy."

George Haynes opened the door, and Tamryn introduced herself and Jay. They knew he was older than Hannah, and today looked even older than he actually was. He appeared tired, and his pale face sadly lined. There was a resemblance between the siblings; both of them were non-descript, the kind of people who blend into the background of life.

George led the way into the kitchen, where something on the stovetop smelled good. Tamryn just realized she'd forgotten to eat lunch. The room was cozy in shades of rust and cream, with a honeyed wood floor and a seating nook in front of a window overlooking the back garden.

"Is it OK if we talk in here?" George asked. "I need to keep my eye on my cooking. Split pea soup. If you forget about it, it will stick to the bottom of the pan."

"No problem," said Tamryn with a smile as she and Jay slid into the nook opposite George. "It smells delicious. First, let me say how truly sorry we are for the loss of your sister. It must be devastating for you and your family."

"Thank you," George responded quietly. "It's been horrible. Hannah was such a bright light. I can't believe I'll never see her again." He reached for a handkerchief in his pant pocket and dabbed his eyes. "Not sure I'll ever get over this." He looked up. "I've already talked to the police. Is there something else you need to know?"

"There is," Tamryn said. "I'm new to Port Stirling, so please forgive me if this is a stupid question. Did Hannah have a child?"

George blanched. "What makes you think that? The answer is no."

"We have two reasons for thinking she might have," Tamryn said calmly. "When Dr. Ryder performed the autopsy, there were some physical indications that Hannah had given birth at some point in her life."

"Ridiculous," George interrupted.

"So," Tamryn continued, "we did some investigating into Hannah's past, and that led us to a hospital in Boulder, Colorado. A young woman named Hannah Haynes gave birth to a daughter there in 1998. We are wondering if that woman was your sister."

"Absolutely not," George sputtered. "Hannah went to college in Boulder, but there was never any baby. There could be lots of women with the same name."

"So, you're telling us," Jay said, "that to your knowledge, Hannah doesn't have a daughter? Just to be clear, you understand."

"If she does, I don't know a thing about it. I'm her older brother. You would think I would know something like this." He looked from Tamryn to Jay and back again, as if searching for an answer himself.

"Were you in close contact with your sister during her college years?" asked Jay.

"Yes, I would say that I saw her regularly. She came home on breaks, and the family would get together. Like people do," he added.

"Did she come home every summer?" asked Tamryn.

George thought. "I think she stayed in Boulder one summer, but mostly she came back to Buck Bay. She usually had a summer job at the ice cream shop down by the port. The owner is a friend of our family, and both Hannah and I worked there off and on while we were in school."

"The summer she stayed in Colorado, would you say that was early or later in her college years?" Jay asked.

"I know she came home after her freshman year because she didn't want to go back. She was homesick. But mom and dad made her return. After that, I can't really remember which summer was which."

"Would you have noticed if your sister was pregnant?" Tamryn asked.

George flushed and sat very still. "I think I would have, or my wife would have for sure. Candace was pregnant at about that time, and she would have been hyper aware. I really think you're barking up the wrong tree here."

"Is your wife home?" asked Jay. "Could we talk to her?"

"She's at work," George said, shaking his head. "She works part-time at the library just to get out of the house. Or away from retired me."

"That's what my dad says about my mom," smiled Jay.

"Thank you, Mr. Haynes," said Tamryn. "We know this is difficult and our questions seem weird, but we need to cover all the bases. I'm sorry if we upset you."

"Comes with the territory, doesn't it?" George said. He slowly rose from the table, and Jay and Tamryn followed his lead. He walked them out of the kitchen down the hallway to the front door. "I hope you can find out what happened to Hannah. It might help all of us process this better."

"If you or your wife think about anything else that might help us, especially on this child angle, please give us a call," Tamryn said, scribbling her new department phone number on a page from her police notebook.

Jay stopped in front of a family photo hanging midway down the hall. "This is nice," he said. "You, your wife, and your daughter, I'm guessing?"

"Yes, that was taken at our daughter's graduation. Her name is Annie."

"They're both beautiful," said Tamryn. "And you clean up nice."

That got a trace of a smile out of George. "Thank you. I'm lucky to have both of them."

"How old is your daughter now?" asked Jay casually.

"She's twenty-five. She works for the city of Buck Bay as a landscaper. She loves plants," George said and smiled.

Tamryn and Jay walked to the car without looking at each other or saying a word. Once they were out of the driveway and around the first corner, Jay pulled off on the shoulder of the road, his hands gripping the steering wheel.

"Annie Haynes is the spitting image of Hannah Oakley," Jay said. "There is a photo of Hannah on Robert's desk, and the two of them could be twins."

"And she looks nothing like Candace Haynes. Candace has gorgeous bone structure and thick blond hair, plus she's taller than George."

"Hannah had a baby daughter and gave her to her brother and his wife?" Jay supposed. "Can that happen in America?"

• • •

Matt punched the intercom button on the Bowens' gate.

"Yes?" came the disembodied voice of Blake Bowen.

"Blake, it's Matt Horning. Patty Perkins is with me, and we need to ask you and Alex a couple more questions. Please open the gate."

Without sound, the gate slowly began to creak open, and Matt pulled up in front of the house. Before they got out of the car, he turned to Patty and said, "We're going to play this by ear, and react to how they answer our questions. That alright with you?"

"Yes," Patty said. "I have an open mind at this point. Honestly, this case is baffling, and I don't know what to think."

"I think the Bowens are involved up to their pretty little necks. For me, a lot depends on how they handle the next thirty minutes. Let's go, detective."

Blake Bowen opened the door. She was frowning. Big time frowning.

"This is starting to feel like harassment, Mr. Horning," she said.

"It's Chief Horning, and it's not harassment if we have probable cause to believe you are somehow involved in Hannah's death. And we now have probable cause. May we come in?"

Blake held the door open and made a dramatic sweeping motion with her free arm. "By all means, please come in. Mi casa es su casa," she dripped with sarcasm.

She was wearing a colorful, flowy caftan that looked Mexican. It was paired with gray fleecy slippers trimmed in dirty white fur, which spoiled the festive Mexican look.

"Is Alex at home?" Patty asked.

"No, he drove to Eugene for a fundraiser tonight."

"When will he be back here?"

"Tomorrow morning. What's this about?" She plopped down on the living room sofa, leaving them to fend for themselves.

Not the way I was brought up, thought Matt. *Beverly would be mortified.*

"Detective Perkins got some new information today and we'd like to run it by you," Matt said.

Patty dove in. "In the past twenty-four hours, I've spoken with your agent, the captain of the plane who flew you home from Mexico, and the cabin attendant on that plane," said Patty.

She watched as Blake's face lost some of its luster and her squarish jaw slackened. But then, following quickly, she saw a betrayed woman's anger in Blake's eyes. It blazed for just a moment, before some internal mastery took over. She sat up straighter, folded her hands in her lap, and said, "Yes? What do you want to ask me?"

"I think you know," said Patty.

"Sorry, I don't."

"Then I'll spell it out for you. Your agent is still lying on your behalf, in case you want to know," Patty said. "But Captain Woods and Lily Wong told me the truth. That they flew you home from Mexico on Wednesday, the day Hannah disappeared, not on Friday as you told us. How do you account for that?"

"I can't," Blake said, as firmly as she could manage. "They're obviously lying to you for some reason. I returned home on Friday."

"No, you didn't," Patty said. "I checked the flight records with both Rancho Miguel Splendida's airport, and with Buck Bay. The flight plan filed by Captain Woods and the timing of it jive precisely with what he and Ms. Wong told me. Why did you lie to us, Blake?"

She sat still for a split second, and then said, "I could have sworn it was Friday. Must be the Mexican sun…the days all run together." She looked from Patty to Matt, daring them to contradict her.

"So, you're saying you just got the days confused?" Matt asked.

"I guess so, if Woods said he picked me up on Wednesday, I must have."

"Why did you leave two days earlier than you were planning to?" Matt again.

She thought for a minute. "My best friend had disappeared. I remember thinking that if I was home I might be able to help find her."

Matt and Patty exchanged a quick glance, and Matt nodded.

"The plane picked you up at 4:00 p.m. on Wednesday," Patty said. She leaned in closer to Blake. "Robert didn't even realize that Hannah was missing until almost 7:00 p.m. How did you know she had disappeared?"

"He called Alex earlier," Blake said, sounding a little frantic now. "And Alex called me. I was immediately worried she'd done something stupid. I needed to get home."

"So, you do remember that it was Wednesday not Friday," Matt said, laying it on the table.

"Well, now I do," she said with a trace of belligerence. "And, this will probably sound crazy, but I'd had a distressing feeling about Hannah for a couple of days."

"What do you mean? Distressing?" asked Matt.

"Like something was wrong with her. I don't know exactly, just something unpleasant in her life." She shrugged. "Some intuition you get regarding your friends once in a while, you know? I could feel that Han needed me."

Matt, unsure how to respond to that, looked at Patty.

Patty stared at Blake, and you could almost see the gears grinding in her head. "I'm going to ask you a question, Blake, and I don't want you to answer it immediately. I want you to take your time and think carefully about your answer, OK?"

"S'pose," Blake said.

"Are you protecting Alex? Did he kill Hannah? Did he call you after he did it, and beg you to come home?"

Instead of taking her time as Patty had requested, Blake, composed, said, "No, I'm not protecting Alex. He did not kill Hannah. I don't know who did. I came home because I wanted to help find her. I didn't lie to you, I just got confused about the days. Is there anything else?"

Matt placed his hands on his thighs and pushed himself up to a standing position. "OK, then, that's it," he said. "Do you mind if we have a look around before we leave? Your garage? Outside? We won't trouble you any further today."

Flustered but trying to fake it, Blake said, "No, I don't think that's a good idea, Chief. You need to leave now. And in the future, please make an appointment if you want to talk to either me or Alex. We've had enough of your insinuations."

"Guess we'll need a warrant," Patty said to Matt. "See you soon, Blake. Enjoy your evening."

CHAPTER 23

Matt called Fern as he and Patty were driving back to Port Stirling from Buck Bay. Sunset was nearing, and as so often happened in winter late in the day as the storms moved inland, brilliant sunshine reflected off the tame waves.

"Can you see the ocean where you guys are?" Fern asked. "Is it as beautiful right now as it is here?"

"Yep. Nice evening. Never gets old, does it?" Matt answered. "Say, Patty and I want to come to the house and talk to you. Does that fit with your plans?"

"Sure. I'd love to see her. What's the occasion?"

"We just had a troubling discussion with Blake Bowen, and we want to talk it through with you to see if it sounds as crazy to someone who wasn't in the room as it did to us."

"OK," Fern said. "I'll open a bottle of wine."

"We'll stop at city hall and pick up Patty's car, and then we'll be there."

Twenty-five minutes later, Matt drove into his garage and Patty parked in the driveway. By now, the sun was just about ready to drop into the ocean, and the sky was a dazzling display of color: pink, purple, red, orange.

"Wow," said Patty, stepping through their foyer and over to the floor-to-ceiling windows in the living room. "That's a sunset for the books. Look at your white pillows! The sun is turning them different shades. Spectacular!"

"I thought it would be a dud tonight," Fern said. "When you called, the sky was clear, but then it streaked up with those clouds at just the right time." She handed Patty a glass of white wine and gave her husband a bottle of beer.

The three cops toasted to friendship and sat quietly for a minute staring out to the vivid sky and sea.

"So, how is Blake Bowen doing these days?" asked Fern.

"Your husband and I feel like we've just visited the Twilight Zone," Patty said. "We know Blake and Alex both lied about when she returned from Mexico. Our investigation turned up that Blake was back in Oregon by 10:30 Wednesday night, not Friday like they both told us."

"How does she account for the lie now?" Fern asked.

Matt snorted. "She had a woo-woo feeling that 'Han' was in some kind of trouble, and she wanted to get home early to help her," he said. "Yeah, and I was born yesterday."

"That's the best she could do?" Fern asked, wide-eyed.

"She did offer that Alex called her around the time the plane took off from Burbank to pick her up," said Patty, "but that would have been around 4:00 p.m."

"It doesn't add up," said Matt.

"Not unless Alex killed Hannah sometime before 4:00 p.m. and called Blake immediately," Fern said.

"That's my theory," Patty said. "Nothing else makes any sense for why Blake came home early. I could understand her coming on Thursday morning once the dam broke Wednesday night and Robert knew Hannah was missing, and especially after McCoy's guys found her car at Mourning Bay. But there was no reason for Blake to fly home on Wednesday night unless Alex called and told her to."

"But I have trouble believing Alex is a murderer. He just doesn't seem the type," said Fern. "Although…" Her sentence dropped off into space.

"Although what?" Matt asked her.

She looked at her husband. "Well, I didn't want to tell you this because I'll get another lecture." She smiled to soften her words. "I met with Alex yesterday to go over the budget for his non-profit. And, I saw a little different side of him."

Matt glowered. "You what? You promised me you wouldn't talk to him again while our case was ongoing."

Patty rose and went to the kitchen to refill her wine glass. The Hornings were aware of why she left the room.

"I didn't think it was a big deal," Fern argued. "I thought you were being unreasonable and controlling."

Matt interrupted her. "That's not fair."

"Fair or not, I'm not used to a man making decisions about my life. And it doesn't really work for me."

"I don't do that."

"You did in this particular case."

"He's a suspect in a murder case, for cryin' out loud. He may have killed a woman. You're a woman. A woman I love. What part of that don't you understand? Where did you meet him?"

A sheepish look crossed Fern's face. "At his house," she said quietly.

"Well, that was stupid," Patty said, coming back into the room.

"Thanks, girlfriend," Fern said.

Matt, speechless, shook his head in disbelief.

"Why are you telling Matt this now?" Patty asked. "I wouldn't have told him, knowing he would react this way." She smiled sweetly at Matt.

"Yeah, why are you telling me this?"

"Because Alex acted a little weird. Blake wasn't home—which I didn't know before I got there, so don't yell at me anymore!—and he flirted with me. It wasn't overt, more subtle, but it creeped me out."

"Oh, for God's sake," Matt said, still red-faced. "He's the type alright. Thinks he charming, but it's too flashy and smarmy. If I may ask without being unreasonable and controlling, did you fall for it?"

"Of course not. I told you; it made me uncomfortable, and I left in a hurry. But here's the reason I'm telling you now. I got a look at the file for his business. He had it out on the table, and he left the room briefly to take a phone call. We'd been talking about the expense categories so I could learn how to structure our non-profit, and one of them struck me as odd." She took a sip of her wine and set it back down on the end table.

"Odd, how?" Matt asked.

"One of the categories was Administrative Expenses, which he described as what he paid their attorney and accountant. The amount for last year totaled over one-fifth of his entire budget. More than rent, employees, and everything. I took photos of the breakdown and some other budget detail pages while he was out of the room, and when I was reading them this morning, I also noticed something else that seemed off to me."

"What?" Patty asked, listening intently.

"Sarah Forrester shared Rainbow to Hope's budget with me, too. They're about two million annually, and they have four full-time employees. They hire some contract counselors when they need extra help. Alex's budget is just under ten million, and he lists twenty-nine employees. I would have expected that number to be closer to twenty, or, five times Rainbow's staff."

"Maybe they do more grant-writing or put on more events — that kind of thing," Patty offered.

"I think they do, but even accounting for that, it seems like Alex is staff-heavy," said Fern.

"Sounds to me like your boyfriend Alex might be padding his budget and pocketing more than his salary," Matt said.

• • •

Jay and Tamryn sat in the squad car in the parking lot of Port Stirling city hall as the day's light began to fade.

"What shall we do next?" Tamryn asked him.

"We could go in and write up our report on our visit to George Haynes," Jay said. "Or, I can take you to your hotel now, and we can write it up in the morning."

"What would you do if I weren't here, and you'd just figured out what we think we just figured out?"

Jay thought. "I'd probably call Matt and ask him if we could talk now."

"Then let's do that," Tamryn said.

"OK," Jay grinned, pulling out his phone and pressing 'boss' on his Recents.

"Jay," Matt answered.

"Where are you?"

"Home. Talking to Fern and Patty. Where are you?"

"City hall with Tamryn. We have something we want to tell you."

"Come on over. We'll have a party."

"You're sure?"

"Be here in five," Matt said.

And they were.

"OK, so your view is better than mine," Tamryn said, gravitating to the windows like everyone who entered Matt and Fern's house did. "Mary-Lou found me the perfect rental house this morning, and I'm moving in tomorrow," she told Fern and Patty excitedly. "I have a view of the ocean, too, but it's not quite as spectacular as this."

"And you will both know the house," Matt said. "What do you drink?"

"I'll have what you're having," Tamryn pointed at his beer.

Fern headed for the kitchen. "Don't talk about your house until I get back! I want to hear everything."

Fern grabbed two beers from the fridge—she didn't have to ask Jay what he would have—and flew back to the living room.

"So, where's your place?"

Matt answered for Tamryn. "It's the house south of here that Clay Sherwin was renting. Tamryn knows its past history and doesn't give a rip, right?"

"Right. I'm not the superstitious type. It's a nice little house, perfect size for me. I never dreamed I could afford an ocean view, so its history worked in my favor."

"That is a great little house," Fern agreed. "Although it creeps me out."

"The owner is lucky to get you," Patty said. "So much better to have a long-term renter rather than short-term rentals."

"Especially someone like me who won't be home that often," Tamryn said. "I couldn't be more thrilled to find it."

"What is it you two want to tell us?" Matt asked.

"Tell them, Jay," Tamryn said.

"The background is that this detective," he crooked his thumb at Tamryn, "discovered that a woman named Hannah Haynes gave birth to a daughter in Colorado in 1998."

"Oh, my," said Patty. "George Haynes is Hannah's brother, so that's her maiden name. Bernice was right."

"Hannah has a child?" asked Fern. "Sorry, I'm out of the loop — please continue, Jay."

"We paid a visit to George this afternoon, and he denied knowing anything about his sister having a baby."

"That's certainly possible if she had it in Colorado," Matt said. "Hannah might not have wanted her family to know. She didn't tell anyone and gave it up for adoption. Wouldn't be the first time a young woman has done that."

"True," agreed Tamryn. "However, Jay and I think that's not exactly what Hannah did." She nodded at Jay. "Tell them what you found."

"As we were leaving George's house, I happened to look closely at a photo on the wall in his hallway. It was George, his wife Candace, and his daughter. The daughter looks exactly like the photo of Hannah in Robert's house. And I mean 'exactly'," Jay said.

"He's right, Matt," Tamryn confirmed. "We stopped by Robert's after we left George's house so I could see the photo of Hannah. George's daughter and Hannah look like twins. It's actually kind of eerie. Plus, the daughter looks nothing like George's wife, Candace. Different coloring, body type, height, different hair — everything. I'd bet the farm she is not Candace's daughter."

"Wow," said Patty. "We've got a couple of options. You two could go back to George and confront him with what you think you know."

"Or," interrupted Matt, "we could go straight to DNA testing and try to get a sample from the daughter. Nice work, you two." He smiled like a proud father.

Patty pointed her index finger at Matt. "What he said. Let's cut to the chase with DNA. And, yes, brilliant work!"

"Does the daughter live in Buck Bay?" asked Fern. "At home with George and his wife?"

"She lives in the area," answered Jay, "but we don't know exactly what her housing situation is. George volunteered that she works for the city of Buck Bay. We didn't want to ask him too many questions or to let on that we suspected this. Wanted to talk it over with you guys first. Neither she nor Candace Haynes were home when we were there."

"Jay and I agreed that we'd go back first thing tomorrow morning if everyone decided that we needed to quiz George on our suspicions," Tamryn said.

"This is going to be tricky," Matt said. "We can't demand the daughter give us a DNA sample; it would have to be voluntary. We can't arrest her on suspicion of anything, and she's not even a suspect."

"She might be a suspect," Tamryn argued. "She might have learned the truth about her mother and been pissed off."

"Or Hannah changed her mind after all these years and wanted to acknowledge her as her own daughter," Fern said. "She told George and Candace, and one of them killed Hannah to silence her before she could talk."

"That's probably more likely," Patty mused. "Which is another good reason why we need to know the truth about the daughter. We have probable cause to suspect that the girl is Hannah's child. That should get us somewhere."

"Why? Because Jay thinks she looks like her aunt?" Matt said. "Kinda flimsy."

"Added to it that we know Hannah had a child, and the ages match up," said Jay. "It could turn this case upside down. Should we call Jeri at the D.A.'s office and get her take on how we should proceed?"

"Yeah, that's a good idea," said Matt. "I don't want to step in anything regarding DNA testing. I'll call Jeri tonight, and then we'll kick off Monday morning with a crime team meeting at 7:30. That OK with everyone?"

CHAPTER 24

W hat I love about this group is that each of us has a role in every case that comes before us," Matt told the assembled major crime team huddled around the table in the lower level of Port Stirling city hall. "This morning, I'm singling out Bernice."

"What did I do?" Dr. Ryder asked with a raised eyebrow.

"You told us that, in your view, Hannah had given birth at some point in her life," Matt said. "We now believe that to be true, and it might be the key to her murder."

Matt recounted what they'd learned about the Colorado birth, and the daughter of Hannah's brother George and his wife for the benefit of Bernice, Ed, the sheriff, and Dan McCoy. Interim D.A. Jeri Schrader, also present, was brought up to speed in a phone call last night with Matt.

"When you say George's daughter looks like Hannah, how striking is the resemblance?" asked Ed.

"It's like they could be twins," said Jay. "Now, we were just looking at a photograph of her, but the resemblance jumps out at you. It's what caught my eye. I can hardly wait to see her in person."

Matt said, "We'll need to talk with George and Candace first and see if they are willing to shed any light on this situation. Jeri, please tell the team what you told me last night."

"Yes. It would be the best thing for your investigation if the parties involved tell you the truth," Jeri said. "Otherwise, it will be very difficult to force the daughter—what's her name, by the way?"

"I think George called her Annie," said Jay, "but we haven't had time yet to research."

"It will be hard to force Annie to give us a DNA sample," Jeri continued. "If she has no idea that Hannah might be her mother instead of her aunt, she might voluntarily submit to a test. But if it goes the other way and she doesn't want anything to do with this news, your hands are pretty much tied. Unless you trick her into drinking a cup of coffee or something. And I didn't say that."

"What recourse will you have if Hannah's brother continues to deny it?" asked Bernice.

"We can request that they produce the birth certificate for their daughter," said Patty. "If George told Jay and Tamryn the truth—that he knows nothing about Hannah ever giving birth—then he shouldn't mind that request, right?"

"In theory," agreed Matt. "And if he and his wife don't want to cooperate with us on any level, we can easily do a records search on their daughter. If George is lying and their daughter is really Hannah's daughter, we can uncover the truth, one way or another. The daughter is my main concern. This will be a shock to her, assuming she doesn't know. If I were her, I'd want to submit to a DNA test to know for sure."

"So would I," said Bernice. "But some people might want to stick their head in the sand, especially if it risks upending the status quo."

"And what if the daughter does know, and she killed Hannah?" said Tamryn. "In that scenario, she won't cooperate at all. Jeri, if we come back to you with probable cause that Annie is Hannah's real daughter, like there is no birth certificate on record that she is George and Candace's biological daughter, would that be enough to force a DNA test on the girl?"

"Maybe," Jeri said. "This is a tight call, and a different situation than I've encountered. She's not a suspect, not yet anyway. But this determination could materially impact your case in that it gives you three possible suspects who might want Hannah dead. From my desk, we're just going to have to play it out and see where we end up. Talk to George and Candace first and let me know what transpires there. There's a chance this may go easier than we're all thinking it will."

"Who's going to confront George?" Jay asked.

"It's your hunch," said Matt, "so, do you want to go back?"

"I think he lied to Tamryn and me before," Jay said. "His body language was all messed up when we asked him if Hannah had ever given birth. I'm not sure if the two of us go to talk to him again we'd get any different response. Even if we point out the physical similarities between his daughter and Hannah. I think you should go. And take Ed. Let's try to intimidate him."

"I am good at that," smirked six-foot-four-inch, substantial Ed. "I can also represent the Oregon State Police lab where the DNA tests are run. Give him something else to think about."

"As much as I would like to be in the room," said Patty, "I agree with Jay—send in the heavy hitters so if he is lying, he knows we're serious. Besides, I have Blake Bowen issues."

"It's settled then," Matt said. "Ed, how's the rest of your morning look? Can we do this next?"

"The Coast Guard wants me to stop by sometime today to look at some photos of a ship at anchor off the coast south of here. Let me do that first and then I'm all yours."

Every eye turned to Matt. "What kind of ship?" he said. "Please tell me it doesn't have Chinese markings."

Nervous laughter around the table.

"It appears to be Colombian," said Ed. "Not related, and only suspicious because it's been in the same spot for two days. I believe Ms. State Department was advised this morning, too."

"Stop me if you've heard this before, but what the hell are we going to do about these drug cartels using Oregon as their playground?" Matt asked.

"We're going to round them up, just like we did the last guys," said the sheriff. "We've got to get these drugs out of my county before every last person in their twenties is living in a tent on Twisty River's main street." Earl's fists were balled up, and it was only a matter of time before he pounded them on the table.

"I'm with you, Earl," said Matt. "But first, we're going to find out who killed Hannah and bring them to justice. And, moving on, Patty and I have a request of you, Jeri. We want a search warrant for Blake and Alex Bowen's property."

"What's that about?" Jeri asked.

"They both lied to us about Blake being in Mexico on the day Hannah disappeared. We have proof she was back in Oregon that Wednesday night," Patty said and filled in the team on her investigation. "She wouldn't let Matt and I look around, and we really want to examine their cars, in particular."

"Why?" asked Jeri.

"My personal theory is that Alex Bowen killed Hannah," said Patty. "I'm not sure why yet, although Fern had some interesting info last night that Matt will share with you. He then immediately phoned his wife in Mexico and told her to come home. I believe he needed help disposing of Hannah's body in the forest, and Blake got a plane ride home fast. I want forensics to go over any vehicles on their property."

"My wife, in her private role, met with Alex Bowen yesterday," Matt said, jaw clenched. "We're starting a foundation, and she was meeting with Alex to understand the non-profit budgeting process. Fern thought there were some irregularities in Alex's budget. This is highly confidential, and it won't be admissible evidence, Jeri, but coupled with the lies Patty and I got out of those two, we are highly suspicious that they might have been involved in Hannah's death."

"Do either of you have a motive for the Bowens' involvement?" Jeri asked.

"Not specifically," Matt said. "But there's lots of little things that may add up to one big thing."

"Such as?" asked Jeri.

"I think Hannah and Blake may have had a falling out of some sort," Patty offered. "Blake appears to be jealous of Hannah in recent Facebook posts and in how she talked about her once to me."

"Based on Fern's report, I think it's possible that Alex has been skimming off the top of his business," Matt added. "I'm going to follow-up with a board member of his today and see if I can learn anything. Maybe

Hannah found out and told Alex the jig was up. Or, to quote, 'It's over', the so-called suicide note. I realize it's a stretch, but in my mind, it fits. Maybe Alex met with Hannah to explain, but it got out of hand, and he went into a rage and strangled her."

"I might be able to help you out on this one," Jeri said. "Judge Hedges doesn't like it when people lie to the police during investigations. That alone might be enough for a limited search warrant. I'll talk to her."

Matt and Patty made a 'high five' gesture across the table at each other. "Thanks, Jeri, you just made our day."

"Let's don't forget about Justin Sorenson," grumped Earl. "That guy has no alibi, and he's a major-league loser. It could have gone down the way you just described for Alex Bowen, Matt. Sorenson finds out Hannah is ending his gravy train, arranges to meet to change her mind, and then loses it completely and kills her. Just as likely."

Matt nodded. "Your theory works for me, too, Earl. Sorenson bugs the hell out of me, and he's not telling us everything, for sure."

"But he loses if Hannah dies," Tamryn said. "The only person who benefits, from everything we know now, is Robert Oakley. And if Patty and Matt are right about the Bowens, they've acted on one of the classic reasons for murder — to shut up someone who could hurt them. Same if Jay and I are right about George Haynes and his family."

Jay looked thoughtful. "Remember when Justin Sorenson declined to tell us what his phone call with Hannah was about on the day she died? Said it was a 'family matter'."

"Yes," said Matt.

"Maybe he's known about Hannah's daughter all along and decided to blackmail her if she went ahead and cut off his support. She wrote him the letter that her attorney said she planned to, and he retaliated by informing her that he would tell her daughter the truth. Hannah called his bluff when they met that Wednesday, he realizes he's lost, and kills her. He's got the 'It's over' note in her handwriting, too."

"Yeah, we can't forget about that note," Matt said. "Whoever killed her had a note in her handwriting saying, 'It's over'." He rubbed his chin. "But all we're doing is speculating. Any of these people are plausible suspects for having that note in their possession. But, if I'm honest, so is Robert. Hannah could have written those two words in so many different contexts. She could have written a note to Robert that said, 'I've had it with Comcast. It's over.'" Laughter.

"You laugh, but it's true," Matt continued. "Bernice, you're sure there were no other fingerprints on that damnable note?"

"I'm sure. Only Hannah's prints," Bernice said.

"If the killer wore gloves, that tells me it was pre-meditated," said Tamryn. "Not a spur of the moment reaction."

Patty shook her head. "Not necessarily. It still might have been a fit of rage, but the killer was calm enough to wipe the note and her glasses clean once the deed was done."

"We need to focus," said Matt. "Let's talk to George Haynes and his wife first. Then, run a forensics check on Blake and Alex Bowen's cars, if Judge Hedges allows. We'll know a lot more after those two things than we know now."

• • •

OSP Lieutenant Ed Sonders called Fern after the crime team meeting. "You want a ride over to Buck Bay to meet with the Coast Guard? I'm coming back to Port Stirling when we're done there."

"That would be nice," Fern said. "Joe Phelps wants me at your meeting. I can't believe we're talking about suspicious foreign ships again."

"I'm sure it's nothing," Ed reassured her. "It's just the CG dotting the i's and crossing the t's."

"Hope you're right. It's still a little raw for Matt and me. I'm ready whenever you get here."

"Leaving city hall now."

• • •

Matt took George Haynes' phone number from Jay and called him to set an appointment. They agreed to meet at 1:00 p.m. at the Haynes' home.

That would give Ed plenty of time to do what he needed to do. It was now almost 9:00 a.m.

Then he closed his office door and called his wife. He had an uneasy feeling and needed to hear her beautiful voice.

She picked up and said, "You heard, huh?"

"I heard. What does Joe think?"

"Probably the same thing you think; it's a Colombian drug cartel that's made billions off the backs of American teenagers. And they're looking for an out-of-the-way place to set up a new shop. Somewhere not in Mexico where they keep having to kill Mexicans who get in their way."

"We don't need this right now," Matt said. "It already feels like there is something evil around here. I keep expecting another body to turn up in a grave somewhere."

"You don't really think that, do you?" she asked.

"Naw. I guess not. Hannah's murder feels like she was specifically targeted by someone who knew her. We have at least three suspects, all of whom might have a good reason for wanting her dead. Seeing her buried in that grave was startling, though, even for someone as grizzled as me."

"It must have been awful for you guys. It's still hard for me to realize that something like this can happen here."

"Different from when you were a kid here, right? The whole world has changed, Fern, and not for the better."

"You sound down, honey. Is there anything I can do to cheer you up?"

"Give me a good report after you meet with the Coast Guard, OK?"

"Hope so."

CHAPTER 25

Sylvia, as requested, brought Matt a list of the Healing House—Alex Bowen's Eugene non-profit—board of directors. There were six names, all with phone and e-mail contact information.

"This is off their website, and it looks current," said Sylvia. "Anything else you need this morning?"

"Yes. Can you call the Whale Rock Inn and ask about their new Retreat Center? I want to rent it for one day for our department and a couple of invited guests."

"When do you want it?"

"That's the tricky part," Matt answered. "I can't in good conscience schedule this until we're further along on Hannah's murder case. Taking everyone off the case for a day feels irresponsible."

"On the other hand," said Sylvia, "if you are able to get Tamryn and the rest of the team on the same page, it might lead to a quicker resolution. I assume that's what this is about."

"Pretty transparent, huh?" Matt smiled at his wise assistant.

"The boys were always going to react this way to her out of the gate," Sylvia said. "She's different. Most men aren't drawn to 'different' women. Plus, she knows her stuff and she's outspoken."

"How do you feel about her so far?"

"She's not Fern. I don't feel lovey-dovey to Tamryn, but I understand why you hired her. She brings a lot to our small-town table in terms of her experience, both in life and on the job. Therefore, I'm welcoming her with open arms because she's probably just what we need. And, she's growing on me already. Sheldon says, 'it's a Boston thingy'." She smiled.

"I appreciate your attitude. How is Sheldon?"

"Sheldon is terrific," she said. "Not that you care, but he and I have settled into a nice routine. We complement each other, yet we have our own lives. It's a nice relationship, to tell you the truth."

"You know I care. And this makes me happy to hear."

"I know you do." She headed to the door. "I'll let you know about the Retreat Center."

· · ·

After Fern talked to Matt and knew that the crime team meeting was over, she called Tamryn's cell phone.

"Fern. To what do I owe the pleasure?" Tamryn answered.

"I'm wondering if you got the paperwork signed for your rental house yet?"

"The owner is on her way down to city hall right now — she just called me. She wants to meet me in person. I'll sign the lease, give her two months' rent upfront, and then I get the keys. How excited am I?"

Fern could feel her happiness through the phone. "Very, I'm guessing."

"You got that right."

"Listen, I have to run over to Buck Bay for a quick meeting, but when I get back how about I help you move from Whale Rock into the house? I can take you grocery shopping and show you the ropes. Matt said you're getting a rental car tomorrow, but I figure you might want to get moved as soon as you can."

"You would do that?" Tamryn asked. "That would be so wonderful, Fern. Whale Rock is lovely and comfortable, but it's not mine, you know? What time will you be available?"

"I should be back by noon at the latest. I'll call you when I'm on my way to pick you up. Do you have any time commitments in the office?"

"No. Have I mentioned what a nice boss I have? He told me to take whatever time I need to get settled."

"I've heard he's a good guy," Fern chuckled. "See you this afternoon."

• • •

Matt sat quietly, staring out his office window. He'd been making notes on the questions he had for George Haynes. The thought of ripping this family apart added to his general sense of uneasiness. He shifted in his chair and turned back to his desk to review his notes. It was a list of four questions, but Matt knew only the top one was relevant: *May we see the birth certificate for your daughter?* If George showed it to them, and they were wrong about her being Hannah's daughter, then that was that. If he wouldn't or couldn't show it to them, it meant the police had to keep digging, no matter what the impact on George's family and Robert. *Dammit, I hate this case.*

He jumped up, grabbed his jacket and UT 'Hook 'Em Horns' cap off his coat rack, told Sylvia he was going for a walk. "Need to think," he'd said, and quickly left city hall before anyone could stop him to chat.

He crossed the highway and headed for the coastal path that ran along the top of the bluff, stuffing his hands in his pockets to ward off the cold wind. Last night's colorful sunset had been replaced by drab clouds that were quickly turning a furious black. Matt turned south where the path divided at the western end of North America, and the bitter wind punished his face with stinging salt spray. He leaned into it and moved vigorously.

We're making progress, he said out loud. No one around, just him and the wind. *It's likely that our killer is either Blake or Alex Bowen, or Justin Sorenson, or one of the members of the Haynes family. We need to nail down alibis, really nail them down, not just take their word at face value.*

Personally, Matt had removed Robert from his suspect list. He knew Tamryn was correct about the statistics in a case like this, but one of his best skills was his ability to read people in times of crisis. Robert was sincere; in his grief, in his desire to learn what really happened to his wife. Matt would bet on it, and, in a sense, he was betting on it by taking his investigative focus off Robert.

Rounding a corner in the earthen path where it headed inland for a few hundred yards, he came up to a bench partially protected from the wind by a large stand of gorse. He rested one foot on the bench, punched in Jay's number, and watched a mini sand tornado rise up from the path.

"Jay, I want you to call Alex Bowen and go over his alibi again for the Wednesday Hannah disappeared. He says he was working from home alone all day, but I want you to pin him down—can anyone verify that? Did he get any deliveries, did anyone call him, did he wave at the mailman—anyone at all who saw him that day at home."

"OK."

"Be mean." Matt hung up. Then he dialed Earl, and the sheriff picked up. "Earl, did we check Justin Sorenson's work shifts at the Growler to see if he was at work like he said he was when Hannah disappeared?"

"Yes, I personally talked to the manager, and she said she thought he was there all day."

"Thought? Don't they keep any records? Payroll or something?"

"She said she had to find them and would call me."

"Jesus, Earl, this might be important," said Matt, growing even more frustrated. "Put some pressure on her. Put some pressure on Justin."

"I will do that, Chief Horning," Earl said formally. "I can also tell you that I just submitted a search warrant request to Judge Hedges for permission to search Sorenson's car. Somebody transported Hannah's body to that grave, and I know you think it was the Bowens, but Sorenson is just as likely in my book. I want to look at his vehicle just as much as you want to look at the Bowens'."

Matt didn't like his tone. "That's fine, Earl," he said stiffly.

"And furthermore, I'm just as frustrated as you are, and you can go to hell if you think I'm not."

"I never said…"

The sheriff hung up.

Okayyy. We're all tense. Having a killer on the loose will do that. Matt resumed his walk, pushing determinedly into the gale until his face was raw.

. . .

Buck Bay Coast Guard Captain Bob Adams welcomed Ed and Fern into his office.

"I'll cut right to the chase," he told them. "We first spotted this ship at anchor just off Cape Douglas three days ago. I sent a crew out in the cutter yesterday to make contact with her." He pointed to a board where several photos of the ship were tacked up. Fern moved closer and looked carefully at each photo, hands on her hips.

"Since they are in our territorial waters, we could have boarded. But we decided to keep it friendly and ask for permission to come aboard, but they denied."

"Do you suspect them of illegal drugs or weapons smuggling?" Ed asked.

"It's my job to be suspicious," Captain Adams replied. "But their spokesman told my crew they are fishing the western Pacific from the coast of Oregon down through Mexico and Central America."

"And, is it a Colombian ship as you thought?" asked Fern.

"Yes. He told my crew that the fishing is no good in South America these days, so they're having to go further afield."

"That sounds fishy to me," Ed said. The Captain and Fern laughed.

"That's what I thought, too," Bob said. "So, we're going out in the helicopter tomorrow morning if it's still there and do a flyover. If it's really a fishing boat, we should see evidence on deck."

"My boss will want me to accompany you," Fern said. "Does that work for you?"

"I figured as much, that's why I called you this morning. Sure, and same goes for you, too, Ed. In an ideal world, they're a fishing boat, but, if not, you two need to be looped in. We'll go out early, as soon as it's light, about 6:30 a.m."

"Sounds good," Ed said. "I hope to hell we're not dealing with more foreign trouble." He looked at Fern.

"You and me both," Fern said. She was having some very unpleasant flashbacks.

On the way back to Port Stirling, with a gloomy rain keeping time with Ed's windshield wipers, the two friends chatted. Fern was comfortable in the passenger seat of the state police car, and loved riding with Ed. He drove like a sane human being, unlike her husband at times.

She would change into her jeans later to help Tamryn with the house stuff, but she'd worn a slim black Ponte dress topped with a royal blue cropped jacket, and dress shoes to visit the Coast Guard Captain. Fern had a lot of respect for Bob Adams. He had a tough job, and it had been crucial that the two of them had bonded so nicely, considering her new role. Jay was the PSPD contact with the Coast Guard, but she got to know them well during the Anselmo case. Dressing conscientiously for work, especially when meeting with the always-dashing Captain in his pristine uniform, was Fern's way of showing her respect to him.

"Has Matt filled you in on the latest in Hannah's case?" Ed asked her now.

"If you mean that she might have a daughter living in Buck Bay, yes. Have you ever heard any rumors about this?"

"No, but then I only knew Hannah by reputation. It sure seems to surprise the people who knew her well, though…like Bernice. And Matt says that he's convinced Robert doesn't know anything about a daughter either. If that's true, it's a tough one for him."

"Everything about this case is tough for Robert, and Matt is taking it hard. He likes the guy," Fern said. "For some reason, he feels responsible for him. Kinda crazy."

"Not crazy in my book. The world needs more police chiefs like your hubby. More people in general. People who want to help others. I just hope to hell that Robert didn't kill Hannah."

"Is that what you think?"

"Not really. But I don't have enough evidence to attach blame to anyone yet. My gut feeling is the Bowens are involved, but this possible child of Hannah's has me all mixed up."

"Matt, too. It opens up several possibilities, none of them good. I'll be anxious to hear how it goes with George Haynes and I'm glad you're going with Matt—I'd like to hear both of your takes. I'll call my boss and fill him in on the Colombian ship, but after that I'm helping Tamryn move into her new rental house this afternoon. Call me when you are headed for home and let me know how it goes, OK?"

"Sure thing, but you'll get the scoop from Matt, I presume."

"Yes, but you're a double-check for my personal comfort level that he's not overlooking something just because it might hurt Robert further. You're not personally involved like he is," Fern said. "And don't worry, I'll tell him I wanted to hear your thoughts, too. We don't hide anything." She laughed. "Sometimes we shouldn't be quite so honest with each other. He says I have no filter."

"As long as it doesn't turn nasty, that's a good thing for a marriage. When Milly gets upset with me—which hardly ever happens since I'm so perfect—she clams up. Won't say a word to me. I'd much rather know what she's thinking."

"Well, Matt always knows exactly what I'm thinking. Whether he wants to or not."

. . .

Back in the squad room, Matt shook off the rain from his jacket, and brushed the sand off his shoes.

"Fine day for a walk, chief," Tamryn said with the trace of a smile.

"Just a little wind, wet stuff, and blowing sand. Did I mention that you have to have a thick skin to live here?"

"You may have mentioned that. Although, in an effort to lure me here, you also told me that Oregonians exaggerate how bad the weather is so that people won't move here."

"I wasn't talking about days like this one," he grinned. He moved to her desk and plopped down in her side chair. "Any luck finding a birth certificate for George and Candace Haynes' daughter?"

"No," Tamryn said. "Sylvia's been looking, too, and talked to her contact in Salem...is that the name of the state capitol?"

Matt nodded.

"Nothing so far."

"You think you won't find one, am I right?" Matt asked.

"I'm doubtful," Tamryn said. "It's too big of a coincidence with the Colorado birth. Hannah had that child and, for whatever reason, gave her to George and Candace. What I don't know is if it has anything to do with Hannah's murder."

"Ed and I are going to meet with Mr. and Mrs. Haynes this afternoon. It's gonna tell us something."

"You're nervous about this, aren't you?"

"Wouldn't you be?" Matt said. His shoulders slumped a little, unusual for him. "Put yourself in the shoes of the people involved. If Hannah is the girl's biological mother, and they've all kept this secret for over twenty years, look at the damage it could do."

"You can't look at it like that, boss," Tamryn said. "What if this secret led to Hannah's murder? That's all that matters to me. If there's collateral damage, so be it. I'm sorry if that sounds cruel."

"No, you're right. Hannah's body lying in that grave is the cruel part." He pushed himself up with the chair's armrests. "So, I'm sucking it up and putting on my tough cop hat."

"Guess what I'm doing while you're doing tough cop business?" Her eyes twinkled.

"Don't know. What are you doing?"

"Your wonderful wife is helping me move into my new home this afternoon." Tamryn dangled two keys in the air. "My landlady was just here, we signed the contract, and I'm moving in! Fern's going to show me where to shop for food and things I'll need for the house."

"That's great," Matt said. "You're in good hands."

She looked serious for a minute. "Nobody in my former squad ever reached out to help me. It means a lot. Thank you, Matt. For everything."

"I'm the lucky one," he said, and meant it. "Make sure Fern takes you to her fish monger — it's our favorite shop in town." He gave her a salute and went into his office.

. . .

Interim District Attorney Jeri Schrader and Chinook County Sheriff Earl Johnson sat in front of Circuit Judge Cynthia Hedges' desk.

"Wow, a double team on Monday morning," said Judge Hedges. "This must be important. What can I do for you?"

"We need search warrants, your honor," started Jeri. "It's in relation to the Hannah Oakley murder case. The sheriff, the local police departments, and the state police are working hard, and are making some progress."

"Good to hear," said the judge. "I'm not particularly fond of a killer out and about in my territory. I was even a little spooked last night when the wind was howling about. Downright creepy."

"Yes, it is good news," Jeri continued. "However, the progress is slower than all involved would like it to be, and it's because they're running into some dead ends with potential suspects."

"Somebody, or several somebodies, are lying to us," added Earl. "We believe our murderer is one of four or five people, and if we are allowed by you to search their vehicles, we might be able to get the evidence we need."

"Tell me about your suspects, sheriff," the judge said.

Earl laid out the case for each potential suspect, carefully giving her the facts they'd uncovered to date. "In summary," Earl said, "there is no forensic or other evidence that Hannah was killed on site at Mourning Bay. We have been over every inch of that county park and turned up nothing of interest. Therefore, we all — and it's unanimous — believe she met her killer there, got into a vehicle with that person, and was either strangled in that vehicle or transported elsewhere. Either way, if we can locate that vehicle and run forensics on it, we think we'll have our killer."

"Thank you for updating me, Earl," said Judge Hedges. She smoothed down her glossy black hair. "There's some good detective work in what you've told me, and I understand your suspicions of these key people. But you're shooting in the dark. Just going on hunches. What am I supposed to do with that?"

"Blake and Alex Bowen lied to the police," Jeri inserted. "That's more than just a hunch. Why did they lie if they aren't somehow involved?"

"Yeah, I'm not wild about lying to the police," the judge said. "There's usually a good reason for it. And Sorenson, the ex-husband, apparently hasn't told you guys everything he knows either. And you have to ask yourself, as you've done, Earl, why is that? What's he hiding?"

"He's a snake, your honor," huffed Earl. "You would meet him for five minutes and know what a lout he is."

"But what's his motivation?" Hedges asked. "I don't see what he gains from her death."

"I think he tried to reason with Hannah about ending his support, it went badly, he became furious and strangled her in a rage."

"Possible, of course. Same with the Bowens. What could possibly be their motivation?"

"We have a couple of theories on them," Jeri said. "But again, at this point, we only know for sure that they lied about Blake not being home."

Judge Hedges placed her hands palm down on her desk and leaned toward them. "OK, here's what I'm going to do. The Hayneses are off-limits for now. They either have a birth certificate for their daughter or they don't, and until you figure that out, you're not allowed to search them. Understood?" She looked from Earl to Jeri.

"Yes, your honor," they both said.

"I may deeply regret this, especially in the case of the Bowens, but I'm going to allow you to impound any vehicles on their property and do a complete forensics search. Nothing in their house—electronics, offices, etc—OK? I'll allow the same for Justin Sorenson. Are you happy now?"

Earl beamed, and Jeri smiled and said, "Thank you."

"You might not be thanking me, Jeri, if this goes tits up," said the judge, smiling back at her. "It's lousy timing for your political career if you're wrong here and the Bowens sue us all. Him," she pointed her finger at Earl, "he's sheriff for life in this county and he can afford to be wrong. But you can't. If I may be direct—because I like you and want you to be elected—you're a woman and a lesbian. Voters don't know much about you. You need to get this case right."

Jeri's smile disappeared.

CHAPTER 26

By design, Ed and Matt pulled up in front of the Hayneses' home in Ed's state police car. They didn't have the lights flashing, but they might as well have for the impact the car had on the quiet neighborhood. If the neighbors wondered what was going on, they were even more alarmed when Ed unfolded his big body in full state police uniform out of the car and approached their front door. Matt was wearing his uniform as well, and the two cops were intimidating in their full cop presence.

A woman answered the doorbell.

"Mrs. Haynes?" Matt asked.

"Yes, I'm Candace Haynes. Are you Chief Horning?" She looked warily at each of them. Dressed in black jeans and an ivory sweater over a black tee shirt, she looked like a practical woman. Tall, almost Matt's height, with thick blond, no-nonsense hair cut short, and sharp blue eyes. Early fifties, Matt guessed.

"Yes, I talked to your husband this morning. This is Lieutenant Ed Sonders, he's with the Oregon State Police. We have just a couple of questions for you. May we come in?"

Wordlessly, she opened the door. Matt could see George coming up behind her. He introduced Ed to him. Jay had told Matt where the photo of the daughter was, and he was on the lookout for it as they progressed down the hall to the living room.

He paused and took a good look at her when they came to it. Matt shivered. It was like looking into Hannah's grave all over again. "Is this your daughter?" Matt asked Candace, walking beside him, in a friendly tone. "What's her name?"

"Yes, that's our Annie," said Candace rather tonelessly.

They took seats in the living room, the coffee table in between them.

"What is it, Chief?" asked George. "Why are you here? We answered all of your detectives' questions yesterday."

Matt leaned forward, placing his elbows on his knees. As he did so, his gun belt and holster made a creaking noise, and both of the Hayneses shifted on the sofa and took a quick glance at his gun.

"I'll be honest with you, Mr. Haynes. Detectives Finley and Gesicki weren't convinced you were telling us the truth. And when Lt. Sonders and I are working a homicide case, we have to make sure we're getting the full story from people we interrogate. People like you who may have a stake in the case."

"We don't have anything to do with Hannah's death," objected Candace. "We don't know anything that could possibly help the police. She was George's sister, that's all we can offer you."

It was clear to Matt that she was trying to be helpful, but she was unable to keep a steeliness out of her voice. He said, "Sometimes in our business, the truth leads to new avenues, new clues. It may not seem important to you, but it can often be helpful in solving the case. That's why Lt. Sonders and I are here again today. We have two questions for you, and we need you to tell us the truth." He nodded at Ed.

"Question one," said Ed. "Is your daughter Annie really Hannah's child? And that is a yes or no question."

Silence for a moment or two, and then George spoke. "How could that possibly make any difference in solving Hannah's murder?" His eyes teared up, and he quickly looked away from Ed.

"Yes or no, Mr. Haynes," Ed repeated, his voice deep and steady. "Did Hannah give birth to Annie?"

But it was Candace who answered. "Yes," she said quietly, and twisted a bracelet around her wrist.

"Do you have a copy of Annie's birth certificate?" asked Matt.

"We do," answered George in a choked voice. "We keep it in a safe deposit box at the bank. No one but Hannah, my wife, and I have ever seen it."

"Does Annie know the truth?" Matt asked.

"She does not," Candace said. "Although, now that she's older, she may have guessed. As you have no doubt noticed, there is a startling resemblance between the two of them. But she's never raised the issue with us, and didn't with Hannah either, as far as we know."

"Why the deception?" Ed asked. "How did this happen?"

George and Candace looked into each other's eyes, and she nodded at him. "We were unable to have children after we were married," George said. "We were planning to adopt because we really wanted kids. Then, at the end of Hannah's junior year at university in Colorado, she got pregnant at a fraternity party. She came home and told our parents, and they were horrified. She was so close to her degree, and they wanted it badly for her. Hannah was the first person in our family to go to college, and it was important for all of us. That's when Candace and I stepped in."

"You convinced Hannah to let you raise her child?" Matt asked.

"Yes. She was opposed to having an abortion, even though the circumstances probably warranted it. The boy wanted nothing to do with Hannah and behaved abominably. But she also wasn't ready to deal with a baby. She desperately wanted to finish college and have a career. She was barely twenty-one years old, just starting out. So, Candace and I offered to take the baby at birth and raise her as our own. That's what we did."

"Who knew about this arrangement?" Ed asked.

"Mom and dad, Candace and I, and Hannah, of course. That's all, just the five of us. Nobody else knew, and it actually worked out quite well. Hannah could see Annie whenever she wanted and watched her grow up. We all lived in the same town, and they were close as aunt and niece."

"Do you think there's a chance that Hannah told Justin Sorenson, her first husband, about Annie?" Matt asked.

Their heads whipped around, both looking astonished. "No!" shouted Candace. "Hannah would never have told a soul; that was our deal. Why did you ask that question?"

"I'm afraid I can't really say," Matt said. "Just that one of our theories is that someone was blackmailing Hannah. It may have backfired and led to her death."

"She never would have told Justin," said George. "I don't believe it."

"Hannah was seduced by Justin, and she was crazy about him in the beginning," allowed Candace. "Who knows what went on between them?" She put her hand on her husband's knee. "I think we need to consider that she might have confided in him."

George shook his head violently. "No, I will never believe that Hannah betrayed us. You won't tell Annie, will you?" he pleaded.

Matt didn't answer. Instead, he asked, "Are you sure Annie never found out? Is there a chance she did discover the truth?"

"No, I don't think so," Candace said. "She would have confronted us. She's a very strong young woman, secure in who she is. George and I have an honest, loving relationship with her."

"Would she have confronted Hannah? Maybe angry and upset because you've all lied to her all these years?" Matt asked. "Is that possible?"

George got a terrified look on his face as he realized where Matt was going with this question.

. . .

Tamryn unlocked the door of her new home. She wasn't the type, but she felt like squealing with delight as the key turned and she stepped inside. Inside to freedom. Inside to safety. Her own home.

Fern was right behind her, pulling a wheely suitcase. She paused inside the front door, looking around and remembering the last and only time she'd been in this house—the day after Clay Sherwin's body had been found. No matter how much time had passed, she still felt a pang in her stomach when she thought of Clay. Fern hoped that this house wouldn't be bad juju for Tamryn.

Tamryn set her backpack down on the dining room table and opened her arms wide. "This is so great," she said.

Fern shook off her misgivings and grinned. "It is the perfect house for you. Where do you want this suitcase?"

Tamryn took off down the hall toward the primary bedroom on the ocean side. Waving, "C'mon, in here." Fern followed her to the small walk-in closet and deposited the suitcase on the lone luggage rack. She recalled going through Clay's suitcase, realizing at the time that he would never wear the clothes again.

"We need to take inventory and make a list of what you need," Fern said, ever the project manager. "You should decide what you want for at least until next weekend, and we can pick up those items. I'll take you to any of the stores you need."

"I plan to stock up today," Tamryn said. "There will be no weekends off for us until we find Hannah's killer. So, we'll cram as much in your VW as we can, OK?"

She moved to the bedside nightstand and tried the light. It was a three-way bulb and came on perfectly. "Good," she said. "Reading light all set. This is an important one for me, and I always check it in hotels first thing. This and the coffee pot. Let's go check out the kitchen and make sure it works!"

"You do that while I check your bathroom and make sure you have a starter supply of soap and towels," Fern said, but Tamryn was already jogging down the hallway.

After a quick look around, the two women decided the house was well-equipped. The owner had even left a bottle of Oregon wine, some Port Stirling cheese from the local creamery, and a packet of chocolate-covered hazelnuts with a welcome note. "That's very sweet of her," Tamryn said.

She sat at the dining room table and made a quick shopping list. "I'll need a supermarket, preferably with a good takeout deli, a liquor store, and a hardware store. Oh, and Matt said you should show me your fish shop," she smiled. "Where do you buy your coffee? I like to grind my own beans, although it's not crucial for now. I can pick up some ground at the supermarket."

Fern shook her head. "No, that's not acceptable. I will take you to my specialty coffee shop. You're in Oregon now—we grind our beans fresh."

"I guess I am in Oregon now," Tamryn said somewhat wistfully. "I hope I can stay…" Her sentence trailed off.

"Do you want to talk about your husband?" Fern said gingerly.

"You mean, my soon to be ex-husband?" Tamryn said with a wry smile. "Honestly, there's not much to tell. He's a horse's ass who couldn't deal with my professional success. One night, his frustration escalated, and he hit me a couple of times, causing me to tumble down about four stairs in our apartment."

"That's awful."

"It was the shock that he would actually do it that was most disturbing to me. He was never the sweetest guy, but he had his moments. He also had a temper, but I thought I knew my way around that. The suddenness and the violence took my breath away."

"What did you do?"

"He slammed out of the apartment, and I called 911, crawled to the front door to let them in, and they took me to the hospital. I never saw or talked to him again. A friend packed up my belongings for me two days later when he was at work and took them to my parents, and my lawyer handled it the rest of the way. Case closed."

"That is a truly terrible story, Tamryn. I'm so glad you're here." Fern embraced her and the two held the hug.

"So, you see why I so desperately want this job to work," Tamryn said. "And why I'm so grateful to Matt for giving me a chance at a fresh start."

"It will work for you. We'll make it work!"

"Not sure I'm off to a great start with my colleagues."

"They'll come around," Fern said. "They didn't all take to me at first either. I had to bust through the old-boy network, and you will, too, once they can see that you're a cop's cop. Plus, you've got Matt on your side, and he has a whole lot of street cred around the county, even the state, for that matter. His leadership in solving some recent ugly cases in the area turned him into an overnight sensation. Matt is a rock star in Chinook County, and his words carry a lot of weight. You'll be fine."

"Hope so. I really want to contribute to finding Hannah's killer," Tamryn said.

"You've already helped. Finding the birth record in Colorado might have been the big breakthrough. Just don't try too hard," Fern advised. "Work with the team, let it come to you."

Tamryn nodded. "Good advice. I tried it with Jay, including him on the first interrogation of George Haynes, and it seemed to work. He was friendly and responsive. He's a good cop, isn't he?"

"He is. And he's an even better human being. Jay sees things that none of the rest of us do — he's done it on every case we've had. Like noticing that photo of Annie Haynes on the wall; I probably would have walked right by it."

"I did! And I'm a terrific detective."

"That's Jay. He has a nose for the little details. That's why he and my husband are a great team. Matt sees the big picture and is an expert on human behavior, while Jay comes along and nails the details. Remind me to tell you about him and bloody shoes in the county dump. But now, let's take your list and get shopping."

• • •

Annie Haynes drove into her parking spot in the family garage. She'd told her supervisor, the Director of Parks for the city of Buck Bay, that she was going to run home for a quick late lunch. A childhood friend who lives across the street from the Hayneses texted her that there was a state police car and two cops at her house, and Annie decided to run home and find out what was going on.

She came in through the kitchen door, heard voices in the living room, and made her way there.

"Hi, I'm Annie," she said entering the room. "What's going on?" she asked her dad but was looking at the cops.

Matt and Ed stood to greet her, Matt extending his hand as he walked toward her. The young woman was dressed in denim coveralls over a black ripped tee shirt, her brown hair spiked high. But the most conspicuous thing about her was the pierced rings in her nose, lip, and eyebrows. That and the black, goth-like eyeshadow.

"It's nice to meet you, Annie," Matt said. "I'm Chief Horning with the Port Stirling police, and this is Lt. Ed Sonders with the state police. We're talking to your parents about the murder of your aunt, Hannah. I'm so sorry for your loss."

Annie shook his hand firmly and said, "Yeah, thanks. It's been hard. She was a neat person and I already miss her a lot."

"We thought you were working on the west side today," said Candace. "What are you doing here?"

"Yeah, we finished that job about noon, and I decided to come home to grab some lunch. June texted and said there was a cop car here, so I wanted to check on you guys, too."

"We're fine, dear," said George. "Just trying to help the police solve Aunt Hannah's death."

"Do you know who did it?" Annie asked.

"Not yet," Matt said. "But we're exploring a few leads. We'll get them. Do you have any thoughts on who might have done this? We understand that you and your aunt were close. Anyone you know have a grudge against her?"

Annie tugged on a dangling earring and looked thoughtful. "Not really. Almost everyone liked her. Maybe Justin Sorenson. They were married before she met Uncle Robert, and she didn't like him anymore."

"Do you know why that was?"

"She told me he was a parasite and not to fall for anyone like him." Annie smiled.

"Great advice," Ed said. "I'm sorry if this is painful but we're asking everyone, Annie: When is the last time you saw your aunt?"

"I had breakfast with her the day she disappeared."

"Tell them why," her mother interrupted.

"Aunt Hannah and I both worked downtown, and it was our routine to go in early together once a week, eat breakfast and catch up. We went to different places all the time and she always paid. It was fun." She blinked fast a few times.

"How was her mood that Wednesday morning?" Matt asked.

"Fine, I guess. She might have been a little jumpy," Annie said. "Told me she hadn't slept that great."

"Did she say why that was?"

"No. But it was unusual. Both Aunt Hannah and I are great sleepers. It's one of many things we have — had — in common." Annie looked at her parents.

CHAPTER 27

As instructed by his boss, Jay paid another visit to the Bowen house Monday afternoon. The occupants were not happy to see him.

"You can come in, Detective Finley," Alex said through the gate intercom, "but you can only stay fifteen minutes. Blake and I are headed out."

"I won't take long," Jay replied into the speaker as the gate swung open. *I hate this gate*, he thought. *Who is so important they need to keep people out? And why is it always raining when I'm here?* He shook the raindrops off his arm that had reached out to the buzzer.

They settled in the great room in front of the huge fireplace where a healthy fire was burning away.

"Chilly out today, isn't it?" said Alex. "We're ready for real spring."

"I hear you," Jay said. Friendly like. "So, we're working on alibis today for the day that Hannah was murdered, and we could use some verification for yours. You told us you were here, working all day."

"That's correct. Blake was in Mexico, it was a quiet week at my office in Eugene, and I was here catching up on paperwork."

"What kind of paperwork exactly?"

"I was writing performance reviews for my staff," Alex explained. "They were due in January, and I was behind. People were starting to grumble." He smiled.

"Yes, we staff want to know how we're doing, and especially how much of a raise we're getting this year. Something like that, right?" Jay asked.

"You got it."

"Did you see anyone at all that day who can confirm you were at home? Mailman, delivery person, friend? Anyone?"

"Like I said, it was quiet," Alex said. "Oh, wait. It was a Wednesday, wasn't it? Rosa was here!" He jumped up and moved quickly toward the kitchen. "Rosa, can you come here for a minute?"

A young Hispanic woman, about thirty, came out of the kitchen, wiping her hands on an apron. She had beautiful skin she obviously kept out of the sun and flashing black eyes.

"Yes, Mr. Bowen?" she said.

"This is Detective Finley. Can you please tell him if you were here three weeks ago on Wednesday? It was the week Blake was in Mexico, and I was home alone, remember?"

She looked nervous but spoke in a clear voice. "I'm here every Monday and Wednesday. Mondays I clean, Wednesdays I cook."

"Do you specifically remember that day?" Jay asked her. "Was Mr. Bowen here alone all day?"

"Yes. Yes. Here all day," she said.

"You are sure?" Jay asked again.

"You heard her, Finley," Alex barked. "Please don't harass my cleaner."

Jay ignored him. "What was Mr. Bowen doing while you were here?"

"I don't know," she said. "Business. His work. That's all I know."

"Did he leave at any time and then come back home?"

"No. Mr. Bowen here all day."

"What time did you leave this house?"

She looked down at her hands for a minute, and then said, "5:00 p.m, I think. Sometime around then. It was late."

"Did he ask you to say that?" Jay asked. Doubling down.

"I don't know what you mean?" Rosa said.

"Did Mr. or Mrs. Bowen tell you to say that he was home all day on that Wednesday if the police asked you?"

She wiped her hands on her apron and looked Jay in the eye. "No," she said. "I tell truth."

"That's enough, Jay," said Blake Bowen, coming into the room. She was dressed to go out and had her coat on. "Thank you, Rosa." She turned to her and smiled. "You can get back to work now. The policeman is finished."

Rosa turned and went back to the kitchen.

"You are finished," Blake said firmly. "Alex and I have to leave now, so that means you have to leave now."

"I'm going," Jay said politely. "Thank you for your time, and please thank Rosa for talking with me."

Jay headed for his car and saw them watching him from their window. He waved and got in his car. But he didn't completely leave. He drove out of their driveway, yes, and headed for the highway. But he took a fork in the road that veered off to the right once he was out of sight of their house. He turned around quickly and parked facing the road in some reeds that concealed his car. And he waited.

• • •

"What'd you make of Annie?" Matt asked Ed as they left the Haynes residence.

"I think she's a scary person and she killed her mother."

"Really?"

"Probably not," Ed said. "But I'm not ruling her out. She knows the truth, she confronted Hannah, became enraged, and the next stop was Hedgehog Mountain forest."

"It's not an impossible theory. We should bring her in for questioning, shouldn't we?"

Ed raised an eyebrow. "You know we should. Why are you hesitating?"

"Because if she didn't have anything to do with Hannah's murder, and she doesn't know the truth about their relationship, it could ruin her life," Matt said. "I hate that thought."

"And if she did kill her mother and dump her in the wilds of Oregon, she should get away with it? C'mon, that's not the Matt Horning I know."

Matt looked resigned. "George seemed beside himself," he said. "Very antsy and emotional. What about him?"

"My take on George is that he is a loving father who is scared to death of losing his daughter-slash-niece. Who has just lost his sister. He has every right to be a little looney."

"I take that to mean that you don't believe he killed Hannah?"

"I don't. No."

"What if Hannah told him she was going to tell Annie the truth?"

"Doesn't change my mind. George Haynes isn't a killer. Neither is Candace. They are two milquetoast Oregonians who have always tried to do the right thing in their lives."

"You got all that in the short time we spent with them?"

"I've lived here all my life," Ed said. "I know who the good guys are, and I know who the bad guys are within five minutes of meeting them."

"Are you ever wrong?"

"All the time," Ed said.

• • •

Blake and Alex Bowen drove out of their driveway about ten minutes after Jay. He saw the front end of their black SUV coming around the corner, and quickly ducked down further into his seat. He waited another five minutes to make sure they didn't return, and then drove himself back to the house.

Rosa's car was still in the parking area up ahead of him. Jay doubted that she would open the gate when the Bowens weren't home, so he brazenly left his car in front of the gate and climbed over it.

He rang the doorbell at the top of the stairs and waited. No answer. He walked around to the front of the house where the huge windows looked out to the ocean. Rosa was dusting a table just on the other side of the window, headphones on, and she almost jumped out of her skin when she saw Jay. He grinned and waved to show her he was harmless and pointed at the door handle.

She opened the door—it wasn't locked—and reached up to turn off her headphones.

"I'm sorry if I scared you," Jay said quickly. "I want to ask you another question."

"You left?" Rosa looked puzzled. "Mr. and Mrs. are gone."

"I came back to see you. I need you to come downtown to the police station so we can talk to you in private. Without Mr. and Mrs. Bowen. Can you do that for me?"

Rosa frowned, but said, "OK, when I finish here."

"Sure. What time?"

She looked at her watch. "One o'clock."

Now it was Jay's turn to puzzle. "I thought you said you worked all day."

A flush started on her neck and moved upward. "No, I work here until twelve o'clock."

So, she lied in front of Alex. Interesting, thought Jay. He handed her his card. "Come to the police department in Buck Bay city hall and ask for me. I'll be there waiting for you."

She nodded. "OK."

• • •

As Ed drove his state police car, Matt answered his buzzing phone. Patty Perkins.

"Hi, Patty. What's up?"

"I'm about to make you a happy man."

"It's about time somebody did," he joked.

"Jeri and Earl were able to convince Judge Hedges to let us search both the Bowens' vehicles and Justin Sorenson's car."

"Hot dog!"

"We don't have the physical warrants yet, but Earl said to tell you we should be in possession of them by 4:00 p.m. How do you want to play it?" Patty asked.

"I can't believe Cynthia is allowing this, but it's awesome," Matt said. "I'm with Ed in his car right now. Let me talk it over with him, and I'll call you right back. What did the judge say?"

"Basically, she doesn't like people who lie to the cops in a homicide investigation. Or, in Sorenson's case, refuse to tell everything they know."

"I couldn't agree more with her," Matt said. "Does the fact that you're calling me with this news mean that Earl still isn't talking to me?"

"I have no idea," she said, "but he had to go to court, so it's probably that. Did you two kids have a fight?"

"He got mad at me, mom, and hung up his phone on me."

Ed laughed so loudly in the background, Patty could hear him.

"I'm sure he's over it by now," she said. "When I left him he was grinning from ear to ear. Just play nice and you'll be fine."

"Thanks, Patty. Talk soon."

"Earl really needs to eat a burger and fries," cracked Ed. "He lost weight when you got shot, and he's been cranky ever since. I think he's just hungry."

Matt didn't laugh. He knew his relationship with the sheriff had taken a hit the minute he decided to look into Robert's claim about Hannah's disappearance. And Matt hadn't made it any better, implying that Earl was dragging his heels on their case. He would have to fix things with his old friend because it was making a hole in Matt's heart.

"Judge Hedges is letting us search the Bowens' and Justin Sorenson's cars—full forensics. What do you think?" Matt asked.

"Call Bernice right now and check her team's availability," Ed instructed. "As soon as we know that, let's see how many men and women in blue we can round up on short notice."

"I want to go in tonight," Matt said.

"Agreed. Time is of the essence…before Cynthia comes to her senses and changes her mind about the warrants."

Matt hit Bernice's cell phone number, and said to Ed, "Do you think it's a bad sign that the medical examiner for Chinook County is the third number on my call list?"

"It's not good," Ed said.

"Bernice, we need your help," Matt said.

"At your service," she said. "What do you have?"

Matt explained about Judge Hedges' search warrants and Bernice cheered.

"You tell me where and when, and I'll have my full team there," she said. "Let's start with the Bowens' place. My friend Patty doesn't like or trust either one of them, and that's good enough for me."

"We have a surplus of suspects all of a sudden," Matt told her. "It would be great if we could eliminate a couple and narrow it down, so this is a very helpful move by Judge Hedges."

"Who else is on your list?" Bernice asked. "Not Robert, I hope."

"Robert hasn't been officially crossed off our list, but I'm not pursuing him at the moment. The additions are the George Haynes family—and this is highly confidential at this point. George and Candace Haynes just admitted to Ed and me that their daughter Annie is really Hannah's child. Hannah had the baby in Colorado, and George and Candace took her home with them, and kept it a secret. We met Annie, and I'll fill you in later. Thank you, Bernice. We never would have learned this without your sharp eye. And Jay's."

"What did Jay do?" she asked.

"He spotted a photo of Annie when he was in George's home. She is the spitting image of Hannah. You won't believe it when you meet her."

"Wow. You think she was involved?"

"Don't know yet, and that's all I can say for now," Matt told her. "Can you have your team ready to go at the Bowens' property by 4:00 p.m? Ed, Patty, and I can get our teams together by then, I think. And I'm sure Earl is on it, too, and will take Justin Sorenson's search. I'll coordinate with him. The Bowens' house is probably about fifteen minutes from your hospital."

"Yes, I know where they live, and I'll be there with my guys at 4 o'clock. We'll wait at the gate until you coppers arrive."

"Plan for a long night, Bernice."

. . .

Jay was waiting in the lobby of Buck Bay city hall when Rosa Hernandez arrived at 1:10 p.m. There was a young, good-looking man with her, about the same age.

"This is my husband, Daniel," Rosa said as Jay approached them. She pronounced it dan-YELL. He smiled shyly at Jay and held out his hand to shake. Jay took it and said, "Thanks for coming in. Please follow me. We'll go to a private room down this hall."

Jay had asked Chief McCoy to join him, and he was waiting in the room. Introductions were made, and the four took seats around the table.

Jay told McCoy that Rosa was here voluntarily, and then asked her if it was OK if he taped their conversation. If not, he would take notes. Rosa said, "Taping OK," and Daniel nodded his agreement.

"Thank you," Jay said and looked down at his notebook. "For the record, you are a part-time housekeeper and cook for Blake and Alex Bowen. Is that correct?"

"Yes."

"What time did you leave the Bowen house on Wednesday, January 25?"

"About noon," said Rosa in a clear voice. "I always finish cooking for them at noon." Jay saw Daniel give her hand a comforting squeeze.

"Was Alex Bowen home while you were working?"

"Yes. In his office."

"Did he leave the house at any time while you were there?"

"No, I don't think so. He was busy at his desk, and I saw him go into the kitchen to make coffee."

"Was Blake Bowen at home?"

"No. In Mexico. That's what Mr. Bowen told me," Rosa said.

"And you did not see her that day?"

"No."

"Why did you tell me earlier today that you were at the Bowen house until around 5:00 p.m?" Jay asked softly.

She opened her mouth to speak, closed it, and swallowed before trying again.

"Take your time, Rosa," Jay said. "This might be important, and we want you to be sure of your answer."

"Mrs. Bowen told me that if the police ever talked to me that I should tell you that Mr. Bowen was home all day. That I was with him until evening. And that she wasn't there."

"She wasn't home, right?" Jay wanted to be clear on that point.

"True. In Mexico, like I said. That part the truth."

"But the truth is that you don't know if Mr. Bowen was home that afternoon or not, because you weren't there," Jay said. "Is that correct?"

"Si. Yes."

Jay looked at Dan McCoy, who nodded.

Jay stood up. "Thank you for coming. We really appreciate it, Rosa. Please don't leave town for a few days until we figure all this out, OK?"

"Yes. We are here," she said.

"Daniel, take your wife out to dinner tonight," Jay smiled. "She's had a difficult day, but she's very brave."

Daniel put his arm protectively around Rosa's shoulders. He said, "I know. She is brave. And I will do as you suggest."

Both Hernandezes were smiling as they left the room.

Dan McCoy, who had been silent during the interview, now said, "There are only two reasons why Blake Bowen would tell their housekeeper to lie to us. Alex Bowen killed Hannah that afternoon, or he really was home alone and didn't want to be a suspect because he couldn't prove it."

"Wonder which one it was?" Jay said.

CHAPTER 28

By 3:00 p.m. Matt had assembled his department, including Tamryn whom he'd reached while she and Fern were unpacking her groceries. They had headed to city hall immediately, Fern dropping off Tamryn and then reluctantly heading for home.

Patty had called and informed Matt that she and Earl had the warrants, and she was heading straight to Buck Bay. She told him that Earl had five of his sheriff department's deputies ready to go, and they would handle Sorenson's search as soon as Bernice finished up at the Bowens'.

"Does Earl know where Sorenson and his car will be?" Matt asked her.

"Yes, they think so. Earl checked with The Growler, and Justin is working the evening/closing shift tonight, so he should be at work," Patty said. "They're going there first. He said to tell you that he would call you when they found him in case you wanted to join them. Also, that he wouldn't hang up on you."

Matt snickered. "That's good to know. I think I will go with Earl."

"Let him run the show, Matt. He needs it. And if Justin Sorenson is our killer, Earl will nail him to the wall," Patty said.

"I hear you. I will watch and learn from the master."

"That's the spirit. I'll wait for your crew at the fork in the road about one-quarter mile before the Bowens' gate. You can hand them the warrant, while Jay, Ed, and I cover you."

"I don't expect them to be violent," Matt said. "There will be a great deal of pissing and hissing, a real show no doubt."

Patty laughed. "I hope so; it'll be fun. But if one of them is the killer, they might feel like they don't have anything to lose. I'm not eager to see you get shot again, Chief."

"Yeah, I'd like to avoid that, too. And with you three sharpshooters along, I'll be fine."

"Believe it," she said. "See you soon."

Matt went out to the squad room where Jay, Tamryn, Walt, Rudy, and Sylvia were gathered. He filled them in on he and Ed meeting Annie, and the confession from George and Candace.

"Thank you to Tamryn and Jay for excellent police work, and getting us to this point," Matt said.

"What's the daughter look like in person?" Tamryn asked.

"How do I say this?" Matt asked rhetorically. "If Hannah were twenty years younger and had piercings all over her face and a goth look going, they would be identical twins. Same hair, same build, same bone structure. Annie is about six inches shorter than George, and about seven shorter than Candace."

"So, in other words, the same height as Hannah?" Jay asked.

"Correct. Genes are a powerful thing."

"We knew she had to be Hannah's child, didn't we, Tamryn?" Jay said. "It was all too coincidental—the timing, the same surname, the looks."

"Yeah, it all fit," Tamryn agreed. "Do you think Annie knows the truth?" she asked Matt.

"I think there's a good possibility that she does," Matt answered. "She made mention of the things she and Hannah had in common, and she strikes me as being an intelligent young woman. I believe she's probably put it all together."

"But the question remains," Sylvia said from her desk, "does it matter in this case? Could Annie, George, or Candace really have killed Hannah?"

"Ed believes Annie could have and he has a theory. I haven't ruled out her parents. Keeping a secret like they were could be a potent motive for murder. So, we'll get through tonight and see what we learn, and then focus on all three Hayneses' alibis for the day Hannah disappeared."

. . .

Patty was already in the agreed-upon location when the Port Stirling PD arrived. Bernice and her team drove up about five minutes later. It was straight up 4:00 p.m.

As Jay had probably already noted, it was raining when they arrived. It had turned colder, too, not the bitter cold of last month, but enough to get your attention. The frequent showers now were morphing into a squall and included occasional bursts of hail.

As there was now no reason for subtlety, Ed drove his state police car up the Bowens' driveway with lights flashing. Riding with him were Matt, Jay, and Patty. Walt, Rudy, and Tamryn followed in the Port Stirling squad car, with Bernice and her crew in the forensics van right behind them.

"If they are going to sue us," Ed noted, "they will sue us no matter how we do this. Might as well have some fun." He pressed the gate's intercom buzzer, and Blake Bowen said, "Yes? Who is it?"

"This is Lieutenant Edward Sonders of the Oregon State Police, and we have a warrant to search your property. Please open the gate now."

"You've got to be kidding me," Blake replied. "This is outrageous. Who do you think you are?"

"Hissing and pissing," Patty whispered to Matt in the back seat.

"I just told you, ma'am. I'm Lieutenant Edward Sond…"

"I know who you are, asshole." The gate slowly creaked open.

Alex Bowen came flying out of the sliding glass doors onto his deck that overlooked the driveway. As the four cops in the first car got out, Alex shook his head in disbelief and laughed. He shouted down at them, "What do you hope to achieve with this farce?"

Matt took the stairs to the deck, with his three colleagues close behind, hands on the butt of their pistols.

"We're sorry for this intrusion, Alex," Matt said. "We aren't coming into your house and won't bother you and Blake." He held out the warrant and Alex took it to read.

"Circuit Judge Cynthia Hedges has authorized us to do a forensics search of your vehicles in the matter of the homicide of Hannah Oakley," Matt continued while Alex read. "If it's any consolation, yours is not the only search being conducted today."

Alex, holding the document with slightly shaking hands, looked up at Matt. "So, cars only?"

"Yes."

Blake came out on the deck and stood beside her husband.

"Please unlock your garage if it's locked and then go back inside your house," Matt instructed. "We will advise you when we're finished."

"What do you expect to find, Chief?" Alex asked, trying to sound polite and cooperative.

"We believe that Hannah Oakley was transported from Mourning Bay, where her car was discovered, to the place of her murder," Matt explained. "She may have been killed inside a vehicle."

Blake Bowen roared with laughter. "And you think you'll find her blood or whatever inside one of our cars? How stupid are you? Whoever killed Han has already cleaned their car. This is a waste of time. Get out of here!" She violently waved her arm dangerously close to Matt's face.

Detective Patty Perkins stepped around Matt, holding her gun pointed directly at Blake. "Chief Horning has presented our warrant and instructed you to open your garage. You need to shut the fuck up and do as he says. Now."

Alex put his hand on his wife's arm. "It's OK, honey. Let's make this easy, please." Blake glared at Patty, whipped around, her royal blue caftan flying, and went back inside the house.

"I'm sorry, Matt," Alex said. "It's just the shock of this. The garage is unlocked, and you'll find our two cars. Mine is the black SUV, and Blake's is the turquoise T-bird convertible. There's also a riding lawn mower in there, but I don't suppose that will interest you."

Matt put his hand on Alex's shoulder and said, "Thanks for your understanding. We'll be as quick as possible."

Matt, Ed, and Jay headed back down the stairs. Patty lingered on the deck. "I'll just hang out here for a while," she said to her colleagues, her gun still in her hand.

"Do you want company?" Jay asked.

"Only if he's a handsome young detective," Patty said.

To Matt and Ed, Jay said, "That's me then, I guess." Jay went back up the stairs and took his place beside Patty.

• • •

Bernice and her team of three technicians, looking like aliens from another planet in their white jumpsuits, goggles, hairnets, and booties, surrounded the two vehicles parked side by side in the Bowens' garage.

"Damn," Bernice said to Matt, "I can't believe Blake Bowen owns the car of my dreams." She stood next to the antique turquoise Thunderbird.

"I never pictured you as the antique car type," Matt said. "You're more the latest BMW sports car with all the gadgets." Which was precisely the car Bernice drove.

"Well, yes, but this would be my 'Sunday drive when the sun is out' car. Isn't it cool?"

"Yes," Matt agreed, "but only if it doesn't have Hannah Oakley fragments in it. I assume you're taking this one?"

Bernice turned to one of her assistants. "Jake, you're with me on this beauty." To Matt she said, "Of course. I'll want to make sure my boys aren't too rough with her."

• • •

It took Bernice and her team just shy of three hours to complete their work on the two cars. Matt, Ed, Tamryn, Walt, and Rudy guarded the outside of the garage so the forensics work could proceed uninterrupted, while Patty and Jay made themselves comfortable on the Bowens' deck.

When sunset approached, ragged patches of blue were visible in the sky overhead as a stiff wind blew off the Pacific Ocean and caused the clouds to scurry along. The rain had stopped — for the moment, at least — and the respite was welcome. The view from the Bowens' property was amazing, and the cops silently enjoyed the scenery while they waited for Bernice to come out.

Darkness fell, and the rising moon over the sea produced a silvery, shimmery moonlight.

"Wow," said Bernice, coming out of the garage and looking out to the ocean, "what a spectacular night."

"What did you find?" asked an impatient Matt.

"Nothing obvious, I'm afraid," she said. "But we'll run our tests and see what we come up with. The vehicles were both pretty clean."

"As in recently washed, vacuumed, etc.?"

"Maybe," Bernice said. "Like I said, our tests will tell us." She stopped talking and stood looking at Matt. He got the picture.

"OK, are you going to The Growler now? Want me to call Earl?"

"We're going through a drive-up to get burgers first. My guys are starving. But, yes, tell Earl we're on the way and will park around the corner, on the north end of the building."

"Do you have room in your van for results from both tests?" Matt asked.

"Yes. We stored the Bowens' tests on one side, and we'll put the Sorenson tests on the other side. We won't mix them up, Matt. Please let me do my job."

Matt grinned his sheepish grin. "Sorry. I'm obnoxious, aren't I? This case is bothering me, and I'm letting it, for some reason."

"It's because you saw Hannah buried in a shallow grave in the forest. It's getting to me, too, and I wish I'd never seen her lying there. It's a creepy image, and I'm not sure I'll ever get it out of my head."

"But you and I have seen all sorts of harrowing things that people do to each other. Why is this one so tough for us?"

"Partly it's because she was such a good person who didn't deserve that ending," Bernice said thoughtfully. "But I think it also has something to do with the location. Our beloved Oregon forests are like cathedrals to us. They are sacred and beautiful places we go to commune with nature and shed the stresses of our daily lives. They aren't supposed to be the scene of this kind of violence. I think I'm more offended than anything."

CHAPTER 29

The story was the same from the forensics team after they'd finished with Justin Sorenson's vehicle, an older model Jeep. No visible signs of Hannah, but there was more to sift through here — lots more hairs, dirt, and stains in his car than in the Bowens'.

Sorenson had not been thrilled when the sheriff presented him with the search warrant either.

"I don't know how many times I can tell you morons that I didn't have anything to do with Hannah's disappearance," Justin said.

"Actually, it's Hannah's murder not disappearance," Earl told him. "A fine distinction, but let's be clear."

"Can I object and refuse to allow you to do this?" Justin asked in all seriousness.

"Sure," replied Earl.

"What happens then?"

"I haul your ass off to the county jail where you can sit and rot indefinitely."

Sorenson considered this option, as Earl folded his arms across his prodigious belly and waited patiently.

Sorenson reached into his pocket, pulled out his car key, and handed it to the sheriff. Then he went back to work.

"I really wish Justin would stop calling us morons," Matt said, slapping Earl on the back.

"I like it. It makes me feel like I'm doing my job when a scumbag like Sorenson thinks I'm dumb," Earl said. "That's when I know how brilliant I truly am."

Matt laughed and waved at Bernice to approach the Jeep. "We're going to solve this flippin case, Earl."

"No doubt about it. I'm sorry I hung up on you yesterday. Just frustration," the sheriff said.

"I'm the one who's sorry," Matt said. "My tone was disrespectful. I'm deeply bothered by this case, and I took it out on you. Please accept my apology…because I really mean it, Earl."

"We're square, Matt. I felt like shit all night because of how I acted."

"I was upset, too. You and I have been through too much together to have any bad blood between us."

"Agreed. We're cut from the same cloth, you and me. I hope you didn't tell Fern what I did. I don't want her to think bad of me, too."

"I've barely seen my wife in the past 48 hours, and when I did I was too tired to talk much. So, your secret is safe between us."

"Why don't you go home now and see her?" Earl suggested. "Bernice doesn't need any of us. My deputies and I will stay to keep an eye on Sorenson, but you don't need to be here."

"I would like to catch up with Fern. Sure you don't mind if I skedaddle?"

"Go."

. . .

Matt drove into his garage at 7:30 p.m. after stopping at Port Stirling's lone Chinese restaurant to get takeout. He'd over-ordered, buying Fern's favorite three dishes and two of his. The BBQ Pork Chow Don and Spicy Eggplant smelled dang good in his car. *Probably because I haven't eaten for eight hours.*

"Your delivery service is here," he said, coming in from the garage. "Is the lady of the house at home?"

Fern came flying down the central staircase. "I thought you wouldn't be home until late tonight."

"I oversaw the Bowens' search, and met Earl at Justin Sorenson's, but he told me to go home, so here I am." He set the food down on the kitchen counter and gave his wife a hug and lengthy kiss.

"I brought Chinese," he said and grinned.

"I can smell it. Delish. I was going to have popcorn in your absence, but this is way better. Did you get the spicy eggplant?" she said and started opening the cartons.

"I did, and two more of your favorites — Salt & Pepper Tofu and Shrimp Chow Mein with soft noodles."

She laughed. "This is enough food for a week. And, yay, I won't have to cook."

They chowed down at the kitchen island while they shared the day's activities.

"How did the Bowens react?" Fern asked. "I hated to be left out of that one. But I'm starting to get used to the idea that it's not my job anymore."

"You'll transition, Fern. It will start getting easier," he said. "The Bowens' reaction was interesting. Alex was cooperative for the most part, but Blake went off the rails. To the point where Patty had enough, and unholstered her gun, accompanied by some spicy language."

Fern's eyebrows shot up. "Wow. Did that calm Blake down?"

"It did. She went back inside the house while we did our job. Patty can be very effective."

"Good for her. Now I'm really sorry I missed it. Did Bernice find anything?"

"Don't know yet. She said, 'nothing obvious,' and wouldn't entertain further questions from me."

Fern laughed. "You're so patient."

"Right. I hope we know more tomorrow. My other interesting tidbit is that Ed and I met Annie Haynes today — George and Candace Haynes' daughter. Or, factually, Hannah's daughter."

"Is she really?!?" Fern exclaimed. "How do you know that?"

Matt recounted the visit to their house.

"That changes everything, doesn't it?" Fern asked.

"Maybe. Depends on what forensics turns up on our suspect's vehicles.

We're certainly going to investigate that family's alibis. I got the feeling that Annie knows the truth about her mother, which opens a can of worms." Matt spread some of the Chinese mustard on the BBQ pork and took a big bite. "Tell me about the helicopter surveillance of the Colombia ship. What did you find?"

"It was just me and the Coast Guard guys since Ed got pulled off on your gig. We flew directly over the ship and doubled back, and it looked like it really is a fishing ship. They had large containers on deck that held several fish species, and about ten smaller float boats with fishing gear in them. The crew all smiled and waved as we flew over and didn't appear to be hiding anything. It was disappointing."

"Why do you say that?"

"Because I'm kinda bored and thought it might lead to something where I could actually do some work on behalf of my country. You know, my job."

"You mean like gun smuggling, scary drug runners, and deplorable human traffickers? You need to find a hobby, my love." He grinned.

"Speaking of which," she said, "did you find time today to call any of Alex Bowen's board of directors? I studied the photos I took of his budget, and maybe it's the hungry detective in me, but I'm convinced something is off with that business."

Matt shook his head. "No, it was next on my list, but I didn't get there. Why don't you do it tomorrow morning? Under the guise of our non-profit fact-gathering?"

Fern leaned over and kissed him on the cheek. "I was hoping you'd say that. I've got a couple of innocent questions that might clear up my suspicions."

"That sounds good. Just don't mention our homicide investigation. If Alex is innocent, we don't want to set ourselves up for defamation of his character."

"Is he innocent? I thought you were leaning toward him."

"Hell if I know," he said and shrugged his shoulders. "Do I have more gray hairs since you last saw me? If so, it's because of this case. Every time I talk to one of the suspects, I change my mind. They all may have a reason for wanting Hannah dead, but I'm stuck on whether or not their reasons are compelling enough to commit murder. Nothing adds up."

"What does Ed think?" she asked.

"He's suspicious of Annie, and I am, too, after today's meeting. She's got this goth look going. Spiky hair, black around her eyes, and a bunch of piercings."

"Which, being from Texas, you find shocking, right?" she teased.

"It's not my cup of tea. I prefer beautiful redheads with peaches and cream complexions."

"Like the one sitting next to you?"

"Exactly like the one sitting next to me." He took her in a close hug and kissed her, knocking over her water glass.

Fern laughed and stood up. "Let me wipe this up."

Matt pulled her back tightly to him and whispered, "Let it go."

• • •

Matt's phone buzzed on the nightstand and woke him up. It was 5:30 a.m.

Bernice said, "You're up, right?"

"Guess so. Why are you calling?" he whispered and slid quietly out of bed and into the bathroom, shutting the door.

"We found about ten hairs in Justin Sorenson's Jeep that share similar characteristics with Hannah's hair."

"Can you tell how old they are?" Matt asked. He was now fully awake and excited.

"Not officially. Not unless I send it to the state police lab, and we pay for more forensic testing."

"Can they do it?"

"Yes," Bernice answered. "But it costs more, and Ed will have to request it, not me."

"What's your best guess at the age of these hairs? I won't quote you; just want to hear your experienced take."

"I think they're more recent than when Justin and Hannah were married, if that's what you're after, Matt. But his vehicle is old, about ten years, so it's possible she lost the hairs during their marriage."

"Where did you find them?"

"Mostly on the floor around the passenger seat. Some on the back of that same seat."

"So, if Hannah had climbed into the Jeep and sat in that passenger seat, and Justin strangled her, and she fought back, it's possible some of her hair would have fallen out during the struggle."

"More than possible, I would say. In your scenario, it's likely that a female victim with neck-length hair like Hannah's would lose some hair."

"OK, call Ed, tell him what you've just told me, and request his lab take it to the next step. We need to know the approximate age of those hairs."

"Will do."

"What about the Bowens' cars?" Matt asked. "Anything there?"

"Nothing," Bernice said. "Clean to the point that I'm highly suspicious."

"What do you mean?"

"They were so clean that they must have been professionally detailed. And recently. Carpets sanitized — the full nine yards."

"Hmm. Just like Blake Bowen said the killer would obviously do," Matt said.

"Yes, exactly like she said."

CHAPTER 30

Fern was vaguely aware of Matt whispering before dawn, but she rolled over and went back to sleep. When she awoke a few minutes before 7:00 a.m, he was gone.

It was very cozy in bed, and she snuggled down even further, thinking about what she would do today. Specifically, she was thinking about her adorable husband. *I love him so much. I've got to stop whining. I know he loves me no matter what, he's proved it over and over again. But I want to make him proud of me, and the best way to do that is figure out my own life. I need to succeed in my job, and Joe Phelps will give me every opportunity to do so. But if I can also take Matt's family money and make this foundation into something real and vital, it will make him happy and proud.*

Maybe I should have a baby. Heck, maybe we made one last night. She smiled at the thought. *No, I'm not ready. Maybe soon, but not now. I can't lose myself and everything I want to achieve just yet. Get this foundation off the ground. Get up now and do it while your real job is slow.*

She contemplated a run on the beach, but a quick look out of her bedroom draperies discouraged her — drippy with swirling fog. Instead, she took a shower and dressed in yoga pants and a sweater. Coffee first, then yogurt, blueberries, and granola for breakfast. Then she'd be ready to face the world, which now consisted of her telephone and computer.

Remembering her mother's admonition that it was not polite to call anyone before 9:00 a.m, Fern patiently waited for that hour. She chuckled to herself thinking that Bernice had clearly not learned that lesson from her mother. Bernice and Patty were both inspirations to Fern. Both strong, intelligent women who had waited to have their children, giving their careers a head start. She thought Patty was forty when her son was born, and both he and his sister, born fifteen months later, had turned out great. *I just need more time with the State Department, and then I'll be the best mother on the planet.*

She dialed the number for the chairwoman of Healing House that Matt had given her. It was the same area code as Port Stirling and Eugene, so she must live somewhere in this part of Oregon.

"Hello?" a woman's voice answered.

"Hi," Fern said. "I'm trying to reach Donna Beck."

"Yes, that's me. Who is this, please?"

"My name is Fern Byrne and I live in Port Stirling. I'd like just a few minutes of your time if this works for you."

"I've heard your name. It's quite distinctive." She chuckled.

"Yeah, I get that a lot," Fern said with a smile. "My parents had, and continue to have, a good sense of humor."

"Aren't you a policewoman? Why are you calling me?"

"I was, yes, but now I have another job and that's why I'm calling," Fern explained. "My husband and I are establishing a non-profit foundation focused on improving health care in the region. Alex Bowen has been helpful in educating me on how to put a budget together, among other things. I have a couple of questions on what he's shared with me so far, and I can't reach him today," she lied, "so I thought I'd try to talk with you. I found your name on the Healing House website."

"If you're a friend of Alex, you're a friend of mine," Donna said. "What can I answer for you? And thanks to you and your husband for trying to help. We have a lot of needs in Oregon."

"That's what we think, too. And we want to make sure we do this right. We've hired an attorney to help us with the start-up, and she's waiting to see our budget. One thing puzzling me on the Healing House budget that Alex shared with me is the allocation for Administrative services, which he told me were legal fees and accounting."

"Yes, that's the primary two items in that budget category," Donna confirmed. "Both our lawyer and our accountant volunteer some of their time, but we pay them a stipend."

Fern was speechless for a moment. "But almost two million dollars between the two seems like a large amount, especially if they volunteer some hours," she said.

"No, that's incorrect," Donna said firmly. "I don't have my file in front of me at the moment, but I believe we allocated about $200,000 for the category last year. That also includes small amounts for miscellaneous board expenses, and occasional HR recruiting fees. But that's it, I think."

So where did the rest of that money in Alex's budget document go? Fern thought.

• • •

Matt left a note taped to Sylvia's computer: "I'm in Buck Bay — back later this morning."

Matt's brain had been stuck on Annie Haynes when he woke up, and he'd driven directly to Buck Bay city hall and was parking his car when the doors opened for business. He looked on the directory in the center of the lobby and found the Parks and Recreation Department, located in suite 110.

The door was open, but there was no one at the front counter. Instead, he found a bell with a small sign that read, "Ring me if desk is unattended." He did so, and a woman came around the corner carrying a pretty bowl full of burgundy-colored hellebores.

"Good morning," she said cheerfully. "How can I help you?" She sat the bowl on a corner of the counter.

"Those are nice," Matt said, pointing to the bowl.

"The Parks and Rec Department should always have something alive on our front desk, don't you think?" she said pleasantly.

Matt smiled. "Yes, I suppose you should. I'm looking for one of your employees, but I don't know when she works. Annie Haynes. Do you know her?"

"Yes. You just missed her. She's checked in and gone to today's work site with the crew."

"Can you tell me where that is? How do I find her?"

"They are down by Mourning Bay County Park," she said. "The city is responsible for the access road before you enter the park, and I think that's where they are again today."

"Oh? Have they been working in that area for a while?" Matt asked.

"Excuse me, but who are you?" she asked.

"I'm sorry, I should have introduced myself," he said, reaching into the pocket of his rain jacket for his police badge. He was dressed in regular clothes today, no uniform. "I'm Matt Horning, chief of police in Port Stirling. I'm working on the homicide case of Annie's aunt, Hannah Oakley, and I need to talk to her this morning."

The middle-aged woman touched her hair briefly. "Awful, wasn't it? Everyone here was devastated at the news. Poor Annie and her family. It's been terrible for her."

"Yes. It's a tragic case."

"Do you have any leads yet?" She looked hopeful. "Everyone has been on edge, including me. The sheriff was here yesterday talking to Chief McCoy, but they said they didn't have any news yet."

"We don't," agreed Matt. "But we might be getting close, and we will identify Hannah's killer—won't stop until we do."

"Promise?" she smiled nervously.

Matt put his hand on his heart. "On my honor, ma'am."

• • •

He found the Parks crew working on brush control about one mile before the entrance to Mourning Bay. He waved at Annie and approached her and her work partner, a young man in his early twenties.

"What are the cops doing out here?" Annie asked. She was holding an industrial-sized weed whacker.

Matt laughed. "If you put down that weapon, I'll tell you."

Her work partner snorted. "She is dangerous with that thing," he said.

"I need a few minutes of your time, Annie. Can we walk down this road?" He pointed toward the park entrance.

"I guess, but we need to finish this job by Friday," she said. "There's too many cars on this road on Saturday."

"Got it," said Matt. "This won't take long."

"Be right back," she said to her partner, who nodded.

Annie and Matt walked away from the crew. He didn't want them to hear his questions. He shoved his hands into his pockets and tried to look casual. The heavier rain had now turned into a light drizzle, and there were patches of blue sky above. He couldn't see the Pacific from here because of trees and vegetation, but he could hear and smell it, as some of the salt spray drifted in with the drizzle. Ahead of them, two seagulls were fighting loudly in the middle of the single-lane road over a McDonald's cardboard container. Matt picked it up when they reached it.

Annie was silent, waiting for Matt to tell her why he was here. *I think you know why, Annie,* he thought and began.

"You had a good relationship with Hannah, is that right?"

"I loved her," Annie said. "She was always good to me."

"I had an aunt I loved growing up, too," Matt said. "She was my dad's sister, and I was her first nephew. She lived nearby during my childhood years."

"Where was that?" Annie asked. "I remember reading about you after our earthquake, but I can't remember where you came from."

"Dallas area, Texas. I've been here three years. You haven't left," he noted.

"No, I went to community college in Portland, but I missed the ocean. Guess I'll probably stay forever. I was just starting to look for a small house I could buy when Hannah was killed."

"Gonna get your own place?" Matt asked.

"I want to, but I can't leave mom and dad now. Dad's a zombie since Hannah died, and they're clinging to me more than usual. I'll stick for a while until things calm down. I owe them that much."

"Do you know if you are in Hannah's will? Did she leave you anything?"

Annie stopped walking and looked at him. "Why would she do that?"

"Because the two of you were close. It wouldn't be surprising," Matt said.

She stared hard at him, not moving. "You mean because I'm her daughter?"

Now it was Matt's turn to stop and stare.

"Yes, I know," she said finally. Still looking at Matt, trying to gauge his reaction. "No one has ever told me the truth exactly, but I have eyes and a brain. When I was eighteen, I did what you all have probably done; I looked up birth records in Colorado the year I was born."

"Neither your parents nor Hannah ever told you?"

"Nope. But I don't blame them. It was better this way. George and Candace have been wonderful parents—the best. And I always felt the love from Hannah. There was simply no need to rock the boat."

"You weren't bitter? Angry, maybe?"

"That my mother gave me away?" She shook her head. "By the time I was an adult and understood what had happened, I was totally sympathetic to her. The thought that I could have another human being to worry about is the worst possible thing to me in my life right now, and Hannah was even younger than I am."

"That's pretty big of you," Matt said.

"Maybe. But you men don't understand the responsibility women take on when they give birth."

"Some of us do."

"OK, some of you more enlightened men do. But whoever got Hannah pregnant obviously didn't, or I would know him, wouldn't I? She did the right thing. She knew her older brother and sister-in-law would take the best care of me, and they have."

"Do you wonder about your real father?"

"Yes, of course. Wouldn't you? But it doesn't run my life, I'm just curious is all. It's enough for me to know that Hannah was my true mother. And to answer your earlier question, no, there won't be any special consideration given to me in her will. And the simple reason is that they don't want to acknowledge that Candace isn't my biological mother. But knowing Hannah, she would've guaranteed that George had enough resources to make sure I am solid forever."

"You're very mature about this," Matt noted.

"What's the alternative? Cause a big scene? Yell and cry? Not my style, chief."

"So, you didn't confront Hannah, lose your cool, and strangle her?"

She laughed. "Is that what this is about? You think I killed her? I loved her. I just told you."

"Love can turn to hate. I've seen it happen. Perhaps Hannah not owning up to your truth finally got to you and you snapped. And your being so down with it now is just a charade to throw me off the track."

"I did not kill my mother. I miss her every single day."

"OK," said Matt. "Let's talk about your work here. How long have you been working in this area? You know why I have to ask."

"It's a coincidence," Annie said. "Nothing more. We started on this road about a month ago." She looked sideways at Matt. He didn't visibly react.

"Were you working here on the Wednesday she disappeared?"

"Yes. She waved at me when she drove in."

"Jesus H. Christ!" Matt bellowed. "Why didn't you tell us this?"

"Because that's it. End of my news. I never saw her again."

"Did you talk to her?"

"No. I was up on a bank clearing brush, and she honked, waved, and kept going."

"And you didn't see her come back out?"

She looked at him and rolled her eyes. "Nooo. You cops found her car still in the park, remember?"

"You didn't see her ride out in someone else's car?"

"I would have told you if I did."

"How many cars went in and out that afternoon, say, after 1:00 p.m?"

"I can't tell you exactly. Not many. Maybe only three or four. But we left about 3:45 because we had to take a load to the transfer station."

"I assume your colleagues can verify you were with them and in sight all afternoon."

"Yes. Same crew."

"Do you remember any of the vehicles?" Matt asked. "Anyone you know?"

"Honestly, I wasn't paying attention. Most of the time, I was halfway up that bank pulling out gorse." She gestured behind them at the ocean side of the road that was mostly sand dune interspersed with the invasive yellow brush.

"Would you be able to recognize a car if we showed it to you?"

"I could try, but I doubt it. I was just working, chief. I'm sorry."

"Go back to work," Matt said. "I'll need to talk to your buddies later, you understand, right?"

"Do what you have to do." She strode off to join her partner.

CHAPTER 31

Matt retrieved his car, continued down the road, and parked in the Mourning Bay parking lot. He didn't know it, but he parked in the same space Hannah had parked in almost three weeks before, on the day she lost her life.

The swath of clouds overhead was being chased off by more and more blue sky as he looked out to the breathtaking view of the bay. The narrow opening between two extensive rocky promontories produced violent wave action as they smashed ashore onto the perfect semi-circle beach, and Matt found it hypnotizing.

He needed some time alone to sort through his thoughts and prioritize his next moves. After days of nothingness, things were starting to move, and he had a fear he was falling behind, missing something.

He shut off his phone, cracked his window an inch or so to breathe in the tangy air and to provide the soundtrack for his view, and retrieved his police notebook from the passenger seat. He began to jot down fragments of thoughts and 'to do' items, which, in fitting with his need for order, he numbered:

1. *Check Buck Bay car washes/detailing places to see if the Bowens had visited. If so, when? Call Patty.*

2. *Ask Justin Sorenson how Hannah's hairs got in his Jeep. Talk to Earl—he handles.*

3. *Have Jay interview Annie's co-workers about the day Hannah disappeared. Had she gone missing anytime that afternoon? Had they noticed any cars?*

4. *Talk to Robert again—did he know that Annie was Hannah's daughter? Be honest.*

5. *Do I have to ask George and Candace if they killed Hannah because she was going to tell Annie the truth?*

6. *Call Michelle Wayne—reading of the will tomorrow morning!*

7. *Did Fern talk to Alex's board about his budget? What's the scoop?*

8. *Bernice send hairs to state police lab? How soon? Call Ed.*

What's first? Matt turned his phone back on and called Fern.

"I was just about to call you," she said. "I've got news. I think."

"You either have news or you don't," he said, smiling. "Did you talk to one of Alex's board members yet?"

"Yes, Donna Beck, the chairwoman. And I think it's news, but I don't know quite what to make of it. That's why I was calling you."

"Go ahead."

"She told me—and she was firm and convincing—that Healing House only spent roughly $200K on Administrative costs in their last budget year, not the almost two million Alex had on his budget that I saw."

"Really? That's interesting. Who else sees his budget documents?"

"He told me that this one was recently submitted to Health & Human Services for a federal grant. Which they got, by the way," Fern added.

"You need to find out the amount they gave him."

"Alex told me that the grant amount was equal to one year's operating expenses," Fern said. There was a hush on the line. "Oh my God. They doled out an amount equal to what he documented to them his annual costs were, and then…"

"And then, Alex Bowen pocketed $1 million plus, and no one was any the wiser," Matt said.

"Surely someone would have noticed," Fern said.

"Maybe Hannah noticed. Hold tight, and we'll talk about it when I get home."

. . .

Matt kept coming back to "It's over." Hannah wrote that to someone, and that someone killed her. He called Earl next.

"Earl, it's Matt."

"I know. We have caller ID now."

Matt laughed. "I know. I just think it's polite to announce myself."

"Southern mother, right?"

"You know it. Listen, I want to make sure that Bernice told you what they found in Justin Sorenson's Jeep."

"You didn't hear me shouting for joy at the news? Seriously, I think it's him, Matt. I believe those hairs from Hannah's head are recent, and that she got into his vehicle to listen to him try to talk her out of cutting him off. She wouldn't budge, and he strangled her."

"I'm leaning your way, Earl. I keep revisiting the so-called suicide note. The thing that makes the most sense is her writing that letter to Sorenson—that her attorney swears Hannah was going to write—and telling him 'It's over.' It could mean anything, but based on what we know, it's the most logical."

"Agree. Ed is driving to Salem right now with the hair samples. His lab said they would put a rush on dating them. We should know something soon. I'm considering arresting Sorenson this afternoon. We can get him off the street, and hold him for 48 hours, by which time we should have the lab results. What do you think?"

Matt considered what Fern had just told him about Alex Bowen, and his new fact that Annie Haynes knew Hannah was her mother and was in the vicinity of Mourning Bay most of that day. "I've got two other issues that demand taking a look into, Earl." He related what he'd learned today so far.

"Well, those are not insignificant discoveries," Earl said, pausing. "That gives possible motives to both Alex and the daughter that we didn't have until now. Maybe I should hold off with Sorenson."

"I think we could wait one day, if you're sure the lab will come through," Matt said. "Although, I don't like Sorenson roaming around free if he is a killer."

"It's one day, Matt. How much damage could he do? Especially when he knows I'm watching him like a hawk."

• • •

"Top of the mornin' to you, Patty."

"Back at you, Matt. What's the latest?" she asked. Patty was in her cubbyhole of an office in the basement of the county courthouse, not too far from the sheriff's office. She had a stack of newspaper clippings piled on her desk that the Twisty River PD's admin had scrounged up for her; they all featured Blake Bowen in her prime days as a singing star. Patty was looking for any tidbit that could give her more insight into her past and character.

"Two things," Matt said. "I want to make sure that Earl told you what Bernice found in Justin Sorenson's Jeep—some hairs that have similar characteristics to Hannah's."

"Oh, god, yes. He's been prancing around here all morning," she said. "Did he tell you he wants to arrest him?"

"Yeah, we decided to wait until the state police lab can tell us an approximate age of the hairs. If they're recent vintage, we'll throw him in the slammer. I think it's him, Patty. But I need your help with one other lead."

"Sure. What can I do?"

"Bernice told me that both of the Bowens' cars had been recently cleaned, probably detailed, too. Do you have time today to check the car washes in Buck Bay and see if they did the Bowen cars shortly after Hannah's murder? Like that Wednesday, or up to a week after?"

"Good idea. I took photos of both cars when we did the search, and I've got a description, so I'm all set. How many places are there, do you know?"

"Not sure, but there can't be that many," he said. "Port Stirling only has one, so Buck Bay probably has about five."

"I'm on it," Patty said. "I'll check online, make a list, and head out within the hour. All I'm doing now is reading about Blake Bowen's celebrity days and it makes me want to puke."

"You can't shoot her because she's famous, Patty."

She laughed. "Too bad. I don't like suspects who lie to me."

"You made that perfectly clear to her."

"It saved us time, didn't it?"

"Yeah. Getting Blake to shut up isn't an easy feat," he allowed. "Call me if you find anything, OK?"

• • •

"Hi, boss. What's shaking?" Jay said into his phone. "And where are you? I'm in the office and you aren't here."

"I'm sitting in the parking lot of Mourning Bay park, but I've been busy this morning. I just talked to Annie Haynes, and I've learned something and need your help."

"What?"

"Annie knows that Hannah is her mother, and she was working near Mourning Bay the day Hannah died."

"No shit?"

"Yeah. She says she doesn't harbor any grudges, didn't kill her, and didn't see anything that day. I want you to come over and talk to her work colleagues. Bring Tamryn with you if she's in, or Rudy if not. There are four of them and they're clearing brush from the access road to the park."

"Tamryn's here, and we can be there in thirty minutes," Jay said. "How do you want us to handle it?"

"Start by asking them if they saw anything on that Wednesday; do they remember any particular cars or people that may have passed them on the road? Did they hear anything? Did they see Hannah come or go? Find out the timing of when they arrived and when they left. And then, as subtly as you can, ask about Annie's presence that day. Was she there all day with them? Did she leave for any period of time? Maybe couch it in with the others; did anyone leave for a while in the afternoon? How does that sound?" Matt asked.

"We can do that," Jay said. "Did you believe her? That she didn't do it?"

"Not sure," Matt said. "I wanted to. She's an intelligent young woman, mature for her age, and she said all the right things. But like Ed said, she's a little off. And don't ask me what that means, I'm not entirely sure. But I'm hoping you can eliminate her from suspicion by talking with her co-workers. And, both you and Tamryn should spend a few minutes talking with Annie. I want your read on her. All you know is that she is Hannah's niece, OK? Be sympathetic."

"Got it. I'll check in with you later."

"Please tell Sylvia I've got two more quick stops in Buck Bay, and then I'll be back. Ask her to schedule a meeting with the major crime team for 4:00 p.m. today, and everybody who can be there should be. Things are starting to move, and I want everyone in the loop. I don't mind telling you, I'm confused as all hell, and we need to talk this out."

• • •

The clouds had cleared off, and the sun was sparkling on the bay's waves now. The stiff breeze had been tamed into a warmer, softer cat's-paw. Matt got out of his car and walked down to the shoreline, the only person on the beach. He tried to imagine walking into the bay with the intention of killing himself, but it was unimaginable; his will to live was too strong.

Matt had a taste of what it might feel like to drown when he was overcome by the tsunami the night of the earthquake, and maybe there were worse ways to go, but he would never, ever choose it. He was glad Hannah hadn't chosen it either. *For her sake, I have to find her killer.*

His next phone call went to Michelle Wayne, Hannah's—and now his—attorney.

"Hi, Matt," Michelle answered.

"Howdy. I'm in Buck Bay and wonder if I could stop by your office briefly?"

"Of course. Is this about your foundation or about Hannah's case?" she asked. "I'll get ready."

"Hannah's will. I've learned something new, and I want to talk about it with you. I'll be there in ten minutes."

Michelle Wayne's office was on the second floor of a building on Main

Street in downtown Buck Bay. Her door, with her name stenciled on it, opened directly off a hallway near the open staircase. It was a small space, two rooms—an anteroom for reception, which no one inhabited now, and Michelle's larger office through a textured glass door that provided privacy.

"You found me," she said, coming out to greet Matt. "Come through." He followed her into the inner office and took the chair facing her mid-size traditional oak desk.

"What's going on?" she asked.

"If you don't already know what I'm about to tell you, I need your word that you will keep it confidential," Matt said.

"You have it," Michelle said, raising an eyebrow. "Sounds mysterious."

"Annie Haynes, George and Candace Haynes' daughter, is really Hannah's daughter. Did you know that?"

Michelle looked stunned. "No, I did not know that." She placed her hands on top of her desk and leaned toward Matt. "But it makes Hannah's will make more sense to me."

"I need to know what's in it, Michelle, and I need to know now if Hannah made a special provision for Annie."

She swiveled to grab a legal file sitting on top of a credenza to the right of her desk, and she opened it now, moving it in front of her. "One of the provisions is for George Haynes," she said, then hesitated.

"Read it to me," Matt said.

She looked up at him, and then reached for her reading glasses. "To my brother, George S. Haynes, I leave the oil painting painted by our grandmother currently stored in my garage, and the sum of $100,000 to be used in future support of his daughter, Annie Haynes."

"Secret to the end," Matt mused. "It looks like Hannah never realized that Annie had figured it out. Is that the only mention of her in the will?"

"Yes. It's the only major provision; Robert Oakley is the primary beneficiary."

"Have you ever been contacted by Annie Haynes or discussed this provision with George?"

"No to both. I suspect George knows he's getting something, but I think he'll be surprised at the amount of the bequest. And you must keep that confidential for now, Matt. The will is being read to Robert, the Haynes family, and Blake Bowen tomorrow."

"Blake Bowen?" Matt asked, surprised. "What's she getting?"

Michelle shook her head. "Nothing much, just some childhood things that Hannah thought she would want as a remembrance in case she died first. They were close friends throughout their lives, apparently."

Matt nodded and stood to leave. He shook Michelle's hand and said, "I owe you a big thank you. There are only three people, other than me and my police colleagues, who are sworn to secrecy, who know the truth about Annie. Please help us keep it that way."

"I will, you can count on it. My profession calls for secrecy, too. I'm really looking forward to working with you and Fern on the foundation. She tells me she's figuring out the budget now."

"She is. She's done a lot of research and work on it. She ran into one little blip, but I think she's about finished. Keep working with her, and then as soon as we solve this case, I'll come by and the two of you can update me. It is exciting for us."

"Sounds good, Matt." She walked him to the door. "Good luck. We all have our fingers crossed that you catch Hannah's killer soon. I still think it's Sorenson."

"Getting close," he said and waved as he headed down the stairs.

I hope that's true, he thought.

* * *

One more stop in Buck Bay for Matt — Robert. He pulled into the driveway and sat in his car for a minute. He was still undecided about whether or not to tell Robert the truth about Annie.

If I can get him to admit that he knew she was Hannah's daughter, and worried about Hannah leaving her money to her, it would put Robert squarely back in the suspect category.

But if Hannah never told him, it would break his heart even further. Plus, there was no need for him to know. Annie would be taken care of as Hannah wanted.

I have to ask him. It's my damn job. He got out of the car and approached the house.

Robert opened the door. He looked hopefully at Matt. "Any news, chief?"

"I do have some news for you. May I come in?"

Robert opened the door wide and said, "What's happened?"

"We found some of Hannah's hair in a vehicle we searched. We're sure it's hers because it shares all the same characteristics. It's been sent to the Oregon State Police lab in Salem for age dating purposes, and we should know soon if it's recent or not."

"Who does the vehicle belong to?" Robert asked, his face clouding over.

"I can't tell you that quite yet," Matt said. "I'm sorry. But if we learn that the hair is recent, we will be making an arrest, and, of course, I will tell you that instantly."

"That's wonderful news, Matt! Thank you!" He grabbed Matt in a hug and held on tight. "Thank you," he repeated. "Is it someone I know? Please, let's sit down."

"I can't tell you that either. It's a person of interest at this point until we get this additional piece of evidence, and it could still go either way, depending on what the lab finds. But I hope to not keep you in suspense for too long." Matt leaned back in the chair next to Robert's fireplace. "In the meantime, I need to ask you a couple of questions."

"Sure thing," said Robert, smiling broadly.

"Do you know that Annie Haynes is Hannah's birth daughter? Did Hannah ever tell you?"

Robert's smile disappeared in a heartbeat. "That can't be right," he said. "Annie is Hannah's niece, George's child. She and Hannah were close, but that was because she was her only niece."

"Hannah gave birth to Annie when she was a college student in Colorado. There is a birth record at the Boulder hospital, and both George and Candace have confirmed that Hannah gave up her baby to them to raise so she could continue her schooling. She was barely in her twenties at the time. Annie figured it out a while back, but never admitted she knew to anyone until she told me this morning. It's the truth, Robert."

Matt shut up and let Robert digest this news.

"Why didn't she tell me?" he said, finally.

"Only her parents and George and Candace knew the truth. It's a small town, Robert. In Hannah's defense, limiting the knowledge to her blood relatives was smart. She and George never wanted Annie to know the truth, and it worked for years. But Annie is smart like her mother and put it together eventually. You must have noticed how alike they are?"

"I did. Yes, of course I did. But Hannah and George are alike, too. I thought it was just strong Haynes family genes." He paused, twisting his hands around in his lap. "Why are you telling me this now? Does it factor into Hannah's case?"

"Only if you knew the truth about Annie and were worried that if anything came between you and Hannah, she would give all her money to her daughter. Worried enough to kill Hannah while you were still the primary beneficiary of her will."

"That did not happen, Matt. You know in your heart it did not happen."

"I think I know," Matt said, "but do I really know?"

CHAPTER 32

The Chinook County major crime team, with the addition of former member Fern Byrne, who Matt had asked Sylvia to invite, gathered at 4:00 p.m.

"Is it Happy Hour yet?" Patty said to the room at large as they all took their regular places around the big table.

"It might be soon," Earl said.

Matt, serious, walked to the whiteboard that held photos of the victim and all possible suspects, with lines of pros and cons written below each name. At the very top of the board, he wrote in big letters "IT'S OVER" in all caps.

"This is our best clue," he said to the group. "It's written in the victim's own handwriting, and the killer had to be in possession of it. Who could it have been written to, and for what reason?"

Earl raised his hand. "As your senior statesman, I'd like to go first," the sheriff said to twittering laughter. "My theory is that Hannah did indeed write the letter to Justin, her ex-husband, telling him that the gravy train was over. "It's over," in her exact words. Her attorney told us she was planning to write it, and so did Robert. Hannah wrote the letter, Sorenson received it, he called her on the day of her death to arrange a meet, they met, Hannah wouldn't back down, he lost his cool, and killed her. He then bundled her body in his Jeep, where Bernice found some hairs belonging to Hannah, drove her to Hedgehog Mountain, and buried her. Means, motive, opportunity," Earl clicked off on his fingers.

"I agree with Earl," said Matt, still standing. "Sometimes the logical, obvious explanation is the correct one. Add to what your sheriff just outlined, I would also say that Sorenson has been uncooperative and is holding back information, we believe. That we think Hannah wrote this letter to him has been corroborated by two people. The only piece that doesn't fit for me where Justin is concerned is that he had no real motive for wanting her dead. He was almost better off the longer she was alive."

"But that game was over," Earl sputtered. "He knew he'd lost, and it sent him off the deep end."

"Most likely," Matt agreed. "We've seen examples of his temper. What do the rest of you think of Sorenson as our perpetrator?"

"Hannah's hair in his Jeep does it for me," Jay said. "Hard physical evidence. Unless we discover that the hairs are ten years old from when they were married." Everyone looked at Ed.

"Still waiting," Ed said. "The lab has had the sample for over twenty-four hours now and told me that the night shift would work on it last night. I expect to hear soon."

"I'm with Earl, too," Tamryn said. "That makes it a spontaneous crime, not pre-meditated, which, as a newcomer, seems to fit with the vibe around here more than someone she knew setting out to kill her. The evidence is slim, but what we do know about the letter, along with the hair in his car, fits. A volatile, tossed-aside man down on his luck with an ax to grind—it's a classic portrait. Will you arrest him, sheriff?"

"Matt and I agreed to wait on the lab report, because there's some other news that might also be relevant," Earl said. He waved at Matt to continue.

"And for the first interesting new tidbit," Matt said, "I introduce to you my wife, Fern."

"We wondered why she was here instead of being ordered to go home," Bernice said. "Delighted to see you, of course, Fern."

"It's nice to be included," Fern said and looked pointedly at her husband. Everyone laughed.

"My tidbit is that I may have discovered that Alex Bowen embezzled over one million dollars from Healing House, his non-profit organization. Or, more accurately, from the U.S. Department of Health & Human Services."

Mouths dropped open around the table, and Fern gave the team her full story.

"If this is all true," Tamryn said, "how did Hannah find out?"

"I don't know that piece," Fern admitted. "I only figured it out this morning after I talked to Alex's board chairwoman. And Alex may have a completely rational explanation for the difference in their numbers."

"Or he may not," Patty said, her jaw set in a firm line. She may even have been grinding her teeth. "Adding to what Fern said, I've learned this morning that Alex and Blake brought both their cars—the ones we searched—to a car detailing operation on the Thursday after Hannah was killed."

"Wow," said Matt. "Nice work, Patty. And Bernice, for giving us a heads up. Which one was it?"

"CarGuy on the south end of Buck Bay," Patty said. "I spoke to the owner, and he knows the Bowens and their cars. That's my only problem; he says they're regular customers. It could be a coincidence that they came in on that day."

Matt shook his head. "I don't know. Your wife's best friend is missing, she's flown home in a panic, and you're taking your car in to get washed? Doesn't wash for me. What time were they there, did he say?"

"He said they arrived shortly before closing, left both cars with him overnight, and he gave them a loaner. They picked up their cars the next day, also close to closing time at 6:00 p.m."

"Did he say what kind of shape the cars were in?" Bernice asked. "Like extra dirty, muddy, hair, blood, etc.?"

"I did ask him that question," Patty said. "But he didn't personally clean the cars. Said he would talk to the two guys that did and let me know. If I may, Matt, let me summarize why I believe one or both Bowens killed Hannah. While we don't have any physical evidence yet like we do on Sorenson, there's plenty of circumstantial and suspicious behavior by these two. First, they lied to us about when Blake came home from Mexico. Why would they do that? To make sure she can't be connected to the crime is the only reason I can see. And they compounded that lie by asking her agent and the pilot of the plane who ferried her back to Oregon to lie on her behalf."

"Which means it was real important to Blake that the police think she was in Mexico," Jay interrupted. "Then, Blake tells her housekeeper, Rosa, to lie and say she was at their house all that day cleaning and that Alex was home, too. Why?"

"Maybe they just didn't want to get involved and risk the hassle of a police investigation," Tamryn offered. "We are a pain in the ass."

"True," Patty laughed. "But still, lying when it's easier to tell the truth? Suspicious in my book. Bottom line is that neither one of them has a real alibi for Wednesday night, and Alex doesn't have an alibi from noon on. And then they take their cars in to be sterilized. Circumstantial, yes, but coupled with Fern's discovery, highly suspicious."

"So," Matt said, "Hannah somehow finds out that Alex has embezzled the government out of a million, writes him a note saying, "It's over, unless you return the money and turn yourself in", he calls her the morning he reads it to set up a time to talk about it, he calls Blake and fills her in, and then Blake calls her BFF to beg her not to rat on her husband. Hannah agrees to talk to Alex, gets in his car at Mourning Bay, he kills her and stages the suicide. Blake gets a fast ride home, and together they take Hannah's body to Hedgehog Mountain and bury her. The next day they take Alex's car in to remove all traces of Hannah."

"Also possible," Earl said. "But why would they take Blake's car in for cleaning, too?"

"Because that's what they usually do," Patty said. "I asked the owner if they always bring in both cars at once and he said, 'Yes.' They wanted it to look like business as usual."

"We have to confront Alex on his budget discrepancy," Tamryn said. "How are we going to do that without implicating Fern?"

"Sadly, you can't," said Fern. "I've already asked my boss in D.C. to get a copy of the HHS grant that was given to Healing House. If the dollars add up like Alex had in his file, which, by the way, I looked at when he was out of the room for a minute…"

"Of course, you did," Ed said, shaking his head. "Kinda like plucking a raft off the beach on someone's private property, no doubt."

"…we will have to show it to Donna Beck, and let her question Alex first," Fern finished, winking at Ed. "No matter whether he killed Hannah or not, if he stole that money from the U.S. government, I have to track it down."

"And, wait—there's more!" Matt said. "This absolutely cannot leave this room." He paused and looked purposefully around the table. "Hannah Oakley is Annie Haynes' real mother. She gave birth in Colorado while a student and gave the baby to her older brother George and his wife. Three of the five people that knew have confirmed it to me. Annie herself was one of those people." He related his conversation earlier today with Annie.

"And," Jay said, "I talked with her work crew, and two of them said they thought Annie 'disappeared' for a while on the Wednesday in the early afternoon. They can't remember the actual day exactly but said that one day when they were working out by Mourning Bay, she went into town for a long lunch."

"Shit," said Matt.

"Had a feeling you'd say that," Jay said.

"I can't believe that young woman could have killed her mother," Matt said.

"Why on earth not?" Ed asked. "She's a freak."

"Ed! You can't say that," Fern said. "Maybe I steal rafts off the beach, but at least I don't call people names."

"You haven't seen her yet, I have," he said.

"You're an old fogey," Bernice said. "You think all young people are freaks."

"She is a little on the strange side," Jay said, coming to Ed's defense.

"How so?" asked Patty.

"All sorts of scary body piercings," Jay said, "and those were the ones I could see. Who knows what's going on under her clothes. And black lipstick and black all around her eyes with weird spiky hair." He shuddered and made a noise that sounded like "eewsh."

"I get the picture," Patty said. "Aside from her scary look, is our theory that Annie found out Hannah is really her mother, not her aunt, confronted her all upset, and was so betrayed and angry that she strangled her? A crime of passion?"

"It's possible," said Matt glumly. "I believed her when I talked to her this morning, and I was hoping Jay could get a firm alibi for her, but his interrogation means we have to put Annie on the suspect list. And we still don't know if George and Candace have an alibi either. I hate this family angle."

"Whether you hate it or not, you know the stats, Matt," said Tamryn. "We can't sweep the Hayneses under the rug. Not with what we learned today."

"I know. I know!" Matt said. He gently banged his fist on the table.

"Now you're acting like me, son," said Earl to everyone's amusement. The sheriff had been known to pound the table on occasion. "What I'm hearing is that we have more work to do before we can successfully elim…"

"My phone's buzzing," interrupted Ed. "It's the lab." Into his phone, he said, "It's Ed. OK if I put you on speaker phone? I'm in a crime team meeting." He pushed a button on his phone and set it in the middle of the table. "Monte, you're on."

"Hi, Ed and all. I'm the manager of the state lab, and two of my staff who worked on your case last night just gave me the results. All the hairs Bernice's team found in the vehicle are a complete match with those she removed from Hannah Oakley's body. And they are recent, almost an exact match with the autopsy timeframe."

"Monte, it's Ed. So, you're saying that Hannah Oakley was in this vehicle shortly before her body was found. Do I have that right?"

"Yes. Perhaps as recent as a few days prior, and not more than a couple of weeks. Anything else I can do for you folks?"

"Not at the moment," Ed said. "Thank you so much, you may have solved our case."

"Hope you get your killer, Ed. See you next time." The line went dead.

"Bring in Justin Sorenson, sheriff," Ed said.

CHAPTER 33

The arrest of Justin Sorenson for the murder of Hannah Oakley did not go smoothly.

Deputies from the Chinook County Sheriff's Department, led by Sheriff Earl Johnson, surrounded Sorenson's small apartment complex on the north side of Buck Bay. His unit, one of eight, was on the ground floor facing the parking lot, and Justin saw the three county squad cars arriving just as he was getting ready to go to work.

Earl, noting that Sorenson's car was in the parking lot, knocked hard on the door. "Open up! It's the sheriff." Sorenson did not immediately respond, so Earl knocked again, this time with even more force. "Don't make me break the door down, Justin!"

From within, Earl heard, "I'm coming out, sheriff. Tell your guys to back off."

Earl waved off the deputies and said loudly, "Retreat. He's surrendering." They moved away from the door and back toward their cars, except for the two cops stationed around the back of the building in case Sorenson decided to make a run for it.

Justin Sorenson opened his front door. He was holding a handgun, and it was pointed at the sheriff. Earl, surprised, made a quick dodging move but Sorenson fired, catching the sheriff in his upper arm. The bullet tore through Earl's uniform, blood spurted everywhere, and the force of it knocked him to the ground.

Paul Leland, a deputy who had served almost twenty years with Earl, heard the shot just as he was entering Sorenson's unlocked back door. He raced through the studio apartment and tackled Sorenson to the ground, placing his gun barrel at his temple. "One move and I blow your fucking head off!" he screamed.

Earl staggered to his feet as two other deputies came to his aid, immediately applying a tourniquet to his bleeding arm. "I'm OK," Earl said, and then promptly fainted.

Between the three sheriff's deputies, who would later receive commendations for their bravery and quick action, they called 9-1-1 and got an ambulance for Earl within six minutes. Simultaneously, they disarmed and handcuffed Justin Sorenson, and placed him in a squad car for the ride to the Chinook County jail in Twisty River.

After they read Sorenson his rights, he began to cry and sobbed most of the ride, claiming, "I didn't do it. I didn't kill Hannah," at various interludes. Leland, who remembered Justin Sorenson from high school, told him to shut up after he'd said the same words four times. "I didn't like you in high school, and now I like you even less. You shot my boss, and it would be in your best interests to not talk again until you get a lawyer."

That seemed to do the trick, and Sorenson didn't utter another word until he, with a public defender at his side, was interrogated by Ed Sonders and Matt Horning in a bleak room in the basement of the county courthouse at a few minutes past 8:00 p.m.

Matt calmly laid out their case against him, starting with the letter they believed Hannah wrote to him ending his spousal support, to the discovery of her hairs in his Jeep. Justin began to cry again, but without the histrionics he'd displayed during the ride to the jail. Silent tears ran down his handsome face, and his substantial shoulders occasionally shook.

"What we need to hear from you, Justin," said Matt, "is whether or not you planned to kill your former wife in advance, or whether you got angry at her for cutting you off and just lost it. Which was it?" Matt sat back in the uncomfortable metal folding chair while the lawyer handed her client a glass of water and whispered in his ear. He took a sip and set the glass down.

"I didn't kill her," Justin said, staring directly at Matt.

"OK, you didn't kill Hannah," Matt said. He drummed his fingers on the table. "Then let's go through some of the issues that cause us to believe you did. How about that?"

"Whatever."

"Why did you shoot the sheriff and try to get away when they came for you if you didn't kill Hannah?"

"Because I knew he would try to pin this on me, and I can't prove I didn't do it. I was scared. I'm scared now."

"You look scared, Justin, and I understand that," Matt said. "Let's start at the beginning. Did you get a letter from Hannah stating that she was cutting off your support?"

Justin looked down at the table and wrapped one hand around his water glass. He stared at the glass as if he was considering taking a drink from it to stall, but then he let loose of it.

"Yes," he said. "She did write me a letter telling me that."

"Do you still have the letter?" Ed asked.

"No. I burned it."

"Why did you do that?" Ed again.

"I was hoping she would change her mind, and it would all just go away. And, I didn't want to think about it anymore."

"Did what Hannah wrote include the words, 'It's over'?" Matt asked.

Sorenson had a puzzled look on his face. "No. Why do you ask that?"

Matt ignored his question and instead said, "Do you remember what she did write to you?"

He smiled a sarcastic smile. "Oh, yeah. Word for word. It was short and to the point. She said, 'I've petitioned the court to end your monthly spousal support after eight years. I thought I should tell you before you get a letter from them. Hannah.'"

"And what did you do when you received this letter?"

"I called her and asked if we could meet to talk."

"Was this on the Wednesday Hannah disappeared?" Matt asked. "The call you made to her shortly after noon on that day?"

"Yes."

"Did she agree to meet you?"

"Yes."

"And did you meet?"

"Yes. I went to her office and parked around the corner. She came out and got in my car and told me she only had a few minutes to talk because she'd ordered lunch."

"How did that talk go, Justin?" Ed asked.

Justin glared at Ed. "Not my way," he said finally. "I could usually talk her into things, but not this time. She was determined. Said 'enough was enough'."

"Did you suggest that you would blackmail her and reveal a family secret if she didn't keep paying you?" Matt said. He leaned forward close to Justin's face. The lawyer held up her hand. "That's close enough, Chief," she said.

Matt gave her his Texas grin and said, "Just want to be sure I don't miss your client's reaction on this one."

"I have no reaction, asshole," Justin said. "I was not blackmailing Hannah and I don't know any family secrets."

"Really?" Matt asked. "You don't know something that Hannah would have done anything to keep you from telling?"

Sorenson looked at his lawyer. "What the hell is he talking about?"

She shrugged her shoulders. "Don't know. What the hell are you talking about, Matt?"

Ed and Matt shared a quick glance.

"Moving on," said Ed, "did you stay parked downtown or did the two of you take a drive out to Mourning Bay?"

"We stayed downtown," answered Sorenson.

"Did anyone see you?" asked Matt.

"I don't know," Justin said. "Oh, wait a minute. We were parked in front of that Thai restaurant she likes, and she waved at the owner. That's where she was getting lunch. He would probably remember."

"Did she say where she was going after lunch? Or if she had a meeting with anyone?"

"She said she had a meeting at 2:00 p.m," Justin said. "That's why she was in a hurry. She wanted to eat before her meeting."

"Did she tell you who she was meeting?" Matt asked.

"Nope. Too bad. That's probably who killed her, right?"

"How did it end with her?" Ed asked.

"We talked for a few more minutes, but I could see it wasn't going any-where. She said she had to go pick up her food, ran a brush through her hair, and checked her makeup in my mirror. I said, 'See you around,' and she got out without saying another word. I drove home. The end."

"So, your statement is that's how her hair ended up in your Jeep, cor-rect?" Ed asked.

"I guess. She'd been in my Jeep before. It's not all that surprising. We were married, you know."

"Do you know the age of the hairs you found?" the lawyer asked Ed.

"Our state police lab has dated the hairs, yes," said Ed.

"Are they recent?"

"Yes."

Sorenson shifted in his chair. "Well, yeah, three weeks ago Hannah was in my car. I just told you. It's the truth." He started crying again.

. . .

After they booked and processed Justin Sorenson into his new home to await arraignment, which would occur tomorrow at 11:00 a.m, Matt and Ed drove to the hospital in Buck Bay.

Earl was sitting up in bed talking to Bernice and his wife, Sharon. He looked pale instead of his usual ruddy complexion. Sharon looked a lit-tle pale, too.

"I knew you two couldn't wait to see me in a hospital bed," he groused as they came in.

Bernice stood and hugged both men. "He's going to be alright," she said, loud enough for Earl to hear, too.

"Damn straight," said the sheriff. "First time I've been shot in the line of duty, and that asswipe Sorenson is not going to be the one who brings me down. Have you interrogated him yet?"

Now Sharon stood, too, and said, "That's my cue to go get some dinner for my charming husband." She patted his good arm and said, "I'll be back soon. Take it easy."

Bernice said to Earl, "I'll help her get something good for you, and I second the take it easy bit." She gave Matt and Ed the eye, and they knew what that meant.

"He says he didn't do it, Earl," Matt said, taking the chair closest to the bed.

"I didn't shoot myself."

Matt and Ed laughed. "No, we mean he says he didn't kill Hannah."

"Don't they all?" said Earl.

"S'pose so," said Matt.

"Please don't tell me you believed him."

"We're not sure, Earl," Ed said, and then repeated their interview with Sorenson.

"So, go talk to the Thai guy and see if he remembers them sitting in front of his restaurant," Earl said. "Was he telling you the truth when he didn't know Hannah's secret about Annie?"

"Unless he's Robert Redford trying to win an Oscar, he doesn't know about Annie," Ed said. "I don't believe he was blackmailing Hannah, at least not with that information."

"Yeah, Ed and I agree on this one," Matt said. "But I'm not convinced that what he said was in Hannah's letter was all that was in it. He's not stupid enough to not realize that we were talking about 'It's over.' Convenient that he burned it."

"We aren't saying that he absolutely didn't kill Hannah," Ed said. "It's only that some doubt is creeping in. It was painful for him to admit to us why he met with her—to beg for her compassion—and it rang true."

Not buying it, Earl harumphed. "If he's slick enough to convince successful women to marry him, he could probably also fool you two."

"Jeri's prepared to arraign him on both your shooting and on Hannah's murder," Matt said. "He can cool his jets in jail for a while so we can check on his story. Has Bernice said how long you'll be in here?"

"Did you have any luck getting a straight story out of a doctor?" Earl said to Matt but didn't wait for his answer. "Thought not. Me neither.

Probably a couple of days. I could stand to get some rest, so I'm not going to fight them."

They noticed his eyes were getting heavy and said their quiet good-byes. "Talk tomorrow," Matt said, but Earl was already asleep.

CHAPTER 34

Fern had a phone call with her boss, Joe Phelps, the next morning while Matt was still sleeping. After he'd arrived home late Tuesday night, they'd stayed up even later discussing Hannah's case, and talking about Earl, and Matt needed the extra sleep this morning. He'd been upset about Earl getting shot and was concerned about him after visiting the hospital last night.

"He looked awful, Fern. Old. Sick."

"You looked awful after getting shot, too, remember? And look at you now — handsome and healthy."

"I'm twenty years younger than Earl. I'm not sure he's going to bounce back as quickly. Maybe this is a message he needs to hear."

"Don't you dare suggest to that lovely man that he should retire," Fern said, that spot on her cheeks starting to redden. "Getting wounded on duty can happen to any cop, I don't care about the age. It's a very personal decision, and he will know when it's time. And Sharon will nudge him along in her quiet, tactful manner when she feels the time is right."

"I know," Matt agreed. "It just hurt to see him like that, so defenseless. Dying in a hospital with a gunshot wound is not how Earl should go out."

"Again, not your decision. That may be exactly how a seasoned, excellent cop would choose to 'go out.' And he's not going to die. He got shot in the arm, and Bernice fixed him. Earl may have a long recovery and his fishing may suffer, but he'll be fine."

But in the middle of the night, Matt had a bad dream that woke them both up. Fern had soothed him, and he went back to sleep, but she knew he was worrying about Earl. So, she'd crept out of their bedroom, happy to see him still asleep, and gone downstairs to her office to call Joe.

"Joe, we need your help on Hannah Oakley's murder case," Fern started.

"What's that got to do with the United States government?" he asked.

"Good question. Let me explain. Do you know anyone at Health & Human Services in the healthcare grants arena? I need to talk to someone who can look up a recently awarded big grant to a Eugene, Oregon, non-profit. There might be fraud involved, and there's a slim chance it might relate to our murder investigation."

"I'm having trouble making the connection," Joe said.

"Alex Bowen is the exec director of the non-profit, and he may have skimmed approximately $1.8 million off the top of a year-long grant that HHS awarded his company. Hannah Oakley may have somehow discovered the fraud, called Bowen on it, and he killed her. It's a long shot, and Matt thinks they've got her killer, but if he stole from us, shouldn't we find out?"

"Sweet Jesus. Why can't people just get a job and be honest."

"I know. It's possible there's a logical explanation, but it smells bad to me, Joe. All I need is to see the budget attached to the actual grant and share that with the chair of Alex's board of directors. They're supposed to be oversight, but Alex has a sterling reputation in the non-profit world, and he pretty much told me he runs things the way he wants to. He's been advising me on how Matt and I should set up our foundation, and I discovered this document by accident."

"Tell me the name of the organization and his name again," Joe said.

"Healing House, Eugene, Oregon, and his name is Alex Bowen, maybe Alexander Bowen for professional purposes. The line item I'm interested in will be the total for a budget category entitled 'Administrative Services'. It should say $200K, but I'm afraid it will say $2 million. And we should also know how the grant is being awarded. Probably in quarterly chunks, but maybe it's one lump sum. Hope not," she added.

"I'm in my office now, and I know who to call. Are you around all day?"

"All day except between 10:30 and noonish. Going to an arraignment at the county courthouse with Matt. If you lay hands on the budget doc, can you fax it to my home office? Or, take a photo and email it to me?"

"Yes. I'll have something to you by the time you get home. You'd better keep me posted on this."

"I will. Thanks, Joe," Fern said. "Is this the part where I say is this the day you're paying me for?"

"Might be." He hung up.

• • •

"Justin Lucas Sorenson," Judge Cynthia Hedges read from the bench in Chinook County courtroom number one, "you are being charged with two felony counts. I will name the charge for each one and you will enter a plea. Do you understand these proceedings, and are you represented by an attorney of law?"

"Yes, your honor," Sorenson answered. He was trying his hardest to look like Brad Pitt. If he resembled the actor a little, it would have been after Pitt had spent a month in a Russian prison.

"The first charge is attempted murder on the person of Chinook County Sheriff Earl Johnson. How do you plead?"

"Not guilty, your honor."

Judge Hedges raised her eyebrows, but silently made a note.

"The second charge against you is first-degree murder in the homicide death of Hannah Sorenson Oakley. How do you plead?"

"Not guilty, your honor." A little shakier on this one.

Fern, sitting between Matt and Robert Oakley, squeezed both their hands. Robert, ashen faced, began to cry.

"You are remanded to the Chinook County jail for pre-trial detention, and bail is set at $1 million. Adjourned." Judge Hedges banged her gavel.

Sorenson's public defender tried to get his bail reduced on the grounds that he didn't have the resources to be considered a flight risk, but her motion was denied.

• • •

Matt and Fern took Robert out to lunch, pledged to keep him informed of all the proceedings, and then headed back to Port Stirling and home. Matt was going to visit Earl again this afternoon, but Fern begged off; she wanted to wait until Joe sent her the info she was seeking.

Matt stopped at Sheldon Weinstein's deli and bought a quart of his coleslaw, Earl's favorite, to take to the hospital.

Fern was changing into her sweats when she heard the bell on her FAX machine ring. She raced down the stairs and into her office, just as the machine spit out four pages. Fern compared the budget document from HHS to the photo she'd taken at Alex's house. They were identical.

"Dammit," said Joe when Fern called him with the news. "How do you want to handle?"

Fern had thought about this before she phoned her boss, and the one thing she knew for sure was that she didn't want to be involved. She told Joe that now and shared her plan with him.

"I can't risk muddling Hannah's murder case until we know if what I suspect of Alex Bowen is true or not, and I can't confront him. So, it would be best if someone at HHS contacted Donna Beck, the board chairwoman, and told her they were investigating the recent grant. They could say, 'we're concerned now that some of Alex Bowen's math doesn't add up,' or something like that."

"You're pretty sure about this, right?" Joe asked.

"I am, Joe. Donna was quite forceful when I threw out the $2 million number that it was incorrect. She gave me details that were totally in opposition to what HHS awarded. Alex is defrauding them, and who knows what else he is up to. But please keep me out of it if you can."

"I will. He doesn't need to know. HHS is good at this stuff, and if he's stealing, they will know. As usual, Fern, this is good work. Eagle-eye Fern, that's your new nickname. And the beauty of this job is that I can hand it off to another agency and earn some points with them that, down the road, you and I might need."

. . .

Ted went along with Patty to Justin Sorenson's arraignment because he wanted to give his condolences to Robert, and because the couple was going over to Buck Bay afterward to visit Earl in the hospital.

Leaving the courthouse, Ted took Patty's hand and said, "That was heartbreaking. I felt so bad for Robert, and I kept thinking how I'd feel if I lost you."

"You're not going to lose me," Patty said. "Not gonna happen. If nothing else, the actuarial life tables say I'll live four years longer than you."

"Well, that certainly makes me feel better," Ted said wryly. "We'd better start having even more fun than we do now."

"Let's start by cheering up Earl, what do you say? Then we should plan something fabulous for right after spring break — I'm due a vacation."

"I was beginning to think you forgot the meaning of that word. What do you have, like a million hours of PTO coming to you?"

"It's been a little busy around here, don't you think?"

As if to prove the point, her phone buzzed. CarGuy, said the caller ID. "Oops, I need to take this," she said. "You drive."

"Hi, this is Detective Perkins."

"Hi. This is the owner of CarGuy, we talked yesterday? You said to call you if my employees had anything to say about the Bowens' cars, right?"

"Yes. Did they?" She held the phone up close to her ear.

"I don't know if this is important or not, but my guy who cleaned Alex's car, the black SUV, said it was a real mess. He said it's usually got some sand — they live near the beach, I guess — but this was way more than usual. Lots of dirt in the trunk, and heavy mud on the undercarriage. Oh, and he found a broken necklace under one of the seats."

Patty didn't know if it was possible for blood to actually run cold, but it felt like hers suddenly was. "What did he do with the necklace?" she asked, almost afraid to.

"He threw it away. Said it was in too many pieces to repair. It didn't look expensive, just junk."

"Did he throw it in CarGuy's garbage or somewhere else? This is important."

"Our dumpster out back, I think. Do you want me to check?"

"Yes, please," she said, letting out a breath. "I'm headed your way now. If you find it, even a piece of it, please hold on to it. Do you understand?"

"You got it, lady cop. I'll go look now."

· · ·

"Girlfriend," Bernice said. "What's up?"

"This is business related," Patty said. She was standing on the tarmac behind CarGuy, where the owner had just pulled pieces of the necklace out of the dumpster. "Do you take autopsy photos of, like say, Hannah's neck and chest area?"

"Of course. Why?"

"We've found a necklace that she may have been wearing when she was killed. I'd like you to look at some of the pieces and compare it to your photos."

"Are there any sharp, maybe pointed bits?" Bernice asked.

Patty looked down at the ground where the CarGuy owner had placed the pieces as he found them. "Yes. Two pieces look like some kind of fake animal tooth, like an alligator or similar. Pointy on one end."

"Bring them to the morgue. I'll meet you there. Try not to touch them with bare hands. Hanging up now!"

· · ·

Ted went upstairs to visit with Earl while Patty went to meet Bernice in the basement morgue. With gloved hands, Patty carefully laid out the necklace pieces on a slab for Bernice to inspect, magnifying glass in hand. She looked at each of the six pieces, and then zeroed back in on one of the pointed tooth ones, studying it for a good thirty seconds.

When she stood up straight, Bernice was smiling and trying her hardest to suppress a laugh, which would be inappropriate in this room. "If you know who owns the vehicle these were found in, I believe you've solved the murder of Hannah Oakley." She turned quickly and said, "We haven't released her body yet. Take a deep breath and follow me."

Bernice opened a locker and pulled a slab out of what she privately called the "Death Wall". She held the magnifying glass up to a puncture mark on Hannah's neck. "See that?"

"Yes, I see it," Patty replied. "You think that necklace tooth made it?" Tough as Patty was, she looked away quickly.

"Positive," Bernice said. "The tooth has a minute piece of dried blood on it. Hannah fought her attacker, and the necklace was broken while she was strangled. I would say that this piece of it was between Hannah's throat and the killer's hands."

"Alex Bowen," Patty said, and looked at her friend.

CHAPTER 35

M att," Patty said into her phone, "Justin Sorenson didn't kill Hannah. Where are you?"

"About three floors above you. I'm talking with your husband and the sheriff. Ted told me you were in the building. What's happened?"

She told him.

"Stay there. I'm coming downstairs. I have to make a quick call to Fern first, but I'll be right there."

Matt hung up and hit Fern's name. When she answered he said, "It's Alex Bowen, Fern. Stay away from him. We need to talk."

"You've got that right," she said, surprising him. "Joe and I have discovered that he likely committed fraud against the Health and Human Services Department—we have proof, we think. I couldn't wait to tell you, but I didn't want to interrupt your visit with Earl. How do you know?"

"The CarGuy who detailed Bowen's car found pieces of a broken necklace and called Patty. She brought it to Bernice, and she says one of the pieces has blood on it and matches a puncture wound on Hannah's neck. It's the piece of physical evidence we need. And you, my brilliant wife, have discovered his motive. 'It's over,' Hannah wrote to Alex Bowen, and he had to kill her to save himself. Jesus."

"No wonder Blake had to get home in a hurry," Fern said. "How awful. Her husband killed her best friend."

"And she helped him," Matt reminded her. "Maybe not the actual murder, but Blake is certainly an accomplice after the fact. What a friggin disaster this case is. I'll be home as soon as I can."

. . .

"What do we do now?" Patty asked Matt, who was panting after running down three flights of stairs and a long hallway.

"Don't mind me," he panted, bending over, hands on his knees. "First time I've moved that fast in weeks."

Bernice patted her former patient on the back and answered for him. "First, I confirm that the blood on this necklace matches Hannah's — that won't take me long."

"I will call Jeri and ask her to drop the murder charge on Sorenson as soon as you tell me it's Hannah's blood," Matt said. "Let's don't tell Earl yet; it might upset him, and he doesn't need that now."

"Agreed," said Bernice.

"We need Fern's evidence on Bowen's fraud," Patty said. "With that, and the necklace, and Rosa blowing up his alibi, and their persistent lying to us, that should be enough. When will Fern know if HHS nails him?"

"Likely tomorrow. According to Joe Phelps, the head honcho in the grants department will talk to Bowen's board chairwoman first thing. Fern says the paper trail evidence is black and white, and they will likely arrest Alex immediately if Donna Beck cooperates."

"That's great," said Patty. "That gives us time to pull together our pieces of the puzzle."

"We're only missing one piece that I can tell," Matt said. "How did Hannah figure out what he was doing?"

"Could there have been a whistleblower in his operation who discovered it, didn't know who inside to trust with it, and called Hannah?" asked Patty.

"That makes sense," Matt said. "Someone at Healing House had to know."

"So, we sit tight until tomorrow, with the exception of telling Jeri," Patty said.

"Sit tight but keep a close watch on the Bowens today and tomorrow,"

Matt said. "I'll coordinate with Dan McCoy, and we'll put round-the-clock surveillance on them."

"Put me down for a shift," Patty smiled. "I'd like nothing better than for Blake Bowen to try to make a run for it."

"When did you become so bloodthirsty?" Matt asked her. "You're not going to shoot Blake."

"Spoilsport," Patty joked. "Seriously, though, give me tomorrow morning."

• • •

Earl's room was crowded. Ted, Patty, Bernice, Matt, and Earl's wife all crammed in.

"It's a party," Earl said, straight-faced.

"How are you feeling this afternoon?" Bernice, aka Dr. Ryder, asked her patient.

"My arm hurts like hell," he growled. "Can't you give me something?"

"I did, you old grouch. See that button in your other hand? You're supposed to press it when your pain becomes worse."

Earl looked down as if seeing the button for the first time. "Oh, yeah, I forgot it was there." He pressed it.

"That's a good boy," Bernice said in a sing-songy voice. "I'll leave it to all of you to see if you can get a smile out of the codger. I have work to do." Patty hugged her and whispered, "Thank you." Bernice whispered back, "No, thank you."

• • •

Alone in his car on the way home, Matt called Jay.

"Does it seem like I call you a lot?" Matt asked.

"Homicide investigation, dude."

"Amen. Wait'll you hear." Matt told him about Patty and the necklace, and about Fern, Joe, and the big fraud.

"So, wrong guy in jail?"

"I'm afraid so. I feel bad, but Justin made it so much worse than it needed to be."

"Justin Sorenson is not playing with a full deck," Jay said. "Honestly, he's lucky to have made it this far. If he didn't have a pretty face, he'd have been toast decades ago."

"Thanks, I needed that laugh. And I need one favor from you."

"Round up the gang and start watching the Bowens' spectacular ocean-front home?"

"Bingo. Tell Rudy to make coffee; he's got tonight."

"I'll go with him," Jay said. "I don't much care for Alex Bowen, so this will be a labor of love."

"I thought you had a date tonight?"

"I do, but she will understand. That's what's so great about Amy."

"Please tell her I'm sorry, and I hope she didn't shave her legs for you."

"Smart ass."

· · ·

Chief Dan McCoy and his sergeant took the first shift, heading out within an hour of Matt's call to Dan, whose response to the latest was, "That couple has been lying through their fucking teeth to us since day one. Let's nail them to the wall."

"You sound like Patty," Matt said. "Try not to shoot anyone this afternoon, Dan."

"Nope. I'd rather go visit them in prison," McCoy said. "Listen, Matt, I want to apologize to you. I resented you calling into question my verdict on Hannah's suicide. But you were right to do so. Earl and I took too much at face value on this one, and I'm grateful you didn't."

"No need, Dan. I made a promise to Robert, that's all."

"Yeah, I need to do something for him. I dismissed him too quickly. It wasn't right."

"He's going to need all the help we can give him for a while. But right now, we have to give him Hannah's real killer, which will come as another lousy shock to him, I'm afraid. Let me know when you end your shift," Matt said.

"Sure thing. Two of my guys will take over from me at 5:00 p.m, and then Jay and Rudy at 11:00 p.m, correct?"

"They are drinking coffee now," Matt smiled.

"Youth is wasted on the young, huh?" McCoy said.

* * *

Bernice called Matt at 4:00 a.m, not that he was asleep anyway.

"The blood on the tooth of the necklace matches Hannah's."

"Positive?"

"Positive," Bernice said. "I also got a partial thumbprint off one of the other necklace stones, and it doesn't belong to Hannah. I ran it through our database, but it doesn't match anyone on record."

"Blake and Alex will be fingerprinted when we arrest them," Matt said, steel in his voice. "Then we'll have a match."

"When will that be?"

"Later today, I think. Once we know if Alex's board chairwoman confirms the fraudulent HHS grant, we're going in. Until then, we've got round-the-clock surveillance on them. I'll keep you in the loop."

"Thanks, Matt. This is going to sell newspapers. Be ready."

"Arresting the biggest celebrity to ever come out of Oregon will be just the same to me as any other arrest."

"If I were you, I'd put your new detective in charge of PR; she'll handle the reporters that will descend with her Boston attitude. And don't forget to call Bill and tell him what's about to happen," Bernice warned.

"Who?"

"Bill Abbott. Your boss."

"Oh, shit. I haven't told him we arrested the wrong guy!"

"My point," Bernice said.

* * *

The night before, Blake and Alex Bowen left their home at 6:15 p.m. and were discreetly followed to a restaurant in downtown Buck Bay. They returned home at 8:00 p.m. and didn't leave the rest of the night.

● ● ●

Thursday morning went without incident. The cops smoothly effected their shift changes, and the only action was the mid-morning delivery of mail to their mailbox at the Bowen gate.

About 11:00 a.m, Blake Bowen strolled down her driveway in an elaborate dressing gown paired with rubber boots, retrieved the mail, and went back to the house.

Alex Bowen came out on the deck briefly at the same time, and that was the only sighting of the Bowens until 2:00 p.m. when all hell broke loose.

● ● ●

First, Stewart MacIntosh, the senior director of grant making for the Department of Health and Human Services, discovered in a lengthy phone call with Donna Beck, chairwoman of Healing House, that Alex Bowen had indeed scammed his grant makers to the tune of $1,768,000.

Donna had suspected Alex of budget shenanigans for almost a year but didn't trust the rest of her board of directors to not be in on it. Approximately one month ago, she met privately with Hannah Oakley, a longtime friend, to discuss her fears, and to compare their budgets. The two women decided that Hannah would tell Alex that she knew about the HHS fraud—leaving Donna out of it, for now—and that if he didn't confess his 'mistake' to the government and return the money, Hannah would expose him. In essence, 'It's over.'

When news of Hannah's murder became public, Donna panicked. She was terrified of Alex and two of her board members, and she, regretfully now, stayed quiet. When Fern found out and approached her, Donna realized that Fern would take steps to expose Alex to HHS, so, still, she kept quiet, fearing for her own safety.

Stewart MacIntosh called Joe Phelps directly, and Joe immediately phoned Fern. Fern, with Matt and Ed in Matt's office waiting for his call, put him on speaker phone while he described everything he'd learned in D.C. this morning.

"Alex Bowen needs to be arrested immediately," wrapped up Joe. "Fern will be the federal government's representative on the charge of conspiracy to defraud the United States government. Matt and Ed, whatever you decide to do regarding the homicide of Hannah Oakley is fine with us. Put this creep in jail, OK?"

Matt stood up. "Off we go," he said into the speaker.

CHAPTER 36

In less than one hour, the murder charge against Justin Sorenson was dropped. He would remain in jail and eventually answer for the charge of attempted murder on the sheriff, no small crime. Judge Hedges said to Jeri, the interim D.A, "You're a lucky woman this didn't come to trial, Jeri. Perhaps we could use some luck in the district attorney's office." She smiled and waved her out of her quarters.

Robert Oakley had been notified in a call from Matt to stay home, and that he would come by this afternoon to discuss a "new development" in Hannah's case.

Arrest warrants had been issued for both Blake and Alex Bowen. Her charge was accessory to murder after the fact, a felony in Oregon. Alex's charges were first-degree murder, and conspiracy to defraud the government. Matt, Ed, and Fern would be the arresting officers on Alex; Patty Perkins and Tamryn Gesicki would arrest Blake.

Jay, Rudy, and Earl slept through the whole event.

• • •

Blake and Alex were home when the cops arrived a little after 3:00 p.m. Ed disabled the mechanism on the Bowen's gate, and, in three vehicles, they approached the house unannounced. Matt rang the doorbell at the top of the stairs.

"What now?" Alex snarled at Matt. "And how did you get past my gate?" He looked around Matt and saw his gate gaping open.

"Oops," said Ed, pulling himself up to his full height beside Matt. "I may have broken it. So sorry."

"Alexander Bowen, I am arresting you for first-degree murder in the homicide of Hannah Oakley." Matt quickly read him his rights, and then said to Ed, "Please cuff the suspect."

Ed turned Alex around somewhat roughly and handcuffed him before Alex could even speak. Over his shoulder, he yelled at Matt, "You're crazy! You can't do this!"

Fern stepped forward and said, "If he's crazy, then so am I. Alexander Bowen, as a representative of the federal government, I am arresting you for conspiracy to defraud the government of the United States, and specifically the Department of Health and Human Services."

"But, wait, there's more," said Patty, stepping up alongside Fern in their well-choreographed plan and dangling a second pair of handcuffs. To Blake Bowen, cowering behind her husband, Patty said, "Blake Bowen, I am arresting you for the charge of accessory to murder after the fact. Ed?" she handed the cuffs to the big guy, who promptly placed them on Blake Bowen.

"My wife had nothing to do with this," said Alex, subdued now. "I killed Hannah, but Blake had nothing to do with it."

Blake moved within a foot of Patty and with rage on her face, and straining against her handcuffs, spit out, "I wish I'd killed her! I wish I'd been home when it happened. I got here as fast as I could, and I enjoyed burying her deep in the woods in the darkness of night. It felt so right. You should have left her there to rot into the earth." Her face was purple with fury, there was spittle on her chin, and Patty took a step backward.

"What could Hannah have possibly done to you to warrant this?" Patty asked her, genuinely curious.

"She was going to expose Alex and we'd have to give back all that glorious money. How dare she! But it was more, wasn't it, darling?" she said to her husband, flinging her hair in an unsuccessful effort to remove a loose strand from her cheek. "Han was trying to outshine me. She wanted to be the star. Homely Han, can you imagine? I've been Oregon's princess for all my life, and she thought she could overshadow me? What a pathetic joke. Just by working hard and being nice to people? Please. It takes star power, and I have it. She never would. Honestly, she's better off dead."

"That's enough, Blake," Alex said, his voice croaking. "Let's wait for our attorney, OK, honey?"

"That's an excellent idea, Mr. Bowen," Matt said. The cops, who had seen almost everything in their combined experience, were all dismayed at Blake's outburst, and silently marched the couple to their waiting squad cars.

• • •

Earl, his wounded arm in a sling, was preparing to leave the hospital. Once the Bowens were transported to jail, Matt called Earl to bring him up to speed.

"What happens next?" Earl asked. "Has Justin Sorenson had his bail reduced?"

Matt was dreading this conversation. "Yes, but he'll stay in jail until they can schedule his trial for shooting you."

"So, I failed Robert twice, didn't I? Not taking him seriously, and then putting him through the trauma of arresting the wrong person. Fuck me."

"The evidence against Sorenson was very strong, Earl. Hannah had been in his car recently. We had every reason to believe he'd killed her. Justin brought this on himself by not being honest with us from the get-go. I'm going to Robert's next to tell him what's happened, and, yeah, he's gonna take this hard. His wife's best friend and her husband. I think Blake's hatred for Hannah and her love for money caused Alex to lose his cool when he strangled her."

"And she will only get about ten years for accessory, and Alex will probably spend the rest of his life behind bars. Nobody ever said life was fair."

"Amen."

"So, I'm checking myself out of this dump now, and I will meet you at Robert's house. What time?"

"I knew that was coming," Matt said. "Why don't you just let me handle it this one time, and you go home with Sharon and stay put for a couple of days?"

"Because I don't want to," Earl said. "I want to explain to Robert why I believed Sorenson was the guy. Then I'll go home and be Sharon's prisoner."

Knowing when he was defeated, Matt said, "Four o'clock."

• • •

"Are there any more surprises for me, Matt?" asked Robert after Matt had explained what happened. "Not sure I can take much more. I need to get off this roller coaster."

"All my fault, Robert," Earl said. He shifted on the sofa, trying to get comfortable. The sheriff explained to Robert why they'd arrested Justin Sorenson, and added, "Like you, I'm guessing, I wanted Sorenson to be the bad guy. I hate his type of man, and I hated what he did to Hannah all those years ago. I wanted to put him away. I'm sorry, and I apologize to you again."

"It was easier knowing it was Justin," Robert admitted. "It will take me a while to process that Alex and Blake were responsible for Hannah's death. I can't imagine Alex with his hands around Hannah's neck. She must have been terrified."

Quickly, because he worried Robert was about to break down, Matt said, "Alex confessed, and Blake confessed to helping him after the murder. There will be no more shocks. They are in jail and will be arraigned tomorrow morning. If you want to confront them, I will drive you to the courthouse."

Robert touched his fingertips to his temple, lightly massaging his head, and stared off in the distance. Matt and Earl knew he was gathering his thoughts, and they sat quietly and waited.

"No, I think not. Maybe I'll attend their trial, but I'm going to move on. I've also decided how I will adjust to the news of Annie being Hannah's child," Robert said. "This, too, has been a real blow, but after thinking it over, and hearing Hannah's own words at the reading of the will, and seeing the Haynes family's obvious pain, it's best if we all let sleeping dogs lie. I hope to be a little more involved in Annie's life, but I won't push her."

"That's very wise," Matt said. "The three of them will deal with the truth or not, but your decision is the best for the family."

"I'm going back to school next week," Robert said. "It's time to let my poor substitute teacher off the hook." He smiled. "Earl, if you want to make amends, there's one thing you could do."

"Anything," Earl said. "Name it."

"Show me your best fishing hole on the Twisty River. I used to fish before I became an alcoholic, and I'm thinking I might try it again."

"Oh, I don't know," Earl said, shaking his head. "You'd have to promise to not tell another living soul if I take you there." He grinned.

. . .

As Bernice predicted, reporters from all over arrived in droves, camping out at the courthouse for a glimpse of singing star Blake Bowen. Interim district attorney Jeri Schrader and Port Stirling Detective Tamryn Gesicki handled the press conference, fending off outlandish requests from the media in a calm, controlled, professional manner. Bail had been denied to both of the Bowens, as they were considered a flight risk.

On Friday, about twenty-four hours after their arrest, a photo of Blake Bowen in an orange jumpsuit, her unwashed hair hanging limply around her lined, tired face had been leaked to CNN.

Jeri Schrader, putting on a good show of outrage, had vowed to find out the leak. She would later be elected to replace former D.A. David Dalrymple in a landslide.

CHAPTER 37

The Port Stirling Police Department, with the additions of Ed Sonders, Earl Johnson, Patty Perkins, Dan McCoy, Dr. Bernice Ryder, Jeri Schrader, and Fern Byrne, were gathered in the sparkling new retreat center at Whale Rock. Located on a small hill behind the inn and restaurant, it had once been a maintenance shed, now remodeled into a mid-sized event space that Port Stirling sorely needed.

The day-long retreat had been billed as a re-hash of the Hannah Oakley case and mini-celebration at the arrest of her killer, but Matt had another agenda, too.

After everyone had gushed over Earl's return to work, and they had all participated in what went wrong, thankfully followed by everything that went right in the capture of the Bowens, Matt took over.

"This is also a welcome party for the newest member of my department, Tamryn," he said. "Because of Hannah's case, most of you haven't had the opportunity to get to know her as well as I have. She will hate this" — he smiled over at Tamryn — "but I want her to tell y'all a little about her life and what led to her coming all the way out here to join our department."

Tamryn rose from her chair at the end of the large U-shaped table. Jay, sitting next to her, helped pull back her chair.

"I needed a change in my life," she said haltingly. Her voice was as deep and firm as always, but she was clearly choosing her words carefully, going slowly.

On the other side of her, Fern helped her out. "Why was that?" Fern asked.

Tamryn looked at her. "Well, unlike you, I did not have the best husband in the world." That got a big laugh. "The short version is that after a few years of verbal abuse, my ex-husband took it physical one night, and I ended up in the hospital for a few days. My good Polish family turned out to not be great in my crisis, and my Boston PD colleagues were pure shit." She looked over at Sylvia. "Pardon my language, Sylvia."

Sylvia wiped a tear away and nodded at Tamryn.

"So, I decided to leave Boston, and about a week after I'd made the decision and started searching for PDs looking for a cracker-jack detective, Matt Horning called me. Your chief was properly appalled at my story, seemed like a good guy, and I decided that 3,000 miles was about the right distance from my life in Boston." She opened her arms as if to embrace everyone, and said, "In the short time I've been here, I think I finally understand what it is to work with a team. It was the right decision." Tamryn sat down.

Deep silence around the room.

"Wow," Earl said. "That's a story. I feel your pain, Tamryn, especially the hospital part. They suck."

Jeri raised her hand and looked at Matt. "I don't know about your fellow cops," she said to Tamryn, "but I welcome you with open arms, and I want to say that I'm thrilled you're here. For those of you who haven't been paying attention, Tamryn was a rock during and after Hannah's case. I never could have handled the media as well as she did. It was her cool demeanor — and possibly a great suggestion from her — that finally got rid of them. For which I will always be grateful. Welcome, detective, I look forward to working with you for many years."

"Thanks, Jeri. My pleasure," Tamryn said and winked at her.

"Once again, I'm partnered with a woman who's smarter than me," Jay said. Tamryn elbowed him. "But it's probably a good thing. Plus, she's already found a better donut shop, which has added a lot of value to my daily life."

Fern's phone buzzed, and she stood and excused herself. Looking at Matt, she said, "Oops, my other boss."

Out in the small lobby of the center, looking out the huge window to the Pacific Ocean, Fern said, "Hi, Joe. What's going on?"

"I'd like you to go for a ride in a boat with me tomorrow. Can that happen?" Joe said.

"Here, you mean? In Port Stirling?"

"Yes, I'm flying out tonight, and the Coast Guard will take us out to an island a few miles off your coast tomorrow about noon. I'll meet you at their HQ in Buck Bay."

"There's no island off our coast," Fern said. "What are you talking about?"

"That you don't know about it is a good thing," Joe said mysteriously.

Authors thrive on reviews. Please consider leaving one for this book, and any of my other books you've enjoyed. It does make a difference. Thank you from the bottom of my heart.

If you want to stay in touch, please go to my author website at

WWW.KAYJENNINGSAUTHOR.COM

and sign up for my occasional newsletter.

ACKNOWLEDGEMENTS

Titling a book is an especially difficult process because the title has to do so much. It must indicate the story's genre, be in sync with other books in the series, lend itself to a great cover design, and have relevance to the story within. My deepest gratitude goes to my editor, Peter Senftleben, for this perfect title. I was struggling, and he came through big-time. He does other great stuff, too.

I like to call Claire Brown the best book cover designer in the free world. To me, she is. I give her about five words to communicate what I have in mind for the next book, and, somehow, she continues to design the perfect covers.

Sarah Forrester is a fictional character. However, there is a real Sarah Forrester in Rhode Island, and she won a contest in my newsletter to have a character named after her in this story. Congrats, Sarah! Who knows if your character will continue in book seven? I rather liked her.

In my previous life, I once worked for a non-profit organization, and all my colleagues were dedicated, wonderful people — nothing like the villain in this story.

Between whisking me off to the desert in the dead of an Oregon winter, to expertly wrapping the Cryo Cuff around my repaired knee, to restraining himself from asking me when I was going to start writing again, my brilliant husband, Steve, continues to be the glue that holds all this together.

And finally, I want to acknowledge you, dear reader. Whether you buy books, nag your library to get them, write reviews or simply rate what you've read, you are the motivation for authors to keep writing. And my motivation to continue to improve. Thank you.

Kay Jennings, 2023